WED TO THE WILD GOD

RUBY DIXON

Copyright © 2021 by Ruby Dixon

All rights reserved.

No part of this book may be reproduced in any form or by any electronic or mechanical means, including information storage and retrieval systems, without written permission from the author, except for the use of brief quotations in a book review.

Cover Design: Kati Wilde

Edits: Aquila Editing

Interior Map: Ruby's awesome husband

Interior illustration: @bonkyconk

❀ Created with Vellum

WED TO THE WILD GOD

When I find a gorgeous stranger in an alley, covered in blood, you'd think the logical thing would be to go to the authorities.

Not me. I take him home.

I've got my reasons, though. See, Kassam is cursed with hedonism. He's a god from another world, accidentally stuck in ours. Anyone (and everyone) around him falls under his spell. It's impossible to resist. Like scratching an itch. And being around Kassam? *Boy*, do I itch.

But trying to send the god home to his world is a near-impossible task. Between everyone we meet trying to kiss him and the gods of *this* world trying to get rid of him, I'm in over my head. There's only one solution that will keep me safe -- marry him. Being the wife of a god will protect me from immortal machinations.

Now, I just need to figure out a way to protect my heart from Kassam himself.

Godspine Mountains
Adassia
Blood Glacier
CHANDRILHAR
Dirtlands
Aventine
BALSINGRA
Ghosthollow
Murk
SUNSWALLOW
Sea of Storms
PORT TIDEWATER

PANTHEON OF AOS

The High Father

The Twelve (as of the last Anticipation)

- **Magra**, Lady of Plenty
- **Tadekha**, Goddess of Magic
- **Riekki**, Peacekeeper and Knowledge-bringer
- **Anali**, Lady of Light and Health
- **Belara** - Goddess of Beauty
- **Aron**, Lord of Storms, Butcher God of Battle (Bound to the Battle God)
- **Kalos**, One of the two Dark Brothers, Lord of Disease
- **Gental**, God of Family
- **Kassam**, Lord of the Wild (Wed to the Wild God)
- **Rhagos**, Lord of the Dead, one of the two Dark Brothers (Sworn to the Shadow God)
- **The Spidae**, Lords of Fate
- **Vor**, God of Seas

A NOTE ABOUT CONTENT

As always, please be aware that some of my books sometimes contain objectionable content. This is my effort to let readers know so they can be alerted and prepared for such things in their reading...or skip the book entirely! It's up to you what your limits are.

If you don't want to be spoiled, skip ahead to Chapter One! If you are here for spoilers, continue on.

SPOILERS AHEAD SPOILERS AHEAD SPOILERS AHEAD SPOILERS AHEAD SPOILERS AHEAD SPOILERS AHEAD SPOILERS AHEAD

First and foremost! These books contain themes of death and rebirth, as do all the Anchor and Aspect books. If you find death triggering or thoughts of impending death triggering, this might not be the read for you.

At a few points in the story, the heroine is assaulted. Not sexually, and not by the hero.

There are mentions of an abusive parental figure and drug use.

Also — the hero is the Aspect of Hedonism, which means he is Up. For. Anything. And while the hero and heroine in this book are utterly faithful the moment they meet, there are references to the pansexual hero's adventurous past. He continues to be adventurous with our heroine, and between them there's a bit of light bondage, light spanking for both parties, toy action, and pegging. Oh, and someone turns into a tree during sex off-screen.

I felt it would be inauthentic to Hedonism to make him totally vanilla so Kassam is definitely a bit more in the spice department. If you are looking for a spice rating, my normal books are probably a warm three, this one would be a four, and a five would be no-holds-barred.

SPOILERS DONE SPOILERS DONE SPOILERS DONE
SPOILERS DONE SPOILERS DONE SPOILERS DONE
SPOILERS DONE SPOILERS DONE SPOILERS DONE
SPOILERS DONE SPOILERS DONE SPOILERS DONE
SPOILERS DONE SPOILERS DONE SPOILERS DONE
SPOILERS DONE SPOILERS DONE SPOILERS DONE

Enjoy!

— Ruby

1

(Author's Note: If you are reading this on a device and it skipped straight here, please page back to read the content warnings if needed. Thank you! — xoxo Ruby)

CARLY

"I'm telling you, sweetie. Be careful out there. You never know who to trust in a city like this."

I lift my shoulder, using it to hold the phone to my ear as I clean a mug behind the bar. It's almost opening time, so I need to make this call to my mom short, but I can hear the worry in her voice. "Have you seen anything weird outside your apartment, Ma? Any weirdos at work?"

"No! I'm not worried about me. I'm worried about you. You know they never found those two girls that went missing from that building." Her voice drops a worried note. "They were both young and pretty like you."

It's nice of my mom to think I'm pretty, but that might be a mother's love affecting her there. I'm sure I'm cute enough—my shaggy reddish blonde hair with thick bangs and my sprinkle of freckles across my snub nose ensures that I get decent tips—but I'm not a model. "One of them was a client of yours, wasn't she?"

"The blonde one, yes. I did a card reading for her right before she disappeared. Weirdest thing." My mom pauses. "Carly...I didn't tell you, but I did a reading for her after she disappeared because I wanted to see what would come up. I did a three card spread and do you know what I got?"

"No, what?" My mom lives by her card readings.

"Death. The King of Pentacles. And The World."

"Okay."

"I remember reading her and she got Death and King of Pentacles that day, too."

I pick up another mug, wiping it down to get rid of any water spots. "I thought you told me that didn't mean actual death."

"It doesn't. It means a big change in life. But...Carly..." I can practically hear my mother swallow on the other end of the phone. "I've done three more readings for that young lady and those three cards come up every time."

Goosebumps prickle over my skin. "No shit?"

"No shit."

"Did you shuffle well?"

"I know how to use my cards, Carly." My mother sounds offended. "This is what I do for a living."

"I know, I know. I'm just trying to understand how that could happen."

"The cards are trying to tell me something. That's how it happened. She's dead. I know it. I just don't have any proof and her killer is out there somewhere."

"Did you do a reading for the other girl?" I ask absently, glancing at the clock. Five minutes until four pm, which means I need to get a move on. I've got to cut some limes and change out one of the kegs, and it's easier if I get it all done before we open our doors. Charlie saunters in from the back with a fresh load of beer steins for me to wipe down, and reaches over to turn on the TV behind the bar. I gesture at my phone, indicating I'll end my call, and he nods and walks away. "The one you didn't know?"

"I did."

"And?"

"Death keeps coming up on hers, too. First card I turn over every time. And then the Lovers. The Hanged Man is always the third card—self-sacrifice. Do you think she gave her life to save the other girl?"

"If she did, it didn't work, judging by your other cards."

"Carly!" My mother admonishes me in a sharp voice. "I'm worried!"

"I know, Mom, and I love you, but we're about to open up and I can't be on the phone." I glance over at the doors to the bar, and I see one of our regulars peering inside, waiting to get his first after-work beer. Shit. I set the mug down. "I really have to go," I tell her, hopping out from behind the bar and grabbing my phone before it drops from my shoulder. I head for the door. "Can I call you tomorrow?"

"Stay safe, baby girl," my mother warns me. "I did your cards, too."

That makes me pause. It shouldn't bother me, because my mother is a psychic. She has the little shop downtown and everything, and rubs crystals to channel her energies. That's just who Mom is, and ever since I was a kid, she's been reading my cards and giving me advice. I don't believe in it like she does, but maybe it's our conversation, or the timing, but goosebumps prickle up and down my arms. "And? What did you see?"

"The Lovers—a relationship. The Fool. And Death."

I frown, my hand on the handle of the front door. "You sure

there isn't something wrong with your deck? Sounds like the same cards keep popping up all the time. Maybe they're too worn out. Or the cards are stuck together."

"My cards are fine!" my mother exclaims, affronted.

I know it's an insult to question her ability, but I can't help but ask. "I'm sorry. It just seems...weird."

"I know. So I tried two other decks and I got the same results for you every time. Just...be careful, okay? I love you. You're all I have."

"I know, Ma. I'll be careful." I think about the cards. Lovers. Fool. Beginning a relationship. Yeah, that's not going to happen. The bar's the only place I go and most of my customers are older, married, or drunks. The last relationship I had, I ran away from the moment it started to get serious. "You don't have to worry. I'm not seeing anyone."

"Just be careful," she warns me again. "I'm sure this means something."

I'm sure it does, in her eyes. To me, I'm not entirely sure that the cards aren't just a little too well-loved. But it's sweet of her to worry. I'm twenty-eight years old and my mom still acts as if I'm fourteen. "I'll text you when I get home tonight. I promise. Love you."

"Love you too. And wear your crystals that I gave you!"

I cringe. I am definitely not doing that. "Will do," I lie, unlocking the front door to let in our first impatient customer. "I really have to go."

∼

I FORGET all about the conversation with my mother, because work gets crazy busy. There's a game on tonight, so the bar is packed with people by the time it starts until close, and then it's such a mess that cleaning the place takes longer than usual. Charlie balances the till and cleans the machines while I put chairs atop tables and mop the floors. We work in silence. After a long day of being "on" behind the bar and chatting with people to make them comfortable (and bring in tips), a little bit of quiet headspace is more than welcome.

After I clean out the bathrooms, I grab the garbage bags and nod at Charlie, who's splitting out the tips for the night. "Be right back. I'm taking these to the alley."

"Wait, Carly." Charlie frowns over at me. "I'll go with you."

He's never volunteered before. "Uh, why?"

"Because it's late and it's dark."

I stare at him as if he's grown another head. He's being chivalrous after all this time of working together...and he's got a damn boot on his foot? Charlie broke two toes last week and has been limping behind the bar all night, his foot in a black, oversized medical boot. I swear if I have to hear his story about it one more time, I'm going to scream. "It's always late and dark. I'll be fine. I have pepper spray." I pat my pocket.

"You have pepper spray?"

"I'm a woman alone in the city. Of course I have pepper spray." I make a face at him. "Now can we just finish up? I really want to go home. I have some leftover pizza that's calling my name and I'd really like to collapse in bed." I gesture at the garbage bags on the floor in front of me. "The longer we do this, the longer it takes to get home."

Charlie hesitates, then goes back to counting, shaking his head. "If you aren't back in two minutes, I'm coming after you."

"I'll let the murderers know," I tease, grabbing the garbage and heading out the back exit into the alley. Even though it's nice of Charlie to offer, I'm glad he backed down. Charlie tends to work at a slow, deliberate pace, and he's a stickler for cleanliness. That's great and all, but at almost three in the morning when I just want to crawl into bed? I know it'll go faster if I don't take him with me. He'll be slow as molasses in that boot, and I know his foot is hurting him. Besides, the alley is always deserted. Our bar's in a business district and no one's around this time of night. That...and I have pepper spray. I've been taking the garbage out late at night for two years now and it's never been a problem. I'm always careful and aware of my surroundings.

I can take care of myself.

I pull the pepper spray out of my pocket and grip it in one hand, the garbage bag handles tightly gripped in the other hand as I head into the alley. Of course, tonight's the first night that the street light's out. Fucking great. I glare up at the sky, but there's a full moon at least so it's not completely and utterly dark...just mostly. I think for a moment about getting Charlie, but then I think about his foot in that boot. And I scan the alley. It looks clear, the rows of dumpsters on the far side of the street framed by a couple of parked cars down the way. There's some garbage and wet crap puddled in the middle of the alley, and one of the dumpster cats is prowling around, but nothing seems out of the ordinary.

All right, then. No big deal. Get this done and go. I head down the steps, moving with purpose toward the dumpsters.

A low groan echoes in the alley.

I freeze, dropping the garbage bags in a clatter of cans and broken bottles. It makes a terrible racket but I don't care. I flick the lid off my pepper spray and hold it up, turning around. I don't see anyone, but the hairs on the back of my neck are standing up. "Charlie? You got that other bag?" I lie, in case someone's watching me and ready to spring. "Need me to hold the door open for you?"

There's no sound other than that of my harsh breathing, and my tense muscles start to relax. Did I hear a cat in heat, then? Or a skunk—

The groan comes again, but it sounds more pained than threatening.

I swallow hard, tempted to head back inside and grab Charlie. Sure, he's a hundred and twenty pounds soaking wet, but someone else nearby would be welcome, and if someone's injured out here...well, I don't know that clean-freak Charlie would be much help after all. "Hello?"

Another low sound, and it sounds like...pain. "Help...me..."

Ah, fuck. Really, universe? Despite my better judgment, I head for the sounds. If someone's dying and I abandon them, I'm going to feel terrible. Of course, if someone murders me, that will also feel terrible, but I feel like I don't have a choice. It's like I'm being compelled to head into the shadows, where the darkest parts of the alley aren't lit up by moonlight. "Who's there?"

Something soft and wispy brushes over my face. I fight back a scream as I realize it's just...cobwebs. Somehow I've managed to find the only spider in the area who's making a web, and I shudder, scrubbing at my face.

"Hello?" I call again.

There's another groan, and my feet hit something hard and solid before I realize I've nearly tripped over the man. I bite back another scream, stumbling as I struggle to keep my balance, and drop my pepper spray—

—right next to a hand.

Oh fuck. Oh fuck.

The hand is spattered with blood, the palm facing the sky, the fingers half-curled. It's a man's hand, and as I look up the tattooed arm, I see even more blood, and then a dark, huge body nestled amongst the trash bags.

The whole guy is covered in blood.

"Oh my god," I whimper, pressing my fingers to my mouth in horror. This guy's been murdered. Even as I think I'm going to be sick, I'm horrified to realize that my nipples are pricking and my pulse is throbbing between my legs. What the fuck is wrong with me? Why am I reacting like this?

The man groans again and to my surprise, he opens his eyes

and looks right at me. I stare into a pair of stunningly silver eyes, so intense that it takes my breath away.

"Carly?" Charlie calls from the bar's back door. "Are you out here?"

"There's a man over here," I call back. "I think he's hurt! He's covered in blood!"

The stranger just looks at me. His hand on the asphalt twitches, and then he lifts it toward me, as if asking me to take it.

Automatically, I reach for it. "You're going to be okay," I whisper to him. "You—"

The moment our fingers touch, my entire body shudders. To my horror...I orgasm.

Then, I black out.

2

"Carly! Carly? Wake up, please."

A hand taps me on my cheek, over and over again, and I groan, opening my eyes. My pulse is throbbing through my entire body and I feel both exhausted and curiously blissful.

I'm lying on something hard, and there's a stink of garbage all around me. I squint, trying to make sense of the shadows, and see Charlie's frantic face.

"Oh thank god," he breathes. "Are you all right?"

"There's a man," I murmur, memories flooding back. "A man covered in blood."

"What? Did you hit your head? Can you sit up?" His hand moves to my shoulder, tugging on me.

Slowly, I sit upright. I don't feel...bad? If anything, my pulse is throbbing and my head fuzzy, but I don't understand why I collapsed. I put a hand to my forehead, trying to remember what happened. The man in the alley was covered in blood....silver eyes...he touched me...

Oh boy.

I shift my hips a little, and the sensation of my pussy, wet and slick and sensitive, hits me like a ton of bricks.

I totally orgasmed and passed out. What the ever-loving fuck?

Swallowing hard, I look around. It's as dark as ever, but I don't see anyone nearby. "How...how long have I been out?"

"I don't know. A few minutes? You were taking a while and I came out here to see what was wrong and found you sprawled." Charlie's face is full of worry. "Do you need me to take you to a hospital?"

"There's no...man?" I blink at him. "There was a man here."

"Did he hit you? Attack you?"

I glance down at my hand, and there's still blood on it. I didn't imagine things, then. How do I explain to my co-worker that a stranger touched my hand and I came so hard that I blacked out? "Uh..."

"That does it," Charlie says. "I'm taking you to the nearest doc in the box. We're going to get you looked at."

"I swear I'm fine," I protest. God, what am I going to tell a doctor? That I spontaneously orgasmed because of a bloody hobo? "Help me stand up, please?"

Charlie wraps an arm around my waist and helps me get to my feet, and oddly enough, his touch bothers me. I think of Charlie like a sibling—a little annoying at times, but harmless and friendly. But he's standing close, trying to help me stand, and...I don't want him to touch me. I don't want anyone to touch me.

Well, no, that's not completely right, I realize. Because I imagine the silver eyes of the stranger, and my pussy clenches all over again.

"I'm good," I say to Charlie, a bit more abrupt than I should. I push his arms away and take a step. Then two. I brush off my clothes. "I think I'm fine?"

My co-worker just stares at me as if I'm insane. "I'm not sure you are, Carly. Have you been getting enough sleep? Have you —" He pauses, his eyes going wide. His storky, long throat moves, Adam's apple bobbing. And he blinks. And blinks again.

I turn around, looking over my shoulder to see what he's staring at.

There's a large figure at the end of the alley, hidden in shadows. He stares out at nothing, and I dimly see tail lights on the neighboring street. He turns back toward us, and then begins to head in our direction.

Maybe I should feel fear, but weirdly enough, all I feel is a prickle of anticipation.

"Is that your attacker?" Charlie asks in a hushed voice, moving to stand closer to me again.

I discreetly step away, because again, Charlie's nearness is bugging me. It's like I don't want anyone to be close to me except...him. The stranger striding in my direction. "He didn't attack me," I tell Charlie. "I think he's hurt. He was covered in blood."

Charlie cups a hand to his mouth. "Who are you?" he calls out.

The man doesn't answer. He just moves toward us with purpose, and as he moves closer, I find myself frozen in place.

And I feel...strange. Languid. Happy. Pleasant.

Sexy.

I watch him move, and even as he comes into the light and I see just how filthy and plastered with blood the man is, he looks...sensual. He moves like a panther, a predator...a sexy damn beast.

My pussy clenches again.

"Oh..." Charlie breathes, and when I look over at him, he's got an utterly besotted look on his face. Okay, so it's not just me. There's something about this man, I think.

He approaches us, all bloody hair and naked chest. His

pants cling to his legs, soaked and outlining his muscles. His hair looks long, his beard clinging to his jaw, and his eyes are such a bright silver in his face that they're positively overwhelming. As he comes closer, I realize just how massive he is. He's big and muscled, his shoulders broad and intimidating. When he comes to stand in front of me, I don't even make it to his shoulder.

The man completely ignores Charlie, his attention focused entirely on me. "What's your name, my light?"

I don't know if I want to giggle with glee or drop to my knees in front of him and beg to let him fuck my mouth. "Carly," I breathe, swept up in his spell. "I'm Carly."

And I'm all yours.

I don't say that part out loud. I'm not crazy. But I mean it. There's something about this man that is just making my hormones scream awake. I'm both horrified and fascinated, because I've never felt like this before, ever. I enjoy flirting. I enjoy getting to know a guy. I've never been so viscerally attracted to a man that I wanted to have sex the moment I saw him.

Especially not a man I found in an alley covered in blood. Yet...here we are.

The stranger puts his hand out to me again, palm up.

I reach out...and then pull back. "I'm not falling for that again." I sound breathless and apologetic as I say it. "Sorry."

His face broadens into a perfect smile, all white teeth and cocky tilt to his lips, and I get weak in the knees all over again. I think Charlie does, too. He makes a weird noise behind me, but the guy doesn't even look over at him. He's looking at me and only me, and I'm entranced by that beautiful grin. "I am called Kassam."

"Are you all right? Do you..." I stare at his bloody face, his chest, his long, wet hair sticking to his skin. "Do you have somewhere to go?"

"Can I go with you?"

I should say no. I absolutely should say no. Stranger danger and all that. Instead, I make a wobbly noise in my throat. "Sure."

"Or me," Charlie says, speaking up. He surges forward, practically pushing me aside. "You can come stay with me if you want. I've got plenty of room."

Kassam's smile doesn't fade, but he finally looks over at Charlie. "No," he says. " I have everything I need with Carly."

The way he says my name makes me flush with heat. Oh boy. I can't think straight. Not when he's watching me with those incredibly haunting eyes. My whole brain feels like it's fogged with lust. "Are you...hurt?" I ask Kassam. I reach out and put my hand on his bare chest. I don't know why I do it, just that I feel like I have to, and when I do, I want to close my eyes with how good it feels. I don't care that he's sticky with blood and a stranger—I'm about ready to shuck my panties and climb him.

"Better now," Kassam murmurs.

"Where..." I lick my lips, and it's hard to concentrate when Kassam watches that small movement. "Where's your shirt? Your wallet?"

He shrugs.

"We...we should lock up," Charlie says, and he sounds as dazed as me.

Lock up. Right. The bar. I stare at my hand on Kassam's bloody chest, and I can't seem to pull away from him.

He notices my troubles, I think. Kassam gently takes my wrist and pries my hand from his chest. "Go on. I am not going anywhere. We have time."

I don't ask "time for what" because I don't care. All I know is I have Kassam and I have time. Time for all kinds of things, and my mind is shotgunning mental images into my head of all sorts of filthy, wicked things to do to this man. I practically sleepwalk through the rest of my tasks at the bar, putting away the cleaning supplies while Charlie readies the cash for the bank deposit. Like we always do, we head out to the bank across the street together, and he puts the envelope in the drop box. Then, he heads toward his car, pausing a few times as if wanting to ask me if he can stay with Kassam.

It's weird, but I also get it. The small part of my brain that's not completely overwhelmed by Kassam totally understands. I head toward my car on zombie legs, my skin prickling as Kassam puts a possessive hand on my shoulder. I open the driver's side door and get in, and he waits beside my car.

And waits.

"Um," I say, gesturing at the other side. "Do you want to get in?"

He nods, moving around to the door, and then fumbles at the handle. It seems odd to me that he doesn't know how to work a car door, but what about this isn't absolutely bananas? I lean over and tug on the handle. The door opens and Kassam folds his big body into the car so very awkwardly I would laugh if my panties weren't completely soaked.

What the fuck is wrong with me? And why don't I care? Right now, all I give a shit about is Kassam coming to my apartment so I can spend more time with him. I don't care that he's a stranger. I don't care that he's covered in blood. I just...need this. Badly. And I can't figure out why.

I glance over at him. He's not wearing a seatbelt, and he's getting blood all over everything and...I still don't care. It's like I'm drugged, this fascination I have with him. "Did you do something to me?" I ask, breathless.

"It is my presence," Kassam says. "It cannot be helped."

"Oh." I think for a moment. "Okay."

My place is just around the corner, and it takes less than five minutes for me to park in my assigned space and turn the car off. Kassam fumbles with the door again, so I open it for him, and I'm rewarded with a pleased grin that makes me feel like

I'm melting. I can't resist putting a hand on him again, and I do, touching his chest. I'm fascinated by how big he is, and how warm, and yet something is...off. Not in a bad way, but in a strange, different sort of way. Like I'm missing something important, some big clue.

Of course, it's hard to think about clues when he's looking at me like I'm making a cake and he wants to lick the spoon... and I'm the spoon.

"Where is your home?" he asks in a sultry voice.

"Stairs," I breathe. "Up the stairs." And I take his hand, noticing mine are covered in blood almost as much as his are, and lead him toward the garage elevator. There's no one around this time of night, which suits me just fine, and I'm practically panting as I get my keys out of my purse as the elevator creeps its way up.

He's just coming in for a shower, Carly, I tell myself. This isn't an agreement for anything.

But somehow, I just know I'm lying to myself. I have this sneaking suspicion that nothing's going to be the same if Kassam comes into my apartment, and I have an even bigger suspicion that I don't care.

Kassam makes a curious noise as the elevator dings for my floor. I look over at him curiously. "The walls are...thin here," he says. "Now I understand."

"Walls?" I echo.

"Between our worlds."

I blink, waiting for that to make sense. It doesn't. "Um...are you on mushrooms?"

He chuckles, the sound rolling through my body like honey. "No, my light, I am not on anything." The look he gives me is pure sensuality, and my toes curl.

"That's good," I manage. "I was wondering because of the blood." I fumble with my keys as I head for my door. "I guess it's not yours?"

"No, it is mine."

I turn, a wordless noise escaping my throat. I scan him, but under all that red gunk, he looks...good? Damn good. I don't see anything that would be causing so much damn blood, either. "Are you wounded?"

He shrugs. "Not anymore." His gaze scans over me, making my skin prickle with awareness. "I find that now that I am free, everything is restored. Good, and bad."

"Free?" I echo as I push the door open. "What do you mean?" My voice sounds all fluttery. Am I really doing this? Am I dragging a stranger? A blood-covered stranger? Into my apartment? This is serial killer territory and yet all I can think about is how utterly turned on I am in this moment. Like I can't think of anything except Kassam and his fascinating eyes. Kassam and his bulging muscles. Kassam and his wicked smile.

Kassam touching my hand and my body spontaneously orgasming. I mean, how does that work anyhow?

I gesture at my apartment as he follows me in. "Home sweet home. The bathroom is the door on the left." My place isn't much. It's little bigger than a studio, with a futon bed-slash-couch propped up against the wall, two windows looking out on the city, and my TV. There's my bathroom, my minuscule kitchen with my tiny, dying herb plant on the counter, and in the next room over is my tiny shoebox bedroom. I cringe at my college-student decor, because I'm not exactly big on decorating or home improvement. I get too distracted for things like picking out rugs or paintings. I'd much rather curl up with a book or take a walk in the park than shop. It reflects in my clothing, too. I'm very much a jeans and T-shirt kind of girl. Looking at Kassam, though, I wish I was a little more sophisticated. I wish I had a bottle of wine and some hors d'oeuvres that I could offer my guest...after he showers, of course.

Because I suspect this is going where I think it's going to go, and I am ten thousand percent okay with that.

Kassam is watching me with fascination instead of heading toward the bathroom to clean up, and my cheeks get hot. I brush past him and move toward the bathroom, opening the door and gesturing that he should go inside. "Need me to show you how to work the shower?"

"Yes."

I should be surprised but I'm not. Actually, there should be a lot of things ringing alarm bells in my head right now, but I just feel kind of pleasant and happy. There's a blissful fog settled over my brain, and it feels as if nothing matters other than enjoying myself. So I'm going to. I smile at Kassam as I slide past him, turn on the water, and test my hand under it. "Warm, cool, or hot?"

"Hot. Very hot." He smiles at me. "I'm tired of the cold."

I can appreciate that. I turn the water temperature up as high as it'll go, hand him my bathing pouf, and gesture at the door, since we're both crowded inside. "I'll be in the living area—"

"You do not want to wash me?"

My mouth goes dry. I stare at his filthy, broad chest. "I shouldn't."

"Shouldn't you?"

"I shouldn't be doing any of this," I protest, even as I step forward and indicate he should get into the shower. "I think you're fogging my mind."

"You're probably right." Kassam sighs. "I will make everything good for you, so you have no regrets at least."

Well that sounds...ominous and sexy both. He climbs into the tub, moving to stand under the spray, and doesn't even bother to take his pants off. Oh. I notice that the water is filthy as it pools around his feet...bare feet. How did I not notice that before? "Where are the rest of your clothes?" I ask him, even as I add soap to my pouf and lather it up. I'm going to wash this man, despite the fact that I'm tired from a full day of work, and he's a stranger covered in blood.

I'm going to wash him and then we're going to do dirty, dirty things to each other, and I'm oddly, bizarrely excited about that.

Kassam leans under the spray, letting it wash away some of the mess on his face and in his long hair. I start to wash every bit of him that I can, since the blood seems to be slow to come off his skin. As I scrub, I can't help but notice that his skin is the color of golden-brown toast, delicious and warm. His hair is long and flows down his shoulders, dark and messy. I wash him as best I can, but my mind is focused on things other than cleaning.

And I finally have to ask. "How come you made me...come?"

He chuckles. "Did I?"

"When we touched hands, yeah. And then I passed out."

"Hedonism. It is just as strong here as it is in my world." He looks thoughtful and somewhat sad. "I wonder what you'd be like if you weren't affected by it."

"I wouldn't be in here washing you, that's for damn sure," I say tartly.

"A god forced to wash himself," he muses in a teasing voice. "Truly a nightmare."

"Are you sure you're not on mushrooms or something?" I ask again. "Because you're not a god."

"I'm not?" Kassam sounds as if he's holding back laughter. "You're certain?"

"I'm pretty sure you would be able to clean yourself if you were," I point out. "And I'm pretty sure there are better people to spend time with if you are a god."

"Than yourself? Why is that?"

I shrug, moving the pouf down his arm. God, that arm. "I'm not exciting. You could find yourself a beautiful actress, or someone with a lot of talent in singing or dancing. Someone that does good things for people. I'm just...me." I grab his arm and force him to turn under the water so I can wash his other side. "A somewhat bossy waitress."

He chuckles again. "But I am with you. And I do not mind your bossiness."

"Of course not. You're going to get laid. Tell me that in the morning."

Kassam throws his head back and laughs, and the breath steals from my throat at how fucking gorgeous this man is. It should be against the law to be so damn...appealing. Like there's never been anyone quite as beautiful as him, or as magnetic. Even his laughing silver eyes pull me in and make me want to touch him.

"I really hope you're not a serial killer," I whisper, fascinated by him.

He gazes down at me, all strong jaw scruffed up by a slight beard. "I am a god."

"Well, parts of you are definitely god-like." I glance down at his wet, clinging pants and there's a massive, hard length straining against the front of his clothing. It's outlined magnificently thanks to the water, to the point that I can see the mushroomed tip of him. My mouth waters.

"Am I clean enough?" he asks.

"For?" I need to shampoo his hair and give him another good soaping. He needs to take his pants off so I can wash the rest of him. And—

Kassam picks me up by the hips, hauls me up against the wall, and kisses me.

3

Oh boy. I wasn't expecting that.

Heat curls through my belly as his mouth slicks over mine, his tongue hot and hungry. He kisses like a frantic beast, like a man that hasn't been kissed in ages. He's all insatiable need, and a moan escapes me before I realize I'm making any sort of sound. His lips on mine feel like...heaven. I've kissed a decent amount of men in the past, but no one's ever affected me like this. Like I'm going to fall apart if his tongue ever leaves my mouth. Like his kisses are the only things holding me together. Like I'm going to burst into another spontaneous orgasm with a few more flicks of his tongue. Even the insistent, abrasive graze of his beard against my jaw feels erotic as hell.

He lifts his mouth for a moment to grin down at me. "I like kissing you."

"Oh...okay." I blink up at him, dazed. "Are we...are we not supposed to like kissing each other?"

He shrugs. "It helps." His hand goes behind my neck, his hips pressing me to the wall, and he kisses me again. This time, the kiss is slower, more languid, and I have a hard time concentrating on anything but the heat of his mouth on mine. He said something about...how liking his kiss helps, and I want to ask more, but then he starts to kiss down my neck, and I'm lost.

Because there's nothing quite like a good neck kiss. A man that knows how to nibble on your throat in a way that makes your toes curl is absolutely a keeper, and it's clear Kassam is very experienced in this sort of thing. I whimper as his tongue glides up the side of my throat, as if he's tasting me. "Jesus Christ," I whisper, legs locked tight around his hips. "You're far too good at that."

Kassam rumbles with amusement, and nips at my throat. "I should be. I have had a great deal of practice."

All right, I don't want to particularly hear about the man's past when we're making out, so I pat his shoulder, trying to get his attention as he skates up to my ear and sucks on my earlobe. Oh god. Ears are just as good as throat, and if he tongues my ear just right, I'm going to be mauling his cock like a shameless hussy in moments. I gasp when his teeth graze my earlobe—and catch a mouthful of shower water. Right. "Kassam," I pant. "Let's...finish...shower...first." I hammer at his shoulder as his tongue sweeps up the shell of my ear, my pussy clenching in response. "Water...cold."

"Mmm. I suppose I can wait. Not for long, though." He gently sets me back down and I realize dimly that I'm still wearing my sneakers from the bar. Jeans, too. They're both waterlogged and I couldn't give a shit. My shirt's clinging to my breasts, outlining my figure, and I notice Kassam's appreciative gaze goes there. I don't have the greatest face and I'm not all that talented at a lot of stuff, but I've got a great body.

So does Kassam. I run a hand down his wet chest, noticing for the first time that under all that grime and blood, he's got tattoos. There are strange, tribal-looking geometric markings across his pectorals. They sweep across his shoulders and down his arms, before fading into his skin. I find them fascinating, but then again, I find all of him fascinating. I let my fingers trail down his flat abdomen and dip into his navel. His pants are slung below it, waterlogged and barely held up by a bloated leather belt. "Can I...?"

"Do what you like," he murmurs. His hand runs through my hair, wetting it, and he looks as if he wants to kiss me again, his lips parted.

I know if he kisses me again, I'm never going to get these pants off of him, and he needs a full body scrubbing if we're going to do this. "How," I ask, ducking my head when he leans in. "How did you get covered in blood like this?"

His belt doesn't seem to have a buckle, but is knotted instead. I fumble with the knot as he brushes his hand over my breast, thumbing my nipple through the thin fabric of my wet shirt. God, this man does not play fair. "I was stabbed."

"S-stabbed?" I stumble over the word, looking up at him.

"It was a long time ago," he reassures me. "My wound is closed. Let us not talk about it. I would rather focus on more pleasant things...like these pretty breasts."

He gives my nipple the lightest pinch and I moan, because even the smallest touch is utterly unfair. I'm so aroused by him that my pulse feels as if it's set up shop between my thighs, and I know without touching myself that I'm aching and wet. I can feel the lips of my sex gliding against one another as I shift, I'm so very wet and turned on. "Can I just point out everything you say doesn't make sense?"

"It will make sense eventually, I promise you." His mouth curls into a hungry little smile, and his thumb moves over the tip of my nipple again. "Hurry and wash me if you must, because I need you."

Oh fuck. I bite back a whimper and jerk at his belt again. The swollen leather stretches and then breaks, and then his pants slip to the bottom of the tub.

And I'm left staring. And staring.

His cock is...well, it's magnificent. It's not a word I'd

normally use to describe a man's penis, but I've seen several penises in my life and not a single one has looked as...perfect as this one. Kassam's dick is something out of a painting, it's so perfect. It's long and thick and smooth, not veiny or overly flushed. The base is framed by a dark swatch of hair that seems to enhance his masculinity, and he's not circumcised. It's my first time dealing with foreskin and I could absolutely not give a fuck. It's just interesting. "Oh...okay. Are you...European?" I curl a hand around the base of his cock, testing his foreskin, and find that it glides over his shaft if I tug on it, and Kassam makes a pleased sound in his throat when I do. "Sorry. I'm not an idiot, it's just my first uncircumcised penis. Tell me if I do something wrong."

"You are doing things very, very right, my little light."

I give another weird, awkward little laugh. "That's kind of an odd nickname, you know. You can just call me Carly."

"Call me whatever you like, as long as you keep touching me," Kassam murmurs, and teases my nipple again.

I whimper, resisting the urge to drop to my knees and just start tonguing his perfect, pretty cock. It curves up at the end, like it's asking to be petted, and I can't stand it. I touch a finger along the head, circling it, and fresh pre-cum beads there.

Kassam gives a ragged groan. "Wash me quick, little light. It has been a long time and my hunger is fierce."

Such a strange way of talking. A strange accent, too. If I was looking at things closely, I'd be full of questions, but right now, all I want to be full of is his dick. "Turn around," I tell him, breathless. I re-soap the pouf and in the next two minutes, I scrub his lower half as quickly as possible, because my hunger is fierce, too. I try not to spend an overly long amount of time on his rock-hard thighs or his massive shaft and balls, or his perfect bubble of a butt. Nope. There'll be time for that later, I tell myself. Right now, I'm all about cleaning this strange grime until his skin gleams with just how clean he is.

Then I shampoo his tangled hair and add some conditioner while he runs his hands all over my body.

"Almost done," I promise him as he tugs at the waist of my jeans. It's like he can't figure them out, but maybe it's the wet fabric that's making him unable to undo them. When he makes an impatient noise, liquid heat flares through me. "You know what? I think we're good. Get under the spray. Hurry."

In what might be the quickest rinse-off ever, Kassam does as I command, and then grabs me by the hips and hauls me out of the tub with him. A stream of water drips on my floors from our soaked bodies, but I find I don't care. I'm panting with need.

"Where?" he asks, burying his face against my wet breasts. "Tell me where or I will fuck you right here."

"Bed," I manage, though I do like the idea of dropping to the floor like animals and just going to town. I point down the hall, at the other door, and he immediately slams into it. I yelp as we crash into the wood, and then he steps back, hoists me over his shoulder higher, and lifts a leg. He kicks down my bedroom door, knocking it off the hinges, and making a godawful racket. I cringe, thinking of the neighbors downstairs. "Um, next time just use the doorknob—"

"Next time," he echoes, but I don't think he's listening. He heads to my bed and dumps me onto my back, his dripping, golden body looming over mine.

Just like that, my mouth goes dry and I forget all about doors. He yanks on my sodden sneakers, pulling them off my feet while I undo my jeans and shimmy the wet material down my legs.

He grabs my jeans and flings them down to the floor, then laughs at the sight of my pink bikini panties. "How many layers are you wearing, woman?"

"The normal amount?"

Kassam laughs as if I'm being funny, then peels my panties

off. I sit up to take off my T-shirt and bra, but he pushes me back down on the bed with a gentle nudge, moving over me. His mouth claims mine again, even as he fits his hips between my spread thighs.

"Oh, are we not doing foreplay?" I whisper, frowning. "Because I need foreplay if I'm going to come—"

He bites down gently on my lip, tugging on it, even as he pushes into my body.

And...oh fuck. I whimper with sheer bliss as he fills me. Nothing has ever felt so damn good. His cock feels as if it's the perfect size, just big enough to stretch me in all the right places, but not so big that it's painful. I lift my legs, locking them around his hips as he thrusts into me, starting a fierce, frantic rhythm. Did I say I needed foreplay? Maybe I need it with other men, but with Kassam, I feel like I'm going to shatter into a million pieces just from this. I make a pathetic little whine when his next thrust rubs against my G-spot, my nails digging into his back.

"I will make it good for you, little light," he breathes into my ear. He gives me another hard, filthy thrust, our wet bodies sliding across the bed. "Always good for you."

"Kassam," I pant as a deep, curling orgasm begins to build in my belly from his thrusts alone. It feels different than a regular orgasm, darker and far more elusive, but I want to feel what happens if it surfaces.

He grabs my hips without a word and moves up, just a little, until his weight is pushing my thighs to my chest and he's fucking me even deeper. That does the trick, and that spiral of pleasure keeps growing until it's racing all through me, consuming my thoughts until I feel as if I'm going to die if I don't come. I choke out his name, over and over again, as he plows into me, until the bed creaks and groans under us and we're in danger of falling off the side.

"Carly," he breathes, and grabs my hand in his, nipping at the fleshy part below my thumb. "You belong to me now."

That's all it takes for me to have the hardest orgasm of my life. I come with such force that my body goes rigid underneath him, my pussy clenching tight around his cock as he drives into me. Kassam thrusts a few more times, then groans, and I feel the liquid heat of his release wash through my body in the most curious way. I've never felt that before, I realize. I've never actually felt my partner's seed inside me. It's...odd.

"We...didn't use a condom," I pant as he rocks his hips against mine one last time. That's bad, I remind my pleasure-addled brain. I'm not on the pill, either. Maybe I need to hunt down a pharmacy in the morning and find a morning-after pill.

Kassam slides out of my body, leaving me feeling ever-so-slightly bereft, and rolls onto his back with a sigh. "What is a condom?"

∼

I WAKE up to a delightfully sore pussy and an empty bed. I yawn, feeling lethargic and yet wonderful, trying to recall the events of last night.

They flash through my mind immediately. Alley. Kassam. Shower. Sex. More Kassam.

Like...four times more throughout the night. He'd just wake me up, roll onto me, and the next thing I knew, we were having incredible sex. No foreplay, no conversation, just a deep dicking that sent me to places I'd never been before.

I look over at the empty side of my bed. The sheets are mussed, still damp from last night's drippy post-shower sex, and the room reeks of fucking, but I'm alone. I hear the distant clank of silverware against a dish and realize he's in my kitchen.

The enormity of what I've done hits me like a ton of bricks. Oh fuck. I found a man in an alley—a stranger!—and took him home and fucked him. Fucked him a LOT. A dirty stranger, to boot. He's probably a hobo.

I had hobo sex and it was fucking great.

I put my hands over my face. What the hell am I doing? How do I get rid of him? My head's clearer now, at least. Last night I couldn't think straight. All I could think about was fucking the guy. Last night, he'd seemed incredibly sexy. The way he moved, the way he talked, those flashing silvery eyes. This morning, though, all I can think about is that I invited a dirty, weird stranger into my home and my body.

We didn't even use a condom.

I bite back a horrified noise and try to remain calm. Maybe I accidentally got splashed with a roofied drink or something last night. Maybe a drop landed on my finger and I—I don't know—licked my finger. Somehow. A roofie seems more logical than me finding a filthy stranger in a back alley and deciding I'm down to fuck.

The more I think about it, the more I'm convinced it's a roofie. Or Spanish Fly. Wouldn't that explain why I spontaneously orgasmed when he touched my hand? That must be it, I decide. Sure, it's awful, but I'll get over it. At least the sex was decent if not particularly creative. Just all business.

My phone buzzes on my nightstand, and I see my Mom's name light up on the message.

Oh god. I resist the urge to crawl back under the covers. My mother. It's like she knows what I was up to last night and is sending me vibes of disapproval through the phone lines. I reach over and flip my phone over so I can't see the screen, as if that will somehow make things better. Okay, Carly, I tell myself. Be rational. You made a mistake last night. Actually, you made a lot of them. Now you get to clean up your mess. Go out there, talk to the nice man—Kassam—and tell him that he needs to go home. Then you go to the pharmacy, get some morning-after pills, and pray that you weren't fertile...and pray that he has no diseases. You learn from this mistake and never, ever repeat it--

A dish shatters in the kitchen.

Fuck. I need to get up before he destroys my place. I close my eyes, visualize myself taking control of the situation, and then get out of bed. I grab a shirt from the pile of laundry in my room, throw it on, and then head out of the bedroom and into the hall. As I approach my kitchen, that languid, foggy, almost dreamlike sensation takes over my senses. Maybe that's why I don't panic when I see Kassam standing in the doorway to my open fridge, buck-ass naked.

Instead, I smile.

I'm aware that my head is messed up again. It's weird in that I know it's messed up, but...I just don't care. It's like all caring goes out the window when I'm around him, which makes it really, really hard to think straight. I came out here for...something. Something.

I think, trying to focus, but all I notice is that Kassam's really incredible butt is staring at me as he peruses the contents of my fridge.

Oh! Right. I was going to tell him to leave. Funny how that doesn't seem half as important as going over to him and just taking a bite out of that bubble butt—

Kassam turns. His face lights up with pleasure at the sight of me, even as he takes a bite out of a stick of butter, the paper still on. "Carly. You are awake."

"What...what are you doing?" I take a step forward. "Why are you eating butter?"

"I am eating everything," he announces cheerfully. "Come, try all these new experiences with me."

New experiences? Gnawing on a stick of butter? I mean, I've never done it, but I've also never wanted to. Kassam takes my hand, leading me toward the kitchen, and I'm not entirely surprised to see wrappers all over the floor. There are open boxes all over the counters, single bites taken out of my favorite breakfast pastries, and coffee grounds everywhere. It's chaos on every surface, melted things pooling on the countertop. Even more curious...my herb plant, the one I got when I decided I might try gardening, the one near death because I also abandoned gardening, has gone crazy overnight. Tendrils snake across the countertops, and it's grown so quickly and so wildly that it covers the entire stove.

What the hell?

For a moment, I stare at it, dumbfounded. Is this one of those weird situations like in the movies where I'm going to find out I've been asleep for three years instead of three hours? "What...my plant..."

"It was dying," Kassam says. "Now it is not." His arm slides around my waist and he pulls me against him, tossing down his stick of butter. "Come here."

Then, he kisses me. His lips taste like butter and his mouth like coffee grounds, but there's no denying that his kiss is utterly intoxicating. I moan as his tongue dances with my own, and he kisses me so hard and so deep that I forget almost everything. My toes curl on the cold floor, and when he drags me forward onto his thigh, I rub shamelessly against it, my pussy hot and wet and ready.

"Ah....I missed you," he murmurs, as if we've been parted for years. Kassam's buttery hands slide to my ass, rubbing it in deep, dirty circles that make me want to go and have sex with him. Again.

Reluctantly, I put a hand on his chest, pulling my mouth from his. "Kassam," I pant. "I...I can't think straight when I'm around you."

To my surprise, he grimaces. "It is the hedonism. I know. You will get used to it soon enough." He leans in and presses one more kiss to my lips, this one light and flirty. "Come. Let me feed you."

Feed me?

I let him lead me to the countertop, and when he hoists me up onto it, I realize he has no intention of using a table or anything mundane like that. My butt and thighs stick to something gritty on the counter—probably spilled sugar—and he rummages through the icebox, looking for things to eat. With delight, he holds up a small jar. "What is this? It looks good."

I shake my head quickly. "That's chopped garlic. It's not a food on its own, just for cooking. Put it back."

His face falls with disappointment, but then he pulls out something else, a bright red ketchup bottle. The look he gives me is boyish. "Is this a food on its own?"

"Not...really? It's a condiment. You can taste it, though?" I reach over and flip the lid open. "Squeeze it and it will squirt out."

Kassam gives it an enthusiastic squeeze and a fountain of bright red ketchup spurts into the air, and then splatters on my floor. He laughs, delighted, and then squirts the next bit into his mouth.

"You're kind of a terrible house guest," I tell him. Something tickles my leg and I'm surprised to see that the plant tendrils are touching my thigh. I didn't realize my plant was *that* big. I run my fingers over one of the leaves, and the darn thing has never looked so damn healthy. "Did you do something to my plant?"

"It is me," he says around a mouthful of ketchup. "I am a god. The plants will respond to my presence."

"I don't understand," I say, shaking my head. I could have sworn I heard him say "god" but that can't be right. "I think my brain is fogged again."

"You will get used to it, Carly," he promises, tossing aside the now empty ketchup bottle and peering back into my perpetually empty fridge. "You do not have many things to taste."

"I eat out," I tell him faintly. When he leans over, I get a good look at his body, and lord have mercy, he's insanely gorgeous. There's not an ounce of fat on him, and his cock, even in its resting state, is a thing of beauty. His hair has dried long and wavy and cascades down over his shoulders in a thick, tangled mane that looks soft and shiny, and he's gorgeous. Even with a mouthful of ketchup and butter in his beard, he's fucking stone-cold gorgeous.

"Eat...out?" Kassam asks, turning toward me. There is a curious look on his face.

"You know, get food from one of the local places?" I frown at him. "How do you not know what eating out is? Is your brain fogged, too?"

He moves toward me, his hands moving to either side of my legs on the counter, and then I'm trapped against his large body. He gazes up at me, so gorgeous it makes my chest ache to look at him, and grins. "My brain is not fogged. I just do not make sense to you...yet. But I will."

I lean down, fighting the urge to kiss him again. As if he can read my mind, Kassam reaches a hand up and caresses the tip of my breast through my shirt, sending a hot, piercing surge of lust through my body. "God, you're distracting," I whisper.

"I want to do this 'eat out,'" he tells me. "Let us go to one of these local places." He leans forward and then nips at my breast through my shirt, and I practically melt into a puddle on the countertop. "Then we will come home and I will fuck you until you are hoarse. Yes?"

Oh god, yes. A thousand times, yes. I let out a low moan as my answer.

"Then let us go," Kassam says.

"Pants," I whimper in protest. "We need pants."

"Why?" he asks, nuzzling my breast. He gazes up at me, his tongue dragging across my covered nipple, and I swear I nearly come all over again.

"Law," I pant. "No one will serve us if we show up naked."

"That is a foolish law," Kassam says, looking up at me with those hooded, sexy silver eyes. "Is it like that everywhere in this world?"

"What do you mean 'this world'?" I'm torn between shoving his head between my breasts again...or shoving him further south. Choices, choices.

"I mean this world," he says, as if that answers everything. "This is not my world. It is yours. I am unfamiliar with its rules. That is one reason why we are now bound together." He grins. "Among others, of course."

I shake my head. "You...you're not making sense." Please put your mouth on my tits again.

"I suspect I am not. Give it time." He grins up at me and gives my flank a light tap. "Where are these pants?"

4

It's a short time later, when I'm brushing my teeth in the bathroom, that I realize I'm no longer fogged. Kassam is in the kitchen, no doubt licking the butter paper, while I get ready to go out and get us breakfast. He's wearing a pair of old sweatpants from an ex-boyfriend of mine, along with an old hoodie, but no shoes, since there was nothing we could find in his size.

I stare at my reflection, curious. Now that he's in the next room, I can think straight. I can think straight and I wonder... what the fuck am I doing? Why have I not told him to buzz off? Why am I going to go have breakfast with him instead of getting rid of him? I think back over our conversations.

This is not my world.

We are now bound together.

He's crazy, I think. Disoriented. Possibly off a medication of some kind? Maybe I should call the police. I spit my toothpaste out, wiping at my mouth, and wonder if I can get to my phone in the bedroom before Kassam's presence fogs me again. Staying away from him is key, I realize. He's cast some sort of... spell on me.

A spell. I didn't think such things existed, but after being in Kassam's confusing, sexy presence, I believe it now.

I think of my mother again. Mom believes in crystals and hoodoo and all that shit. She'd know the answer I'm looking for. The question is, how do I ask without sending her into a panic spiral? I ponder for a minute, and then start to type.

CARLY: Morning, Ma. I'm a little foggy this AM. Late night. What's the best crystal for clearing your mind?

MOM'S ANSWER comes right away, as I knew it would.

MOM: Hello, darling!!
MOM: Clear quartz is best! It will also extract negative energy. You work too hard! Tell your boss you need to leave work earlier. I don't like how late you stay out.
MOM: You need to take care of yourself.

I SMILE. Twenty-eight years old and my mother still hovers protectively over me. Probably always will, too.

CARLY: Thanks, Ma!
CARLY: And I'm fine. I promise it's not a regular thing. And I work at a bar, of course I have to work late.
CARLY: Please don't worry. XOXO

MY MOM WILL WORRY ANYHOW, of course. What's ironic is that she's going to worry about me bartending, which is the least of my worries right now. I'm far more concerned with the big, seductive stranger in my kitchen that keeps fogging my head every time I get close. It has to be some sort of chemical situation, I tell myself. He's dosed in some sort of cologne with pheromones and that's why my body lights up like a firework whenever he's near. That's why my brain can't function properly around him and I end up agreeing to everything. There has to be a simple, logical explanation.

I dig out my jewelry box from under the counter and look for crystals. I have dozens of them, because my mom is nothing if not consistent in her birthday and Christmas gifts of choice. She's given me so many damn crystals over the years I could probably open my own shop. I tug out piece after piece with quartz—a pendant, earrings, a ring, and two silver bracelets with a big decorative hunk of quartz over each wrist. Sure, I look a little...crystal-enthusiastic, but if it helps, I'm absolutely going to roll with it.

Now to test them out.

I take a deep breath and head out of the bathroom, back toward the main part of my apartment. Kassam's not in the kitchen. He's leaning out the window in my living room, practically on the fire escape. He holds out a hand and clucks his tongue, and in his palm is...a bird. It's a tiny sparrow, but it looks up at him with inquisitive eyes, chirping. Kassam smiles back down at it. "Go and see what you can for me, little one."

As if it can understand him, it trills a response and then flies away.

"How...how did you do that?" I ask, shocked.

Kassam looks over at me. He grins, taking in my appearance. I'm wearing a T-shirt and another pair of jeans, because that's all my wardrobe consists of. My hair's pulled up in a fuzzy knot atop my head and my bangs hang over my eyes. It should be a casual look, but I bet it's ruined by all the crystals I'm dripping with, and I wonder if he thinks I dressed up for him. "How did I do what?" he asks, regarding me with a mixture of pleasure and possessiveness. He lifts one big, browned hand and flicks it at me. "Come here."

To my relief, I don't feel any urge to comply. I cross my arms over my chest and silently thank my crystals. For once, my mother is on to something. "First you tell me what's going on."

He lounges against the window. "You'll have to be more specific. What do you mean, 'what is going on'? I fear I am just as confused as you as to our situation. If anything, you probably have more answers than me."

Kassam smiles, and my heart lurches at the sight, my body responding. Okay, so the crystals aren't miracle workers. I reach up and rub one of the earrings, trying to activate the damn thing to work harder. "I mean all of this. Who are you? Why does my brain turn to mush around you? Why were you all bloody in an alley last night? Why did you eat a goddamn stick of butter?" I gesture at my window. "How did you get a bird to eat out of your hand? I was gone for all of five minutes. Where are your clothes? Your ID?"

"That is a great many questions, my light." Kassam doesn't look ruffled by my rapid-fire questioning. "Which do you want answered first?"

"Who are you?" I immediately shoot back.

"Kassam."

"That's not an answer and you know it."

He grins wider. "You can come and sit in my lap and I will answer you truthfully."

"Or I'll push you out that damn window. How's that?"

He throws his head back and laughs, as if both delighted and surprised at my response. "So violent. So angry. Just because you put a few pretty rocks on your wrists? Have I been so cruel to you?" His gaze changes, from amused to sexy, and my skin prickles in response. "I thought I gave you a great deal of pleasure."

"Look." I will not step toward him. I will not. "This...isn't me, okay? I'm not the type of girl to find some guy bloody in an alley and then take him home and bone his brains out. There is something *very* wrong with that situation, okay? And now I wake up and you're not only still here, but you're licking my butter and—"

"You are obsessed with the butter," he points out. "Are you sad because I wasn't licking you? I'd be more than happy to."

"Will you please listen to me?" I'm about to tear my hair out, I really am. "I don't understand what's going on. Did you drug me? Is that what this is? Can you please stop flirting for five minutes and just give me a straight answer?"

Kassam watches me. Sighs. Lifts his shoulders in a slight shrug. "I cannot stop flirting with you, because that is not who I am. I am cursed to be Hedonism, and so everything out of my mouth will be about pleasure, or for pleasure, or an effort to get more pleasure." He tilts his head, regarding me. "Now do you understand?"

"No. If anything, I'm more confused than ever before. What do you mean, you're Hedonism?"

He leans against the window, and as he does, a new bird shows up. A pigeon. He reaches out and strokes it idly with a hand, and the bird just lets him. It hops onto his knee, into my apartment, and coos as he pets it. "Your world does not have Anticipations, does it?"

"What do you mean, my world?" I feel like I'm shrieking into a void. I keep asking questions and he swears he'll answer and yet I'm getting nowhere. "Are you trying to tell me you're not from my world?"

Kassam grins. "That is exactly what I am telling you."

I stare at him.

Then, I snort. "Bullshit."

"No shit at all," he says in that same calm, easy voice. "It is truth. Somehow when the sword was pulled from my guts, the

Spidae saw fit to send me to your world instead of to return me to my own. Perhaps there is a lesson here I am meant to learn, or it is for my safety. Either way, here I am." He shrugs. "I am helpless and alone...except for you."

"Me?" I protest. "Why me?"

"Because you took my hand." He holds his out to me. "The moment we touched, we were bonded."

"Again, I have to call bullshit."

"Did you not feel something special the first time we touched?" He arches a thick brow at me.

I clench my jaw, determined not to blush. I spontaneously orgasmed, and I suspect he knows it. Did I feel something special? Oh, I felt a whole lot of special. "You did something to me," I accuse. I know I'm being shrill and demanding but I'm just so damned confused. All I want are a few answers. I don't think it's that hard.

"Of course I did. I bonded us when we touched. It is how I am able to stay in your world."

"What do you mean, bonded us?"

He holds his hand out to me, indicating I should take it. "It means that we are together, you and I. You are my anchor in this reality, and in this mortal realm. Otherwise, as a god, I will not be able to remain. We are bonded until I return to my divine home."

I stare at him. So much for simple answers. "I'm sorry, did you say you were a god?"

Kassam inclines his head. "I am."

"I don't believe you."

He laughs. "You are so suspicious. Do your people not believe in the gods anymore?"

"There's only one god!" Not that I'm all that religious, but we mostly agree that there's just one god. I think. "And you ain't him, buddy."

Kassam laughs even harder. The pigeon jumps on his

shoulder and nuzzles at his ear, and for a split second, I'm jealous of the pigeon. Clearly I'm insane. Clearly. "No, if you refer to the High Father, I am most definitely not him. I am one of his naughty, naughty sons." The look he gives me is positively wicked. "Some naughtier than others."

"Again, I'm going to have to go with bullshit."

"Take my hand, then. My powers are muted here—"

"Oh, naturally." I roll my eyes. "Of course your powers are muted here."

"—but I can show you a few small things at least." He gets to his feet, pigeon friend still on his shoulder. As I watch, another one flies into my window, looking for him. Did he smear peanut butter on the landing or something? Is that why there's a bird invasion?

I eye the hand Kassam holds out to me. "Dude, you just petted a pigeon. They are hella diseased. I'm not touching you."

"A god cannot get diseases." He thinks for a moment. "Unless you are Kalos of course. Which I am not. If I wash my hands, will you touch me then and let me prove this to you?"

I eye him warily. "Get your birds out of here, too. They don't belong inside."

He nods once, and to my surprise, the birds fly back out the window. Kassam never said a word. Just a coincidence, I tell myself. Nothing more.

Something's definitely wrong with this guy.

5

I desperately need a cup of coffee, and since Kassam has helped himself to all of my grounds (seriously, what the fuck), we head out the door and down to the coffee shop on the corner. It's a place I normally frequent, usually isn't all that busy, and tends to turn a blind eye when I show up in sweatpants and with terrible hair.

Usually.

Today...things are weird. We walk a whole block—far too little for me to bother driving—and by the time we get to the coffee shop, there are people following us. Kassam is barefoot, wearing an old boyfriend's clothing, his long, tangled hair fluttering in the morning breeze, and he looks as if he's thoroughly enjoying himself. He also seems to be oblivious to the crowd we're gathering. People cross the street to stand near him. Random pedestrians follow behind us.

And the damn birds. I've never heard so many birds in my life. Every tree we pass is covered in them in all their chirping, maddening glory.

It just reminds me that Kassam might be who he says he is—a god.

But that's impossible. It makes zero sense. Why is there a god here in Chicago? Why is there a god from another world here on Earth, period? And why does he keep giving me spontaneous orgasms when we touch? Why do people and birds follow behind him like some sort of freaking Disney princess?

I don't get it, but I'm relieved when we step into the cafe and off the street. I want to turn around and go back to my apartment, but I'm a little worried the weirdos will follow us.

There's two people in line at the counter, and we step in behind them. Immediately, a businessman turns around and gives Kassam a broad, seductive smile. "Hello."

Kassam gives him a lazy, assessing look that tells me he's not exactly turning down what this dude is offering.

I pinch the "god" in the side, hard. "Can you turn this shit off for five minutes?"

He leans over toward me. "I cannot. It is my curse."

"Let me guess, you're cursed to be SO beautiful and desirable?" I hiss at him. That sounds like bullshit, even to my salty ass. The line moves up one and the businessman keeps staring at Kassam, lust in his eyes. I snap my fingers in front of his face and point. "Order or get out of line, buddy."

"Right. Apologies," the man says.

I turn back to Kassam. He's not looking at the businessman like he wants to eat him anymore. Now, he's looking at a big glass display of cookies with that same hungry expression. I suppose I should be glad? Instead I pinch his side again. "Hello? What's this about a curse?"

"What are those baked goods?" Kassam asks, fascinated. "Are they tasty?"

"I'll get you one of each if you can answer my questions," I say. He lights up, and I resist the urge to rub my face. At least I found a way to get his attention. "So, for real, what is your curse?"

He leans over even as the man in front of us gets out of line. "I am cursed with hedonism."

"I...oh..." I step up to the counter, flummoxed. As I do, I see the young barista—barely college age, blonde and peppy—get all soft-eyed at the sight of Kassam. She stands a little straighter, her tits pressing against the front of her apron, and her nipples are prominently on display through her shirt. Is he going to have this reaction from everyone, I wonder? "Two coffees and one of every cookie, please."

She doesn't even look in my direction. Just puts a hand to her breast and stares at Kassam as if he's the most stunning thing she's ever seen.

And honestly? I get it. I was totally fucked over last night and in the same situation. So I can't even be mad that she's in a horny daze. So I put cash on the counter, grab the tongs and open the cookie display, helping myself to a stack, just like I promised Kassam. "Here ya go, bud," I say loudly to get his attention.

He turns to me, his expression brightening as I hand him the treats. "Marvelous."

I point at an empty table in the corner. "Go sit over there and I'll bring you a drink."

He heads away, and the girl behind the counter watches him go, her face full of longing. "Two coffees, please?" I ask again, determined to be patient.

She finally glances at me, and her face colors with embarrassment. She grabs two cups, flustered. "I'm so sorry—"

"Don't be, he does that to everyone." Heck, he'd be doing it to me right now if I wasn't dripping in crystals. I touch them absently, making sure they're all still in place. Even with all these on, he still affects me. It's just like standing in winter sunlight instead of hugging the sun directly. I have a feeling it's a sensation I need to get used to if Kassam's going to be sticking around.

And then I wonder if he is. Sticking around, that is. It's something I haven't considered all that much. He just doesn't seem like he has anywhere else to go, and he's content to hang out with me. I add that to the mental list of questions that's growing longer by the moment. I need to get this figured out, because he said we were bound now, and that feels awfully...permanent.

It's strange, because it also feels very...right? Like a puzzle piece sliding into place, I muse as the girl hands me the coffees and takes my cash. Kassam hasn't said anything more than that he's a god and he's played with a few birds and eaten all my groceries and yet...it feels like him showing up was meant to be. Like he's not going anywhere because now we're a team, and I need to protect him.

Odd that I should feel protective of a man that's easily a foot taller (and probably a hundred pounds heavier) than me.

I move to the little table, and it's easy to see which one Kassam picked. It's surrounded by people, from a woman with a baby in a stroller to the same businessman again, everyone in the damn cafe is clustered around the table, watching Kassam take a big bite out of each cookie. "Hi guys," I say brightly as I push my way through. "We need you all to back up a little, okay? Kassam needs his space. Isn't that right, Kassam?"

He smiles lazily at his new disciples and makes a flicking motion with his hand, indicating they should go.

They disperse—very reluctantly and with many longing looks—and I sit down in a newly vacated seat that's still warm. Yech. I take the sugar from the center of the table and pour a heaping amount into Kassam's cup, along with a dose of creamer. "You can't turn this shit off, right?"

"Alas, no. It would not be a punishment if I could." He breaks off a small piece of cookie and holds it out to me. "Let me feed you, my light."

I glance up, startled, and Kassam's got that "let's fuck" look in his eyes. Oh shit. He watches me with that hungry gaze, and I realize that the people around me are not the only ones that need to focus. Kassam needs reining in, too. I take the cookie from his fingers, pop it into my mouth, and then put a lid on his coffee. I offer it to him. "This one is yours. I doctored it up in a way I think you'll like."

"Let us go to your abode and fuck, Carly," he murmurs. "My body is ravenous for yours."

I'm trying to sweeten my own coffee and accidentally spill sugar all over the table at that. "Throw on the brakes, Kassam," I say in a wobbly voice. "I need answers before I'm letting you touch me again."

He growls impatiently.

"Drink your coffee," I say. "Give me my answers, and then let's...we'll talk about you and me."

I suspect he takes that as a "yes, we'll fuck" answer, because his smile widens and he gives me another sultry look before taking a sip of his coffee. His expression turns to one of ecstasy and his head tilts back. He groans, low and deep, and I cross my legs, because my pussy pulses in response.

I'm pretty sure someone a few tables over groans, too.

"What do you mean it's your curse, Kassam?" I ask, leaning in. "Can you tell me more about that?"

"It is my curse to be split into four Aspects of what I truly am." He picks up another bite of cookie and offers it to me. I hold a hand up and he eats it instead, his eyes closing. His long lashes look stunning, and I find myself fascinated by them... and touch the crystals at my wrists.

Focus. Focus. "So there's four Kassams running around?"

"There was...once. I am the last. I was trapped on the mortal plane with an enchanted sword in my guts." He lifts his shirt and touches his washboard abs. I'm pretty sure I hear the barista whimper. "For millennia, I existed without existing. Unable to free myself, and unable to touch my powers. My anchor abandoned me to die, and I assume he died, too." Kassam's gaze grows hard. "He was a coward and deserves whatever fate he has suffered. I hope the fires of the underworld burn him for all eternity. I hope he suffers a—"

"Let's put a pin in the whole 'deserves suffering' thing," I say quickly, before Kassam can get even more derailed. I reach over and tap his hand. "What's an anchor?"

He captures my fingers before I can pull away and lifts them to his mouth, kissing the tips. "You are, my light." And he gives me the flirtiest, most lascivious look ever.

I squirm in my chair. I'm pretty sure others are squirming, too. His sexuality is so intense it practically hangs in the air. Like if the coffee shop spontaneously turned into an orgy, I would not be surprised in the slightest. Everyone seems to be hanging on his every word, even when we talk so low they can't hear us. Kassam is just...magnetic. "You know that's not an answer, right?"

Kassam grins, and he's that fascinating mixture of boyish charm and seductive stranger once more. "It is a better answer than the one I have to give you. Plus, I like thinking about you." He tilts his head, regarding me. "It has been a long time since I had company. I did not realize how much I missed it."

"You know you're a master of not answering a question?"

He laughs, delighted. "So I am. Very well." He thinks for a moment, then takes a long drink of his coffee. His eyes light up with enthusiasm at the taste, and I know my decision to sugar the ever-loving fuck out of it was the right one. "As a god, I cannot dwell on the mortal plane without some sort of anchor to tie me here. My very being is bonded to yours because you volunteered to be my anchor."

"Did I? I don't remember that."

"You held out your hand. I took it. That is enough." He smiles and drains his cup. "Now that we are joined, I am here on this mortal plane for as long as you are."

Well that sucks. It sounds like the choice is all his and zero percent mine. I guess I shouldn't be surprised—if he IS a god, I'm just a lowly mortal and all. "So why are you here on Earth then?"

"Earth?"

I use my thumbs to point at my surroundings. "Here? What's your world called?"

"Aaah." He nods, thoughtful. "Aos. It is called Aos...or it was when I was last present. Perhaps it has changed since then. A lot of time has passed." He tips back his empty cup and then stares mournfully down at it. Wordlessly, I nudge mine toward him, and he gives me a delicious smile of pleasure as he tips my cup back. "You are an excellent companion so far."

A hot blush steals over my cheeks. "What, because I fed you?"

"You fed a lot of my needs last night." The look he gives me over the rim of the coffee cup is positively sultry.

Good god. I cross my legs, because my pussy is reacting to that look he's giving me. "Don't distract me with more of your not-answers. Why are you here on Earth instead of Heaven or wherever it is you hang out?"

The smile he gives me is positively lethal. "Because I've been very, very naughty."

I shift in my chair, heat suffusing my body. Despite the crystals, I still want to race around the side of the table and crawl into his lap and dry-hump his leg. Maybe I need more crystals. Or maybe he's just that damn sexy.

At the table next to us, an elderly couple starts making out. Like, hardcore making out. Tongues-licking-over-each-other's-faces, tearing-at-each-other's-clothing making out. I try not to stare, because it's not polite, but do these people not realize they're out in public? Discreetly, I adjust my gaze to a booth behind Kassam...and see a woman with her hand down her pants, her eyes closed in ecstasy. I look around, and everyone in the cafe seems to be in various stages of...pleasuring. "What the fuck's in the coffee this morning?"

Kassam chuckles and drinks the rest of mine, just as quickly as he did the last cup. "It's my presence."

I look over at him, narrowing my eyes. I think about how much he fogged my mind and how I couldn't take my hands off of him last night. How even right now, it's hard to resist him, and I'm dripping with crystals to clear my head. He oozes sexuality, from the way he licks the last drops of coffee off the rim of the cup to the way he watches me with those fuck-me eyes. "Are you...the god of love?"

"God of love?" He laughs, utterly delighted. "Do you think there is a god of such foolishness?"

I scowl at him. "Why wouldn't there be?" I gesture around us, at the distracted and rather lusty patrons of the cafe. "Everyone's diddling themselves in front of you. You make my hormones go nuts when I'm around you. If you're not the god of love, then what are you?"

"You truly can't guess?" He looks delighted at my question.

"Just tell me."

"I'll show you instead." He closes his eyes, concentrating, and for some reason, a tension headache blooms between my eyes. I wince at the sensation, like I've just given myself an ice cream headache. I need more coffee, I decide, as I squint at my companion.

Something runs over my foot. I look down underneath the table, and there's a rat. Actually, there's several of them, and they all park near his feet.

I let out a cry of horror, backing up. "Oh my god. You're the god of rats?"

Nearby, someone else groans, no doubt jerking it to rats or something fucked up like that. Kassam looks at me and then throws his head back and laughs with delight. "Not rats!" His smile widens. "Or should I say, not just rats."

The door opens and someone cries out. A squirrel scampers across our table, and as I watch, Kassam leans down. The thing crawls up his arm and perches on his shoulder, nuzzling against his ear.

While I can relate to the whole ear-nuzzling thing, I'm getting a little alarmed at the amount of vermin he's calling to us. My head throbs. "Can you not? They're not exactly clean animals, and they sure don't belong inside. We don't need to draw attention to ourselves." Funny how I'm no longer questioning if he's a god or not. There's just too much weirdness that's happened ever since he walked into my life a few short hours ago. Holy shit, has it been less than a day? Incredible. I feel like my life has turned upside down.

And weirdly, I feel like this is just the beginning.

"You do not like my friends?" Kassam makes this sexy little pout and then shrugs. Just as quickly as they arrived, the animals scamper off, eliciting a few startled cries from the patrons. Either that or someone's coming. It's hard to tell. "Can we have more food?" the god asks. "And drink?"

"Not until you wash your hands and give me more answers," I say.

The grin he gives me is sin itself. "You are obsessed with washing. All right. Show me where, and I will answer more of your questions."

6

I get up from the table, and he automatically puts his hand out for me. I slide mine into his before I can think about it, and an orgasm rolls through my body. I make a weird sound, all my muscles clenching, and that devil looks on at me like he's the cat that licked the cream. "You bastard," I whisper, snatching my hand from his.

"Why are you mad? You liked it." He hovers close behind me as we head toward the cafe's bathrooms. "I like pleasuring you, Carly. I like the look on your face when you come. It reminds me how enjoyable it is to be this Aspect."

I clench my teeth, fighting back the urge to scream—or jump his bones. I hate how they're warring with one another so fiercely. It's like I can't even stay mad—or focus on a question—long enough to get anywhere with Kassam. "Hands. Wash. Now." I open the door to the ladies' room, not caring if it's occupied already, and escort Kassam inside. Luckily, the stalls are empty, so I turn on the water on the first sink, give it a few pumps of soap, and then start to wash his hands and arms.

He doesn't move, and when I glance up at him, I notice he's watching me with amusement.

"What?"

"I thought you wanted me to wash myself?"

I look down and I'm soaping his enormous arms up to the elbow, my hands running over his skin like I'm giving him a sexy massage. I've been so messed up in the head I didn't even notice what I was doing. Flustered, I release him, and he immediately grabs me by the waist and hauls me up against him.

"Are you mad that you are responding to me, Carly? Or mad that they are?" His teeth nip at my ear, and my nipples get hard. Heat pools between my legs and I whimper. "Because that is part of my curse. Wherever I go, everyone will be affected by my presence."

"Because you're the god of rats?" I pant, dazed. I watch in fascination as his soapy hand moves to the front of my jeans. He doesn't bother undoing them, just sticks his big hand inside the waistband, heading straight for my pussy. Oh fuck.

One big, soaped-up finger glides over my folds. Oh fuuuuck. I am utterly soaked. I turn, trying to push away from—or against, I'm not entirely sure—his hand. He ignores my squirming, leaning over me with that big body, and begins to pet my pussy. "I am the god of the wild," he murmurs against my ear, his tongue brushing against the shell of it. "The trees, the birds, the creatures—from small to large, they bow to me."

Slowly, he circles my clit and I nearly come undone. I grip the sink, trying to stay upright, and it doesn't matter that we're in a public restroom and he's still a stranger. His hand feels better than anything I've ever imagined and if I don't come again, I'm going to lose my fucking mind.

His big body presses up against mine from behind. "But hedonism...hedonism is my curse. It means that I am condemned to pursue every pleasure known, and to pursue it fiercely. And while it is a great deal of fun," he says, and grazes my ear with his teeth, "it is also highly, highly distracting."

I squirm against his hand. I'm panting, so loud that anyone near the door is going to hear me before it swings open. I feel like I'm losing control—there's not enough crystals in the world to get Kassam out of my head. I look in the mirror, whimpering, and his silver eyes are pinning me in place, his gorgeous form so damn sexy as he presses up against me from behind. His hair is long and wild, but oh god, no one has ever looked better.

"You want to know who I am?" he growls into my ear, leaning forward and pressing me against the sinks. I'm bent over, his hand working my pussy, and I'm so close to coming that I'm panting, mouth open. Even though I don't want to, I rock against his hand, needing that friction so dreadfully. "I am the wild god," Kassam says. "I am the incarnation of pleasure, and you are tied to me. Every day, this will be your fate. You're going to come so hard and so often that you'll salivate when you look in my direction. Your cunt will clench at the sound of my voice. And more than that, you'll completely and utterly belong to me. You are my anchor." He leans over and drags my hair back from my face, revealing my ear. He nips it and then whispers in my ear. "Your pleasure is mine."

I cry out, coming so hard that my vision fuzzes. His fingers keep working my clit, dragging circles around it and wringing the pleasure through me for what feels like an eternity. I keep coming and coming.

And coming.

When the last shudder is wrested from my body, he pulls his hand free from my jeans as I pant, trying to recover my breath. I glance up and he licks his fingers, gleaming from my juices. "Does that answer your question?"

"No," I pant. "It doesn't answer shit." I cling to the sink, waiting for my knees to start working again. "What do you mean you've been cursed with hedonism?"

"The gods misbehaved," he tells me. "We did not fulfill our

duties as the High Father intended. So he expelled us from the heavenly aether and exiled us to the mortal realms. There, he split us into the four aspects of our worst sins—lies, apathy, arrogance, and hedonism. To return, we must defeat these flaws. Only then will we be allowed to return to our home." He pulls me back against him and presses a gentler kiss to the side of my neck. "But I defeated all of mine long ago. I defeated Apathy and Arrogance. Lies was the most difficult but I tracked him down and destroyed him. All that was left was for me to ascend once more, but I was betrayed. That is why I am still amongst mortals, even after all this." Kassam looks thoughtful. "Or perhaps the High Father does not want me back at all. I cannot know."

"Sounds fucked up," I wheeze. I run a hand over my breasts, because my nipples are still far too alert.

"Very."

"What...what are you going to do?" I try to straighten, to pull myself together.

"I am going to return to my world. Somehow." He gives me a seductive smile. "There will surely be a way. And until I figure it out, I will have rather pleasant company, I think."

Lucky, lucky me. "What if I want to call this off? What if I'm not interested in being your anchor?"

"It has already been decided," Kassam says. "You cannot leave my side." He gestures at the door to the bathroom. "If you try it, you will be filled with intense pain until you return."

"That's fucked." I don't try it, though. I like a pain-free existence. "Let's say you get back to your world...what happens to me? If we're tied together?"

Kassam traces a finger along my jaw. "Ah, sweet one. Do not ask me that."

I jerk away from him, chilled by his response. "Too late. I already asked it."

He sighs. Licks his fingertips one more time, as if he can't get enough of the taste of me, and then shrugs. "I cannot ascend while tied to my anchor. Our bond must be severed. Once it is, I'm free to return."

"You mean...."

"Death, yes."

I stare at him in shock. "What the fuck, Kassam? I don't want to die!"

"Well, I have no wish for you to die either, so we need to figure something out." He smiles at me.

I'm utterly aghast. I want to rail against everything. I want to call him a liar, and a fake, and say that he's not exactly who he says he is. That he's not a god. That he's not Hedonism. Except...I can't explain all the people spontaneously orgasming in the cafe. I can't explain why he can command squirrels and pigeons, and why my nearly dead plant doubled in size overnight. I can't explain why my brain fogs whenever he's near me and makes me want to do bad, dirty, naughty things.

Unless he really is cursed with hedonism, and a god.

"Wait right here," I tell him, lifting a finger. "Stay put."

He leans against one of the sinks, crosses his arms, and watches me. "You're going to test things, aren't you? My poor Carly. I'm sorry. I know this isn't what you wanted. If it's any consolation, I'm going to make however long we have together the best time you've ever had." He inclines his head with a mocking little smile. "Courtesy of hedonism, of course."

"You can stuff your hedonism," I say. "I'll be right back." And I march out of the bathroom. People are clustered near the door—ugh, ugh, ugh—and are no doubt waiting for Kassam to come out. He's like the pied piper of pussy, this man. I push through them, making my way through the tables and to the front door. I head out, and then I start running.

I'm not running anywhere in particular—I just want to get

away. Away from a man who's given me more orgasms in twenty-four hours than I've had in the last year, and away from the fact that he's very sorry, but I'm going to die. So I run.

And as I run, pain begins.

I'm maybe one block away before the crushing pain begins in my chest. I slow my run to a brisk walk, and from there, I slow down even more. I'm on my feet all day at work, and I'm reasonably fit, but with every step I take, it feels as if my legs are getting heavier and heavier. Tightness radiates through my limbs, and it feels as if I can't breathe. Like my lungs are shriveling up even as I struggle to gulp down each breath. I turn around and look behind me. A block and a half from the cafe.

I need to rule out that this isn't just a cramp. My hand on my chest, I take another step forward, and it feels as if I'm swimming upstream. It's downright difficult, and every bit of my body feels terrible. It's like the worst flu I've ever had, even as I wheeze for breath. I pause, no longer pushing ahead, and then turn and walk back a few steps, toward the cafe and toward Kassam.

Immediately, the crushing feeling eases.

I pause, turn around, and walk a step away from Kassam. The pain returns, hard and heavy and awful.

Whatever it is that's going on, it isn't my imagination. I stagger backward a few steps, and when immediate relief hits, I walk back to the cafe. With every step I cover, the pain ebbs, but my anxiety increases. How do I fight this? How do I break free from a man that's suddenly trapped me to his side with good sex and a disarming smile? A man that has said, quite pointedly, that for him to go home, I have to die?

Suddenly the entire last day is taking on a sinister tinge. I think of Kassam in the alley, his hand extended out to me. I think of the constant mental fog I have around him. Of how he can make me come just with the blink of an eye.

How he can get whatever he wants from me with just a few

touches and a gentle word. I've been playing right along with him, too, dazzled by his attractive face and gorgeous body and the sex appeal that oozes off of him. He's the pied piper of pussy all right, and I've been dancing to his tune.

No longer. Hearing that Kassam needs me dead is a real eye-opener. I have to figure a way out of this, somehow, because I am not about to give my life up for a pretty smile and a man that doesn't know how to wash his own hands.

Determined, I march back to the cafe and pause in the doorway. Kassam is seated atop the counter, his bare feet dangling as he eats cookies straight from the case. The barista watches him with an adoring expression, and the others sip their coffees and look on as if he's some sort of celebrity...or messiah. At least they're no longer diddling themselves. Or each other. I step inside, heading for the counter, and behind it, I see a few bodies writhing in what can only be an orgy.

Spoke too soon.

Kassam smiles at me, his expression utterly delighted. "You are back, my light. Did you...get what you needed?" His expression is both apologetic and casual, as if he knows it sucks, but he doesn't care all that much. As if to make up for this, he holds a cookie out to me. "Cookie?"

I...need more crystals, I realize. Lots more. I gesture toward the door. "Come on, Kassam. We're leaving."

"Where are we going?" he asks, as if he knows the streets of Chicago himself.

"Does it matter? This is all new to you." I put another twenty on the counter, hoping that covers at least a few of the cookies he's scarfed down, and then grab him by the arm. "If you must know, we're heading to my mom's shop."

"Her shop?" His face brightens. "Your mother is nearby? I should enjoy meeting her. Is she as beautiful as you?"

I look at the adoring people around us. Oh fuck. I can't just introduce him to my mom cold turkey. I whip out my phone and text.

CARLY: Mom, I will be there in 20 with a friend.
    CARLY: Wear all the quartz you've got. You're going to need it. XOXO

7

For as long as I can remember, my mom's had her little psychic shop tucked away in downtown Chicago. It's little more than the size of a closet, with a sky-high rent for an old, outdated shop in an equally old, outdated building, but somehow my mom makes it work. Fortunes and Futures manages to pull in people despite the hokey name, the equally hokey beads and neon signs that hang in the tiny window, and the fact that it's probably all crap to some degree. I've never believed, much to my mother's chagrin.

Today, though? I'm willing to believe.

Even getting over to the shop today was an adventure. By the time we got back to my apartment building, Kassam and I had people following us. I wanted to go upstairs and grab a few things from my place, but I didn't trust the weirdos not to follow us to my door. Instead, I headed straight for the parking garage, got in my car, dumped all my abandoned crafting stuff out of the passenger seat so Kassam could sit down, and drove over to my mom's shop. In the car, I cringed every time we made a traffic stop, wondering if someone was going to try to jump in, or if other drivers would be pulled in by Kassam's magnetic presence through their cars and we'd somehow end up with a caravan over to my mom's store.

"You're a real pain in the ass," I tell Kassam. "You know that?"

He just laughs. "Can I help it if hedonism is the most pleasurable of all flaws?"

"CAN you help it? Can you rein this shit in, even a little?" I find a Park and Pay and steer my car inside, slapping the ticket onto the dashboard with practiced ease.

Kassam shakes his head. "Would that I could. Even hedonism grows tiresome over the years. I would prefer to be cursed with it more than anything else, but it does not mean I do not wish for normalcy. I would like to be able to stop thinking with my cock. I would like to be able to put on human clothes and not get lost in the feel of the fabric against my skin. I would like to watch humans eat and not feel the need to taste everything myself." His lip curls, just a little. "I do not even think the gods are supposed to eat, yet I stuff my gullet every chance I get."

I don't know if I feel bad for him. He seems miserable, but of all curses, it doesn't seem like such a shitty one. "Yeah, well, feel bad for me. I'm the one stuck with you."

His smile broadens. "I am glad you are," he says softly. "And I am sorry if I am a burden to you." He pauses. "Actually, I am not sorry. So far I have found you to be a very enjoyable companion." He reaches out and strokes my arm, fingers sliding over my skin in a sensual way that leaves no doubt in my head that he's Hedonism.

"You're thinking with your dick again, aren't you?" I murmur.

"Very much so." Kassam licks his lips and regards me. "We have enough room in this cart. You could straddle me. It would not take long." His sexy eyes grow hooded with desire. "And I would make you feel very, very good."

God, I have no doubt about that. But I also have enough mental control at the moment that I'm not about to get freaky in a parking lot near my mom's store. "They have cameras recording everything we do here," I tell him, and resist the urge to rub my crystals. Focus, focus, focus. "We're not doing anything here."

"Somewhere else, then?"

"Later," I tell him, and a tiny part of me is disappointed that I'm so responsible. "We need answers before we get all distracted, okay? I don't know if these crystals stop working after a while and I need to do what I can before my brain fogs just from being around you."

"Why does it matter?" he asks, his hand gliding down my arm to take my hand. "What is your plan? To send me home? That will come at the cost of your life, and I am not ready to see that yet, my light. If I have to stay here for a time, I shall." He shrugs. "Time is all a god seems to have. Endless, endless amounts of time."

"I don't want to die," I say. "And if there's a way around it, I want to find it. I also want to find a way to shut this"—I wave a hand at him—"hedonism off."

"Why?"

"So you can make your own decisions instead of being led by your cock? So we can think clearly and figure out what exactly has happened between us and why you're here? Are you supposed to be accomplishing something in my world? Is that why you're here and not in yours?"

Kassam sighs and leans back against the headrest. "I think what I am hearing is that you are not all that interested in straddling me."

"Not right now!"

He takes our joined hands and guides mine to his cock. It's rigid underneath his sweatpants, so big and delicious that I don't snatch my hand away immediately. "But I want you."

"Is this Hedonism speaking?"

Kassam chuckles, the sound slightly weary. "Always."

"Just come on," I say, and get out of the car.

He must be starting to get a hang of door handles, because Kassam is able to exit the vehicle on his own. He moves to my side, his hand automatically seeking mine. I take his without thinking, and the moment I do, I stagger on the sidewalk with the force of the orgasm that rolls through me.

"Goddamn it, Kassam," I whimper, clinging to his arm as all my muscles lock up in pleasurable distress. "You don't play fair."

"I do not. Remember...I am a naughty god."

I wrench my hand from his. "Can you behave for just five minutes?"

He shrugs. "If I must, but I will not enjoy it."

"You don't have to enjoy something every moment of every day," I grumble, but when he just arches a brow at me, I realize how stupid that sounds. Right. Of course he does. According to him, he's Hedonism.

We cross the street, me holding a handful of Kassam's shirt to guide him. It's a silent refusal to hold his hand after the stealth orgasm, but he seems more amused by my actions than anything. I guess if you're Hedonism, you're hard to offend. You're just always having a good time. I know this area of town like the back of my hand, thanks to multiple visits to my mom's shop, and long before I see the neon sign of the hand with an eye in the center, I can feel the warmth of my mom's presence pouring over me, helping me relax.

Mom will know what to do. She might not believe that her daughter's gotten mixed up with a god—not at first—but Mom always has an answer. She'll help me figure out what the hell I'm supposed to do here. I could desperately use some guidance.

I open the door to Mom's shop—Fortunes and Futures—and the scent of incense wafts over me. Her store is empty, but that's not surprising. Mom's store always seems deserted, but she has some die-hard regulars that pay the bills. It's not unusual for one of her customers to come in and spend several hundred dollars on crystals in one swoop, plus she does her readings. The store itself is small, with one wall full of crystal bins and shelves, and another wall covered in occult books of all kinds. I wince at the seashell collage she has hanging on the wall next to a terrible painting I did, both of them missing components to be completed. The seashell collage needs a border, and the painting has a big thumbprint at the edge where I got impatient for the paint to dry, and that I promised to cover up with a tree or something.

But that's me—lots of promises and no delivery.

I move to the glass counter by the register, peering inside, and in the counter itself, my mom keeps the pricier items—silver and gold charms, out of print tarot decks, and the larger, pricier chunks of crystal. Hanging on the wall is a terrible oil painting of a phoenix that I did back when I was in my brief "painting" phase. I hate looking at it because there's no moon in the sky, or stars. It's just a flaming bird rising against a field of dark blue. I've always meant to go back and finish it but...it's just another abandoned project. I turn away, glancing at the back of the shop. There's a small door to the back covered in occult symbols and glow-in-the-dark stars, and I know that's the room she does her readings in.

My mom is nowhere to be seen. She's in the back, then. I turn to Kassam and bat his hand away before he can touch one of the many candles she has for sale. "Don't touch anything."

He arches a brow at me, those silver eyes flashing with amusement. "But you know me. I love to touch."

Heat floods through my body again, and I'm reminded of the bathroom at the coffee shop. And last night. And, well, every time he touches my hand. "Kassam, please," I beg, because the last thing I need is a naughty god pushing my boundaries in my mom's store. While she might not disown me if she finds me on my knees in front of him, I might certainly want to die of embarrassment. "Let me focus, just for a while, all right? Then we'll have some fun."

The god's eyes gleam with enthusiasm. I've got his interest now. "What kind of fun?"

"Snacks and back to my apartment?" I offer. I can't believe I'm having to bribe a grown man with cookies and kisses. Also, I can't believe I'm getting turned on at the thought and my stomach is growling. I know it's his presence that's doing this, but it still feels bizarre. If he really is cursed with hedonism, I'm going to have to figure out how to work with this until he gets home...without getting killed.

Or getting arrested for public indecency, since those gray sweatpants he's wearing are currently stretched tight over a massive bulge. My mouth waters at the sight, and I stare at his body, my hands itching to touch him as he runs a hand down my arm. "Must we wait? I can tell you want me now, my little light. Your body is practically singing for my touch."

It is, and that's a problem. I pull him down against me, give him a hard, quick kiss, and then head for the display of crystals, grabbing the entire box of loose quartz and hauling it against my chest. It helps, but only a little.

Kassam just leans against the counter and grins, all sexy confidence. Oh god, even that is incredibly hot. I am in such, such trouble. "Just behave for a short time, Kassam. That's all I'm asking."

"Look at me, behaving," he purrs, practically devouring me with his gaze.

I bite back a whimper, my nipples tightening under my bra. In that moment, my mother emerges from the back of the store. I don't know if I'm relieved to see her or mortified. Both, I decide. "Hi, Ma," I manage. "I'm here."

Her wide-eyed gaze goes from my flushed face over to Kassam. Her gaze drops to his bulge and her lips part.

"Hello, Carly's mother," he says, voice soft and sexy as he looks my mom up and down.

Oh no. Oh no, no no. This is bad. My mom is a cute older woman—she's round-faced like me, has an awesome smile, and her thick brown hair is only showing traces of gray. She dresses like a hippie, sure, but she says it's part of the gig. Even so, this is not a person I want Kassam looking over with those "wanna fuck" eyes. I race over to my mom's side and shove the box of crystals into her arms. She blinks at me, repeatedly, as if the fog is clearing from her head, and rips her gaze away from Kassam. My mother's face turns a fiery red. "Oh. Oh boy. This is…I'm sorry. I think I'm distracted."

"It's him, Ma," I soothe. "It's Kassam. He causes everyone to lose their shit."

"Hedonism," he agrees, and rubs one thumb down his shirt-covered pectoral, as if he finds himself irresistible as well.

"Long story," I correct, because my mom's not going to know what he means. "I need your help, if you can ignore him for a while."

In a daze, my mother turns back to me. She clutches the box of crystals to her chest and studies my face. "I'm glad you're here, but this is troubling, Carly."

"He's harmless. Mostly." I mean, unless you look like a pussy…or a donut…or a cookie.

My mother shakes her head. "That's not it. Your aura. It's covered in spiderwebs." Her expression grows bleak. "I've seen this before, on that missing girl."

Oh no, not this again. I fight the urge to roll my eyes. My mother "found" an ability to read auras about ten years ago after an ayahuasca experiment. I'm convinced she's just hamming it up for the clients. "Ma—"

"No, listen to me," Ma says firmly, juggling the box of crystals in her arms. "I'm telling you, I've seen this before. The spiderwebs. Except this time, they're attaching you to…" She trails off, ducking her head and nodding at Kassam without looking at him.

"There's no webs—"

"Webs?" Kassam straightens, no longer leaning on the counter. He looks interested. "The gods of fate in my world utilize spiderwebs in their tasks. They must have a hand in this." He gives my mom an appraising look. "Fascinating. Are you a spinner, wench?"

I make a protesting sound. "My mom is not a wench!"

Ma refuses to look over at Kassam, her eyes wide as she stares at my T-shirt. "Carly, honey, he's got massive energy. Massive. I've never seen anything like it."

Well, she's not wrong about that? Wrinkling my nose, I wonder if there really is something to this aura business. I can't believe Kassam's starting to make me believe in all this woo-woo nonsense. Next thing you know, I'm going to be pitching rose petals at the full moon or something. "If I tell you something crazy, Ma, promise you'll listen to me?"

"Of course, Carly. I'm your mother. You can tell me anything and everything."

I glance over at Kassam. "He says he's a god from another world and I think I believe him." I skip the part about fucking him like a wild woman, because this is my mother, after all. "That he's been brought here and he's cursed."

My mother nods thoughtfully. "That lines up with what's going on in his aura. He could be the one I saw in your cards."

My cards. Oh god. It's been such a long two days that I forgot all about the cards. "What were they again?"

She scowls at me and pinches my arm, as if outraged that I'd let something like that slip my mind. "The Fool, and Death." Her gaze slides over to Kassam. "And the lovers."

Right right. "You told me before that the death card isn't bad, right? That it means new beginnings?"

"That's correct, but my concern is that I got a very similar reading for the other girl, and look what happened to her." She purses her lips. "You have the Fool card, though. That means inexperience and improvisation. Being in over your head." Mom grabs my hand. "You want to talk about it, sweetie?" She leans in, giving me a meaningful look and whispers, "Do we need to call the police on him?"

Aw, that's nice of Mom. She's five foot two soaking wet and can't defend me from a flea, much less a god, but that's thoughtful. I squeeze her hand. "No, but I need advice. We have to get him back home and right now the only way for me to be free of him is for me to die."

Mom's eyes go wide. She releases my hand and goes to the door, then turns off the neon psychic reading lights and flips over her 'Out to Lunch' sign on the door. Then, she turns back to me. "Tell me everything, Carly. Start at the beginning."

8

Because she's my mother, I don't tell her everything. I don't mention that Kassam's touch makes me orgasm instantly. Or that we've had sex (or something close to it) multiple times since I've met him. I don't point out that he got me off in a coffee shop bathroom. There are some things a mother just doesn't need to know about her daughter. But everything else Kassam has told me? I don't hold back. All the while, she pulls cards, tutting when the same ones come up over and over again.

The Lovers.
The Fool.
Death.

The cards pop up over and over again, a silent message that returns no matter how often my mother shuffles. "What do I do?" I ask my mother, worried.

She sucks on her bottom lip, thinking. "I'm not entirely sure." Her gaze flicks to me, and then over to Kassam, who is eating a bag of chips I found in my mom's back office. He licks each one with lascivious attention, casting looks over at me between savoring each chip. I'm doing my best to ignore him and pay attention, but it's hard. Even with crystals all around us, it's hard. My mother's starting to sweat. "It's difficult for me to think clearly right now. I'll keep working your cards and see if I can get any answers, but for now, maybe it's best if you head out?"

I sit back in the folding metal chair in her reading room, hurt. She's getting rid of me? "We just got here, Mom. Can't you help me?"

"I know, sweetie. I know." She reaches out and squeezes my hand. "It's just...he's very distracting." And she shifts in her seat.

I glance over at Kassam, who gives me a sultry look and licks his fingers.

Okay, she's got a point. I hate to leave, though. For some reason, things feel under control when I'm in my mother's presence. "I guess we can go. You'll text me?"

My mother nods. "I will. I'll pull more cards and see what I can find out. Is there something specific you think I should ask? How he gets home? Or how you break the bond?" She gives Kassam another look and shifts in her chair once more, her face flushed. "Maybe I should write this down."

"I know how we get back to my world," Kassam offers, speaking up.

We both turn to him, surprised. "I thought you said you didn't know how you got here," I bring up. "You told me it was all a mystery to you."

"And it is." He licks a fingertip again, smiling devilishly at me. "But the answer as to how to get back should be obvious." Kassam peers down into the bag of chips. "Are there more of these?"

"Focus, please." I snap my fingers. "How do I get you home without killing myself?"

"Your beautiful mother has the right idea." My mother makes a sound that might be excitement, might be an orgasm. Shit, I hope it's not an orgasm. Kassam smiles at her, all gorgeous silver eyes and sexy beard, and my legs go liquid. Yeah, these crystals definitely lose some of their power over time, I decide. Every time he looks at me, I'm feeling the urge to get up from my seat and go rub up against him. Kassam continues, "It is the webs."

"The webs," I echo blankly.

"We are connected by threads tied to a web, yes? This is how it works?" At our puzzled looks, he shrugs. "This is how it works in my world. And that web must be tied somewhere. We find where the web is tied, where the walls between worlds are thin, and send out a call. Once they know I am stranded here, surely they will pull me back into my world."

"And what happens to me?" I ask.

Kassam grins. "You can come with me. Serve me there like you do here." The look he gives me makes no bones about the kind of serving I'd be doing.

I clench my thighs together, because that should make me angry, not turn me on. "What if I don't want to go to your world? Don't they want you back in the heavens? And to get you back there, I have to die, right? So it's safer for me to be here."

He licks his thumb again, shrugging. "You are the one that wanted to send me back."

"And what do you want?" my mother asks, her voice throaty and in a tone I've never heard before.

Kassam gives us that languid, sexy smile. "I want to enjoy myself, of course."

"He's Hedonism, Ma. This is useless." I've learned that it's hard to keep Kassam on course. He's far too easily distracted by food and sex. I get to my feet and hug my mother's shoulders. "See what you can find out and text me, all right?"

She nods, a worried look on her face. "Are you going straight home? That's probably best."

"For now." I don't point out that I have to work tonight. I still don't know how I'm going to figure that part out. I can't leave Kassam unattended—actually, I can't leave him at all—but if I don't work, my fridge stays empty. I need those tips. "Love you."

"Be safe," my mother says, and pats my arm.

I feel a little lost as I grab Kassam by the arm and head out of my mom's shop. Immediately, the full force of his magnetism hits me, and I wish I'd brought the box of crystals along. I suck in a breath, glancing over at him.

Kassam just smiles that same wicked smile he always has. "Feel better?"

"Better" is not the right word. Visiting my mother solved nothing. She can't help us, and all I've done is make my mom incredibly horny for my new lover, which makes me cringe to the depths of my soul to think about. Nothing was solved just now. I'm still adrift and alone, and my clothes feel far too constricting in certain areas. I just shake my head and head for the car, unable to voice how frustrated I am. I need answers, and I need help, and all I'm getting is more turned on by Kassam's presence.

The moment I sit in the car, my phone buzzes with an incoming text. I pick it up and glance at the screen.

MOM: Whew. I couldn't think while he was in the room. That man is potent, Carly. Be careful when you're driving.

CARLY: I haven't even left the parking lot yet.

MOM: I had an idea.

OH THANK GOD.

. . .

CARLY: I'm listening.

MOM: You should get married.

I STARE DOWN at my phone, wondering what autocorrect has changed. We should get...martinis? We should get...marked-down sushi? What? My mom keeps typing slowly, so I wait. As I do, Kassam puts his hand on my knee. He squeezes it, and when his hand stays, I realize it's both comfort and need. I want to snap that Hedonism needs to give me a break for an hour, but I know it's not his fault. If he's telling the truth, he's cursed.
What's even more annoying? I want him to slide his hand higher.

MOM: Hear me out. I've read a lot of books about the old gods and faeries and the like. They're not trustworthy, but if you can get them into a binding agreement with you, that's the only safety net you have. Take him to some fly-by-night chapel, make him promise to love, honor and cherish you. He can't get you killed then.

MOM: It sounds squirrelly, but we're dealing with squirrelly things right now.

KASSAM LEANS OVER, pressing his mouth to the side of my neck, and I bite back a moan. "My light," he murmurs. "I need you."
I look over at him, panting and distracted. "Five...five minutes," I manage. Good lord, how am I possibly going to get

anything done if I can't go five minutes without wanting to jump on his dick and ride him? I never thought pleasure-seeking would be a curse, but it's definitely a distraction.

"I can give you five minutes," he agrees, his hand drifting down my arm and then brushing across my breast. He manages a little smile. "I will let it whet my appetite."

That makes me laugh, slightly hysterical. "Whet your appetite? Yours is non-stop."

"Hedonism," he agrees, his thumb drifting over my nipple and teasing it. "It is never-ending. Some think it is the best of flaws, but it can be a bit much."

A bit much. I'll say. I reach over him into the glove compartment and pull out a box of breath mints. "Here. Distract yourself."

Kassam's eyes light up and he shakes the tin, fascinated. "It smells wonderful."

"Tastes even better," I agree, shivering as I pick my phone up again. I have to fight the urge to crawl into his lap and just forget everything for a few hours. Focus, Carly, I remind myself, and slap my cheek. Focus.

I read through my mom's texts again. Get Kassam to agree to marry me in order to protect me. It sounds very fairy tale, but then again....I glance up as one crow, then another, land atop my car hood. They caw in excitement, staring through the windshield at Kassam as if they know him. A few more crows flutter in, and I glance over at the god, who is eating mints by the handful.

Right. This could actually be a fairy tale. My Disney princess here has the requisite birds and animals eating out of his hand, after all. I ponder my mother's words.

ME: I can't believe you're suggesting marriage. Even weirder, I can't believe I'm considering it.

. . .

MOM: It won't mean anything if it's just to keep you safe. Divorce his weird ass the moment you know you're safe...and you're done with the D.

I STIFLE A SNORT OF LAUGHTER. Okay, I love my mother. I send her a couple of heart emojis and glance over at the god of lust and squirrels, or whatever he's calling himself. "Hey Kassam?"

"Yes, my light?" He gives me a minty smile, his gaze flirty.

"If you promised something as a god, you have to hold to it, right?"

He nods and offers me a mint from the nearly empty tin.

Okay, well, that could work. I take the mint from him and pop it into my mouth. "If I'm going to be your partner—"

"Anchor," he corrects.

"Anchor," I amend. "If I'm going to anchor you, I have a few requirements."

"Ask away." He closes the tin with a little sigh and then peers out the window at the gathering crows. "My friends," he murmurs. "Your services are not needed yet. Perhaps soon."

One crow caws at him, pecking at the hood of the car. Then, as if they share a brain cell, they all fly away.

I glance out the window after them. Weird. Just another distraction, I remind myself, and focus on Kassam. "I want to get married."

His brows go up.

"What, do your people not have marriage?"

"No, we do." That lazy, pleased grin curves his mouth. "Shall we bribe a priestess to join our hands and swear undying love for one another? Is that what you require from me, my light? Pretty lies in front of an audience?"

Ouch. "Pretty lies, huh?"

"I like you, my little light," Kassam says, smiling. "But I am a god and you are a mortal. I have used your body to sate my needs, but that is all. We are simply scratching each other's itches."

I stare at him, a little stung. "You're not even trying for romance, are you?"

Kassam gestures at our surroundings, chuckling. "What about this is romantic?"

He has an excellent point. It's like being drugged, being around him constantly. Drugged and somewhat exhausting. "Okay, well, if we're being truthful, I want to get married. Not because I'm in love, but because I need your sacred promise that you'll look out for me and won't get me killed."

Kassam gives me an impressed look. "You're trying to corner me?"

"You cornered me!"

"So I did." He tips his chin, grinning. "I don't regret it. If we're continuing truths..." He leans in, and my belly twists with a hint of dread. Oh god, what now? I don't think I can take much more packed into twenty-four hours. "Your cunt is the finest I've fucked in ages. And I love those little cries you utter when I make you come."

I blink. That was unexpected, but...still pleasant to hear. I guess if we're scratching itches, it might as well be enjoyable. "I'm sure you say that to all the girls."

"I do not. Nor do I fuck just women." He gives me that languid smile again. "I am a god who loves all."

Which brings up another excellent point. "If we're getting married, I need you to be a monogamous sort of hedonist, Kassam." When his brow arches, I shake my head. "I'm serious. I'll sleep with you, I'll help you with all your hedonism needs, but we need to keep it between us."

"Greedy wench." He beams at me. "I like how possessive you are. Very well, I agree."

That was a lot less difficult than I thought. For some reason, with all his talk and sensual teasing, I thought he'd be trying to bring others into our bed. Hell, I'm still trying to get used to the idea of sharing a bed with a god, much less sharing it with multiple people and a god. I can only imagine the shitshow if other people get involved. I picture diseases, or spontaneous orgies, and it makes my head hurt. I'm a traditional girl for the most part, and it's hard enough for me to think of having tons of sex with Kassam just to have sex, zero feelings involved. It's probably a good thing I remembered to set some boundaries, considering Kassam doesn't know what a condom is...

Oh shit.

I start the car. "We're going to the pharmacy."

"What is a pharmacy?" Kassam asks, curious. "Is that where you get married in your world?"

"Nope," I say. "That's where we panic and get a pregnancy test." I'm not sure if it'll work the morning after, but I can stock up and keep testing...and buy Kassam an absolute truckload of condoms.

He laughs. "Is that what you are worried about? Most would be honored to carry a god's offspring."

I shoot him a withering look, which only makes him laugh harder. Things are difficult enough right now—the last thing I need is a half-hedonism baby. "Just shut up," I mutter. The urge to kick him out of the car is overwhelming, but I know I can't leave him behind without subjecting myself to some pretty gnarly pain. And I'm going to marry this guy? Clearly I'm insane. "I wish you'd grabbed Charlie's hand last night instead of mine."

"Ah, but I am very glad I have you as my anchor," Kassam says, his tone achingly sexy. My body instantly responds, and I grit my teeth. His hand smooths up and down my arm, and his touch feels good, but it also frustrates me with how quickly and easily my entire being responds to that small touch. Being with him is making me turn into a person I don't recognize half the time. I'm not this wildly sexual creature that has unprotected sex. Hell, my last boyfriend broke up with me because I didn't want sex as often as he did. Now I'm practically panting at the thought of touching Kassam again.

There aren't enough crystals in the world for me to deal with hedonism, and I don't know what to do.

For a moment, I feel so overwhelmed I want to cry. I want to throw my keys down and just walk away. Walk away from my job, from Kassam, from everything in my life that's somehow led me up to this point. Walk away like when I walked away from college, or from art classes, or ballet.

Just start walking and start over again.

My lip trembles and I stare out the windshield.

A hand unexpectedly touches mine. Kassam grips my fingers and gives them a squeeze. "I am sorry, Carly. I know this is hard. Everyone thinks hedonism is endless enjoyment, but they do not see how tiring it can be. I have been this person for so long that I am...exhausted. And yet I must keep going. I must keep entertaining myself, because if I do not, I will lose myself entirely."

I look over at him, full of mute misery.

He brushes a finger over my brow, sweeping my thick bangs out of my eyes. "We allow ourselves to be miserable for a short moment, and then we seek the next pleasure, because we must keep moving, yes?" He gestures at the windshield. "Now, on to the pharmacy so we may find out if we have babies."

I almost hate the giggle that escapes my throat.

9

aking Kassam to the pharmacy closest to my apartment is a mistake. The moment we go inside, he starts grabbing things, fascinated. I know it's the hedonism that makes him fascinated by everything, so I can't really get angry. Instead, we grab handfuls of candy bars and I let him eat a bag of chocolate-covered raisins while I prowl through the pregnancy test section, reading the backs of boxes. Ten days for a test to show if it's positive or not. I finger one of the tests thoughtfully, then add it to my shopping cart. And another. And I throw in a few boxes of the biggest condoms I can find while the elderly pharmacist behind the nearby counter gives me a disgusted look.

That expression on her face is gonna make asking for the morning-after pill a little awkward.

I linger around the tests, steeling up my courage, when Kassam hands me the empty candy bag and leans in as if going for a kiss. "We are being followed, my light."

Stiffening, I resist the urge to turn around and stare at the other patrons of the store. I remain where I am as Kassam gazes at me, tucking a strand of hair behind my ear. "Like...by security? Are they wearing a uniform?"

It's on the tip of my tongue to ask him if he stole something or ate something without giving me the wrapper when he cups the back of my neck and leans in to kiss me again. I'm so fascinated by his mouth brushing over mine that it takes me a moment to realize he's speaking in between nips. "Not mortal," he murmurs. "We are being followed by something else. You said you did not have gods in your world?"

Panic creeps up my spine. He kisses me again, and I manage, "I'm pretty sure we don't? The main religions all follow one god." But I don't know for sure. I'm not an expert on theology, but there's lots of old myths that had a bunch of gods. To those people, the gods weren't myths. Well, shit. "Why would someone be following us?"

Kassam rubs his cheek against mine and then moves in to nip at my earlobe, and I have to bite back a moan. "My thread would not belong in this weave. If someone is curious, they will come and see. Or they will come to get rid of me if they do not like that I am in their territory."

I manage a glance over my shoulder, clutching my handheld shopping basket against my side. The store looks fairly busy for midday, but I don't see anyone that screams "god." There's an elderly man peering at vitamins a few shelves over, a mom reading a magazine while her kid teethes on a box of tampons, and a store employee that's giving me a disgusted look, a pricing gun in her hand. To be fair, I am showing an excessive amount of PDA with Kassam. To also be fair, I've been cleaning out the condom aisle for the last five minutes. Anyone would think I'm being weird. I bite my lip and glance at Kassam, who's watching me with those glowing silver eyes. "Are we in danger?"

He shrugs, toying with my hair as if he's considering kissing me again. "Let us walk a bit more and see if they approach."

I nod and head down the next aisle, clutching my basket. We head past curling irons and into hair care, and when the scent of the shampoos hits, Kassam has to spend the next while opening each bottle and smelling them. "I like this one," he tells me, holding out a cheap but fruity brand to me. "You should use it."

I close the cap so the shampoo doesn't go everywhere and put it in my basket. "That's now officially your shampoo."

His eyes gleam. "Can I wash you with it?"

My thighs squeeze together tightly and a ripple of lust fires through me. "I mean...sure...later." I move closer. "Are we still being followed?"

"No, they are gone." He picks up a new bottle and pops the cap, impressed. "Oh, I like this one, too."

They're gone and he didn't tell me? Frustrated, I snatch the bottle out of his hands and put it back on the shelf. "You're sure? Focus, Kassam. I'm worried here." I bite my lip. "Are they trying to kill me?"

He shrugs, reaching for another bottle. "I think they were snooping. It was curiosity to see who visits their world."

"Do you know who it was?"

"Not a clue." Kassam holds up the new bottle. "I like this scent, too."

I toss it into my basket. "Come on. We're leaving."

The cashier gives me an odd look as I buy six boxes of condoms, pregnancy tests, a ton of candy, some shampoo, and some random dog toys that Kassam tossed into my basket. I ignore her, and when Kassam smiles at her and she makes a throaty sound, I shoot him a dirty look. "Turn it off," I whisper. "At least until we get home."

"I cannot," he purrs, reaching over to caress my ass. "My needs are overwhelming."

Ah, Jesus. He's affecting me, too. I lick dry lips and help the cashier bag my things to speed the process up, and shove a few bags into the god's hands as we leave. The sooner we get home, the sooner we can see to...needs. His and mine. Part of me hates that I've become sex-obsessed due to his presence, but it's not my fault. This isn't who I am.

I toss the supplies into the car and then slip into the driver's seat, panting. I'm aching with arousal, and when my phone pings with a text, I bite back a groan and check the screen.

CHARLIE: Just making sure you're coming in to work this afternoon?

SHIT. Shit shit shit. I have work tonight. I'd forgotten all about it. I want desperately to call in, especially since I can't leave Kassam alone, but Charlie can't handle the night shift by himself and Trina is out of town for the next week. We're short-staffed as it is. I let out a whimper of frustration, because everything feels like it's collapsing around me.

"You are distressed," Kassam observes.

I press a hand to my forehead. "I feel like I'm being pulled in a million directions. My boss needs me to come in to work tonight but I've got you to handle and we've got the whole issue of being followed and..." I trail off, my face flushing, because I almost blurted out that I really, really want to have sex right now. "There's just a lot going on."

"And the marriage," Kassam prompts.

"Shit." I'd forgotten about that. I flick through my phone, pulling up options for a quick marriage. "I just...I can't handle all this. You need a different anchor," I tell Kassam, panicking. "One that's better equipped to follow through with this. One that can help you. I can't do this—"

"Shh," Kassam murmurs, reaching across the car to stroke

my hair. "It will be all right, Carly. You are panicking, but there is no need. I am here."

"You need a better anchor," I say, fighting back tears. "I'm just a bartender."

"You are everything I need," he soothes, and tugs on my arm. When I give him a curious look, he adds, "I am pulling you into my lap to touch you. Come on."

"We're in my car—in the parking lot."

"So?"

"Someone might see."

"There is nothing to see other than a male comforting his mate." The look he gives me is easy. Reassuring.

All the crystals in the world aren't helping with how overwhelmed I feel right now, and I could really use a hug. I adjust my seat, sliding it back, and then crawl over the center panel into the bucket seat on his side of the car. He immediately tucks me against his chest, curling me against him and rubbing my back.

It's...nice. I didn't realize just how badly I needed comforting.

He strokes my spine, caressing me through my shirt, and says nothing at all. He just lets me tremble against him, until the overwhelmed feeling ebbs a little. I tuck my face against his neck, breathing in his scent. He's big enough that I still feel tiny in his lap, but he doesn't scare me. If anything, I feel protected, and it makes things a little better. Like they're not the worst they could be as long as Kassam is right here to hug me.

"I'm sorry if I'm screwing things up," I murmur. "You smell nice."

"Of course I do." He glides his hand down my shoulder. "I am Hedonism. I am all things that are pleasant. And you are screwing nothing up, Carly. As you said, this is all very new to you."

I squeeze my eyes shut, because the old feelings of inadequacy, of my father telling me I'll never be good enough, rise back up and threaten to choke me. This anchoring, this helping Kassam, it feels important. Far more important than someone like me should be handling. My mother would be better at this than me—she believes in auras and helpful spirits and all that woo-woo stuff. I know...well, I know how to mix drinks and that's about it. Kassam needs a new anchor, a better anchor.

It's just...the thought of Kassam touching someone else makes me want to shrivel inside. I know that's the hedonism talking, that I'm already addicted to him like a junkie, but I can't help it. I know I should give him up...I just don't want to, even if part of me thinks I need to detangle completely.

"I just don't know what to do," I confess, breathing in his warm, comforting scent.

"It is easy. We find a way to bring me home. That is all we must do." He smooths a hand along my hip, a gentle caress that promises more than just comfort. "And we find a way to do so that does not involve your death."

I say quietly, "I would really, really like that."

One big hand squeezes my ass. "I would, too. I like having you around."

I huff. "You barely know me."

"I know enough. I know that you do not annoy me with your questions. I know that you are thoughtful. I know that you are kind and clever." His lips brush against my cheek. "I know that being in your cunt feels better than any pleasure imaginable, and I can imagine a great, great deal."

I shiver at that, hot need flaring through me again. "I have to work tonight. If I lose my job, I'll be screwed after this is over. I need to pay my bills."

"Then we will work tonight," he says, catching my earlobe between his teeth and sucking. A hot rush of need flares through me, and I bite back a cry. "I will keep you company."

Oh, I just bet he will. I imagine endless breaks, racing

toward the stock room so we can fuck again and again...and I'm panting as I envision it. "And we need to marry."

"Yes." His hand slides between my thighs, pressing against my pussy. "But first, we need to pleasure each other. It has been far too long."

"It's literally been an hour," I pant. "Maybe two."

His tongue flicks against my ear again. "Far, far too long," he agrees. "And I have not tasted your cunt yet."

I whimper. I'm not sure if we can afford to be distracted right now, but his hand flicks open the button on my jeans and slides the zipper down, and then he's pressing his big fingers into my panties, seeking my folds. Kassam's mouth is on my earlobe, doing absolutely filthy things to it while his fingertips brush over my clit. I cry out, the heat of his touch nearly choking me with how badly I crave it. My hips jerk, pressing up against those incredible fingers as he teases the hood of my clit, his mouth on my ear as he holds me locked against him.

"Give me that sweetness, little light," Kassam whispers against my ear. "Soak my hand. Show me how good I make you feel."

Oh god. His fingers work against my clit perfectly, making me squirm. I clutch at him, panting, until the need peaks, shockingly hard and swift, and I cry out, grinding against his hand as I come. He croons praise at me, pressing soft kisses to my neck and continuing to slowly rub my clit until I'm spent, and I collapse against him, panting. I let out a low moan, exhausted...but somehow feeling better.

"Mmm," Kassam murmurs, scraping his teeth against the side of my neck. "I liked that. You're going to make everyone jealous."

Everyone...?

I open my eyes, and through the steamy windows of the car, I can just make out someone trying to peer inside. A stranger.

With a squeak of alarm, I wriggle out of his grasp and hit the car horn, making the peeping tom scatter backward. "Is that—"

"Our curious deity?" Kassam chuckles, licking his fingers with a sultry look in my direction. "No, that's just someone who wishes they were you."

God, this hedonism thing is a mess. Shaky, I slide into my seat and start the car. Get home, I tell myself, and everything will be fine.

But when we get home, my apartment is filled with greenery and house cats.

Two problems.

The only plant I have is the one that was dying...and I have zero cats. I shoot Kassam a look as I step inside. Immediately, the cats swarm him, meowing and rubbing against his legs. "Did you leave the window open?" I ask, trying to hide my exasperation.

"Perhaps." He shrugs, picking up one fat, fluffy Persian and snuggling it under his chin. "They simply wish to say hello."

It's hard to stay mad at a man cuddling a cat, so I just shake my head at him. "I need to shower and get ready for work. We're ordering a pizza, and then you're going to come with me, so we need to find you shoes." I glance down at his gray sweatpants, which outline everything and leave nothing to the imagination. My mouth waters at the sight, which means they're dangerous. "And new clothes."

"I shall let you be in charge, Carly," he declares, and scoops up another cat. "I must talk with my friends."

Right.

10

"So...you and that guy."

I look up from the keg that I'm changing out. Charlie is hovering by the bar, a nervous look on his slender face. He's been avoiding me since I got here, but I thought it was because we've been absolutely slammed. I don't think I've had time to breathe since I arrived. At least the tips will be good...I hope. I frown at Charlie. "Huh?"

"You and that guy." He licks a finger and smooths an eyebrow, which strikes me as slightly bizarre. "You...together?"

"Maybe?" I say defensively. "Why?"

"I can share," he blurts. "I just...I wanted you to know that."

I stare at him. And keep staring. Charlie, last I checked, was straight. And married. "Ew?"

He puts his hands on his hips. "Look, I'm not proud, okay? I just...I'm really into him." He glances out at the crowded bar, into a particular corner of the room that I know is absolutely inhabited by one lusty god of the wild (and probably every rat in the cellar, let's be honest). "I've never felt like this before about anyone."

I can relate. Even so, I'm cringing at how awkward this is.

"He's with me, Charlie. And we don't share." As Charlie's face falls, I'm glad I made Kassam promise to be monogamous. Something tells me it wasn't on the table until I asked. "We're getting married tomorrow, actually."

My co-worker looks as if he's about to cry. "Oh. Right. Okay." He turns away, flinging the bar towel over his shoulder, and then pauses. "Open marriage—"

"No," I bark. "Not open." I finish hooking in the keg and test the spout, making sure the nozzle works. "You just need to forget about him, okay?"

Charlie just stares at me, as if the thought of forgetting Kassam is impossible. I want to say that I know how he feels, but, truth is, it was a mistake coming in to work. It's made an already frustrating afternoon that much longer, and thanks to Kassam's presence, the bar is shoulder to shoulder. I glance at the back of the barroom, but I don't see him. I know he's around—I'm starting to get used to the tiny tugs on the invisible tether between us that tell me when he's moving away from me, or me moving away from him. I just have to get through today, I remind myself as I fill a glass with a draft beer and set it on the nearest tray. Then I'll call in sick to work tomorrow and...we'll figure something out. I'll tell the owner, Jim, that it's my wedding day and I need time off work. Hopefully that'll do it, even if the timing of it is lousy.

Because it's becoming very obvious to me that I can't work with Kassam around.

I'm wearing every piece of my crystal jewelry, and I'm managing not to break down into an orgasming mess. The others around me? Not quite so lucky. There's been a crowd around Kassam's table constantly as he's sat in the back, sipped drinks and ate snacks, and his sheer magnetism pulls person after person in from the street. Charlie's crush is a problem, though...as is the fact that I caught a girl trying to drag Kassam into one of the bathrooms with her. I shut that shit down fast, feeling both incredibly possessive and annoyed at the same time.

I finish filling the second beer even as Charlie opens his mouth, no doubt to ask me again about sharing my "boyfriend." "The answer's no," I call to him over the din of people. "Whatever you're going to ask, just...no." Grabbing the tray, I head out from behind the bar and drop the drinks at one of the tables. Just a few more hours.

Mom has a plan. I texted her again after I got to work, because I've run into a snag with the marriage idea. Kassam has no identification, and we'd have to file for a marriage license. My mother has offered to handfast us, Wiccan style, and promised to spend tonight trying to read more cards. She says they're being blocked, which sounds worrying.

Almost as worrying as the fact that we were followed earlier.

"You might want to get your boyfriend, honey," a woman at the bar tells me. "He's up to no good."

I glance at the woman—middle-aged, a long cigarette hanging from full lips, and a tired expression on her face. Her dirty-blonde hair is pulled into a messy knot atop her head, and she's nursing a whiskey, neat. I open my mouth to tell her she can't smoke in the bar, but she tilts her head to the corner of the room, where I'd left Kassam with a roll of quarters for the old jukebox. All I can see is the back of his head, and someone else with him, hunched over...which is no good.

Hauling ass, I race over to the back table, threading my way through the crowd. "Kassam?"

The silver-eyed man looks up in delight at the sight of me. The thin, slightly dirty-looking man and woman with him? Less thrilled. "My light," he calls, beaming in my direction. He extends a hand out to me, which I take, pushing my way to his side. "We are just about to smoke something! What do you call it again?"

The couple looks shifty, and I notice the woman hides her lighter.

Oh no. No, no no. I shake my head, a hard, frozen feeling churning in the pit of my belly. I remember finding my father hiding out in the bathroom too many times, his lighter in hand. I remember a childhood full of missing spoons and kitchenware stolen, only to be found in the bottom of a closet, covered in foil and charred. I remember how my father's personality would change when he was smoking up. I remember being wary of coming home from school to find him itching and cranky, and how he'd always turn on me and pick everything I did apart. Fighting back nausea and old memories, I lean in to Kassam. "If you touch drugs, we are done."

He looks surprised at my anger. "You do not approve?"

"I don't do drugs. I don't want to be around anyone that does them."

Kassam studies my face. What he sees there must convince him, because he nods. "Hedonism does not have many limits. I never know what is appropriate in a mortal form and what is not. If this upsets you, I will forego it."

"It upsets me," I say tightly. I turn to the couple. "And if I catch you two smoking anything, you're banned for life. Understand?"

"Bitch," the man mutters, tucking something back into his pocket.

To my surprise, Kassam jerks to his feet. There's no pleasure on his face, only rage. His silvery eyes blaze and his fists tighten. "You did not call my woman a foul name, did you?" He grabs the man by his collar and hauls him up against the wall, a dangerous gleam in his eyes. "I can find just as much pleasure in destruction as I can in nose spices, my friend. So say something again. I dare you."

Things are just going from bad to worse. I race over to

Kassam's side, pulling at his arm as he hauls the man effortlessly up against the wall. "No, Kassam, no. Don't—"

His intense gaze pins me. There's heated lust in his eyes, but also a banked rage. "Shall I kill him for you, my Carly?" he purrs.

Oh god. "No. No killing. *Very* frowned upon," I say, tugging on his arm again. I give his wrist a little squeeze, my fingers moving over his tanned skin. It zings me with a light, pleasant orgasm that makes my toes curl and my pussy clench, but I manage to hold my shit together anyhow. Kassam's look goes to pure heat and he drops the man, his focus entirely on me.

God, that focus is epic, too. It's like nothing else in the world exists but me and him, and the air practically crackles with sexual energy. Someone in the back of the bar grabs a man by his collar and starts making out with him, and I have a feeling there's going to be an orgy here if I don't do something. I let go of him and hold out my hand. "Come on," I say, and my voice is nearly drowned out by the sound of the packed bar. "Give me ten minutes. I'll wrap things up and we'll get out of here and go be hedonistic at home."

Kassam practically purrs at that. "I like the way you think, my light."

He reaches for me, but I just give him a naughty wink and gesture at the bar. If he touches me again, I'm never going to stay focused long enough to cash out. "Can I get you to sit there for a few minutes? I'll pour you some shots and you can guess which one is my favorite."

I can tell that intrigues him, because he follows me to the bar—well, not follows as much as "stalks." I feel very much like a prey animal, and I'm reminded that he calls himself "Kassam of the Wild." I shiver, and it's not from cold or fear, but from a tendril of pleasure snaking through my belly. Distracted, I duck behind the bar and pour him five shots, tapping the wood and indicating he should sit. People make room for him and I glance around for Charlie. I need to leave, but I can't just bail out without letting him know. I don't see him anywhere, though...

But I do see the cigarette-smoking woman at the far end of the bar. She's holding it up, one brow arched in my direction, and then chugs her whiskey. She sets the tumbler down and taps it, indicating she wants more.

I move toward her, grabbing the bottle of cheap whiskey she'd preferred and pour her a refill. "Thank you for the heads-up," I say. "About my boyfriend."

She shrugs one shoulder, looking surprisingly elegant despite the fact that she's wearing a plain white T-shirt. "When you get to know people like I do, you learn their hard limits pretty well." She stubs her cigarette into her napkin. "I figured that was a hard limit for you, and there'd be nothing he could do to win your good graces again."

"You're not supposed to smoke in here." I indicate her cigarette. "Sorry."

The woman tilts her head, smiling at me. "Then I suppose it's a good thing no one can see me but you." She pulls out a new cigarette, deftly maneuvers it between her fingers, and then lifts it to her lips. The moment it touches her mouth, the end flares with heat, as if it lit itself.

11

The room grows cold around me. I can see people at the bar, looking impatiently in my direction to get more drinks, but I'm frozen in place. All I can do is stare at the woman in front of me. She's neither young nor old, that middle range of age that could be anywhere from thirty to fifty with a good skincare regimen. Her hair is a bland color and her face is nondescript, but her expression is knowing. Bored.

Almost tired.

I lick my lips, moving closer. "Were you the one following us earlier?"

One of her brows arches again. She takes a drag on her cigarette and then pauses. "Were you followed? No, honey. That wasn't me. Sounds like you might have more interest than I thought. That could be a problem." She points at me with her cigarette. "Tell your mom to stop, by the way. She's going to get herself hurt."

I feel like I can't breathe. "Leave my mom out of this."

The woman gives me a patronizing smile. "Would love to. I actually like her. She's very scrappy. However, she keeps pushing at things she doesn't understand, and I can't be held responsible if she gets slapped down. I've warned her several times." The woman tilts her head, shrugging. "Maybe the warning will mean something coming from you. She's trying to read your future, but there isn't anything for her to read."

I glance down the bar, worried. Kassam is there, sniffing one of the shots I poured for him with a fascinated look on his face while some old man yammers in his ear. Satisfied that he can't hear our conversation, I move closer to the woman, leaning over the bar. "Is it...because I don't have a future? Is that why? Am I going to die?"

She shrugs again, flicking the filter-end of her cigarette with an impatient thumb. "No one knows, honey. That's why I'm here. I should know. That's my job. But someone's hijacked your destiny and now I can't read shit."

"Who are you?"

"I thought that was pretty obvious, but I'm Fate." She gives me a cool smile. "One of three, anyhow."

She's fate? "But...I thought you guys were spiders. That's what Kassam said."

"Mmm. Our counterparts in his world are." The stranger smiles. "You can call me Lachesis, but it doesn't really matter, since you won't be seeing me again. I shouldn't be here to begin with, but..." She gives a little shake of her head, as if fighting annoyance. "I hate a mystery, and right now, you two are a mystery. So I thought I'd find myself a few answers, but all I have are more questions."

Wait, I'm confused. "Our world has fates?"

The woman—Lachesis—shrugs. "Everyone believes in something. We're mostly retired at this point, but once you're created, you don't just disappear because people no longer pay attention to you." She takes another drag from her cigarette and then flicks the ashes. "Like your friend. His worshipers are long gone, but he's still around."

"They...are? Where did they go?"

The woman gives me a strange look. "You don't know? Did he tell you why he's here?" At my blank look, she leans in, her voice dropping. "Did he tell you anything?"

I suddenly feel incredibly stupid. There are big gaps in Kassam's story and I've been too dazzled to ask about them. "Um...that he's the god of the wild and he's stuck here."

"Did he say why?" When I shake my head, her brows go up. "Don't you think you should ask?"

"He said I had to die for him to return to his world. I have to admit, I kinda stopped asking after that."

Lachesis snorts. "A string may look flimsy, but it always has two ends. Remember that." She points her cigarette at me. "The rules are different in each world, too. Remember that, as well." She stubs out her cigarette and gets to her feet. "And I'm sure I've said enough to get me in trouble, so I'll be going."

"Wait," I say, reaching for her hand. "I have so many questions—"

She snatches her hand away before I can touch her, shaking her head. "You don't want to do that." Her expression looks worried more than offended. "Just trust me. And tell your mom to stop."

"But I need help, and you have answers," I say, following after her as she gets up from the bar. I duck under, pushing through the throng of people on the other side and race up to Lachesis's side. "Please, help us. How do I send him home?"

"You'd think that's an easy question, wouldn't you?" The woman shakes her head, a few stray tendrils of hair drifting loose. "But therein is the problem. Where exactly are you sending him and how? A better question is...how did he get here? And who sent him? That's where you'll find your answers." She purses her lips, as if angry with herself. "I've already said too much, though. Good luck, honey."

Before I can follow her further, the crowd closes around me and she disappears into the throng. By the time I fight my way free from the patrons crowding the bar, I can't find her anywhere. I bite back a growl of frustration and turn toward Kassam, heading for his side. The mob is thickest here, even if he's ignoring them, and I'm not entirely surprised to see he has a ferret on his shoulder. "Where did you get that?"

"Carly, my light," Kassam says, turning toward me with a brilliant smile. He shrugs at the ferret, rubbing his nose against its fur. "It is my friend."

"I know which drink is your favorite." He holds up a shot glass that has a cherry stem in it, only a hint of grenadine and cherry liqueur at the bottom. That's right, I'm a bartender with the tastebuds of a sorority girl. Cherry bomb is my favorite. "Did I guess correctly?"

"You did, and now we have to go." I hold a hand out to him, ignoring the groans of the patrons around us. "We've got a lot to do tonight."

"Do we?" Kassam purrs, and hot pleasure shoots across our touch.

I brace myself against it, tugging him toward the door. Coming in was a mistake, but Lachesis gave me things to think about. I need to call my mom and get her to stop casting my cards. I need to quiz Kassam and find out what's really going on before he distracts me again. Most of all, we need to get out of here before some other god figures out where we are and shows up. Lachesis said she wasn't the one following us earlier, which means we've still got an unknown quantity out there.

And I don't know if it's friendly or not.

Dragging Kassam behind me, we're nearly at the door when Charlie calls my name. "Carly! Stop! Wait!"

Ugh. I grit my teeth and turn as he races toward us. "I can't stay, Charlie. I'm sorry."

His eyes are wide. "You can't leave me. We're packed—"

"I know. I can't stay. It'll ease off after we leave, I promise." Since Kassam won't be around to pull people in like a magnet,

I'm pretty confident in that prediction. "I just...there's too much going on."

Charlie's normally easy-going face turns dark with frustration. "If you leave, you're fired."

I just shake my head and pull the god toward the door again. I can't work anyhow. Not until this situation with Kassam is solved. I'll just...have to figure something out. Somehow. "Goodbye, Charlie."

"Carly, please!" There's desperation in his voice—he's looking forward to a night of angry customers who won't tip for shit because of slow service, and I don't blame him for being upset. But he doesn't realize that I can't stay. Not with things like they are. So I take a deep breath, promise myself I'll make it up to him someday, and lead Kassam out to my car. I hate having to leave work so quickly after arriving, but if we stay, I don't know what sort of nonsense will happen next.

I can't take Kassam anywhere.

The realization is a slightly disturbing one. I move to the driver's side of my car, keys in hand as Kassam gets in on the other side. How am I supposed to do anything when I've got to take one very horny god wherever I go, and he causes a scene? How am I going to be able to do life's smallest chores if he—

"Bitch!" A hand snags in my hair from behind. Before I can register what's happening, my assailant slams my head into the roof of my car.

12

I collapse onto the ground, head ringing. There's a red and black haze of pain that makes it difficult to think. How did I fall? What happened?

Then the roaring starts, and I realize through the din in my ears that someone is furious...and that someone is Kassam. Easy-going, always laughing Kassam is snarling with rage.

"She stole you!" a man cries. "She stole you from me!"

Holy shit. Dizzy, I struggle to sit up, because that voice is familiar. It's not... Charlie?

"Human, I will tear your spine from your body and toss it into the rubbish heap," Kassam seethes. He sounds completely different than how he normally does, and the haze in my brain makes it difficult to concentrate. The air is heavy and ominous, and thunder crackles overhead. "Get away from her."

"It's not fair," Charlie cries. "I want you, too! We both saw you at the same time!"

"Human." There's a hollow, horrifying timbre to Kassam's voice. "Touch her again and you will regret it for the rest of your life."

Something skitters over my leg. A bug, maybe? My head

swims, and I can't concentrate enough to look. Then another, and I hear the skittering sound of thousands of legs—a swarm of insects rallying as the air grows thicker and heavier around us. It's like a storm is about to break...and I fear that storm is Kassam.

I roll onto my back and try to assess my injuries. There's something wet on my face, and my nose feels as if it's been flattened. I touch it gingerly, pain flashing through my face. It's broken. As I open my eyes in time to see Kassam throw Charlie across the parking lot. My co-worker goes sailing and slams into another vehicle, the car alarm going off. I crawl to hands and knees. "Kassam," I croak. "No—"

"*Carly.*"

He's immediately at my side, scooping me into his arms. This time, there's no blatant orgasmic flash as he touches me, just a gentle sort of pleasure that reassures and makes me feel better. He bridal carries me, and stars flash in front of my eyes again. Now that Kassam has me, the dizziness that I've been fighting sweeps me away.

I pass out.

When I wake up a short time later, it's to the sound of Kassam's borrowed flip-flops (the only thing I had in my closet for him to wear on his feet) smacking as he goes up stairs. I moan, my entire head throbbing and my stomach queasy. "Where..."

"Hush," Kassam says in a gentle voice. It's strange to hear, after he lost his shit and sounded like he was going to tear Charlie's throat out. I'm still sorting between that Kassam and the normal one I'm used to, who loves to lick each potato chip as if it's special, and who laughs constantly.

The angry god in the parking lot felt like a stranger. A terrifying one.

"Need...to drive," I protest. "We can't stay...here."

"We are almost home, Carly," he tells me, tone soft. "You do not have to drive. I will take care of you."

That doesn't make sense to me. My pain-addled brain tries to focus, but I can't seem to figure it out. Tonight's problems swirl through my head in a jumbled mess.

Bar.
A ferret.
Drugs.
Charlie.
An army of insects.
Lachesis?

I moan, touching my face. "I think my nose is broken."

"It is not," Kassam reassures me. "You will be all right. You are still beautiful, my little light." He shifts my weight in his arms, and I vaguely feel him opening a door. A dozen meows call out the moment it opens. "We are back, my friends. You will tell me your news soon. I must see to my anchor for now."

I clutch at Kassam's shirt, blinking hard even as enormous black dots swirl behind my eyes. "Need...to talk..."

"When you feel better," he promises me. "We will talk then. Rest now."

He steps inside, murmuring to the cats as he does, and they are everywhere in my apartment, crawling over countertops, sitting outside on the balcony, curled up on my sofa. There's no surface that's not covered in house cats of every shape and form. "I'm not supposed to have pets," I say weakly. "Against...rules."

"Did I not tell you to hush, my stubborn female?" A tender hand caresses my cheek. "You will sleep, and then we will talk." He crosses into my bedroom and lays me gently down on the bed, tucking the blankets around me.

I want to protest. I want to get out of bed and figure out what's going on. I want answers.

But my throbbing head wants me to close my eyes and

sleep, and when Kassam brushes his fingers along my jaw, I lean into that comforting touch and drift off.

∽

WHEN I WAKE UP, my face feels like fire and I'm pretty sure there are at least six cats curled up against me in bed. There's a heavy weight on my chest, and when I open my eyes a crack, I see the black and white face of a large cat, licking its paw as it nestles against my boobs. The room is dark, moonlight pouring in through my window. "Kassam?" I manage to croak. "Are you here?"

Heavy feet pound on the floors and in the next moment, I see Kassam peek his head in.

At least, I'm pretty sure it's Kassam? But he looks different. His long, bushy beard is gone. In its place is a smooth, strong jaw. His thick, wavy hair is pulled atop his head in a knot and there's a long, slinky-looking tabby cat hanging over his shoulders. He looks boyish and young, and utterly delighted at the sight of me. "My light! You are awake once more. This is excellent news."

I rub my face, biting back a whimper as I accidentally brush my sore nose. "Why are all these cats still here?"

"Because they help me focus. I am learning that if my powers are siphoned off, my hedonism is less potent. So I am using them to siphon some of my energy. It might cause you a headache, though. Tell me if it pains you too much?"

As if I can notice any sort of head pain beyond my throbbing nose? But I manage a nod. "I think I'm okay."

"Excellent. Wait here. I will get you food and drink."

As if I'm going to leap out of bed. I want to just crawl back under the covers, but there's a fat cat shoving its way underneath the blankets as if they belong to him. I sit up slowly, wincing at jostling my tender head. My shirt slides off my shoulder, and I realize I'm in my loose sleepshirt. Kassam must have taken me out of my work jeans and polo. My bra and panties are gone, too. I reach over to turn on the lamp beside the bed. The moment the lights go on, I stare in shock at the greenery covering my walls. Wild vines cover every inch of my room, curling around my hanging art and dancing up the corners of the walls to the ceiling. I gaze at the trailing leaves and tiny flowers, and I notice that a lot of them seem to be coming out of the window itself, pushing in through the edges of the frame like determined fingers.

Uh oh. When I left my apartment, I didn't have plants in the bedroom. Wincing, I climb over the cats and out of bed, moving toward the window. A quick peek outside shows that massive vines are crawling up the side of the normally plain building front. Shit. Shit shit shit. The landlord is going to crap himself and I am going to get in so much trouble.

"My little light! What are you doing out of bed?" Kassam scolds me as he returns, bearing a glass of water and a box of donuts. "You should be resting."

"The greenery," I protest, gesturing at the window even as I move back toward the bed. "That can't be here."

"If anyone is upset, I will talk to them." He sets the food down on the nightstand and picks up a cat, moving it so I can climb back under the blankets. "Come. Rest."

Oh. I didn't think about that, but it's an excellent idea— Kassam can talk anyone out of their panties, even my asshole landlord. I curl up against the pillows as he leans over, fluffing them for me, and then sits on the edge of the bed. He offers me the box of donuts, which makes me pause. "When did we get donuts?"

"One of your neighbors," he says. "I went to one of the doors in the hall and told them you required food. They were quite gracious."

I'll bet. I can only imagine what that must have been like. "I hope they're not going to show up and try to bang my head in, too."

Kassam flinches. "I knew he was affected by my nearness, but I did not realize he'd take it out on you. It has been a while since I have been myself. Some of my knowledge is not what it used to be."

I nibble on a donut as another cat hops onto the bed and begins kneading the blankets. Chocolate cake donuts. My neighbor has decent taste. "That reminds me. You haven't told me your full story."

"Haven't I?"

"No, you haven't," I stress again. "You told me that you're the god of the wild, and that you're cursed with hedonism, and that I'm your anchor. That you can't return to your job until I die, but something tells me I'm not getting the full story."

He shrugs, his big shoulders moving. Kassam rubs his jaw. "Do you like my face like this? My beard tore up your thighs. I did not realize you were so sensitive."

I blink, chewing the chocolate donut slowly. Did he undress me while I was unconscious? I touch a finger under my nose, and there's no blood there, so I'm guessing he washed and changed me like a mannequin or a doll. I'm not sure how I feel about that. "Thanks, I think. You're changing the subject again."

"Ask your question. I will do my best to answer."

Sure he will. "You *are* the God of the Wild?" When he nods, I ask, "How many gods are there in your world?"

"Twelve, and the High Father who rules over all."

"So where is everyone else?"

"Back in Aos, I imagine." He tilts his head, thinking. "Some have returned to their planes, but I imagine others are still walking the mortal realm. Death was, I know for certain. I met him and his anchor." He looks thoughtful. "I am not sure what happened after they freed me, though."

"Freed you?" When Kassam's eyes narrow, I want to throw

the donut I'm eating at him. Unfortunately for me, it's delicious and I shove the rest of it into my face and reach for another one as I chew. "Go on. Freed you from what."

The god gives me a tight look. "The Blood Glacier, where I'd been trapped for a thousand years." He thinks for a moment. "Maybe two thousand."

13

I choke on my donut. Coughing, I take the water he hands me and manage a few sips, waving my hand to indicate he should continue. Lachesis was right. There's more of a story to what's going on and Kassam (and okay, me) has been too distracted by hedonism to pay attention. "What do you mean, you were trapped? What happened?"

The look he gives me is boyishly sheepish. "A goddess wanted to marry me. I refused her. She did not take to it kindly."

Did I think my donut was dry before? It's sawdust in my mouth now. "Goddess...?" Here I'd asked him to marry me to protect me and he's been turning down goddesses? That's...not going to go over well. "Who is she?"

"The fair Riekki," Kassam says dramatically, scooping up one of the cats and cuddling it against his chest. "The Peace-keeper. The Knowledge-Bringer." He leans toward me, conspiratorial. "Bit of a bore." He nuzzles the cat, who eats up the attention. "We were lovers at the dawn of time, but she became very possessive and I decided I did not wish to join to her. Or be in her presence at all, really. Riekki did not take that well." He strokes the cat's triangular ears. "Thus began a thousand years of Riekki trying to pull me to her side. She tried whatever she could to entrap me, and her priests attacked my worshipers regularly. She hunted my *conmac*, my forest lords."

I frown. "I thought you said she was the Peacekeeper? That doesn't sound peaceful to me."

"And thus you see the problem with Riekki," Kassam agrees. "It is all peaceful as long as it is done her way. Her priests feel it is their duty to convert others to their ways. Only then, can peace be acquired."

"That's fucked." I pull out another donut. I have no idea why I'm starving so badly, but these donuts are the best things I've ever tasted and I can't stop eating them, even when one of the cats licks some of the glaze. "So she's crazy."

"She is focused," he amends. "Riekki is a very determined goddess. And because she is the keeper of knowledge, she believes that only she has the answers and we all should listen to her, regardless of how we feel."

A narcissist. Not ideal to have one of those as a goddess. Between her and easily distracted Kassam, I'm starting to see why the High Father is cleaning house over there. It sounds like a damned mess. "So you turned her down and she imprisoned you?"

"No, I turned her down and Riekki sent her priests to destroy my forests and my faithful. She thought she could control the wild, which, by its very nature, cannot be tamed. And when that did not work, she vowed a full-scale war against me and mine. Before she could do it, however, the Anticipation happened."

"The clean-up," I say, biting down on my donut. I wonder if these things have crack in them. They're seriously so good. I can't stop eating. I'm ravenous. "The big guy sent all the little guys down to the mortal world to shape up."

Kassam nods. "We were split into our four greatest flaws—

hedonism, arrogance, lies, and apathy. There are more flaws, of course, but those are the most deadly for a god. It is a punishment that is handed down time and time again, to purge us of the worst of our sins. The four Aspects are bound to the mortal plane until there is only one remaining. That Aspect—be it Hedonism, Lies, or whatever—is allowed to continue on as he is. The High Father does not value perfection, after all. Everyone must be flawed to grasp mortal concepts, because mortals are the most flawed of all."

I squint at him when he chuckles, as if this observation is vastly amusing.

"In the last Anticipation, I had just dispatched Lies. I was the last Aspect left, and set to return to my home, the Great Endless Forest. Instead of talking to me, my anchor, my very bond with humanity, betrayed me. He was in league with Riekki's wizards, and shoved an enchanted blade into my gut. With that, she broke the tether I had binding me to my anchor. He was free and I was...well, dead. Except the gods are not supposed to die in the Anticipation. Perhaps Riekki figured if she could not have me, no one could. I floated in the Abyss, the plane between the mortal realm and the divine aether, for I do not know how long. I was vaguely aware of my body. Of the sword nestled in my gut, here." He puts a fist to his chest, below his heart. "I was neither alive nor dead, divine nor mortal. I could not be killed, but because of the enchanted sword gutting me, I could not free myself, either. So I laid there and bled. And bled."

The donut in my mouth tastes like ash. I set it down in the box, horrified at what I'm hearing. "No one came after you?"

"No one," Kassam says with a faint smile. "It made me angry for a time, but then I realized...I had angered the goddess of knowledge. It would be a small thing for her to obscure my location. It would be an even smaller thing for her to spread the word that I am lost. That I have never returned from the Anticipation, and that there is no point in looking for me. So I remained where I was." He strokes the cat in his arms intently, as if his entire focus is suddenly on that small feline. "I remained there as the seasons changed, and so did humans. I bled and bled as armies rose and fell, the gods returned, fell once more, returned again. I remained where I was as cities crumbled into the ocean and were forgotten, just like me. I started to think I would be lost for all time. That no one would ever remember who Kassam of the Wild was."

My heart breaks for him. He tries to keep his tone light, but I can hear the pain in it. I can't imagine how horrible it was for him to be stranded like that, never mind the pain. He must have felt so alone. I reach out and touch his hand, and I don't even mind when it sends a ripple of pleasure racing through me. If it gives him pleasure, too, I want that. "Okay," I say softly. "So your dick of an anchor betrayed you and Riekki's a selfish ass. I think I'm up to speed now. None of the other gods tried?"

"If they did, Riekki likely obscured my location or the fact that it was me in the Blood Glacier, that it was my blood pooling in the desolate mountains of the east." He shakes his head, his gaze drifting off, and I can tell I've hit a nerve. He's wondering why no one else came after him, too. They're supposed to be gods, but no one gave a shit when he just up and disappeared for a thousand years.

I can't imagine. I just...can't.

I rub my thumb against his hand, squeezing his fingers. He seems to need to be touched, and when he clings to my hand, I decide I can do more. I pull the cat out of his grasp, setting it down at the foot of the bed, and then push the others aside. I lie down and indicate he should join me at my side. Instead, he rolls me onto my back and presses his cheek to my breasts, resting his head on top of me. His arms go around me tightly, and I feel so, so terrible for bringing it up. It's clear that his time spent trapped for so long that his blood made a fucking *glacier* has traumatized him. I pull his long, tangled hair free from the knot atop his head and run my fingers through it as he holds me tightly. "Okay, so everyone you know is a dick." When that elicits a chuckle, I feel a little better. "How did you get free?"

"There is another Anticipation going on even now," Kassam murmurs against my chest. "The god of death and his anchor found me. They pulled the sword from my guts, and the moment it was free, I felt the thread that bound me snap free. The world went black. I woke up, and you were standing over me."

"So you were sent here," I muse. "Maybe someone's protecting you from Riekki and her crazysauce?"

"Mmm. Perhaps."

I think for a moment and then venture, "Is it possible that you're not supposed to return home at all? That whoever sent you here wants you to stay?"

He props up on one elbow, looking down at me. His gaze devours me, and for a moment, I think he's going to kiss me and we're going to fuck and he'll forget all about answering me. But Kassam just shakes his head, thoughtful. "If that were the case, would I not be split? I was very aware every time the High Father tore me into the four aspects of myself. Right now, I feel like…Hedonism only. I am a left-over shard from my world, and I think I must get back. You could be right that someone brought me here to hide me, but I have been gone millennia. My worshipers will have dwindled to nothing. And if a god has no one to pray to him…what happens then?"

"I don't know," I admit. I think about the woman at the bar and offer, "Lachesis—she said she was fate of this world. She suggested we think about who sent you here, and we'd find our answers there."

"Lachesis?" Kassam's eyes go wide and the thoughtful look

disappears from his face, changing to one of worry. "She approached you?"

Is that...bad? "She was at the bar, smoking a cigarette. She told me that my mother was—oh god, my mother." I've been unconscious, and I haven't passed on Lachesis's warning. I grab Kassam's hand. "Where is my phone?"

"What is a phone?"

Oh boy. Frantic, I sit up, pushing him aside. My head throbs —the pain focused around my nose, and I jump from the bed. "The phone. You know, the square thing I'm always typing on? Please, Kassam, I need it." Like most people nowadays, I don't see the need for a landline, and right now my phone is my only way to get ahold of my mom. She checks her email maybe once a week, so that won't work. Did I leave my phone in the bar? In the parking lot?

"Wait, Carly, we need to talk about Lachesis. I don't like that she's coming to you—"

"My phone," I cry again. I grab a pair of jeans from the floor, shake the nesting cat off of them, and shove my foot through one leg. "Lachesis gave me a warning for my mother. Said she has to stop reading our cards. That she could hurt herself. I have to call her and tell her to stop—"

"I do not have your small box," Kassam says apologetically. "It was important?"

I press my hands to my face and then wince, because that hurts like the dickens. I finish shoving my jeans on and stumble toward the bathroom, just in case my phone ended up there somehow. The moment I flick the light on, I reel in horror at my face. My nose is swollen twice its size, and there's an ugly bruise on one side of my brow and scratches along my jaw, probably where I hit the gravel. Good lord, I look rough.

No phone, though. I'll lament over how bad I look some other time. I race back into the bedroom and hold a hand out for Kassam. "Come on, we have to find a phone somewhere. I've got to call my mom and warn her."

He gets up from the bed lazily, languidly, and I'm hit with a blast of need that makes my knees buckle. "Carly," he murmurs, pulling me into his arms and palming my breast through my T-shirt. "It will be all right. Do not panic."

"Need...to help...Mom," I pant, even as he rolls my nipple under skilled fingers and plucks at it. "You're distracting me."

"I cannot help myself. I need to touch you." Kassam toys with my nipple, his expression hazy with arousal, lips parted just inches away from mine. "I think my magic is drained and the only way I get it back is giving in to my curse." The smile he gives me is so sexy and hungry that it makes me squirm. He pinches my nipple, fingers light enough that it makes me gasp at the sharp sensation. "Help me focus."

Focus? When he's touching me like this and I just want to drop to my knees in front of him? I moan, pressing my face against his bared, tanned chest. I'm inches away from his nipple, and it'd take nothing for me to lean over and lick that small, dark bud and see how he reacts. I slide my hand to his cock and my wrist feels curiously light. I glance down at it and notice scratches on my skin, encircling my wrist.

"Oh," I breathe, lifting my hand to examine it. As I do, Kassam takes my wrist and latches onto it, sucking on the tender skin of my inner wrist. "Oh, fuck, that's hot."

He tongues my pulse, the heat in his eyes full of promise. "Help me focus," he says again. "Carly, please."

I'm entranced by his mouth on my wrist. "Sure," I mumble. It's hard to think when he's touching me like this, his lips tracing the red scratches on my skin. "Scratches..."

"From your bracelet, yes. I took it off when you were hurt."

Bracelet. I squint at my skin even as he rakes his teeth over my flesh, sending shivers directly to my pussy. I should be wearing a bracelet.

Oh fuck, my quartz bracelet. I pull out of his grasp and touch my ears—the quartz earrings are gone, too. "Where's my jewelry?"

"Took it off." He thumbs my nipple again.

I bite back a whimper, but somehow I manage to pull free. "Can't think like this," I gasp. "Hedonism..."

"I know," he purrs, and when I take a step away, he grabs my hips and pulls me back against his cock. "We can contact your mother after I make you come."

"First," I pant. "Need to call Mom first." I scan my messy room, and when I see the jewelry on the floor next to an orange cat's flicking tail, I nearly sob in relief and disappointment both. I grab the quartz jewelry, clutching it to my chest. The moment I do, some of that delicious, twisting need fades. The fog clears from my thoughts and I glance at Kassam.

He palms his cock, watching me with eyes the color of smoke.

Okay, mental note, don't look at Kassam when I'm trying to get ahold of myself. I get to my feet and fasten one of the bracelets on his wrist. "I need to think straight," I remind him. "We can't do this right now."

Kassam nods, still rubbing his cock. "Too much," he murmurs. "I used too much of my magic. Even as it drained, the curse hit me like a bolt of lightning. It's still hitting me right now."

I can tell. He's still rubbing his shaft through his sweatpants. And god, I want to do the same. I stare as he drags his fingers up and down his length, outlining it through the soft material, and I've never wanted a man to flip me around onto my bed and rail me so badly.

"New plan," I say breathlessly. "We call my mom quickly. Make sure she's okay. Then we come back here and we fuck until dawn."

A sensual smile plays at Kassam's mouth, and he squeezes his length. "Very well."

It should absolutely not feel like I've somehow lost a bet when he agrees to that. Yet somehow, it does. I rub the crystals as I put them on, wishing they were a little more potent. But there aren't enough crystals in the world to counteract what Kassam is throwing off. Not enough in two worlds, probably.

14

My neighbor does not look thrilled to see me. If anything, he looks slightly terrified. "Y-your face," he mumbles as I come to the door. "What—"

"I know I look a little strange," I say quickly, fighting every instinct to push my way inside. "But I need to borrow your phone."

He doesn't answer me. In fact, he stares right past me. His lips part, and then he makes a wordless little sound that might be sexual. Right. Because Kassam is two steps behind me. I shouldn't be surprised.

Nor should I be jealous, but as he gives Kassam an intense stare, I want to snap my fingers in front of his eyes and shout, "That's my boyfriend." Except...he's not my boyfriend. What did Kassam say earlier? That I was helping him scratch an itch? Now that I've got the crystals back in place, I'm a little peeved by that. Scratching an itch, indeed. Is that all I am to him? A back-scratcher? The thought bothers me. "Phone, please?"

My neighbor—a nice-looking guy in his mid-thirties and probably divorced—pulls out his phone, wordlessly types in his password and holds his cell out to me. His gaze never leaves Kassam, even when some of the cats head inside, meowing and twisting around our legs.

"This better not be the donut neighbor," I mutter as I swipe my finger over the screen and start dialing. I don't know why I'm jealous. I don't.

"It does not matter if it is, my little light," Kassam says in a voice that sends curls of heat through my body. "You asked me to be monogamous, and I shall be."

My neighbor looks at me then, and his gaze is sheer hatred. It's calculating, too, and an alarmed part of me is starting to realize just how dangerous it is to be Kassam's anchor. Charlie attacked me because he was jealous. If this guy came to my door in the middle of the night with a butcher knife, I'd absolutely believe it. Cradling the phone, I step behind Kassam as it rings.

And rings. And rings.

My mom doesn't pick up on the first eight rings and it goes to voicemail. A hard knot of panic starts in my chest and I hang up, then re-dial the number. To my relief, this time my mom answers. "Hello?"

She sounds tired, her voice thick. "Mom?"

"Carly? Is that you?"

"Yes!" I cry, so relieved I could scream with sheer joy. "Are you okay?"

"Just a rotten headache," my mother says. "I was taking a nap to try to get rid of it. What time is it?"

"Late," I say, though I don't know how late. Just that it's dark out and my neighbor is in his pajamas. "Listen, Ma, I need you to stop using your cards to help us out, okay? Whatever you were doing, just stop. I got a warning that you can't continue."

"What do you mean, you got a warning?"

I glance over at my neighbor, not sure if he's listening in or not. Even if he does, does it matter? I'm not entirely sure he'll remember. Hesitant, I lower my voice and turn away. "You know I told you who and what Kassam is? Do you remember?"

"A god. From another world."

"Yup. Well tonight at the bar, one of the locals showed up. Said her name was Lachesis and gave me a warning that we were messing with things and for you to stop."

My mother pauses. "Lachesis, like...one of the three Greek fates?"

"Right. That's the one." She'd mentioned fate, but I didn't know the rest. "Just...no more cards, okay? I don't want you getting pulled into this."

"No more cards," my mother agrees. "I couldn't find out anything anyhow. It's like someone's blocking me."

It could be Lachesis for all I know, but I don't point that out. The goddess could be our enemy, but I'm still going to take her warning to heart. "Just...be careful, okay? Are you feeling all right?"

"I'm fine. Just headachey."

"Want us to come over?" I glance at Kassam, who's holding my neighbor entranced with a sensual smile. "We could protect you."

"No, no no," my mother says, a fussy note in her voice. "Now that I'm awake, I'm going to work on your handfasting vows. Make sure that they're good and binding so he can't slip out of his promises to you. I can't do that when he's around." She chuckles. "I can't do anything when he's around, actually. I don't know how you think straight."

"I'm not sure I do," I admit. "Okay, well, if you need me, I lost my phone. We'll be there in the morning first thing, all right?"

"Be ready to get married," my mother tells me. "We're going to make sure he keeps you safe."

I try not to think about Charlie's attack, or the fact that my neighbor probably wants Kassam for himself...or hell, the goddess Riekki, who wanted to marry Kassam and will probably shit a brick when she hears I have. Fuuuuuck.

One problem at a time. "Be safe. Love you."

"I love you too, sweetheart. Kiss your pretty man for me."

I hang up with my mom, a little amused at her comment to kiss my "pretty man." He's not mine, and he's not a man, but a god. But...he's definitely pretty enough. I hold the phone back out to my neighbor, a thank-you hovering on my lips, when he gives me a dirty look and turns back to Kassam. "I could treat you better than her."

And just like that, any gratitude I have toward my neighbor vanishes. "Your phone," I snap, wagging it at the neighbor. "We're leaving."

"Think about what I said," he murmurs to Kassam.

"My needs are met," Kassam tells him, that smile constantly on his face.

His needs. I'm growing less amused by the moment. First I'm scratching his itches, now I'm meeting his needs. I don't know what sort of response I expected from him, but this bond between us feels...bigger than having just needs met?

Because here I am helping him, and in return for some mind-blowing orgasms, I'm getting my life torn apart. I just lost my job, my boss attacked me, I'm pretty sure I'm going to get tossed out of my apartment building, and now my mom is in danger. All because I'm helping him "scratch his itch."

For a moment, hot resentment flares. It feels like I don't matter to him, and that hurts. I know it's only been a short time since we touched hands in the alley, but...can't he even feel some sort of appreciation for me? As a person? Not just my pussy?

Kassam keeps blithely smiling as we head out into the hall. The cats mill around us, meowing for attention as we walk the short distance back to my apartment, and unhappy thoughts stew in my head. I'm tempted to remove the quartz jewelry entirely because I'm much happier with Kassam when I'm being orgasmed out of my mind. If I have time to think about what a shitty situation I'm in, I start to wonder what the hell I'm doing.

I stumble over one of the eager cats, and Kassam catches my arm. He sees the expression on my face and that dark brow goes up. "You look upset, my little light. What's wrong?"

"I kinda hate the effect you have on everyone," I grumble.

He nods. "Not to worry. You are the one I am using for my needs."

My jaw clenches. Is that what I am to the gods? Just the human version of a pocket pussy? A convenient receptacle for Kassam's lusts while he figures out how to get home? Now that I'm slightly less dazzled by him, I'm starting to realize what a raw deal I've been given. It's not in me to stew endlessly, though. If something isn't working for me, I bail out quickly...as evidenced by my long string of short-term relationships and all of the unfinished art projects scattered around my apartment.

And my three-page résumé.

And the fact that I changed my college major six times before dropping out.

But...whatever. That's beside the point. "You and I should probably talk about our situation."

He blinks at me, puzzled. "Why?"

"I'm feeling a little railroaded at the moment," I begin, twisting my quartz necklace. "Do you realize just how much this is messing up my life right now? With—"

I break off, because Kassam places a hand over my mouth to silence me. That slippery, coiling pleasure slides through me, coupled with outrage. What the hell does he think he's doing, shushing me? I push at his hand, irritated, but he wraps his other arm around my shoulders and hauls me against his chest, my back pressing against him.

"Shh," Kassam whispers. "Wait."

I go still, because the urge to obey him is always present. Not only that, but there's something in his voice that makes me worry. I move my lips against his fingers, indicating that I want to talk, but he keeps me pinned against his chest, cradled in front of him.

Kassam leans in, whispering in my ear. "Do you feel that?"

Feel? I wait, trying to see what it is that Kassam "feels" in the hall. Around me I see nothing but the plain halls of my apartment building, slightly dingy and a boring, corporate gray. There's a plastic ficus at the far end of the hall, by the elevator, just like normal, and the doors across the hall are all closed tight. My door is cracked open, a cat trotting out to meet us. Someone has mail stuck to the clip outside their door, but other than that, everything looks normal.

I don't see anything. I'm tempted to bite his hand, but he makes a low sound in his throat that pauses me.

And...then I feel it.

The small hairs on my arms rise. The air feels charged, heavy like it does before a storm. Not quite the same as when Lachesis was in the bar, that subtle attraction that told me to go to her, but something else. It's strong and potent and not quite human, like someone poured pure energy into my building.

It's coming directly from my apartment, too. Whoever—whatever—is waiting there wants us to know that they're there.

I'm frightened. I clutch at Kassam's hand. "What is that?" I mumble against his fingers.

His mouth brushes against my ear as he whispers. "Whoever is following us found you. Are you ready to fight?"

Fight?

Is he serious? I don't want to fight. I want to go home, push a few cats off the bed, eat the rest of the donuts, and gripe that he's treating me like a thing and not like a person. All of that doesn't matter right now, though. Not when there's some sort of strong, worrying entity in my apartment waiting for us.

Lurking.

I shake my head and his hand moves away from my mouth. "I don't want to fight," I whisper. "Do we have another option?"

"Run?"

I nod. Yeah, I like that one. "Running's good," I hiss. I grab his hand and turn around, racing for the fire escape stairs. He goes with me, our bare feet padding down the metal stairs as we go down several flights toward the street. I race out of the front of the building, and I keep racing without stopping until we get to the corner store at the end of the street, the twenty-four-hour one with a few gas pumps, a Slurpee machine, and bright, bright lights in the parking lot.

For some reason, those lights feel like safety. Having people around feels like safety.

I step inside the electronic doors, my toes curling on the mat near the entrance. The middle-aged woman behind the counter frowns at me as I walk forward, but her expression melts into one of adoration the moment she catches sight of Kassam.

Behind me, Kassam breathes deep, inhaling the scents. "What is this fascinating place?"

Fascinating? I look over at him and he's got that hedonism look in his eyes. Maybe it's the scent of the hotdogs on the world's oldest grilling machine, or the bright colors of the snack foods, but I can see how this is exciting to him. He picks up a plastic package of pink frosted cakes and sniffs it. "This is a corner store," I say, watching the cashier. "People get food and gas here." I pat my pockets, but I already know they're empty. "We don't have any money, though."

"Hi," blurts the woman behind the counter. "I'm Shirley."

"Greetings, Shirley," Kassam practically purrs, turning his gaze toward her. "Do you mind if we visit your store?"

Like a schoolgirl, Shirley giggles and tucks a gray lock of hair behind her ear. "I don't mind. And if you forgot your wallet, you can start a tab here. I'll cover you." She gives Kassam a meaningful look. "But don't tell anyone."

He puts a finger to his lips and holds the pink cakes out to Shirley. "Do you find these tasty?"

15

I pace around the store's low, dusty shelves, pretending to examine the contents while Kassam works his charms on Maggie. I don't feel anything, though, and as I continue to watch the door, no one comes in or out. When Kassam finally hands me a bright red slush to drink, I take it and slide into the booth at the back of the store, gazing at old lottery ticket advertisements that cover the window. I can't see out into the parking lot or the street, but maybe it's for the best. I don't know that I'd be able to see a god approaching anyhow, unless he was in mortal form like Kassam. If he's a god, he could be anything—a bird, a horse, a gust of wind...

Instead of sitting across from me in the booth, Kassam sits right next to me, blocking me in against the wall. He grins, his lips reddened from his slush, and spills his snacks on the table. He's got a hot dog from the machine, three bags of chips, four kinds of candy, and those pink cakes he was so fascinated with. "Are you hungry, my little light? Shall we eat?"

I'm ravenous, despite the donuts I had just a short time ago, but I shake my head. I don't feel like eating, especially not when we're being pursued. "Are you done flirting now? Can we focus on the fact that someone's following us, please?"

"They are gone," Kassam says, frowning at the plastic wrap on the cakes. He licks it cautiously, a thoughtful look on his face. I snatch the package from him and open it, and his smile grows again. "I do not feel anything anymore, do you?"

"No," I admit, handing him back the food. "You don't eat wrappers, FYI. Just the contents."

"Aaaah." He takes a bite of the pink cake and grunts. "It looks better than it tastes."

"A lot of things do."

He gives me a sultry look from under his lashes and licks the frosting. "You both look delightful and taste delicious."

Heat prickles through me. I rub my bracelet instead, trying not to watch him as he tongues a cheap snack cake. "So do you know who—or what—that was? In my apartment?" It's hitting me now that someone was in my home, lurking there. Waiting for us. I'm not sure we can ever go back. Despair hits me. No job, no apartment...I'm starting to feel invisible walls closing in around me. It's been two days since I was bonded to Kassam.

At this rate, we're not going to last a week.

Kassam sets down the remnants of the cake he's licked clean of its frosting and picks up his Slurpee again. "I did not recognize the power signature. A god from this realm, perhaps, but one that is unknown to me."

"So what do we do?"

He sips from his straw, which makes me wonder how he figured that out, and then sets his drink down. "It depends on who it is that is seeking us out. It could be someone allied with Riekki, or someone seeking to use us for their own gain. You seem sad, Carly." Kassam puts an arm across the back of the booth, hugging me closer. "Are you all right?"

Am I all right? "We're being chased down by gods I didn't know existed in my world, I just lost my job, my neighbor hates me, my apartment is lost to us, and you want me dead. Of course I'm not all right."

At that, Kassam frowns. "I do not want you dead, Carly." His free hand slides to my thigh. "You are my anchor. If you die in this world, I might be trapped here."

Well, great. I'm *thrilled* that his only reason for wanting to keep me alive is so he won't be trapped. Heaven forbid. "You're kind of an asshole, you know that?"

"You are mad at me, and I am being honest with you, Carly. I wish nothing but to be honest." He shrugs. "Would you rather I give you pretty lies?"

I glare at him. "Maybe I'm tired of being told that I exist purely to service your needs. Meanwhile, my life is in danger and I'm being chased out of my home by gods that are pissed you're in their territory. And here I am, in your eyes, existing solely to scratch your itches."

Kassam blinks. Then, his grin slowly spreads across his face and he chuckles, the sound low and throaty. "Are you developing feelings for me, Carly?"

Ugh, this man. I want to choke him and kiss him at the same time, and I know the kissing is only because of his hedonism curse. "The only feelings I have right now are sheer frustration that I'm utterly powerless in my own life and no one seems to care. I feel like I brought a stick to a sword fight. Better yet, a stick to a gunfight."

He gazes at me with amusement. "If it helps, you are nothing to these other gods. They are only interested in me."

Not exactly the comforting words he was looking for. "Do you know if they are coming to kill you?" Because if they are, I'm fucked. "Or to push you back to your world?"

"I am not certain, but it did not feel like a well-meaning deity behind that door," Kassam admits. He squeezes my thigh again, this time his hand a little higher up my thigh. "Do not worry, my little light. I will keep you safe."

Somehow I have my doubts. "I'm not even sure you want to."

"I do." Kassam's big, warm hand slides higher. "Who would scratch my itches for me if not my pretty Carly?"

I glare at him, even as my body quivers with need. It's like he can sense how he affects me—either that or I'm wearing a hungry, needy expression on my face—because he slides his hand into my pants and starts touching me. I'm wet, because my body's determined to betray me. I bite my lip, holding back the needy sound that threatens to escape.

"Feels like I am not the only one itching," Kassam murmurs. "Do you like my touch, my light?"

My body clenches around nothing, and I hate that when he rubs my clit, everything in me responds. I lift one foot to the other bench across from me, spreading my legs under the table so he can touch me better. My head falls back, and I press against his shoulder. He leans in to kiss me—

And I turn away. "N-no," I breathe, because somehow, him kissing me feels like a betrayal.

He pulls back in surprise, still toying with my aching clit. "Why 'no'?"

"Because." Because I need to hold something back from him. Because I don't want to catch feelings for him only to be constantly hurt when he reminds me that I'm nothing more than a convenient vessel for him. "Kisses are for romance, and you've made it quite clear there's nothing romantic about what's going on between us."

"But what if I like kissing you?" He shifts his hand, pushing a finger deep inside me even as his thumb works my clit, and I grab onto his shirt, clinging to him. If someone walks past, they'll see us. Hell, we're probably on the security cameras. But if someone asked me to move away in this moment, I don't think I could. "What if I like capturing that lovely mouth of yours, Carly?"

Kassam's lips hover over mine even as he fucks me with his hand, trying to push me into giving in.

"I'd tell you..." I manage, our mouths brushing, "too bad. You can have my body, but you can't have my kiss."

He chuckles. "The gods love a challenge, my little light. If you're trying to make me lose interest, you're failing."

I don't care. All I know is that I have to keep something for myself or I'll go crazy. He's got his hand in my pants at a convenience store, and I am shamelessly grinding against it. He's turned me into a person I don't even recognize anymore.

If withholding a few kisses helps me keep my sanity, I'm all for it. If nothing else, it feels good to be able to say "no" to Kassam on something. He watches me with a strange new curiosity, as if I've surprised him.

I'm guessing the gods don't get refused a lot of things.

16

After spending a miserable night in the convenience store, we head out before dawn.

Shirley—the lovely woman behind the convenience store counter who's fed us and let us hang out all night—drives us downtown to my mom's shop the moment she gets off her shift. She's been casting hungry looks at Kassam all night long, but they've fallen into discussions about what kind of snacks are best for late-night binges, and spent the last few hours taste-testing types of candy while I flipped through bridal magazines, ate my weight in stale packaged cookies, and waited for dawn impatiently. I can't go home. I'm not sure I can ever go home again. Not with something evil waiting for me there.

One day at a time has turned into one hour at a time.

Shirley pulls up to the building that houses my mom's shop and idles her car at the curb. "You sure I can't do anything else for you, baby?" She gazes at Kassam intently, ignoring me. I'm starting to get used to that, though, and this time it doesn't hurt my feelings. Considering that Kassam's low-key flirting with this woman kept us fed and safe all night, I'll take it.

"You have been more than enough, my dove," Kassam

murmurs, taking her hand and kissing her knuckles. "We would be lost without you."

She looks fascinated at his touch. "I work the overnight shift again tonight if you're around."

"Thanks, Shirley," I say, climbing out of the car. The pavement of the sidewalk scratches at my bare feet but it doesn't look incredibly filthy, so that's a plus. Kassam follows me and we head toward Mom's shop, moving down the empty street. Downtown Chicago is busy a lot of times of day, but the crack of dawn is not one of them. The storefronts are all dark, and Mom's shop is as deserted as the rest of them.

I try the door, just because I don't relish the thought of sitting on the sidewalk in front of her shop for hours, and I'm surprised when it opens, the chimes clanging against the glass as I pull it open. "Ma?"

"In the back, darling. Stay out there!" my mom calls, voice muffled. Sure enough, there's a line of light under the stockroom door, so I usher Kassam inside and lock the door behind me.

I glance over at Kassam. "Feel anything unusual?"

He shakes his head. "All is quiet. If one of the gods of this realm is chasing us, they have not found your mother."

"Good. I want to keep it that way." I bite my lip, because even being here right now feels like it puts her in danger. "Make sure you don't use your powers, all right? No plants, no birds, no squirrel parade showing up at the door. None of that."

"If I do not release something, the hedonism will grow stronger," Kassam says, a vaguely hurt look on his face. "I was doing all of that to help you."

Help me? I guess. After I was clobbered by Charlie—Kassam's fault, I might add—I wasn't exactly feeling like having some sexy romps. But I didn't want him drawing every cat within a six-block radius to my apartment, either. Yelling at him feels like a lost cause, though. I'm frustrated because I'm tired and cranky and scared. I scrub at my face. "Can you bottle up the hedonism for just a little while? Please?"

"If I could, don't you think I'd try?"

"Honestly? No." I put my hands on my hips. "You're enjoying yourself far too much." I gesture at him. "You like eating all the snacks and kissing all the ladies. You like people falling all over you. You're having a great fucking time and my life is being completely and utterly destroyed."

Kassam moves toward me. "Carly," he says softly. "If I seem like I do not care, or if I am having a wondrous time, it is because of the curse. You think I would rather be here, eating your pink cakes and enticing your neighbor, than I would be back home, ruling my dominion? I endure this because I must. Because it is the only way to get back to who I was before this all happened." His voice is soft, and he reaches for me, rubbing my arm gently. "My biggest regret is that my presence is making you miserable. I hate that. I want to be your friend."

I bite back a sigh, because now I feel like an asshole. "This has just been really rough, okay?"

"It could be worse," Kassam says, and a dimple flashes in his tanned cheek, a dimple that was hidden by his thick beard before yesterday. "You could be stabbed in the guts with an enchanted sword and left to rot at the bottom of a blood glacier for a thousand years."

Oh sure, just play the trump card. "Okay, you win," I mutter. "That's a far shittier scenario than me losing a bartending job."

The look he gives me is wry. "I am aware this is hard for you, Carly. Trust me when I say I will make it up to you."

"How?" I have to ask, because I'm genuinely curious.

He thinks for a moment. "Endless orgasms?"

"Is that all you've got to offer? Because I have a vibrator, my friend, and it offers the same." I poke a finger in his chest. "And it never got me fired or invited two dozen cats into my apartment."

But Kassam's eyes gleam with interest. He catches my finger, tugging me closer to him, and the scorching heat is back in his gaze. A hot current of pleasure flares between us. "What is this 'vibrator'? Tell me more."

Oh no, I'm not falling for that. With a chuckle, I escape his grasp, backing up a few steps. "None of your business."

His brows furrow together and he looks...annoyed? Just then, my mother steps out of the back room, and my focus goes from Kassam to her. She flicks on the lights, a smile on her face, and I'm relieved to see that my mother looks the same as she always does. There's dark circles under her eyes, but overall she looks good. Best of all, she's whole and healthy, and I want to sag with relief at that realization.

She's also wearing every single piece of quartz in the shop. Her head glitters with a mix of duct tape and quartz stuck to a headband, and her sweatshirt is covered in bands of more tape, all with crystals of various sizes underneath.

"Ma," I breathe. "I'm so glad to see you." Some people don't get along with their parents, but despite my disdain for psychic everything, my mother and I are best friends. I love her and I've been worried sick about her. Not having my phone with me and being able to check in via text has been harder than I realized. Seeing her in front of me, bedecked in crystals and no worse for the wear, has taken some of the stress of the night off of my shoulders.

"Oh honey," my mother breathes, her gaze horrified. "Your face."

"Is it that bad?" I touch my bruised nose.

"Yes," Kassam says helpfully. "But nothing is broken." At my mother's wordless sound of protest, the god adds, "There was a fight at the bar. Carly was pulled in despite my efforts. I made sure they paid, though."

"Good." My mother gives me an assessing look, and I know she was worrying over me, too. "Are you okay, Carly honey? You look rough. Not just the bruises. Tired, too." Her gaze flicks to my bare feet and then over my dirty, wrinkled clothing.

"I didn't get much sleep," I admit. "Long story."

She closes her eyes and holds up a hand. "Say no more. I'm your mother and I don't want to hear details." She points at Kassam. "You—stay across the room. Both of you, actually. Much as I'd love to hug you, I need to remain clear-headed if we're going to do this."

Biting my lip, I nod. Of course it makes sense for us to stay as far from my mom as possible so she doesn't get pulled into Kassam's hedonism spell...but it still hurts. "You didn't use your cards, did you?"

Mom shakes her head, pulling out a few books she had in the break room. "Spent most of the night researching, actually. I looked up Lachesis and various rituals." Her gaze gets wistful. "What was she like?"

"Lachesis?" I have to struggle to recall. "Really...average. She smoked a cigarette and looked like she'd just gotten off work. If I didn't know better, I'd have thought she was just an average person."

"She's the middle fate in Greek mythology," my mother says, clutching the book to her chest, a dreamy expression taking over. "I can't believe she knows who I am. That she was looking out for me. I'm going to have to light a candle and thank her."

"If she's fate, she knows you're grateful," I point out, worried that my mom's going to start futzing with things she shouldn't. I've ignored and humored her spell-casting and rituals all my life, because I thought they were about as legit as Bigfoot or Nessie. Now that gods are real, it's casting a whole new light onto things, and I'm worried. "Just stay off the spells for a bit, maybe? Until things die down?"

She looks disappointed, but nods. "I can't stop seeing auras, though. Yours looks more web-covered than ever." She gestures at Kassam. "And all your threads and webs are stuck to him."

I blanch. "So which one is the fly caught in the spiderweb, me or him?"

My mother looks worried, casting a glance back and forth between me and Kassam as if she can't decide. "That wasn't what I meant—"

"It's okay," I manage, as Kassam puts a reassuring hand on my shoulder. "I know things are a mess right now. I'm just hoping they all get straightened out soon."

"Yes!" my mother says emphatically. "I do, too. I want you safe."

My skin prickles with awareness and I think about the dark presence waiting at my apartment last night. I put my hand over Kassam's, giving his fingers a gentle squeeze and silently asking him not to say anything that might alarm my mother. "Let's get this show on the road, then. We probably shouldn't linger."

I want nothing more than to hug my mom and have her help me with all of this, but I worry if she gets pulled in, it'll be dangerous for her. Better to stay away.

"Yes, of course," my mother says, opening her book again. "While I was preparing my clothes last night, I also looked up handfasting rituals. And I registered to be an official priestess of one religion and a minister of another, so I figure we can make this ceremony stick. A handfasting is just as legitimate as a wedding, and you don't need a license for that, which solves your problem." She gives us a firm nod, flipping open a book. "Give me just a moment and we can get started. No time to waste. The sooner we get you protected, the better."

"Right. Sure."

"Is he certain he wants to go through with this?" my mother asks, licking a fingertip and flipping pages in her book.

I turn toward Kassam. "Well?"

He gives me that lazy, dimpled grin and puts a hand to his

chest, directly over the game logo on his wrinkled shirt. "You mean I get a choice?"

"Honestly, no. You get about as much choice as I do." I give him an insincere smile and reach out, pretending to smooth a wrinkle on the front of his shirt. "But this is to protect me and to bind you to me, and if you want my help scratching any sort of itch in the next while, you're going to do this or I'm abandoning ship right now."

Kassam huffs with amusement. "As if you could. We were bound to one another the moment your hand touched mine."

"That may be, but there's a big difference between a willing Carly who goes along with your schemes and one that won't participate at all. I can make this really, really hard on you." I'm also bluffing, because I'm utterly powerless in this moment and I hope he doesn't realize it. I don't know what I'll do if he doesn't agree to marry me. It won't make a big difference, but my mother thinks it'll protect me and I need all the protection I can get.

He gazes down at me, expression thoughtful. His hand covers the one I have on his chest, and my inner channel contracts with the force of my orgasm, hot prickles rushing through me. Bastard. I can't believe he did that in front of my mother. I glare at him, because I know this is jockeying for the upper hand. "And what do I get out of this?"

Is he serious? "A willing companion? Someone to help guide you on the way home?" I lower my voice so my mother doesn't hear. "Someone who scratches your freaking itches?"

But he just waits. "What else?"

What does he mean, what else? His gaze flicks to my mouth, and then I realize what this is about. He doesn't like that I've refused to kiss him. I wonder if Kassam has ever been refused anything at all. "Not that," I say. "That's mine. But you know that everything else is on the table."

He grunts, his thumb brushing over the back of my hand. "And you will not give me that?"

"Kissing belongs with love. There's no love here, just mutual using."

His eyes spark, as if he's just figured out something important. Kassam leans in, murmuring in a low voice. "I have decided that I am going to make you love me, Carly."

I laugh. Genuinely laugh. "You are talking to the ultimate non-finisher, Kassam. I never go all the way in anything, remember? The queen of unfinished projects?" I shake my head, amused. I've never been in a relationship that didn't go sour quickly. I always bail on the guy when things start to get serious. "Trust me, it's never going to happen."

"We'll see." The challenging look is back in his eyes.

"Are you two going to whisper all day or can we get this handfasting going?" my mother calls from across the store.

17

A short time later, my mother has married-slash-handfasted us in four different ways. We've repeated a half-dozen vows, all of them promising to honor and obey and cherish one another. Several times, Kassam has had to promise to look after me in sickness and in health, and to guide me through all of life's perils. He's vowed to cleave only to me, to protect, and to be true. I don't know how much is Mom's ad-libbing and how much is true, but as Kassam binds a long, red length of cloth around our joined hands, tying us together, it feels...heavy.

Sacred.

I'm married to a god.

A really annoying, really sexually charged god who just wants his itches scratched, but whatever.

"Should we seal things with a kiss?" my mother asks cheerfully as she closes her final book.

Ulp. In that moment, I could cheerfully scream at my mother. She beams at us, oblivious to the can of worms she's just opened. Kassam gives me a look, pulling me toward him.

"Yes, my light, let us kiss and ensure that the ceremony is binding."

He angles his mouth toward mine, and I turn aside at the last moment so he kisses my cheek. When Kassam pulls back, there is a challenging look in his eyes, and I suspect I've waved a red flag in front of a bull. Doesn't matter. I'm not going to give him what he wants just because he demands it.

"Well," my mother says as we pull apart. "You're as safe as I can make you, Carly honey." She clutches the book on ceremonies to her chest, her gaze misty. "Never thought I'd be the mother of the bride quite like this, but we'll get it all figured out, right? Have you had any luck with contacting his world?"

I opt to glaze over the dangerous elements. "Not much yet, but we'll get there. Right, Kassam?"

"Actually," Kassam says, squeezing my sweaty hand. He glances down at the red handfasting ribbon holding our joined palms together. "The ceremony is not complete until we have consummated the marriage, is it?"

I freeze in place, turning toward him. My nostrils flare and my jaw clenches with sheer outrage. That son of a bitch.

"Well," my mother hesitates. "I figured that wouldn't be a problem for you two, but yes, that is part of quite a few of the ceremonies—"

"Then it is best we do so promptly to ensure Carly's safety." He gives me the barest smile. "Since that is what this is all for."

Bastard. It takes everything I have not to blurt the word aloud. Maneuvering, sneaky-ass bastard. I won't kiss him so he's going to turn this into a game? This is my fucking *life*. "I'm sure we can wait a few hours—"

But Kassam looks right past me and at my mother. "The sooner the better. She is already in grave danger. Did she not tell you of last night's encounter?"

Oh, double bastard. At my mom's worried look, I shake my

head, plucking at the red handfasting ribbons on our hands to untie us. "It's nothing, Mom. He's just being dramatic."

"After Lachesis warned Carly, another god showed up in her dwelling," Kassam states. "Someone is seeking her out. This is why we must be careful. If these vows are sacred and will bind Carly to me, then we must make sure she is bound, yes?" He snatches my hand the moment I untie the handfasting bindings and heads into the back room, the one my mom uses for her card readings. "Give us a few minutes. This will not take long."

I make a wordless sound of protest, even as Kassam drags me after him, sending orgasmic pulses through our joined hands. I don't dare look over at my mother, because I'm humiliated as the god pulls me toward the room. "We're not doing this here," I manage to choke out. "Kassam, no—"

"Carly, yes," he says, pulling me into the plain little room and shutting the door behind us. He scans the surroundings—my mom's folding card table, the two cheap metal chairs, and then the counter stacked with tarot decks and rune stones, along with books and more crystals. He sweeps the counter clean, everything crashing to the floor. "You wanted a marriage, you will get a marriage—in all ways."

"You're being an asshole," I hiss at him. "Is this because I wouldn't kiss you? I sure don't want to now."

"No, this is because you are my wife," he says, voice succinct and clear as he turns to me. "And because I have now vowed in front of the gods to keep you safe from harm. So hop onto the counter and I will fuck you appropriately, so we may consummate our relationship and you will be protected."

"I am not doing this here!" Not with my mother outside the door, knowing what we're doing. It violates every rule of mother-daughter-ness there is.

Kassam turns to me, ignoring my protests. He hauls me against him, and I practically stumble, my hands slapping against his chest. He ignores my efforts to push him away, unzipping my jeans and thrusting them down my legs. "Step out."

"I am not," I hiss.

He kneels in front of me, his silver eyes hazy and his expression one of absolute determination. "Carly. You agreed to see to my needs, did you not? We have copulated many, many times already. Your mother knows this. Your body knows this. This will keep you safe. Do not be stubborn."

"You're doing this because you're mad at me," I pant. It's getting harder to think, especially as he gently lifts one foot and pulls my jeans free, then the other. I didn't put on panties earlier when I left, imagining I'd only be gone for a few minutes, and now I'm bare from the waist down. He cups my ass with his big hands, pulling me closer to him.

Kassam squeezes my ass, gazing at my pussy. "Mad at you? No." He glances up at me. "I am doing this because I like fucking you. Because I like those little sounds you make when I am deep inside you. I am doing this because I am Hedonism...and because I owe it to you to make you as safe as I can. If that means we have sex here instead of in another store like the one we were in last night, then I will gladly do so. Unless you have somewhere else you'd rather go?" His hand skims across my hip and down my thigh, and it takes everything I have not to part my legs and just pull him in. "Tell me to stop right now, Carly, and I will. You are in charge."

"I hate you," I mutter.

"Are you telling me to stop?"

I bite back a sigh of frustration. I'm annoyed, but I'm not an idiot. And with him touching me like this? I want him, too. Of course I do. It's his curse that's making me react, but it doesn't matter. I'm still achy with need. So I answer. "No, I'm not telling you to stop."

He glances up at me, and there's triumph in his eyes. "But you do not want me to kiss you."

"Nope." I pop the "P" in the word for emphasis.

"Not even...here?" And he nuzzles at my pussy, his tongue flicking against my skin.

I suck in a breath. We've had sex. We've had a lot of sex, actually, in the last two days. But it's been about him and "scratching his itch," so to speak, so all the sex has been fast and furious, with very little foreplay. I haven't minded. In fact, I've been so out of my head with need that the faster the sex, the better. It never occurred to me to demand that he go down on me. But right now, as he kneels before me with his mouth hovering just above the juncture of my thighs? I realize he's discovered a new angle in which to drive me crazy.

And I am suddenly all for it.

"Kissing...is usually on the mouth," I mention, squirming against his touch. "That's...not quite the same."

"Is it not?" He gently pushes my thighs apart, forcing me to lean against the counter. The room's a mess thanks to his arm-sweep across the countertop, and I should tell him we need to clean up before fooling around, but I can't make my mouth work to form the words. He gazes at the tuft of hair between my thighs and then slides his thumb down the seam of my folds. "If I put my mouth here, is that not a kiss?"

"No." My voice sounds wobbly. Heated, but wobbly.

"Even if I add my tongue?" He licks his lips as that thumb moves over and over, rubbing up and down my slit.

"Still not a kiss."

"Mmm." He glides his hands down my legs, then takes one foot in his grasp. Pressing a kiss to my ankle, he maneuvers my foot onto his shoulder and then over it, sliding forward. His face is between my legs, and I'm half-straddling his face. I'm panting, too, my breath coming in raspy, excited gasps. "Should I stop, then?" he asks, nipping at the inside of my thigh.

"Didn't—didn't say that," I manage.

He gives me a triumphant look. "You're going to fall in love with me, Carly. Wait and see."

"Just because you give me head? You've got a pretty high opinion of...ohhh," I cry out as he buries his face between my legs, his tongue surging deep. His movement is so sudden that I have to brace my hands on his head to hold myself steady. He immediately goes in for my clit, and when he finds it, he makes a noise of pleasure.

Then he tongues it and begins to suck.

I whimper, my legs twitching with the force of the pleasure shooting through me. This isn't some Tinder date that brags about his prowess and lies about his height. I've forgotten in my stance against kissing that Kassam is a god. He's thousands of years old and has had plenty of time to practice how to please a lover. He knows exactly what he's doing, and he wastes no time. He sucks on that tiny bit of flesh like he's nursing from it, and all the while, I practically crawl up the wall, beside myself with how good it feels. I jerk my hips against his face, crying out as he adds a finger into the mix, teasing it at the entrance to my core but never pushing it quite in.

"Oh please," I breathe, wriggling as I try to rock my hips in a way that will get that big finger deep inside me. "Oh, Kassam, please. Fuck, yes. Oh god, your mouth is killing me."

The horrible man chuckles against my flesh, and the feel of it just makes me squirm even more. His tongue flicks against my clit, and he switches to rolling it against his tongue, back and forth, side to side, teasing like a goddamn monster as I keen obscenities into the air.

Then, he pushes a finger inside me, and I sob with how good it feels. A moment later, he adds a second, and I eagerly mount his hand, my pussy making these wet, filthy, squelching sounds as he works me with two fingers. When I finally come, it's with a sob of pure relief, everything clenching magically and sending me into bliss. Kassam continues to tongue me, though his pace slows a little. He languidly teases my clit with the occasional flick of his tongue, and I think he's about to let me go. Sighing, I relax against the counter, vaguely aware that I'm on tiptoe with my one foot that's on the ground. I'm not entirely sure how I managed to keep my balance in all that. Kudos, me. "You can let me up now," I say, detangling one hand from his hair. "You—"

Kassam crooks his fingers inside me and begins to rub. His mouth latches onto my clit again and I make a squawk that's part distress, part surprised arousal as he starts to work me again.

"You..." I begin, only to lose my train of thought as those fucking glorious fingers rub against my G-spot and my legs jerk in response. I let out a weak little cry, digging my hands into his thick, tangled hair once more and holding on for dear life as he works my pussy again. His fingers move faster, thrumming in and out of me with all the speed of a machine, even as his mouth works magic on my clit. I feel another orgasm tearing its way to the surface, and I let out an ugly little whine. "Need...you..."

Suddenly, Kassam's mouth is gone. I'm panting like I've run a marathon as he sets my leg down and surges to his feet. In the next moment, he has me bent over the counter, my tits pressed to the formica counter. There's nothing for my hands to grip and I flail uselessly as he pushes my thighs apart, his weight resting against the cleft of my backside. I hear the shift of fabric and in the next moment, he's pressing the hard, thick head of his cock into me. I'm so wet that he practically glides into my body, and I want to cry with the sheer relief of it.

Yes. God, yes.

He fucks me hard, grabbing my flailing hands and holding them behind my back with one hand, his other gripping my hip. I lose myself to the sensation as he rails me against the countertop, the wall thumping with the force of his thrusts. My pussy clenches around him over and over again, and I make these awful, squawking noises that I'll probably regret later, but it feels so good that I can't help myself, nor can I stop. I'm lost in the moment, and even though we've fucked a dozen times before now, today feels different. This feels different. The air is charged between us, and there's a strange tension that adds to the moment.

This time, when I come, my entire body seems to bow up, my legs leaving the ground as every muscle contracts. Kassam just fucks me harder, making these animalistic grunts as he uses my body for his own pleasure. I barely have time to catch my breath before he pulls out and rubs the head of his cock over my ass and thighs. Hot seed splashes over my skin in ropes, and I gasp for air, stunned, as he paints my backside with his release.

"Now," he breathes raggedly, rubbing some of the dribbles of cum into my ass as he touches me, "You're my wife."

18

By the time I have the courage to emerge from the back room, I've put everything in order again and done my best to straighten my hair and clothes. Luckily for me, my mother isn't around. She must have hightailed it out the moment she heard us "consummating" our marriage, so there's no walk of shame, at least.

She did leave a note on the counter, along with a stack of twenty-dollar bills.

Lock up when you leave, Carly. Get yourself a cab and call me later tonight to check in. I love you, pipsqueak. XOXO Mom

Thank god. She's the best. I feel better knowing she wasn't listening to me getting nailed for the last half hour. Full of affection, I tuck the note into my pocket, along with the money, and pick up the landline phone she has behind the counter. Then, I hesitate. "If I call a cab, where do we go?"

Kassam pulls his wild hair back into another thick, messy knot atop his head. I must have pulled it all free when he was going down on me, and the realization makes me blush hard. His movements are all satisfied and languid as he moves to my side. "What is a cab?"

Oh, right. "A car that will pick us up and take us somewhere." I shrug. "My question is...where? Where is safe for us?"

"So...I have been thinking this morning."

Great. I can only imagine. While I was whining that he needed to fuck me harder, he was contemplating our situation. I try not to let that hurt my feelings too much. Maybe gods can multitask while screwing. I certainly can't. "Go on."

Kassam moves to stand next to me, and he smells like sex, which makes my body perk up again. It takes everything I have not to lean in and just...rub myself all over him. "If whoever is stalking us is a god, do you truly think that hiding at a candy store—"

"—corner store," I interrupt. "It's a corner store."

He shrugs, and I can't stop tracking his movements with my hungry gaze. I wonder if I knocked a crystal off somewhere. "Regardless, do you think some harsh lighting and a change of scenery will stop a god who wants to confront us?" When I wince, he reaches out and runs his thumb along my jaw. "We have two choices, my little light."

I kinda hate that everything he's saying makes sense. "Go on, I'm listening."

"We can continue to try and run, knowing that the gods will approach us when they please..." His thumb strokes my skin thoughtfully.

"Or?"

"Or we confront them head on. We go back to your dwelling, we greet whoever is waiting, and we see what they want."

I groan, because I know he's right. "And what if they want to kill us and like, obliterate us from existence?"

Kassam's thumb skates across my lower lip, sending heat through my body. "You think they would wait for us to approach, then? Why would they not do it now? I do not think they seek that. I do not know what they seek, but I do not think it is our doom."

"Maybe it's another goddess that wants to marry you," I point out, letting my tongue brush against his fingertip. "And she's going to be pissed to find out I beat her to it."

He laughs at that. "High Father forbid. The last thing I need is females fighting over my carcass. One unnecessary wife is enough."

I bite his thumb.

Kassam doesn't pull away, though. His eyes only grow that smoky, dark silver with arousal, and the look he gives me is even more heated than before. If this continues, we're going to return to that back room and go for round two, and while my thighs quiver with joy at the thought, I know we can't stay here. If something dangerous *is* following us, I don't want to lead it to my mother.

"You think this is wise, then? To confront whoever—or whatever—this is?"

"Wise?" He chuckles, dropping his hand. "Oh no. We are long past wise options, my little light. We are just going for the ones we have left."

Fair enough. "Let's get it over with, then. But if I die, I'm coming back through time and space to haunt your ass."

Kassam tosses his head back and laughs, delighted at my crankiness.

∼

OUR CAB DRIVER is so besotted with Kassam that I could pay him nothing and he wouldn't care. Even so, I'm starting to feel like a freeloader, so I make sure he's paid well and apologize a dozen times for the fact that we have no shoes. When we get to my building, I inwardly cringe at the sight of all the overgrown vines crawling up the side of the building directly up to my window. I guess we're not exactly hiding Kassam's location. That's practically a flashing sign right there.

We pause outside the building and I look over at Kassam. He nods at me. "Still there, whoever it is."

A knot of worry forms in my belly. "You can feel it?"

"Oh, yes." He closes his eyes. "Pulsing like a dark heart. You cannot?"

I have to admit, I'm still a little dazzled by Kassam and his nearness. The sex we had a short time ago feels as if it cracked me open. There was something different to our coming together, something a little more raw and needy, a little more intense. I'm still reeling from it, and as he takes my hand in his, I ache with need. "All I feel is you," I say, voice breathless. "You're a little distracting."

"Am I?" He glances down at me, pleased. "Is it because you're madly in love with me now, and you want me to kiss you?"

"Nope. Takes a bit more than one round of sex to make a girl fall in love."

"How many rounds, exactly?"

I just roll my eyes. "Can we focus on the problem at hand?" I gesture up to my window. "Do you think we need weapons of some kind? Wards? Like...vampires hate crosses. Do you think our friend up there has a vulnerability to something?" When he's silent, I glance up at him, and he's giving me an incredulous look, one that says I've grown another head. I can take a hint. "All right, that's a no go, fine."

"Whoever is there is likely thousands of years old and will not be affected by a paltry symbol or two." He shakes his head. "We will try to reason with him—or her—and see what it is they desire. I am near powerless in this world, so a battle is not an option we have."

Considering that he's invulnerable and I'm the one that has to die for him to be "defeated," I agree with that assessment. "And if they want to fight?"

"Then we are doomed anyhow." He smiles down at me.

"You sure are smiley for a guy discussing doom," I grumble.

"I am Hedonism. I take my pleasure where I can. Right now, my pleasure is in how cranky my every word makes you." He grins, pausing and cupping my face. "Want to kiss me now? Before we race into danger and battle the gods?"

I push his hands away. "First of all, you said we weren't fighting anyone. And second...no? What makes you think I want to kiss right now? I want to run for the hills."

He shakes his head and loops an arm around my shoulders, pulling me in close despite my squirming. "Listen to me, Carly. I do not know the rules of this world, but I do know how gods think. We want to make sure that whoever is up there keeps their focus on me and not you. Understand?"

I stop struggling. This time, when he puts his arm around my shoulders, I stay still. "Why would they care about me?"

"I ask myself the same thing," Kassam agrees, and then I just want to punch him in his laughing face. "But then I remember that Lachesis sought you out. Not me, you. So there is something going on, perhaps, that I am unaware of. Either way, it worries me. I have vowed to keep you safe and I will do so." He pulls me in closer, until my face is practically pressed against his chest. "When we arrive, I want you to keep your focus entirely on me. Act utterly besotted. Act as if nothing matters to you but my pleasure. We want them to think of you as weak and useless and thus harmless. Do not let them realize just how clever you are."

Was...was that a compliment? I want to check Kassam's face to see if he meant it, but he squishes my cheek against his T-shirt-covered pectoral, and grabs my butt, squeezing. Right, because he's Hedonism and I'm supposed to be lost to his spell, not fighting it with crystals and every ounce of willpower I have. "Okay."

"Remember," he whispers. "You are completely in my control and you live for my amusement. You are my plaything, my way of passing the time until I return to my world."

"Okay."

"You mean nothing to me at all, but I have you so well trained I should like to keep you," he continues on.

I pinch his abdomen, slightly annoyed at that. He just squeezes my butt again, his fingers dancing over the cleft of my ass and making me quiver. "It's not going to be hard to pretend that I don't mean anything to you," I grumble. "That you're just using me out of convenience."

He tweaks my ear, sending a shiver up my spine. "Whatever you do, never mention that we are married. Understand?" When I nod absently, he grabs me by the chin and forces me to look him in the eye. "I mean it, little light. The gods do not marry mortals. Do not give them any reason to be intrigued by you."

"Got it," I say, pulling away.

"Good. Now, take off your jewelry." He holds a hand out. "If you know this trick about such things, they will, as well."

Wait, what? I pull back from his arms, suspicious. "If I take those off—"

"Exactly." Kassam wiggles his fingers at me. "Give them over. We will hide them somewhere out here so this interloper does not suspect anything."

I frown up at him. If I take them off, I'm going to be hit with the full force of his hedonism. Does he want me to just crawl all over him, panting, when we might be meeting our doom? "What if I say no?"

His eyes gleam. "Then I will pin you down right here and

pull them off of you." At my angry huff, he adds, "Along with all of your clothing."

That makes me go still. "You wouldn't dare," I warn.

"To keep you safe? I absolutely would." He gives me a thoroughly lascivious look. "And then I think I would spank you, just for good measure. I should like to smack that delicious bottom of yours until it's bright red and you're whining for my mercy."

"Oh my god, you are the worst," I sputter. "The absolute worst."

Kassam just looks smugly pleased even as he tugs me against him again. "Do not retreat from me," he cajoles, his voice soft as he wraps his arms around me and hauls me against his chest. He ducks down, kissing my temple, and murmurs, "We might be watched, even now."

"Then it won't matter if I take my jewelry off, will it?" I grump, but my skin is prickling, not just with his awareness, but of that of some *other* nearby. The air feels like it does just before a storm, charged and waiting, and it's making me break out into goosebumps.

"We must be sly," Kassam murmurs against my ear, and then licks the shell of it.

Irritation explodes through me even as hot lust does. He's enjoying this, the bastard. He's going to have me crawling all over him like an oversexed hussy, and he's going to enjoy every damn moment of it. And me, I don't have much of a choice, and that's annoying as hell. It's either be a sex fiend, or risk calling attention to us...and specifically to me. "Let's go inside the building first. I'll take them off in the mail room and shove them into my mailbox." I shoot him a look. "And if I kiss you without my crystals on, it's because I'm out of my mind. It doesn't count."

He clutches a fist over his chest, grinning at me. "I am

wounded that you think I would take advantage of you like that, my little light."

"Be wounded all you like," I say, even as we head for the doors to my building. "But I'm learning none of you gods are worth trusting."

"Good," he says. "Keep that at the front of your mind, because it will keep you safe."

19

To my relief, there's no one in the mail room. I don't have the key to my mail slot, so I glance around and decide to hide my crystal jewelry in the big, dusty plastic fern in the corner. Goodbye, earrings. Goodbye, chunky necklace covered in crystal. Goodbye, three rings with quartz studding them. I slip my bracelets off, too.

I catch a whiff of his scent—and my pussy practically spasms in reaction. I let out a choked sound of need as a wave of arousal washes over me. Oh good god almighty. The change is immediate. I look over at Kassam, at that fine-ass man who looms over me, and decide I need to ride that, right fucking now.

He quirks an eyebrow at me as I get to my feet. "Do you remember what we talked about?"

I link my arms around his waist and go immediately for his nipple, nuzzling at it through his shirt. "Besotted," I tell him, purring the word out. "I'm supposed to be besotted." I bite the hard tip and lick it through the fabric, glancing up at him. "Lost in you."

"That's right," he murmurs, his hand going to the top of my head.

It takes everything I have not to drop to my knees right then and there. I haven't sucked his dick, have I? The realization is shocking to me, and my mouth waters with hunger. Well, clearly I need to fix that. I hook a finger in the waistband of his sweatpants and give him an enticing look. "Give me five minutes and then I'll be ready to go up."

And I palm him through his sweatpants.

He growls with pleasure, his hand covering mine as he gives me a heated look. "Didn't realize how potent those crystals are. I've a mind to toss them into the nearest river if it'll make you like this all the time."

"You like me sassy, too," I say, rubbing him. "Because you like it when I finally cave."

"I do indeed." He grasps my hand in his, pulling me away from his cock, and presses a kiss to the center of my palm. "Let us go up and meet our friend. Do you remember what I told you?"

"Don't mention a certain thing," I parrot, fascinated at the sight of his lips brushing against my skin. "Be lost in you. Pretend to be stupid and very, very mortal."

"Close enough," he says, chuckling. "Shall I carry you up or would you prefer to walk?"

Oh man, just the thought of him carrying me up to my apartment gets me incredibly wet. "Bridal carry?" I ask hopefully, and then a better idea hits me. I make an excited sound. "No, wait! Toss me over your shoulder like you're a sexy caveman and you've stolen a woman to take as your mate. And when you get back home, you can ravish me until I'm so smitten that I agree to be your cavewoman."

Kassam grins at me and then ducks down. In the next moment, my belly hits his shoulder and then I'm in the air, upside down, and he carries me toward the elevator as easily as he would a sack of groceries.

God, that is sexy. I moan, squirming on his shoulder as the elevator goes up to my floor, and by the time he gets back off again, I'm practically panting with need. Just being carried by this man is making my toes curl and my pulse throb between my thighs. I've completely forgotten what our goal is until Kassam stands just outside of my apartment, and the pulse of power is so evident that even I can feel it.

"Your door is open," Kassam says to me. "Are you ready?"

"Play your cards right and my legs will be open too."

He barks a laugh, patting my ass before he ducks inside. "That's more like it."

The moment he steps inside my apartment, my skin crawls with awareness. There's something here all right, and while Kassam's intense vibe feels like sex and sunshine and a strong wind on the leaves of a tree, this feels…darker. Cooler. Far, far more intense. He stops just inside my living room, glancing around my apartment. I don't hear any cats, but the leaves of the plants covering every surface flutter and rustle, and I belatedly notice that the door to my refrigerator has been left hanging open. Vines have crawled all over it now, too.

I'll have to chide Kassam for that later. Better yet, punish. I picture smacking his ass with a paddle, and instead of making me laugh, I whimper with another surge of arousal. "Can you feel that, my little light?" Kassam asks, his voice casual, even as his hand strokes between my thighs, pressing against the seam of my jeans.

"Oh fuck yes," I breathe. "Feels so good."

He spanks me in the next moment, and I yelp—and then moan again, because I liked that far too much. "You're not paying attention, are you?"

"To what?" I pant.

Kassam chuckles, setting me down on the ground. Dizzy, I

cling to his arms as the blood rushes to my head, and he pulls me against him, stroking my back and then squeezing my ass again. "Go change into something pretty," he murmurs. "And skip the panties."

I glance around, but my apartment seems to be empty of both gods and cats. That's a relief. Maybe the feeling here is a leftover from whoever was here before. Doesn't matter—they're gone now. With a little shiver of excitement, I race toward my bedroom, eager to please him. Later on, I dimly realize, I'm going to be so mad at myself, but that's for future me to be pissed about. Right now, just the thought of putting on a cute dress and seeing Kassam smile at the sight of me makes me tremble with anticipation. I throw open my closet, gazing at the stuff there. Lots of jeans and T-shirts. Something pretty, I consider. Something pretty. When has Kassam ever cared what I wore? I don't think he's paid a lick of attention at all. I pull a breezy, pale yellow sundress out of the back of my closet and start to change.

"Show yourself," Kassam says in the living room.

I pause, because it doesn't sound like he's talking to me.

There's a sly, mocking laugh, and then that deep, intense sensation rolls through the air. The atmosphere gets so heavy it feels like a blanket. "I thought you two would never return," comments an unfamiliar voice. "It isn't polite to make company wait."

Terror shoots through me, and I shove my dress over my head, my hands tangling briefly in the spaghetti straps. I look around my room and the attached bathroom for a weapon, but all I've got is a tiny pair of hair-cutting scissors I use on my bangs when they get too shaggy. I snatch them anyhow, padding back toward the living room because a desperate need to protect Kassam floods my senses.

The moment I step through the bedroom door and into the living room, a headache blooms. I sway, distracted by the heavy feel of two gods in my apartment. It feels crushing, as if I'm a bug that shouldn't dare to be anywhere near here. My eyes can't seem to focus, and I stumble forward one step, and then the other. "Kassam..."

"Right here, little light," a familiar voice murmurs, and then warm hands are caressing my bare shoulders. "Is this what you picked to wear for me? I am pleased."

I tremble with pleasure at that, my senses filling with the sight of him again. I drink down his gorgeous face, the thick, tumbling brown hair that frames those tanned angles so perfectly, the silver eyes that glint with amusement as I devour the sight of him. He pulls me discreetly behind him and turns to face the far side of my room. "What do you want?"

The far corner of my living room pulses with formless shadow. The air ripples like a pond, but I can't see anyone. I can feel someone, but when my eyes try to focus, I see no face, no form, no nothing.

Just...power.

I clutch at the back of Kassam's shirt, my fright temporarily overriding my lust for him.

He must sense my unease, because Kassam lifts his chin, facing that strange entity. "Pick a mortal form. You're scaring my anchor and I don't want her distracted with fear when I'd rather have her squirming in my lap."

"Apologies. Flesh is so inconvenient, but if I must." The air shimmers, and that mocking voice suddenly has a face. It's a man, with a long, lean-boned face. He's got brown skin and somewhat short, dark hair with a floppy lock hanging over his brow to give himself a rakish air. His brows are thick, his nose aquiline, his race and age indeterminate. His mouth is full and almost feminine, but the cruelty in his eyes erases that softness. His clothes are as ageless as he is—he wears a long-sleeved white shirt and simple, dark pants, much like a pirate would.

The stranger scans a quick glance over my form and then just as quickly dismisses me. "Better now?"

He lounges back in my computer chair, hands behind his head as if he owns the place.

I decide I'm glad that I'm bound to Kassam and not this guy. Kassam laughs and jokes, and his idea of torturing me is shotgunning orgasms in my mom's store. This guy looks as if he'd rather torture me the good old-fashioned way—with knives and a lot of pain.

But Kassam seems satisfied. He grunts and then leads me over to my sofa. The big god drops down and then immediately pulls me into his lap, settling my ass directly over his very hard cock. I suck in a breath as the hedonism waves pull me under once more. With a moan, I rock against his cock. A small part of me is ashamed to do this in front of the stranger, but I don't think I could stop if I tried. And when Kassam runs a hand down my back and thrusts against me, I know he's pleased.

Right. Because I'm supposed to "act" besotted. As if I can do anything but rub myself against Kassam and pray he gives me an orgasm soon.

"Who the fuck are you?" Kassam asks, his voice a strange mixture between amusement and anger. One big hand clasps over the back of my neck, and he pushes me down against his cock, grinding me against him. "And why are you disturbing me when I want my anchor's full attention?"

The stranger—who is directly in front of me, if across the room—rolls his eyes. He raises his hands in the air. "I come in peace...and apparently I'm not the only one coming." He smirks at me. "You've found yourself a lusty little thing."

"She's mine," Kassam growls. He pushes me forward, dragging my skirts out from under me and then spreading them around his legs. I'm not wearing panties—just as he asked—and this time when I grind down against his cock, the only thing separating us is the too-thin barrier of his sweatpants,

sweatpants that I'm soaking with my arousal. He pushes forward again, slowly thrusting against me, and I gasp at how good it feels, my eyes fluttering closed.

"I have no desire to take what's yours. Play as you like." The man's voice is bored. "As for who I am, I have had dozens of names over the millennia. Which one do you want?"

"Any. All." Kassam's hand steals between my legs, his fingers brushing over my folds before skimming to my thigh and pushing them apart until I'm straddling him, reverse-cowgirl style. It makes my pussy open wide, and I bite back a gasp when he rocks me down against his cock again, my hands flying to his knees to brace myself on him.

"Very well." The man thinks for a moment, and all I hear is my own ragged panting. "I am Mercury to the Romans...who are gone. I am Hermes to the Greek...also gone. I am Loki to the Norse. I am Ea to the Assyrians, and Seth to the Egyptians. You can call me any of those things and I will answer. Does that help?"

I gasp, recognizing some of those names...just as Kassam adjusts his pants and his cock pushes into me under my dress. No teasing, no prepping me, just seating me atop of him in the next moment and dragging me down over his shaft. A choked noise escapes me, and I'm horribly aware of the other god in the room...and the fact that I don't care. Kassam feels so big and full like this, and I need him so badly that it takes everything I have not to lift my hips and start riding him like a wild woman. "C-condom," I manage to wheeze out.

"Yes, yes," Kassam says in a bored tone. He spanks my ass, sending shivers through my body. "Be good and I won't come inside you, little one. Now hush."

"Asshole," I manage, the words dying in my throat when his big hands grip my waist and he drags me down on his cock, rocking against me. The man certainly knows how to shut me up.

"Now," Kassam begins again. "Seth, is it? I am unfamiliar with your names."

"That one works as well as any other," the other god says.

Do I point out that he's a trickster? That Loki is a name that sticks out in my poor knowledge of mythology as someone not to be trusted? I open my mouth to speak, and Kassam swivels his hips, all thought leaving my head. "Ah!"

"My little one is a bit noisy," Kassam murmurs, affection in his tone, and it makes me clench tight around his cock. "You'll have to ignore her."

"Easily done. Mortals don't interest me."

I flick my eyes open to look over at the god—Seth—and he's not looking in my direction. His focus is on Kassam, his gaze narrow and assessing, as if trying to figure him out.

"And yet you are not affected by my curse despite sitting across the room from me?" Kassam asks. "Is it because I am not from your world?"

Seth smiles, showing sharp, white teeth that make me whimper in fear. Kassam's touch soothes me, and he fucks me again, driving into me by raising his hips, and I welcome it for the distraction it is. "I came prepared," Seth says. "I knew something was twisted up in your making, but I didn't realize it was a curse. Is that why you're here, in my territory? When Lachesis told me we had a visitor, I almost didn't believe her. I'm glad I came to see for myself...and to warn you that you don't belong."

Kassam continues to pump into me, slow and steady and deep, sending shivers wracking through my body. It makes it difficult to concentrate on the nuances of the conversation—I can't see Kassam's face and Seth's disappears every time I close my eyes (which is far too often). But I listen and try to remember for later. Lachesis. Territory. Seth.

"Prepared?" Kassam asks. It's silent, but then Kassam chuckles and I feel it vibrate through where our bodies are joined, and so I open my eyes to see. Seth has pulled open the collar of his long, blousy pirate shirt, and revealed what look like runes tattooed—or burned—into his skin. Wild symbols pattern all over every inch of his chest, and as I stare, they seem to glow against his skin. Kassam flexes under me, his hand stroking my back, but I get the impression his focus is anywhere but me. "Very nice. I admire your cleverness, brother."

"Are we brothers, then?" Seth's terrifying smile grows broader. "Friends? You do not come to take your place at our table?"

"Hardly. I merely seek my way home. Until then, I amuse myself with this little tidbit." He reaches around my front and cups my breast, finding my nipple unerringly and pinching it hard enough to make me yelp. I hate that it feels so good that it sends another pulse of heat straight through my body, too. It's like I'm an instrument he knows just how to play....and it's probably the truth. Kassam has had thousands of years to figure out how to fuck like a demon. Unfair.

Seth ignores me, his gaze locked on Kassam despite the fact that I'm grinding over him, our joined bodies hidden only by the flimsy skirt of my sundress. He tilts his head and says, "Tell me about your world. Maybe I can help. Is it like here?"

Kassam chuckles, tweaking my nipple again as I bear down on his cock. "Nothing like here, other than humans have spread everywhere. We do not have such strange buildings or talking boxes."

"Talking...boxes?"

"Phones," I manage to whimper out. "He...means...phones."

"Hush, little light," Kassam tells me again, and this time his hand slides between my thighs and spanks me through my dress. I make a horribly loud sound that is part arousal, part surprise, and he only laughs harder. "Let the important ones speak."

I make another outraged sound, only to get my pussy

spanked again. This time, it sends a quiver of an oncoming orgasm through me, and I clutch at his hand, holding it between my skirts as I come, shuddering hard around him. The blood roars in my ears, and I'm vaguely aware of the two gods talking in low voices, completely oblivious to me riding Kassam, my pussy making wet sounds as I rock over him. When I come back to myself, gasping, Kassam continues to move his hips in languid thrusts, and I realize he's not coming. He's not anywhere close to coming, and I'm stranded, impaled atop his cock as my body clenches around him, desperate to get away—or to release again.

I lose track of the conversation at that point. Dimly, I'm aware of Kassam speaking of his entrapment in the glacier, and how he arrived here and found me. He and Seth talk of worlds, and even though I worry Kassam is sharing too much, he continues on, speaking of his world, called Aos, of farms and mountains and humans that live in tiny huts and caves and eke out an existence. His world sounds pretty dark ages to me.

"Any great civilizations?" Seth asks.

"Not for a long, long time. The Suuol Empire fell before I was entrapped, so I can only imagine what has risen to take its place." Kassam shrugs, and I feel it all through my body, my toes curling. "Before humans rose, the dominant race was dragon-kind. I can only imagine what humans have done in the time I have been lost. For all I know, my world looks like this one."

"Mmm." Seth has gone quiet, which worries me a little. "Yet you were sent here to protect you from another goddess? And the god of death awoke you?"

"Indeed. He and his anchor." Kassam strokes my back, and it takes everything I have not to preen against it. I should be humiliated at what I'm doing. Horrified. But I feel too good to protest even a lick. It's like I'm drugged with his curse, and when another endless orgasm ripples through me, I whimper with the pleasure of it, my legs twitching. Kassam pulls me against his chest, dragging me backward. I'm still on his cock, panting and exhausted, but when he slips a hand under my skirt and begins to toy with my clit, his other hand on my throat, my body lights up again. "You think he sent me on purpose?"

"No, not at all." Seth strokes his chin. I'm no more important to him than a gnat, which is good, because I'm pretty sure the choking, whining, needy noises I'm making are utterly humiliating. "It makes me think the gods still have power in your world, for them to be punished again. If they were useless, the High Father would not care if they misbehaved, because they could do nothing. They would be toothless even when they were at their worst." He shakes his head again. "The gods in your world still have power, and that is exciting."

"Mmm." Kassam nips at my ear, even as he works my clit between two fingers, rubbing on both sides of the hood. He whispers in my ear. "Look at how wet you are for me, little light. How your cunt drips for me. Even on display, you love to please me, don't you?"

I mewl a response like the shameless creature I am.

"That's my girl," he says, and gives my pussy another pat before going back to rubbing my clit. His attention turns back to Seth. "Why do you care so much about my world?"

Seth leans back in his chair and grins, all sharp fangs. "Because, my friend, I aim to join it."

20

Instead of laughing in Seth's face, Kassam appears to consider this. His hand pauses beneath my skirts temporarily, but then he goes back to caressing me, working my clit as another orgasm blasts through me, my pulse pounding in my ears. "How would you propose such a thing?" Kassam asks. "Joining my world and leaving yours?"

Seth spreads his arms wide. "The gods here are nothing but memories. Our powers are neutered, our followers in the dozens instead of the thousands or millions we once had. We are forgotten and useless in modern society. But if I cross over to your world..." He leans in, his expression calculating. "I can start fresh. Gain power for myself once more."

I whimper, opening my mouth to protest. "But—"

Spank.

I yelp as Kassam smacks my pussy again, and another orgasm rips through me. Oh god. I'm going to die from coming. Just stroking out as he strokes *me*. That's how I'm going to go. My tombstone will read *she came so hard her insides exploded*. They'll have to bury me in the fetal position, because my muscles will be permanently clamped up.

Kassam chuckles, as if the thought of Seth grabbing power in his world is somehow fucking funny. "And how would you do so? We already have one trickster god. I do not think my world needs another."

"Ah, but you said there was a goddess that was responsible for your curse, yes?" Seth reclines backward once more, crossing his arms over his rune-covered chest.

"Riekki, the goddess of knowledge."

"Perfect. I'll take her place." Seth grins. "What is a trickster after if not knowledge and power? She has both. It shall be a perfect fit."

"She is also known as the Peacekeeper." Kassam says, amused. He doesn't sound upset over Seth plotting the downfall of the other goddess.

Seth shrugs. "Names change over time. Many, many things change. It will not be such a stretch to replace a useless, broken goddess with a newcomer. Your High Father will see I aim to play by his rules and he will be pleased."

"A trickster playing by the rules?" Kassam rubs my clit, nipping at my ear. "I'll believe it when I see it."

"I can behave with the right incentive." Seth arches a brow, gesturing at me. "Just like your little pet there."

"Speaking of my pet..." Kassam purrs, his tongue gliding along the shell of my ear. "You will need an anchor of your own. We cannot remain in the mortal realm without a mortal to tie us there."

Seth doesn't look worried. "Easily done."

But Kassam hesitates, and I can feel it in his body, even as he rocks his hips, bouncing me on his cock as he works my pussy. Another orgasm fires through me and I whine, both exhausted and overstimulated. I feel like I'm about to fly apart, and yet it keeps on going, the most delicious torture of all time. "How do I know this isn't a trick? Tell me why I need your help when I can find my way home on my own."

"I imagine you can," Seth agrees. He sits up, his lean face full of urgency. "Help me, my brother. I am tired of being nothing but a memory. A god is nothing without purpose."

Damn, he's good. Even I'm won over by that impassioned plea.

Kassam thinks for a long moment as he fucks me, the only sounds in the room that of our bodies make when they come together and my wordless little cries. Just when I'm about to come again, he slows his thrusts, becoming more languid, and begins to speak once more. "I have a condition."

"Name it," Seth says immediately.

"If we work with you, I promised my little light that she would not be harmed." He presses a kiss against the side of my face, caressing my neck with one big hand. "I need you to make the same promise."

The other god shrugs. "Why do you care if a single human lives or dies? They are nothing to us."

I tense, but Kassam takes that moment to thrust deep again, distracting me. He pushes me forward once more, until I'm forced to brace my hands on his knees again. "Ride me, wench."

"I hate you," I grit out, even as I do as he says. How can I not? I'm so close to coming again that I want to scream with the unbearable tension in my body.

He laughs, gripping my hips as he works me over his cock. "Look at how delightful she is," he says to Seth. "I have her perfectly trained. Why would I wish to find another?"

"If you say so," Seth says, and he sounds bored. "So, do you agree to work with me?"

"Do you agree to keep her safe?" Kassam has a smile in his voice, even though I can't see his face. "I know how a trickster works, my friend. I may be new to this world, but I am not new to the machinations of our kind."

Seth laughs again, harder this time. "Very well. I promise to keep your little plaything from harm in exchange for you helping me cross over to your world. We will work together for something we both want."

"Excellent." His hips surge, making me gasp. "Give me a few minutes to finish her off and we'll discuss our plans. She's flagging a bit."

"Take your time," Seth drawls. "I'm not going anywhere."

Like I'm a doll, Kassam pulls me off his cock and slides my skirts down over my hips again. I hate the needy whine that escapes me when he puts me on my feet, and I wobble, barely able to stand. My body is throbbing, and even though I squint to focus, to try and concentrate, I can't think of anything but how badly I need yet another orgasm. I'm so damn close. But Kassam gets to his feet, slipping his cock back into his sweatpants, and then takes my hand. He leads me into the bedroom and I practically shiver with delight at the realization. I don't even look back at Seth, because my focus is entirely on Kassam. Kassam and his glorious body, Kassam and his impressive, wonderful cock. Kassam and—

He sits on the edge of the bed and pulls me in between his legs, nipping at my throat. "You did an excellent job, little light," he whispers. "You made him think you are mindless with lust."

"I am," I hiss at him, even as I bury my hands in his hair and drag him forward, pressing his face to my breasts. "I am so fucking turned on right now that I can't think straight. I'm going to be really mad at you later, but right now—"

"I know. Right now, you would like for me to give you what you want." He brushes his mouth over my nipple. "Do you want it hard and fast, or slow and easy?"

Oh fuck, like I even have a choice at this point. "Hard. Fast." I grab two handfuls of his hair. "Condom."

He looks up at me, all laughing silver eyes. "Do you not feel that hare is out of the trap? But very well." He grabs one from the nightstand and tears the packet open with his teeth, as if he has done this all his life. "I will do as you please. Get on the bed."

I need no further urging. Eager, I crawl forward on hands and knees, hiking the skirts of my long sundress up so I don't trip on them. "Do you need help figuring out how to put on a condom?"

Kassam laughs. "Oh, my little light. As I have said before, I am not new to anything mortals can think up."

"Says the man who wanted to eat a bottle of ketchup," I grumble, but I obediently spread my thighs apart, my pussy clenching with need. God, I am so freaking aroused. How is it that I've come so many times in the last hour and yet I want to come again so badly that my mind feels wrecked with the need of it?

Kassam's weight presses against the side of the bed and I tremble with anticipation. He flips my skirt up and then presses his cock against the entrance to my core. Pushes in just a little, and stars float behind my eyes.

And then waits.

I growl in frustration, arching my spine and pushing back against him.

He laughs at my hungry actions, and then his hands go to my hips and he thrusts deep. I howl with pleasure at being filled again, my hands fisting on the blankets. This time, there's no languid motions, no teasing thrusts. He anchors his hands on my sides and drives into me with single-minded focus, and within minutes, I'm coming so hard that I'm crying, biting down on my blanket as he hammers into me. God, it's so good, even the tenth orgasm in, it's incredible. He smacks my ass with one big hand, making me yelp, and then he's coming too, his thrusts growing ragged and deeper, his movements slowing.

When he's finally done with me, Kassam gives my hip a little pat and pulls my skirts over my collapsed body again. "My good, sweet little anchor. Stay here and rest while I speak with

Seth." He squeezes my butt cheek affectionately and then heads for the bathroom. I hear the snap of the condom as he removes it, the sound of him washing off, and then he flicks the light off. "Rest for a bit. I'll need you again shortly."

I moan against the mattress, collapsed into bed. I should get up and listen at the door, I decide as he shuts it behind him and returns to the living room. Listen at the door and figure out their plans so I know what's going on.

Instead, I collapse in an exhausted, spent heap and doze.

21

Something tickles my nose as I sleep. Annoyed, I rub my nostrils and turn over, only for the tickling to continue. Frowning, I open my eyes...

Only to see a very smug-looking Kassam perched on the edge of my bed, teasing my nose with nothing other than my vibrator.

I jerk upright with a screech. "What the fuck!?"

He grins at me, waving it in the air. "Is this your dildo? Is that what you mentioned when you said you didn't need me?" His silver eyes gleam with excitement as he examines it. "Why does it have all these buttons down here?"

I snatch it from him, horrified. I'm glad he hasn't figured out how to turn it on. I guess they don't have vibes in his world. "How did you find this?" I tuck it under my leg to hide it from his grasp and rub my nose again. "And why were you rubbing it against my nose?"

Kassam shrugs. "I was bored and wanted you to wake up. I should have used it on you instead, yes?" He gives me a sultry look. "Give it back and I promise I'll make you feel good."

I grab my pillow and smack him in the face with it instead.

Now that I'm awake, I feel a little more like myself and I'm remembering what happened in my living room. A god named Loki-slash-Seth showed up and Kassam *fucked me* in front of him. And I let it happen, because I was out of my mind with lust thanks to the lack of crystals. "I hate you. I hate you so much right now."

"Is that a no?" He puts a big hand on my leg. "Can I lick your pussy instead?"

It takes everything I have not to kick him in his face. I bat at him with my pillow again instead. "I don't want any more sex," I snap. "Don't you think we've had enough for one damn day?"

"No."

I huff, my nostrils flaring with irritation, and clutch the pillow against me as Kassam flashes me another easy grin, gets up from the bed, and moves to the window. I touch my clothes, checking myself over. I'm wearing my sundress still, but that's it. The skirt is stuck to the back of my thighs, and I flush with the shame of it. Even though I reek of sex and probably pulled a muscle somewhere, I feel like...myself. A little less sex-crazed, which is an absolute relief. I glance up at Kassam, who's wearing the same T-shirt and sweatpants he always is. "My crystals?"

"Next to the bed. I retrieved them while you slept." He turns and glances down at me. "You're welcome."

I resist the urge to make a rude gesture and glance over. Sure enough, there's my pile of quartz jewelry. Thank goodness. I immediately start putting them on, looking over at Kassam as he watches the window. "What are you looking for?"

"Just looking at the moon," he says. "It is nothing but a tiny slice in the sky. Did you know it's white here? And so small, too."

Interesting. "What color is the moon in your world?"

He gestures with his arms, indicating size. "Very big, very red. Quite magnificent. But I suppose everything is bigger and prouder in my world." The look he gives me is lascivious, and I know he's thinking of his cock.

I roll my eyes. "Not everything is about sex, Kassam."

"It is when you're Hedonism. I could be having an orgy right now." He lets out a wistful sigh. "I truly would like a good orgy, actually. They really do take the edge off."

"Feel free to have one," I say sweetly, slipping the last bit of jewelry onto my wrist. "And feel free to release me from our agreement."

"You know I cannot do that, my little light." He moves to the bed and sits down across from me. "So here I will stay, orgy-less and sad."

I ignore that, glancing at the clock. It's late. I scrub a hand down my face, and my belly rumbles. I'm starving, and I'm sticky, and I'm curiously exhausted. "How about I clean up and change, and then we'll find an all-night restaurant somewhere, okay? We'll get you pancakes. You like pancakes, don't you?"

That gets his attention. "What is a pancake?"

"Oh, you'll love it. Come on. I'm going to shower, and you're going to tell me all about the plans you made with Seth."

"While you shower?" His silver eyes gleam with anticipation. "Can I wash you?"

"Nope." I climb out of bed, making sure to keep the covers over my vibrator before he figures out how it works and decides he wants to use it on me. My pussy clenches at the thought, but she's been working hard lately so I guess I can't blame her for reacting. "You've done enough to me today. But you can talk to me."

I head into the bathroom, undressing as I walk. I'm past all shyness with Kassam at this point. Dude just fucked me in front of a stranger. I have no modesty left. I consider my jewelry, but leave it on. I don't care if it's weird to take a shower with a necklace and a bunch of bracelets on—if it keeps me in my right mind, I'm all for it. He groans and grabs at my ass as I climb into the tub, but I bat his hands away. If he's suffering for a minute...well, good. Payback's a bitch. "You are so beautiful," Kassam groans as I bend over to turn on the taps. "You should let me wash you."

"Here," I say. "Hold this." I hand him one of the new bottles of shampoo, the fruity-smelling ones. He immediately flicks the cap and sniffs it, closing his eyes. "Now, tell me about Seth and don't skip any details."

Kassam inhales deeply, then leans against the wall, watching me as I shower. "He says that he is from an old, old time and that no one worships him any longer. Is that truth?"

I wash my hair, considering. "Pretty much. Out of all the names he listed, I only recognized one and that's from medieval times. Most of the religions I'm familiar with focus on a single god, though I admit I only know of a couple religions. Most people in this part of the world are some branch of Christian, Jewish, or Muslim, I think. I'm sure there are other religions but those are the big ones I know of, and those all worship only one god. All of the religions he mentioned are old-old." I pause. "Lachesis is from an old-old religion, too."

Kassam is quiet. Too quiet.

I glance over at him, and when he remains silent, I hold my hand out for the shampoo. He squeezes a dollop into my hand —a huge dollop—and sighs. "I worry that if I return to my world, that will be my fate, as well. No one will worship me. I will be powerless and forgotten."

Feeling a twinge of sympathy, I shrug. "You'll just have to do something dramatic to remind them all that you've returned.

He chuckles, his mood turning sunny again. "An excellent idea. As for Seth, he says the moon will be new tomorrow night. That will be our time to step between worlds. He says that Lachesis owes him a favor from old, so he is going to approach her. When the moon is gone, he says the connection between our worlds is greater. That it will be easy for Lachesis to tug my thread back to the appropriate spot, and easy for her to slide his over to our web as well." He watches me as I shampoo my hair. "I do not know if I believe him entirely, but it is worth a try. He is most desperate to leave this realm."

"And you think it's a good idea to take him with us?"

"A good idea? I did not say that. But it is an option. If I must choose between a god who is beholden to me or a goddess who seeks to destroy me since I will not have her, I will take the trickster."

Okay, that's fair. If he can make an ally and get rid of an enemy, I can see how Kassam would be all for this. I still think it's because Seth is in a situation that Kassam fears he'll be in—lost and forgotten—and so it hits him hard.

He *understands* Seth.

22

I rinse my hair, pushing water out of my eyes. "Okay, so tomorrow night, full moon, what do you have to do to get ready? Anything?"

"Seth says Lachesis will pull the appropriate threads. We will not have to do anything." He takes another long sniff of the shampoo, his eyes closing with delight. "Just...a blink and all will be well again."

I frown. It seems there is a lot more involved than just "a blink" but what do I know? I'm just a dumbass mortal, good only for being a fucktoy. "And I'm tied to you, right? Where does that put me?"

Kassam shrugs. "At my side, I assume."

Uh. This is something we haven't really discussed in length, and I'm pretty sure I have feelings about it. "In your world?"

"If all goes well, yes."

Yup, I definitely have feelings about this. I stare at him through the shower of water. "To die?"

Kassam hands me shampoo again. "Not to die. I told you, I would protect you. Seth assures me that you will be safe. That to get back to my world, we are circumventing the usual rules. It should not have an effect on your mortality."

"But when you get back home, you're still Hedonism, right? Still stuck on the mortal plane? So you need me to die for you to go fully home." I pick up a bar of soap and my loofah, scrubbing the soap into the sponge. I have to do something with my hands, because this conversation is making me too nervous. "Where is your home, anyway?"

"It is the Great Endless Forest," Kassam says softly. "I miss it like I miss air...or the red moon. I feel as if I have been gone forever, and I wonder how it has fared in my absence."

Poor Kassam. I feel a hint of guilt at his words, but I'm still worried. "So that part of the plan hasn't changed. We get you home, and if I'm with you, I still die." At his silence, I scowl in his direction. "At least be honest with me, unless you plan on taking up the mantle of trickster god, as well."

"That part has not changed," Kassam admits. "I am still working on it."

"Cool, well, I have a simple solution," I say. "You go home, have a great time, and I'll stay here. You get yourself an anchor on your side."

"I want no one but you."

"Well, that's gonna be rough for you because I don't want to leave this world. My mother is here. My apartment is here. My job is here."

His eyes gleam slyly. "I took care of your job."

I flick water at him, enjoying it too much when he flinches back. "I sure don't want to transfer over to a strange world just to die."

Kassam pulls back my shower curtain and steps into the tub with me, ignoring my sounds of protest. His clothing immediately gets soaked, plastering to his skin. He takes the loofah from me, a displeased expression on his face as he gently moves it over my shoulders, soaping them up. "You are now my wife, Carly. I will not let you die. I vowed to keep you safe, and I mean to keep that promise." His gaze flicks to my eyes. "But it only works if we are together, so I can protect you."

But me being in danger is because I'm with him. "I've only known you for a few days, Kassam. How can I trust you when you say you're going to keep me safe when literally everything I've heard is that I need to die to help you?"

"I kept you safe in front of Seth, did I not?" He turns me with a touch of his hand and then begins to wash my back. "He thinks you are little more than a lust-addled cock-sleeve I am playing with. And because he thinks you are unimportant, he will not use you against me."

Ouch. "So that's why you sexed me in front of him?"

"That, and because I enjoyed it." I turn my head and glare at him, but he just chuckles. "You enjoyed it, too. You like being naughty with me."

Naughty? He thinks that was naughty? To me, it was full-on porno, but this is also a guy that's thousands of years old and misses a good old-fashioned orgy. I guess his version of filthy is slightly different than mine. Even so, it makes me want to one-up him. I know he does things to shock me and to make me gasp (as well as orgasm) and it makes me want to turn the tables on him. He thinks he's the only one that doesn't have to play fair? I can play along, too...

Except he's leaving and I don't plan on following.

Oh. Right.

I mull through my feelings on that as he scrubs my back with careful hands. I haven't thought about what comes next. I've been focusing so hard on Hurricane Kassam blasting through my life that I haven't stopped to consider how I feel about him leaving. Will I miss him? Probably a little. I'll miss the intense orgasms and his sunny personality. I'll miss the way his face lights up when he tastes something. But I won't miss the out-of-control feeling that's taken over my life, and I won't miss the fact that he makes me feel insignificant and very, very mortal.

It's going to be really weird to go back to my normal life. The moment he leaves, I'm probably going to be kicked out of my building. I've lost my job. I'm pretty sure I'm ruined for sex with other men at this point. Even so...I don't regret it? I like Kassam and want the best for him after all.

"Say you'll come with me, Carly," Kassam presses.

"No. I'm staying here in my world. I don't want to go to yours."

Kassam continues to wash my back. "Have I not done everything in our agreement? I have cleaved only to you. I have not shared my affections with anyone else. You would force me to return to my world without an anchor and start over? To pull another man or woman into this?"

I frown at the shower, parsing that. "Are you trying to make me jealous?"

"Yes. Is it working?"

I clench my jaw, because it kinda is, and that pisses me off. "You're asking me to go and risk my life because you don't want to fuck a stranger?"

"No." He takes me by the elbow and turns me in the shower, gazing down at me. His clothes are soaked from the shoulders down, and I'd laugh if this wasn't such a serious moment. "I am asking for your help because you are my friend and we make good partners." He runs the sponge down my front. "Did we not make the same vows to one another? To cherish and protect?"

He's got a point there. If the vows work, they don't work just one way. "I hear what you're saying, Kassam. It's just..." I spread my hands. "Let's say the best-case scenario happens and you're able to protect me and I live. Which is fantastic, right? Except... now I'm trapped in your world? How is that fair to me? You get to go home, and I...what? Settle down and have babies with a caveman?"

The look he gives me is downright strange. He goes still, then shakes his head. "You are my wife. Why would I let you go?"

My mouth hangs open. Of all the arguments I thought he'd give me, that one hits me by surprise. "You...that wasn't real."

"Why not?" Kassam brushes the sponge over my breast, teasing the nipple, almost as if he can't help himself. "What if I have decided it was real? The High Father cannot kill my wife without justification. As my mate, you are safe from the machinations of others." His mouth crooks up in a half-smile. "And like you, I do not share."

I...have no words. He wants to make this sham marriage between us legit? I need to argue this...but how? "But...you're immortal."

"And you are my anchor," he agrees, moving to soap up my other breast.

"Who is supposed to be mortal."

He frowns at that, as if the thought bothers him. "But when I return to the Great Endless Forest, you will join me there."

"Are mortals allowed?"

His frown grows deeper. "I...I would figure something out."

Yeah, that's a "no mortals allowed" if I ever heard one. "You see?" I say. "This isn't going to work—"

Kassam tips a soapy finger under my chin, forcing me to look up at him. "I would ask the Fates to intervene and make you immortal. You could prowl the forests for all time at my side."

"Or...you could ask the Fates to intervene and send me home? One seems as easy as the other."

"Would you prefer that?"

I'm not prepared for Kassam's crestfallen look. He's a god— why is he disappointed at the thought of me leaving his side? We're just scratching each other's itches, according to him. I don't understand why he'd be upset if I didn't choose him.

Anyone can scratch an itch, after all? "Let me think about all of this," I say softly. "You're asking me to leave my world behind—and my mother—on the promise that you won't let people kill me despite the fact that everyone says this needs to happen." When he continues to give me an entreating look as he soaps my breasts, I take the sponge from him and sigh. "You're asking for a lot of trust here. I'd be going in on faith alone."

"As a god, I happen to be an expert on faith." The look in his silvery eyes grows intense. "I mean it when I say I will let nothing harm you, Carly. I made a vow, and I intend to keep it."

"I'll think on it," I state again.

"Think quickly. We must leave tomorrow night. It is our best chance."

So says the trickster god. I'm still not sure I want to put all of my faith in that one, but I'm not sure we have another choice. "I said I'd think on it, Kassam. Don't push me."

"Push you?" He laughs, and his hand goes to the wet necklace at my throat. He fingers one of the quartz crystals and leans in. "I could steal your crystals and make you want me. It would take nothing at all for me to convince you to come with me, just with a few licks of my tongue. We both know this."

I slap his hand away, angry and more than a little hurt. "You'd do that to me? What happened to us being friends?"

His expression grows sad. "I would do it to convince you if I must. My domain, my people, have been abandoned for millennia. I do not know what happens to me if I never go back. How can anyone worship an absent god? I fear I will dissolve into nothing at all."

My mouth goes dry. "But Seth...he said people don't worship him anymore..."

"No, he said only a few dozen do. But what happens when I am down to one? And that one loses their faith because I am not there to respond?" Kassam shakes his head. "So yes, I would push you into going with me, if I must, my Carly. Because I need you at my side to help me right things. I need a friend and a companion. I need someone that will tell me when I am too deep into my hedonism." His mouth ghosts a smile. "And I need someone I can trust. I need my wife." He gives me an imploring look. "Please, Carly. Help me."

Damn it. I'm being asked to put my trust in a god who I met two days ago. A god who lives for fucking and eating sticks of butter.

What's even stupider is that I'm probably going to do it.

23

*A*fter a full night of sleep (and a few more rounds of quick, itch-scratching sex with Kassam), I wake up the next morning with a sense of impending doom and determination both. This might be the most idiotic decision ever, but I'm going to help Kassam. Strangely enough, it's not the promise of eternal orgasms or immortality or any of that shit that has decided me. It's not fear that he's going to take my crystals away and like, give me oral sex until I give in.

(I mean, if that's the torture he's talking about, I'm going to volunteer.)

It's that he looked so hurt and lost when I said we weren't married. Like he'd been hoping for someone to count on, and he felt betrayed it wasn't me.

And I haven't finished a lot of stuff in my life, but I can at least see this through. Kassam's right. If the marriage vows keep me safe because he promised to protect me, it needs to work both ways. I can't pick and choose which part of being married to him applies. So even though I'm terrified of what the future holds, I'm going to go through with it.

"We need to see my mother this morning," I tell Kassam after I brush my teeth.

He looks up from tasting a bit of toothpaste he squirted onto his finger. "Why's that?"

My lip trembles. "Because I need to tell her I'm going with you. And if she doesn't see me again, she'll know why."

Kassam's beautiful silver eyes brighten with excitement. He grabs me and pulls me into his arms, hugging me tightly. "I could kiss you right now."

"But you won't, because we agreed no kisses," I point out. It's the hill I've chosen to die on, and I'm not kissing him until this feels less like scratching an itch and more romantic.

The god isn't deterred. He squeezes me against his chest, all boisterous affection. "You still have time to fall in love with me yet."

"It doesn't work *quite* like that," I tell him.

"You're right." He leans over and whispers in my ear. "I probably need to lick your cunt far, far more often."

Hot desire shivers through me. "I mean, that's not a bad start."

Kassam gives me another hug, then strokes my hair. "We will also pull your mother into my world after everything is settled. I have decided this."

I suck in a breath, because it's something I haven't even considered. "Really?"

He nods. "I will owe the Fates a dozen favors, but as long as I am home and ruling my domain once more, let them ask for what they like." A look of determination crosses his normally laughing face. "All that matters is my return."

"And me living," I chirp, feeling the need to point that out.

"And you living," he agrees.

∼

My car keys are missing, and my car isn't in the parking lot. I'm pretty sure it's still back at the bar from the other day. When I ask Kassam how he got me home when I was unconscious, he shrugged and said he walked until someone offered to give him a ride. I find that incredibly odd but not surprising. It's just another bizarre aspect of how strange my life has become in the last week. We take another cab over to my mom's store, and I brace myself, trying to figure out what I'm going to tell her.

She's going to think I'm crazy for following him over, knowing that an anchor has to die for the god to return to his world. But like...if a god can't keep me safe, who will? For now, I'm going to put my faith in Kassam and try not to worry too much.

Ha.

Ha ha.

I twist my hands in my lap as the driver pulls up to my mother's psychic shop. He flicks his gaze at Kassam in the rearview mirror over and over again, but it doesn't bother me. It would have yesterday, before our shower discussion when Kassam told me that he considered our marriage to be a real one. That thought keeps turning in my head over and over again.

A real marriage.

With a god.

Who's cursed with hedonism.

And someone else tried to take out because he wouldn't marry them.

Yep, all of this leads to madness, but somehow I'm determined to race into it, face first. I force back my worries and pay the cab driver in the last of my cash, then get out of the car. Kassam follows behind me, and when he steps onto the sidewalk, he holds his hand out to me.

I take it, not thinking—and he zaps me with an instant orgasm.

A whimper escapes my lips and I turn to him, eyes wide. "What the fuck, dude?"

Kassam just grins at me. "You looked so very serious and sad. I wanted to give you something that felt good."

"I am about to tell my mother that I'm leaving this world," I whisper to him. "Maybe don't make me come while I'm trying not to cry?"

His expression immediately changes to one of consternation. "I forbid you to cry, Carly. I won't like that." He shakes his head, as if that decides it. "Your sadness makes me unhappy."

If only it were that easy to turn it off and on, like a switch. Kinda like he does with the orgasms. I give him a stern look, squeezing his fingers. "You can keep holding my hand, but if you give me another orgasm, I'm changing my mind about going with you."

Kassam's mouth twitches, and he does his best to look serious. "I will be on my best behavior."

Somehow I doubt that.

I head inside the shop, the neon PALM READING sign in the window bright and flashing. It's early in the day but my mom is open already, and I think guiltily of the stack of cash she gave me. Her shop runs on a tight budget, and I know she barely makes the bills. It's a labor of love for her and I hate that she's having to pass me money and even more that I can't pay her back. Ever.

The realization chokes me, and when my mom comes out of the back room with a stack of books in her arms, she looks so familiar and warm and mom-like that I burst into tears.

"Oh, pipsqueak," my mom says sadly. She sets the books down on the nearest counter and holds her arms out to me.

I release Kassam's hand and race into my mom's arms, holding her close and weeping. I haven't even gotten the words out yet, but Mom knows there's something wrong. How am I going to leave her behind? My mom is my best friend and the only family I have. She's held my hand through a dozen broken relationships, and those horrible years when my dad was strung out on drugs and took it out on his family. She's been my rock, for all that she loves to keep her head in supernatural clouds. How am I going to leave her behind?

"You don't have to explain," she tells me in that gentle, motherly voice as she strokes my hair. I notice the jangle of a quartz bracelet as she does, and dimly see Kassam retreating to the far side of the room to give us space. "I know what you're going to say, Carly."

"You don't," I promise her, my heart aching.

She steers me toward the small storage room, away from Kassam, and shuts the door behind her. As I fight to compose myself, my mom just gives me a knowing look, brushing a lock of my thick, straight hair behind one ear. "You're leaving with him, aren't you?"

"How did you..."

A smile curves her lips. "Lachesis came to me in a dream last night." Her expression turns both sad and loving. "She said you were leaving me behind."

That only makes fresh tears well up, and I bury my face against her shoulder again. "Mama, I can't. I love you. You're my family. I can't leave you here alone."

"Oh, my pipsqueak. Don't cry. The goddess said you're needed. That you have a great destiny waiting for you over in the other realm. How can I possibly keep you from that?" She cups my face and brushes my tears off my cheeks, a brave smile on her face. "I'll miss you terribly, of course, but how can I keep you from great destiny?"

I manage a small smile. Most other parents would probably roll their eyes at being given a message from the gods in a dream. My mother, however, believes all of it. She's exactly the kind of person that pays attention to messages from another world, and for the first time, I'm grateful that she's into all this woo-woo nonsense, because she didn't bat an eye when I said I was bonded to a cursed god from another world. She just looked for solutions. And right now, instead of begging me to stay, she understands. She's going to hug me and let me go fulfill my destiny, whatever the hell that might be.

I'm grateful, but it makes me miss her even more. Why do we not appreciate our parents when we have them? I hug her again. "I love you so much, Mama. Will I ever see you again?" Fresh tears roll down my face, and I try to memorize the way she looks in this moment. Her hair is a messy version of my own, more gray than caramel brown. She's shorter than I am, and wider, but god, I love her so much that it hurts. "Did Lachesis say?"

My mother shakes her head. "Just that you were needed, and for me not to grieve."

A horrible, snot-filled laugh erupts from me. "Easy for the gods to say." I wipe at my face. "Kassam says...he says once everything is straightened out, he'll talk to the Fates, see if he can bring you over to the other world. Would you be okay with that?"

"Of course I would, honey." My mom gives me a sweet look. "But don't you worry about me right now. You worry about yourself and that new husband of yours. I'm going to do your cards every day and check in on you. Lachesis promised to help me. And I'm going to miss you terribly, but I know you're in good hands." She squeezes my shoulders. "The gods are involved. Multiple gods, pipsqueak. How could you possibly be any safer?"

How indeed. I bury myself in my mother's arms again and try not to worry too much. This is just temporary. Kassam is going to come through for me. "We'll get everything squared away and settled, and then I'll have him bring you over."

Neither one of us brings up that I've never finished a task in my life.

24

I cry all afternoon as I straighten up my apartment and pack a bag of my most valued possessions. I can't guarantee that anything will be here when I come back—or if I come back at all—so I have to go through everything and decide what I'm taking with me over to Kassam's world. I pack a few shirts, a pair of jeans, a sturdy pair of cute hiking boots, and a pair of comfy pajama pants. I don't know if his world has toilet paper, so I add a few rolls of that, too, and then I see the cross-stitch project on the end of the sofa that I never finished, the one I was stitching for my mom.

It sets me off into a fresh round of tears, as does the half-completed quilt sticking out of my sewing machine. I can't decide if I want to take all my half-finished projects with me or burn them all to hide the evidence, but I cry anyhow. I cry as I pack a couple of foil packs of crackers into my bag and a half-eaten jar of peanut butter that Kassam has somehow missed. I cry and I cry and I cry, even as the bag grows enormous and I have to switch out some of what I've decided to bring.

It keeps me busy, at least. And if I'm busy, I don't have to think about the foolishness of what I'm about to do.

Kassam heads into the living room at some point and watches me try to shove a wrapped bar of soap into the overstuffed bag. "My world has soap, Carly," he teases. "You don't have to bring that."

I just sniff. "Just in case, you know? This is like...an overnight trip. A big one. I'm trying to be prepared." A trip I might never return from and might kill me. I'm allowed to pack heavy, I feel.

"I see." He is quiet for a moment, and then says, "You forgot this."

When I glance over, Kassam holds out my vibrator, a shit-eating grin on his face. I just stare at him. "Are you trying to be funny?"

"Yes." He looks crestfallen that his joke fails, and he waves it at me, then gives up and tosses it down on the bed. "I was trying to make you smile, my little light. I do not like your tears." He sighs heavily. "I'm tempted to tie you down and use it on you until Seth gets here, but I suspect that won't make you smile, either."

I lick my lips, a little pleased that he's trying to cheer me up and clearly doesn't know how. It has to be hard for a party-focused immortal to deal with a sad person. Doesn't feed his hedonism bug at all. But I appreciate him recognizing that I'm miserable, and I sit down next to him on the bed. He immediately takes my hand and this time he doesn't zing me with an orgasm. He gives me a gentle wave of pleasure and laces his fingers through mine, rubbing the back of my hand. "I'm just...sad," I manage to choke out. "I'm all that my mom has, and the thought of leaving her behind really hurts."

"Where is your father?" Kassam asks. "Can your mother not lean on him?"

I flinch. It's an automatic reaction to anytime my father is brought up. He's been dead fifteen years, but the scars still run deep. "He's gone, and even if he was here, my mom couldn't count on him for anything. He was a horrible person."

He gives my hand a squeeze. "I find it difficult to believe that anyone that helped to create you is horrible. You are so charming and fierce."

Charming? I'm thinking he's blinded by sex, but the compliment makes me smile. I lean against his shoulder. "My dad was a junkie." I realize a moment later he probably doesn't know what that means, so I go on. "My father always had issues. When he met my mom, he was addicted to cigarettes and weed. Said he had anger problems and they helped him chill. My mom is sweet and somewhat gullible, so she looked the other way when he used."

"Gullible like believing in crystals and cards?" Kassam asks.

"I would have agreed with that statement a week ago, but given the fact that the only reason I'm not crawling all over your dick right now is because I'm dripping in quartz? I'm not laughing anymore." When he grunts acceptance, I continue. "My mom views the world with rose-colored glasses, though. She likes to believe the best in everyone. She figures if she does the right thing and someone lies to her, the shame is on them, not her. That good intentions trump everything. I think it's one reason why she didn't kick my dad out when she found out he was using harder stuff. He always promised to do better, and she believed him."

"Harder stuff?"

"Crack. Meth. Heroin. LSD. Pills. Anything my dad could get his hands on to try out, he'd do it. He'd smoke up. He'd toke. He'd inject. He'd snort. Whatever made him space out and made him high. I think he was just miserable and constantly looking to escape. He didn't want to be a responsible, working man, and he didn't want to be married with a young child, either. So he'd constantly get drunk, get lit, whatever he could do to alter his brain. And then he'd usually hit my mom." My mouth clenches in memory of that. "He never hit me. My mom always protected me. But when he was on something—which was all the time after a while—he was mean and nasty. He said awful things to me. If I drew something, he mocked it. If I played a sport, he'd tell me I was the worst kid out there. It got to the point that I was afraid to do anything because I'd hear my father's comments in my head."

"Mmm. So it is safer for you to give up than to try things." His gaze goes to an unfinished scarf hanging out of the bottom dresser drawer, knitting needles still in it.

"Bingo."

"And this is why you did not like it when they offered me drugs at the bar."

I nod. "Funny enough, alcohol doesn't bother me. I guess because when Dad drank, he just fell asleep. But the moment I smell weed or see someone shooting up, I get upset." My stomach clenches at the thought. "So yeah. You can drink what you like, but the moment you snort something, you're dead to me." I glance up at him. "It's another rule I think I'm going to enforce, as your wife. Sorry."

He grins down at me, his thumb caressing my hand. "I do not seek the pleasures because of the pleasures themselves. I simply chase hedonism because it is my curse. As long as I have you to sate my urges, I need nothing else."

"Not even butter?" I tease, feeling a little better. Talking about this helps a little. Not much, but a little.

Kassam shakes his head. "Just you."

I absorb his words, basking in the unspoken compliment. I know he's using me, but it's nice to hear that I'm appreciated, even if it's just for my willingness to have sex. The fact that he lets me put conditions on our relationship—knowing that he's a god—makes me feel valued as a partner. It makes me feel like my opinion matters, like I matter, and after the last few days, it feels more precious than gold. I pat his hand, still entwined with mine. "Thanks, Kassam. I know I'm being silly."

"You are not being silly. I have met many, many mortals and experienced many silly situations, and this is not one. You are putting your trust in me and yet your fear is not for yourself, but for your parent."

"I'm just afraid of leaving her alone," I say again, biting my lip. "At least I have you to look out for me. She won't have anyone."

"Lachesis visited her in a dream, yes? The goddess will watch out for her."

Which reminds me. "Are we sure Lachesis wasn't showing up just to lie to my mom and make her feel better about me going with you?"

Kassam snorts at that. "Why would she feel the need to lie? Your mother is a mortal. She is nothing to the goddess."

"An excellent point, and ouch, dude. Just ouch." I guess there's nothing more to do than to hope for the best. I look over at Kassam, at his utterly calm face. He's not worried about tonight in the slightest. In his eyes, I am completely safe despite the fact we're teaming up with a trickster god to switch worlds. It seems like a big deal to me, but what do I know? I'm just mortal. I have to have faith that Kassam (and Seth) know what they're up to. "Just promise me that you're telling the truth, Kassam?"

His brows furrow. "Truth about what?"

"All of this." I release his hand and get up to start packing more shit into my bag, because that at least helps me feel somewhat in control of an increasingly bizarre situation. I shove my hairbrush into a tight corner of the bag, shrugging as I do. "I just need to know that you're not lying to me. That you really are going to protect me. That I'm not going over to your world just to get axed. That Lachesis is going to look out for Mom. That you and I are"—I break off, because I'm not sure what answer I want to hear from him. It's not love. It's not devotion—"committed," I finally manage. "That you and I are a team. I need to know this is the truth."

Kassam leans back on the bed, watching me try to shove a belt into my bag, next to the hairbrush. A belt just seems like something pretty handy to have in a medieval world, and I want to bring it. He regards me for a few, and when I pause to look over at him, he shrugs. "I'm not sure what answer you wish from me, Carly."

Well that makes me nervous. "How about a 'Yes, you can a hundred percent trust me, Carly. Pinky swear.'"

But Kassam doesn't raise his pinky to meet mine. He only gazes up at me thoughtfully. "I will never betray you. I gave you my vow, and I meant it. I cannot control others, though. If Seth means to betray, he will betray us both. But if you are asking if I am using you, the answer is both yes and no. I do not deny that I have used people in the past. Every god does. I have used every anchor I have had in the past, just as I am using you now for my needs. I have ensnared others to do my bidding. Ask the *conmac*, who do my bidding on this plane because I demanded it, when they would rather run free. I told them they were needed to serve me through the Anticipation. That if they wished to live in the Great Endless Forest and keep their wolf-skins, they must obey the rules of the domain. That they must obey *me*. They were bound to me and they resented me greatly, but they still served."

"I don't know who the *conmac* are," I point out. "And this really isn't helping me feel any better about the situation."

"They are fae," he says. "Immortal, wild fae who wanted power and freedom. I gave them wolf-skins and the ability to shift into wolf form, but I made them promise to be my army if it was needed. They are my wild hunt. And when I have need, I call upon them. Because they are wild, they have no wish to help me, so I must force them to do so. I threaten to withhold their skins if they will not answer the call. And they do so, grudgingly. They would tear my throat out if they could." Kassam's smile is faint. "But I am answered at least."

I say nothing. I try to reconcile the laughing, teasing god in front of me who just waved my vibrator to make me laugh with the one he is telling me about, the one who withholds magical wolf-skins if people don't do his bidding.

"I am telling you this, Carly," Kassam says softly, "because I could force you. I could lay you down on this bed and use everything in my power to coax you to stay at my side. I could use my tongue and my cock to make you beg for anything and everything. But I will not. I welcome your refusals, and your challenges, and your questions, because you are my wife and my partner. We are friends. I am sharing the foul things I have done as a god, because I have forced others to my will, but I am not forcing you, and I want you to know the difference."

I nod. It's something that has occurred to me as well. For all that he thinks he is "helpless" here, he still has some degree of magic. The vines outside my window and the clusters of birds that follow us everywhere attest to that. "I'm very aware of the power disparity between us, trust me. But...thank you. Sometimes it's good to have it pointed out." I hesitate for a moment, and then continue on, since we're laying it all on the table. "I'm a little worried about Seth and his motives."

"Who isn't?" The look he gives me is wry. "But we cannot control his actions. It makes no sense to stress over them. If he is going to use this opportunity to attack us, there are easier ways to go about it. We can only control our own actions, Carly."

"Some of us can't even do that," I mutter, and gesture at myself.

Kassam throws his head back and laughs, all delightful, smiling god once more, and I have to admit, seeing him smile like that makes me feel better. Somehow it helps to hear that he's just as wary as I am. That yeah, we don't trust Seth, but screw it, we're doing this anyhow. The god rubs my arm, and then his expression turns from playful to aroused once more. "Do you want to fuck before Seth arrives? One last fling before we cross over? It could relax you."

Typical man to offer that. I give him an apologetic look. "No, but if you're offering a hug, I won't turn it down."

To my surprise, he spreads his arms wide, inviting me in. Kinda feels like a trap, like the moment I get closer, I'm going to find a hand on the back of my head, urging me downward into a blow job, but I go in for the hug anyhow. I'm delighted when he wraps his arms around me and hugs me tight. Just hugs me.

He keeps on hugging me, too, one hand rubbing slowly up and down my back as I cuddle against him. It feels amazing. Other than my mother, I can't remember the last time someone hugged me. Just hugged me to share affection, nothing more. He rests his chin atop my head and just holds me, for as long as I need it. And as Kassam hugs me, I keep waiting for him to turn it into something more, but he never does.

For that, I'm incredibly grateful and pleased. It was nice of him to make this all about me and my needs. When I pull away, I give him a kiss on the cheek. "Thank you for being sweet. The hug really did help."

Kassam touches his cheek, thoughtful. He looks surprised at my kiss, as if it was the last thing he was expecting. It's nice to surprise an immortal. Makes you feel powerful as hell. I'll have to surprise him again sometime, I decide.

If I ever get a chance.

25

I get the first inkling that things are going to be a problem tonight when Seth shows up to my apartment with a blind date.

"Shall we go?" Seth asks, his arm around a stranger's shoulders. The woman looks younger than me, maybe early twenties. She's shy looking, an awkward expression on her face, and wears a retro floral swing dress that she looks deeply uncomfortable in. Her hands clutch a tiny matching purse and her cheeks are flushed as she glances shyly up at Seth, who is wearing a button-down shirt and jeans. Today, when he smiles, his teeth aren't sharp.

I smell a trap. I eye the woman. "Hi, I'm Carly. You are—"

"My companion," Seth says smoothly, squeezing the woman's shoulders. "Again, shall we go? The best window for our project is soon, and we don't want to be late."

"Project," huh? I glance over at Kassam, who hauls my enormous backpack off the couch (I might have overpacked, but whatever) and slings it over one brawny shoulder.

"I'm Margo," the girl says. She blinks at Kassam for a long, hard moment and then focuses on my jeans and hiking boots. Then, she looks back at Seth. "Is this an activity date? I didn't realize."

"Date?" I echo. A fucking date? I look over at Seth, narrowing my eyes. "So does she realize where we're going?"

"To a park," Seth says, glaring daggers at me. That ominous sensation returns, the one of danger, and I know it's coming from Seth. As he glares at me, his pupils flash red, as if he's warning me off. "Do you have a problem with me bringing a date? I thought the intention was to double. You and him, and me and her."

My mouth opens and then snaps shut again. I look over at Kassam helplessly, but he just watches me, clearly not seeing the problem here. I turn back to Margo—pretty, awkward Margo who looks both trapped at Seth's side and flushed with excitement. "Can I ask how you two met?"

"Tinder," she says sweetly. "This is our first date."

I shoot a look at Seth. Did this asshole really pick up a stranger on a dating service just so he could have an anchor in the other world? Does this woman have any idea of what she is getting into? As she gives me a cheery smile, I realize no, she has no fucking clue. This is a problem. This is a big, big problem. I grab Kassam by the front of his shirt and haul him away from the door.

He chuckles at my impatience. "Did you decide you wished a quick orgasm before we leave after all?"

"No!" I hiss, ignoring the tendril of lust that flirts with my pulse. "I have a problem with this situation."

Kassam looks confused. "With what?"

I want to grab him and shake him. Instead, I pull him closer, dragging him toward the doorway to my bedroom. "He can't show up here with a blind date. She has no idea he's a god, and I'd bet ten bucks that she has no idea tonight is about crossing over into the other world. And I have a serious problem with that."

"But she is his problem," Kassam counters. When I put my hands on my hips, he sighs heavily. "Fine. I shall speak with him before we get started." He lifts his head and gestures at the other god. "A word, Seth."

Seth's sharp features are all annoyance as he strides over to join us. "Time is of the essence here, you two. Can we get moving? Lachesis is waiting to meet us and she's not going to sit around all night."

I look over at Kassam, pleading. I can't go along with this unless we're all on the same page.

"My Carly has issue with your anchor," Kassam says. "Have you bonded to her yet?"

The trickster god crosses his arms over his chest. He smiles, but I suspect it's more for Margo's benefit than mine, because the look he's giving me is full of daggers. "A human bond isn't required for me to be in this realm," Seth whispers. "She's my fallback. If I have to bond with someone in your world, she'll be my solution. If not, well, then she's extraneous." He shrugs. "So what's the problem?"

"She thinks you're on a date," I hiss. "Does she know who you are?"

"Seth Anderson, accountant." He pretends to straighten an invisible tie. "At your service. And if you're worried if she's willing or not, I can assure you, she absolutely is. She swiped right on me, after all, not the other way around." He winks in my direction. "She's absolutely thrilled to be going out with a ten, given that she's maybe a five herself."

I sputter with outrage. "That is disgusting of you."

"Okay, I'll give her a six, but it's barely a six." He shrugs. "Listen. I've worked very hard to set this all up." His gaze moves from me to Kassam. "Do you want to go back to your world or not? Because I've already cashed in my favor with Lachesis and she won't give me another. It's tonight or never."

I cross my arms over my chest, unwilling to compromise. "No. Absolutely not."

Seth looks over at Kassam. "Well, if you want to know what it's like to be a forgotten god, you're about to find out for all eternity." He casts an ugly glance over at me. "Unless you get your mortal in line."

Kassam flinches, but he doesn't look over at me. "Carly does not like that you're using that female," he states again, "And this is her world and her rules."

I can tell he's incredibly disappointed, but he's still supporting me. I'm grateful, filled with affection for Kassam... and a little panicky at Seth's words. I try to imagine a future with Kassam here, stuck forever and me stuck to him. What happens when I age and inevitably die? If he's stuck here, what happens then? Better yet, what kind of life am I going to have with someone like Kassam and his hedonism curse destroying everything around me on a constant basis?

We're cornered. Seth knows and just doesn't care. If I balk, am I going to have two gods to have to worry about? Something tells me Seth won't deal well with being thwarted. Frustrated and a little scared, I have to think of a solution, fast. "Is she safe with you?"

Seth chuckles. "I thought we all agreed that a god needs his anchor alive?"

"But is she safe?" Kassam presses, and I realize that Seth was working around the question. I'm so grateful for Kassam in that moment that I decide he needs a kiss later, when all this is settled. Hell, I'll even throw in a blow job. I'm just thrilled he continues to have my back, no matter what.

Seth glares at him, his jaw clenching. "I vow that I will do everything in my power to keep her safe."

"And you'll send her back to Earth the moment you no

longer need her as an anchor?" I push. "Unless she wants to stay?"

The trickster inclines his head. "You have my word upon that."

"Then...I guess I don't have any more objections." I hate that I'm caving in, but what choice do I have?

26

The car ride is an uncomfortable one. Seth drives a cherry-red sports car in a type I've never heard of. It's only got two doors, so Kassam and I have to squeeze into the tiny backseat as Margo chatters uncomfortably about how nice the weather is and how pretty the stars are tonight. I sit atop my overpacked bag (since there's nowhere else to put it) with my legs in Kassam's lap and try not to resent everyone and everything that led me to this moment.

Only the fact that Kassam has supported me this whole time has made me keep going forward with this. I'm doing everything for him, I decide. It's all to get him home and to get him back to his kingdom. To get him back the life that was stolen from him by that bitch Riekki who left him at the bottom of a glacier with a sword in his guts. Just thinking about that reminds me how much I hate this unknown goddess, and how she doesn't deserve to keep her spot. I want Kassam to take her down and make her pay for hurting him...which means we need to cross over to his world, even if Margo is an unwitting pawn.

As for Margo herself, she seems to be besotted with Kassam

instead of Seth. I know that it's all just part of Kassam's curse, but as we drive out of the city, I grit my teeth every time Margo asks Kassam a question and giggles no matter what he says. The looks she keeps shooting to the back seat infuriate me, like she'd cheerfully climb onto Kassam's lap and fuck him with me sitting right here beside him.

It's hedonism, I tell myself. No need to get mad. He has this effect on everyone.

But I didn't go to bat for everyone, and I did for Margo, and so it stings a little.

It seems to bug someone else, too. At one point, Seth glances over his shoulder at Kassam. "Can't you turn that shit off for five minutes?"

"I wish that I could," Kassam says easily. "Carly can attest to how very inconvenient it has been for both of us." He winks at me and rubs my foot through my boot.

"You have no idea." I peer out the window. It's dark, and I've noticed that as we leave the city—we've been in the car for at least an hour, maybe longer—it grows darker and darker. Now we're on country roads, and there are fewer cars and buildings by the minute. I have to admire Margo for going along with this cheerfully, because a first date that wants to take me to a moonlit park? That's some serious serial-killer territory. But maybe she feels safe with me and Kassam along as the double. Who can say? "Are we almost there?"

Seth snorts. "It's amazing how impatient your kind is."

"Her kind?" Margo asks.

He pauses. Glances back at me. Glances at Margo. "Millennials," he says finally. "Are you one?"

She chuckles, seemingly nonplussed. "I'm Gen Z, but just barely. Aren't you a millennial?"

"I'm older than I look," Seth replies.

I cough politely. Kassam merely slides his hand up my ankle and gives me a meaningful look, as if warning me not to push it. His thumb skates over my leg, teasing my skin, and as Margo glances back at Kassam again, I'm tempted to slide into his lap and give her a show like we did to Seth.

Then, I realize what I just thought. What the hell is wrong with me? I touch the crystals at my throat and wrist, then my earrings, checking to make sure everything is in place to banish as many horny thoughts as possible. Kassam has corrupted me, I decide, because the thought of straddling him in the car and fucking while we drive doesn't bother me nearly as much as it should.

I mull on this as Seth finally pulls the car over. "Here we go."

Margo peers out the windows, frowning. "Where are we?"

"Park," Seth says, as if that explains everything, and gets out of the car.

We manage to climb out of the back, and Kassam hefts my pack, holding my hand to help me out. I stretch, wincing at cramped muscles as we get out. Beyond the asphalt parking lot, the trees here are tall and looming in the darkness. Margo looks around in worry as Seth strides off down a path. "Where's he going?"

"Probably to check on the person we're meeting."

She gives a nervous laugh. "Isn't it kinda dark?"

"It is, yeah."

"New moon," Kassam offers helpfully.

Her gaze turns toward him and her expression grows adoring. "Of course." She stares up at him. "Gosh, you're tall."

"Come on, honey," I say deliberately, grabbing Kassam's hand and giving him a meaningful look. "Let's go find Seth, shall we?"

"As you wish, my little light." Kassam looks as if he's laughing inside, and I don't know if it's because of Margo's reaction—or my possessive one. But he lets me lead him down the path after Seth, and a few moments later, Margo trots behind us, her heels clicking on the paved trail.

We walk deeper into the trees, and just when I think Seth has gone and abandoned us, I see a tiny cherry of a light flare in the darkness. Sure enough, there's someone sitting atop a distant picnic table, cigarette in hand. I can guess who that is. I hear a rustle of keys and when I turn to look over at Margo, she has a tiny can of mace in her hand. She looks worried. I don't blame her. Poor thing. I hate Seth for not explaining anything, and I hate me just a little for going along with it.

"Everyone here?" Lachesis asks, her warm, smoky voice as familiar as I remember. She sounds a little...tired. Annoyed, maybe.

Margo steps forward, her keys clanking in her hand. "Um, I have to ask, why are we out here in the middle of nowhere?"

"You can see the stars better, my heart," Seth replies smoothly.

"I'm not your heart," Margo says, and I instantly like her a thousand percent more. "And is there a light around here somewhere? I can't—"

Before she can finish the sentence, light flares from Lachesis's fingertips. She pinches at the air and draws her pinched fingers apart, and between them, a glowing string creates light, flooding the darkness around us and illuminating the cigarette hanging from her lips.

"—see," Margo squeaks, finishing her sentence. Her eyes are round as saucers in the darkness.

I'm only slightly less shocked than Margo. Holy shit. I watch as Lachesis smirks, just a little, and then lifts her hand, tying the string off to an invisible hook. "Better? Everyone can see now, yes?" She casually takes her cigarette from her lips, flicks the ash, and then crosses her legs, grinning at us. "So here's the dream team, eh? Ready to begin?"

I notice she doesn't look at me or Margo, just Seth and Kassam. It's like we don't matter to her. Hell, we probably don't.

"More than ready," Kassam says. "You and Seth have worked everything out?"

"Oh yeah." Lachesis rolls her eyes. Seth just grins, quite pleased with himself. "Let's just say I'm not thrilled, but a debt is a debt."

"Can someone explain to me what's going on?" Margo asks. "How did you do that light strand?"

Seth moves toward Margo's side. "She's a magician," he purrs, sliding his arm around her shoulders again. "Don't be so worried, pet. This is all part of the fun."

"What fun? No one will tell me what's going on."

I look over at Kassam, but he shakes his head at me. He doesn't want me scaring Margo off. Fuck. Fine then. I'll do what I can. I step forward to get Lachesis's attention. "Can you explain to us how this works? Tonight's ritual?"

"Ritual?" Margo asks. "Are you guys witches?"

"Of a sort," Seth grins at her. "Does it offend you?"

"N-no, of course not. I just wasn't expecting this for our date." Her tone turns meek and apologetic. "I'm not trying to offend. Just understand. I didn't know witchcraft actually worked." And her gaze slides to the thread, hanging like a clothesline in midair.

I bite back a groan of frustration, practically stomping my feet as I look over at Kassam. Really? Really we're doing this? It's so unfair to Margo. But he pulls me against him, burying my face in the crook of his arm, and zings me with a fluttering almost-orgasm. I gasp and smack his chest, because that is not playing fair at all. "Just...I need to know what's going to happen. All right? For me and no one else."

And I glare at Kassam.

"Sure." Lachesis stubs her cigarette on the park bench, next to her hip, and then begins to move her hands in the air again. As she does, more shimmering threads dance into view out of thin air. She pulls and pulls, her hands working so fast that they're blurs, and her face glimmers with colors as the threads glow around her. "All of humanity exists in a tapestry. I believe Kassam said that for our brothers on the other side, it is a web. Same sort of thing. When you are born, Clotho spins you into existence. She places you into the tapestry and starts your thread. Then, I take over. I work you into the weave, guiding your thread when it snarls, and seeing the largest intersections. I tease out knots and make sure that important threads cross over with others."

As I watch, she makes a clawing gesture across the sky, and the threads in front of her draw together, clustering into a ball. With a quick flick of her hand, she sends them scattering across the air once more.

I stare in fascination as her hands dance amongst the threads she's pulling from midair. She's like the conductor of an orchestra, and the strings are her instruments. Her face shines with pleasure, as if the act of simply touching the threads brings her joy. In this moment, her plain face is unearthly and beautiful, and I can see her for the goddess she is, instead of just a downtrodden middle-aged mom.

"Here is Margo's thread." Lachesis gently tugs one thread forward, pulling it free from the tangle of threads in front of her face. "And here, we have Carly. Note that they intersect here, at this time, because of your meeting."

My mouth open in fascination, I take a step forward, peering at the threads. I'm disappointed to see that my particular thread looks the same as Margo's—as in, boring. It has a faint blue light, but nothing spectacular compared to some of the threads around them.

"And here we have Kassam," Lachesis says. She nudges my thread forward, and I can see a much brighter, golden one entwined with my own. In fact, it's so bright and dazzling that now that she has it pulled forward, it completely overshadows my own. "Note that Carly's thread is locked into the tapestry of this world." Her finger gestures, following the line of my thread where it disappears into the tangle of thousands of other lights, all in varying pale colors. "Just as you'll note that Kassam is not anchored to this particular tapestry at all. Carly is the only thing holding him here."

The goddess runs a finger along Kassam's thread, and I watch as she gestures outward. Sure enough, both Margo and I are tied to the rest of the strings, but Kassam's brilliant, blinding thread trails off into nothing at all. It's like a random spiderweb out of nowhere that has somehow found its way to my thread and is clinging to it for dear life.

My mouth goes dry at the sight.

Now I see why an anchor has to die. Kassam is tied to me. I'm what keeps him here. If I die, then he returns home because there's nothing to "anchor" him to the mortal world any longer.

I suddenly find I'm far less interested in the thread display.

27

"Where's mine?" Seth asks, leaning in.

"As if I'd forget you," the goddess says playfully. She reaches into the cluster and pulls out a bright, flaming red thread. "Here we go. Ready for action." She lays his thread atop ours, where Margo's thread crosses mine.

Margo gasps and looks over at her date with new eyes.

"Now, here comes the fun part," Lachesis says. "So what the plan is, I'm going pry you two ladies out of your current tapestry, and then I'm going to take one for the team and contact the Fates in Kassam's world by following his thread. I'm going to have to pull a few strings"—she points at us—"no pun intended, and get you four placed in that world's web and out of mine." She dusts her hands and smiles at us. "And then you're someone else's problem. Understand?"

"Why does this have to be done under the new moon?" I ask, curious. This lines up with what Kassam had hinted at, but the whole "moon" thing has me baffled.

Lachesis shrugs. "No big reasons. What we're doing isn't exactly in the rules, and certain moon goddesses are a gossipy sort and like to get people in trouble."

"Even after all these years, Selene hasn't learned to keep her mouth shut." Seth chuckles. "Doesn't she have anything better today?"

"You know she doesn't," Lachesis says lightly. "No one does."

That sobers him. Seth's expression is no longer laughing. His face hardens and he studies the glowing strands in the air, all business once more. "When we reach the other side," Seth asks, "We'll be in the mortal realm, yes?"

Lachesis nods. "They're currently experiencing a crisis and most of the gods are walking the mortal realm. I haven't been able to glean too much from peering in from afar, but yes. I haven't wanted to get involved." Her mouth pulls up on one corner and she gives Seth a wry look. "Until now, when my hand is forced."

"But such lovely hands," Seth murmurs, grinning at her. He reaches out and takes her hand in his, kissing the fingertips.

The goddess just rolls her eyes.

I hug my chest, a little worried and trying not to look at that whole thread mess that I thought was so beautiful just a few moments ago. I don't like the sight of Kassam's thread entwined with mine, overwhelming it, and stretching out into nothingness with me as the only flimsy anchor to this world. I glance over at Kassam to see what he's thinking, and instead of watching Seth flirt with Lachesis or eyeballing the threads, he's watching me. There's a sad, soft expression on his face, as if he knows just what I'm thinking and he's silently apologizing for it. That he knows this is a difficult thing to ask, and he's asking it anyhow.

I move to his side and link my hand with his, showing him that I know what I'm getting into...and I choose him anyway.

The smile he gives me is dazzling and full of promise, and my heart flutters at the sight.

"You're not witches at all, are you?"

Margo's hushed voice makes me pause.

Seth doesn't even look at Margo. He gives Lachesis an impatient gesture. "Let's just get things moving. Quickly."

At Margo's terrified look, I change my mind. I've always been a bit on the fence with the whole thing, and I decide it's time to take a stand. "Actually, this isn't fair to Margo," I say, and ignore Kassam's squeeze of my hand. "She needs to know what she's getting into."

"I thought we just went over that," Seth snarls.

"Don't yell at my wife," Kassam says, stepping in front of me.

"Your wife?" Seth's eyes widen and then he throws his head back, laughing. "You have got to be shitting me. You married a mortal? You? She must have a cunt of solid gold." He shakes his head and grins at Lachesis. "He really is desperate to get home, isn't he?"

"Who are you people?" Margo's keys jingle again and she pulls out her pepper spray, holding it up. "Actually, I take it back. I don't care. I'm getting out of here, and I don't want anyone to follow me. Understand?"

"You're not going anywhere," Seth says, moving back to Margo's side. He plucks the can from her hand as if it's nothing and tosses it away, her keys jangling as they land in the grass somewhere. "You said you'd go on a date with me, and we're not done. I told you we were going somewhere special, and you said you were all for it. That hasn't changed." He grins coldly. "It's special indeed, wait and see."

Margo gives him a terrified look.

"Stop it," I say, moving toward Seth. "This isn't right. You—"

Lachesis pinches the air and my thread jerks. The words die in my throat. I'm frozen in place. I can't move. Can't speak. Can't do anything. I'm not even breathing. I'm not sure my heart is beating. I'm just...frozen in time.

My eyes are open, and even though the rest of me can't

function, I can watch as Margo takes a step forward—and suffers the same fate. She freezes, her mouth parted as if she is going to speak, her hand stuck in mid-air.

The goddess turns toward Seth, giving him a cranky look. She swings that gaze toward Kassam, reproaching him as well. "I thought you two secured your mortals? Do we have a problem?"

"No problem here," Seth says smoothly.

I feel Kassam's hand brush my shoulder, then my jaw. "Let her go."

"Not until we're certain we all want to move forward like this. You told me it was under control," she says to Seth, accusing. "We're going to be in big trouble if I ask the Fates in his world to move over a mortal and then she cries that she was coerced. She has to step across the threshold on her own." Lachesis sighs heavily. "I need a fucking cigarette. Okay, here's what we're going to do. Regroup again. Both of you get new mortals, and we'll try again next month."

"No," Kassam says flatly. "I am bound to Carly. She is my anchor."

"I know, dummy." Lachesis pulls out her pack of cigarettes, and the hold on me wavers as she pulls one stick out and lights it. "Here's the thing. I can move your anchor bond to someone else. You just say who and we'll get it handled. No fuss, no muss. They're such little lights in the cosmic tapestry that no one will ever notice."

Little light.

Kassam calls me little light. Is this why? Because I'm so insignificant to the gods? Hurt and anger blaze through me both, but I'm helpless to do anything. I can't even flip anyone the bird or clench a fist. All I can do is stare mutely at all of them. If I'm nothing to him, of course he's going to switch me out. He'll find someone more ruthless, someone that won't care if Margo's being manipulated. Someone that's eager to join him in his world instead of worrying over her mother."

"No," Kassam says. "Carly is my wife. I made a vow to her and I intend to keep it. Now, let her go."

"She's not hurt. She's just silenced while we figure this out."

"There's no figuring out to do," Seth counters. "We move forward. Margo said she'd go on a short trip with me. This qualifies. I'll deal with her later if she gets upset. She agreed, and that's all that is required, yes?"

Lachesis tilts her head, a reluctant agreement. "If we're splitting hairs, sure, it's an agreement. There might be fallout in the future though."

Seth just gives her a sly grin. "As if I'm not familiar with handling such things. I will take care of it." He looks over at Kassam. "And your mortal agreed. She even packed a bag. So what is the hold-up? Do you wish to return to your world or not?"

Kassam hesitates. He moves to my side, running his knuckles lightly along my jaw as he gazes down at me. I can see the torment in his eyes. He's weighing whether or not my good opinion of him outweighs his need to go home. "I care for Carly, as much as any god can care for a mortal," he admits, looking over at Seth. "But I know you care nothing for yours. I have made a promise to mine to keep her safe. I need you to make the same promise to yours."

"What? Why?" Seth sounds offended. "She's a mortal. She could die from any number of things. Why do I have to vow to keep her safe? Why do you care?"

"Because Carly cares," Kassam says simply.

And even though I'm still angry over the "little light" situation and the fact that Margo's being manipulated, I kinda want to hug Kassam for that. He cares because I care. Because I matter to him. I'd cry a little if my tear ducts weren't frozen.

Seth sighs, the sound a little petulant. "Fine. Whatever. Can we just get going?"

"Do you agree not to harm the female?" Kassam states specifically. "I need a better answer than 'whatever.' Do you swear to protect her with all your might?"

A moment ticks by. Then another. Seth glares at Kassam. "Yes. Fine."

Definitely going to kiss Kassam when this is all over and done with. My guy turns to Lachesis. "And I need a promise from you, as well."

She rolls her eyes, taking a pull on her cigarette before flicking it. "Here we go. Spit it out."

"Promise you will not pull Carly's thread prematurely. Nor this other female."

"Honey, I don't pull the threads. That's my sister."

Kassam gives her an icy look. "Then make her promise."

Lachesis sighs. Her eyes turn completely black for a moment, then flicker to normal once more. "She promises."

Kassam grunts, as if satisfied. "Then I am ready. Send us through."

The goddess nods. "Good luck, you two. Hold on to your mortal, and when you cross over, they'll unfreeze. I don't dare do it beforehand or we're going to be here all night." There's a note of impatience in her voice. "And I'm already growing tired of this. So both of you, snag your humans, and when I start pulling on threads, you're going to see a portal open. I advise you to go through it quickly before someone gets wind of what we're up to. Understand?" She looks between the two gods. "Okay. Great. Let's roll."

Warm hands cup my waist, and then Kassam pulls me—still frozen like a mannequin—against his chest. I can't see anything now but his shoulder. He strokes my hair once and murmurs, "All will be well, Carly. I promise."

Then there's a bright light that sears my frozen eyelids. I

can't blink away. I can't scream. I can only stare at Kassam's shoulder as he gives my back one last pat and then surges forward.

Something hard and painful *yanks*, and for a moment, it feels as if my spine has been ripped out of my body.

Then...nothing. Nothing at all.

28

When I wake up next, it's to a crick in my neck, an ache in my pussy, and my stomach growling.

My eyes flutter open, and I stare at the green canopy overhead. Trees. Big ones. Okay, that's not so weird. Considering we were in a park, that's kinda expected. I raise a hand to my forehead, rubbing it to get rid of a forming headache. I can hear water somewhere, trickling and pleasant, like a fountain.

Something moves into my sight, and then a tongue licks my forehead. I frown, lowering my hand as a big deer with an enormous rack of antlers licks my brow, as if I'm an errant fawn in need of cleaning. I sputter, trying to move away from that licking tongue. "Hey now!"

There's a chuckle somewhere off to my side, and the liquid heat that pools in my belly tells me that it's Kassam. Pushing the insistent deer aside, I sit up.

And I get my first look at my new surroundings.

Wow. Just wow.

It's like something out of a Disney movie. I'm lying in lush green grasses that make a soft bed underneath me. The wind picks up, rustling the leaves out of the tall, fantastic-looking trees all around, sunlight trickling through the branches and dappling the scenery. In the distance, I see a charming waterfall, cascading over rocks into a pool below, and the mist that forms around the rocks is full of rainbows. The air smells like flowers and fresh air, and I breathe deeply, because I've never smelled anything quite so fresh before. Birds chirp and dart through the skies overhead. As I look around, I see deer and small animals everywhere. They nibble on the greenery and wander about in the glade, content.

It's very obviously daylight. Considering it was night when we left my world, I must have been asleep for a long time. Maybe that's why my stomach is growling so hard that it feels as if it's about to start gnawing on my spleen.

A small, yellow bird lands on a nearby moss-covered boulder and watches me, tilting its head. It chirps and then hops over to my shoulder. "Oh, okay," I breathe. "We're doing this, then. Hi. Have you seen a guy named Kassam around here? Kinda big, kinda sexy? Likes to laugh and lick everything in sight?"

That selfsame laughter dances through the clearing, making my body quiver in response. My nipples prick against my T-shirt and I have to bite back a moan at my neediness. Kassam was potent in my world, but here he's downright murdering my pussy with just a sexy laugh alone. Frantic, I reach for my crystals at my neck—scaring off the bird in the process—and find that they're very much in place.

I manage to stagger to my feet as leaves rustle with Kassam's approach. "I think my crystals aren't working," I blurt out as he steps out of the shadows and into the dappled sunlight. "I think..."

The rest of my words die in my throat as the neediest whimper.

God, he is *pretty*.

Kassam strides forward, and he was gorgeous in my world, but here he's just...more. More sensual, more attractive, more magnetic. I can't tear my gaze away from him as he approaches me. His clothes are gone. That's the first thing I notice. He's shed his jeans and flip-flops and T-shirt and is now completely and utterly naked, save for a vine that curls up one arm and tangles into his long, wild brown hair, that seems to have grown twice as unruly and twice as long in the time that I slept. His eyes practically glow silver, his tan is deeper, and a squirrel rests on one shoulder, a crow perched atop the crown of antlers that lofts from his thick mane.

That's...new.

He stops in front of me and kneels, and I notice that he smells good—like a pine forest and flowers both—and his feet are hooves. Fucking hooves. That's new, too. "Hi," I manage to choke out. "You look...well."

I'm proud of myself for not shoving my hand down my pants at the sight of him. Really proud. He'll never know how strong the urge is right now. I'm wide-eyed as I gaze at him, wanting nothing more than to close the distance between us and just lick every inch of his golden-brown skin.

"How do you feel?" Kassam asks. He reaches out and traces a finger along my jaw, and it takes everything I have not to drop onto my back and fling my legs into the air. "Do you hurt anywhere?"

Oh, there's a part of me that's throbbing, but pain? Not really. I'm mostly ravenous and fatigued. "Tired and hungry but...I think I'm all right." I gaze up at him. "You?"

His face wreaths in a smile that's so ecstatic it makes me quiver. Kassam closes his eyes, pressing his hands to his bare chest over his heart. "Words cannot describe how full my heart is, my Carly. I have dreamed of being free again for so long that to be here..." He makes a sound of pure joy and leans over me, cupping my face. He leans in as if he's going to kiss me—

—and then stops. His brows furrow together and then he releases me. Right, because I don't want to be kissed. Why did I say that again? "Thank you," he says hoarsely. "Without you at my side, this would not be possible."

"Of course," I manage.

He smiles at me, his thumb brushing over my cheek and sending skitters of need through my body. "Well. You are hungry, yes? Shall I ask the birds to give up their lives for your meal? Or do you prefer fish?"

Oh god, that sounds weird. I blanch at the thought, my mind racing with images of cute little birds flinging themselves onto a fire to feed me. It's so much easier to not think about where food comes from when you're a child born in a world full of grocery stores. "I'm not sure I want to eat your followers."

"Plants, then? Fruit?"

My mouth waters at the thought. "Sounds amazing, thank you."

Kassam gives me a cocky grin. He gets to his feet, all wild, beautiful god, and looms over me. "Watch and I shall provide."

He stretches a hand out to the ground, and the plants surge forward, growing at incredible speed. One pair of tubers shoot up, starting to resemble celery. The leaves rustle in a tree nearby, and I watch as the flowers wither and fade, fruit springing up in its place and growing so quickly that they look as if they're inflating like balloons.

I'm so fascinated with this sight that I don't notice my headache at first. Or rather, I notice it, but it seems so much less interesting than what's going on with the plants. Something wet drips onto my lip and I absently brush at it, then glance at my hand.

Blood.

I whimper, my hands flying to my face. My nose is bleeding,

blood pouring down my lips and chin, and my head pounds. "Something's wrong," I manage to choke out. I grab the front of my shirt and hold it under my nose. "Hurts."

Kassam hisses between his teeth, dropping to sit on his feet —er, hooves—beside me. "It is my powers. They draw through you. I remember now." He rubs his fingers together and moss forms out of nowhere—and makes blood gush anew from my nose. He growls in frustration, immediately tossing it down. "I keep forgetting."

"You're...not supposed to use your powers?" I ask, my voice clogged and muffled due to the bloody shirt shoved against my nose.

"None whatsoever," Kassam says with a shake of his head. "It is part of our punishment. We are to be as powerless as mortals." His expression turns pained. "It has been so long that I have forgotten. You have my apologies, little light."

I decide to let that "little light" thing go for now. "It's okay. Just...try not to use the powers, all right? It feels like it's squeezing my head in a vise when you do."

"Of course. I will do my best not to forget again." His expression looks miserable. "I don't like that I hurt you."

"It's okay," I manage, smiling under the T-shirt, and then I realize he can't see it. "I should probably wash my face, though—"

Before I can finish the statement, Kassam is on his feet. He sweeps me into his arms, crossing the clearing toward the waterfall. He carries me as if I weigh nothing, and the only sound is the constant falling of water and the thud of his hooves against the grass. I don't even bother to protest that I can walk, because I *like* that he's carrying me. I like that he's fussing over me as if I'm special. After the week I've had, I welcome a little pampering.

He sets me gently into the water, up to my hips, and instantly my sturdy hiking boots and jeans are soaked. I can't really bitch about it, though, because Kassam cups water in his hand and gently washes my face, a look of intense concentration on his handsome, otherworldly features. "I do not like this at all," he murmurs as he rubs the blood from my face. "My curse must have been muted in your world. I could pull at bits of my power and it did not cause this problem."

"Muted" would explain a lot. Because I'm utterly ravenous, to the point that I could toss fistfuls of grass into my mouth, or chew on the nearest lily pad. I'm also horny as fuck, despite the fact that I'm dripping with quartz jewelry. I want to put a hand on his chest and then slide it south. I want to rub his cock until he fucks me in this pool. I want to do so many filthy things to him that there's not enough time in the day to get to it all.

He peels off my shirt, frowning at the blood all over it. "Now we have ruined your fine garments."

"It's a concert T-shirt. It's fine, really." I touch my nose. Other than being a little warm, it's not sensitive or in pain despite the fountain of blood that just gushed from it. Weird. My head has stopped hurting, too. Still turned on, though. I study Kassam as he swishes my shirt in the water, trying to get the blood out. He looks different here. The same guy, of course, but just...more. "The horns are new," I say, feeling a bit lame and stupid. "The hooves, too."

Kassam wrings my shirt, then gently touches my face with the fabric, dabbing at my skin. His fingertips hold my chin steady as he cleans me, and maybe it's the fact that I'm super turned on, but I'm eating this up. I love that he's fussing. "Do you like them?"

"I do. They're just...a surprise." I brush my fingers over his arm. "Your skin actually looks browner, too."

"Brown is the color of the earth. Why would it not be?"

Why not, indeed? "I didn't say it was bad. The hooves just took me by surprise."

He finishes washing my face and then leans in, his thumb

brushing over my lower lip in a sensual way that makes my pussy quiver deep, deep inside. "Do not worry, little light. I will still be able to put you on your hands and knees and fuck you so hard that you scream."

I swallow, entranced by his silvery gaze.

29

My stomach chooses that moment to growl, and Kassam chuckles. He winks at me. "Wait here, and I will get your food." He bounds out of the water quickly, his bare ass dripping and tan as he strides over to the tall stalks of whatever and carefully digs them up. He heads to the tree and plucks a piece of fruit the size of a basketball while I stand in the water, fascinated at the sight of him. The animals seem as entranced with his gloriousness as I am.

When he turns back toward me, his cock is half-stiff and growing by the moment, and it suddenly seems like too much to look at. Gazing at him is like staring into the sun, and I dunk my shirt again, dragging it through the water just to give my hands something to do. I'm painfully aware of my wet bra and my nipples pressing against the soft fabric, of the fact that I'm practically topless as I gaze out at his nude body. I'm tempted to just start playing with my nipples to see how he reacts, but then Kassam moves to one of the rocks at the edge of the pool and smacks the fruit against the surface. It cracks open, revealing wet, orange-pink flesh, and the scent drifts toward me, setting my mouth to watering again.

"Come," he says, holding a chunk out to me. "Eat."

I don't have to be told twice. My hunger overrides my arousal, and I pull myself onto one of the nearby rocks, taking the half of fruit he offers to me. It reminds me a bit of melon, but the first bite tastes more like a deep, ripe peach, and I make a sinful sound of pleasure at the taste. "Oh god, that's good."

"I'm glad. Eat as much as you like." He leans over the water, washing the vegetables, and once they're clean, he offers one to me. It's a bulb of some kind and looks a bit like an onion. I'm not entirely sure I want that after fruit, but since he made my nose bleed for it, it seems rude to refuse. I finish my piece of melon, then take the bulb and bite into it like an apple. It has a strange, earthy taste, but reminds me a spicy bean more than an onion, and I decide I like it. I eat everything, and then when I've licked my fingers clean, I head over to the waterfall and drink my fill.

Once I'm sated, I move back to where my pack is and flop down on the ground, running my fingers over my fruit-distended belly. I ate all of that and it was delicious, but something tells me I'm going to be hungry again quickly. Heck, I could already eat another snack. "I must have slept for a long time to be so hungry."

Kassam drops onto the grass next to me, propping up on his elbows. He regards me with amusement and what looks like... affection. "Remember, since you are my mortal, you will be hungry and thirsty because you are fueling me."

My mortal. I hate how much that word choice makes me quiver with pleasure. "Where are Seth and Margo?"

"Uncertain." He shrugs, and gazes at his surroundings with shining eyes. "I have been trying to decide why Lachesis sent me here. When I left, it was at the Blood Glacier, when Rhagos and his anchor found me. This is near, but to the south. Perhaps Lachesis simply looked for a convenient spot to place me...but then it does not answer where Seth and his anchor would be." He shrugs. "I thought we would end up together, but it does not matter. We will find them soon enough."

I lick my lips, and they taste like fruit. "I kinda hope Margo's giving him a piece of her mind. That man needs to be yelled at."

Kassam chuckles. "He is not a man, little light. You must remember that, first and foremost. He has seen ten thousand generations. What is one human to him?"

I prop up on my elbows, looking over at Kassam. "Okay, well, the same could be said for you."

"It could, yes."

I study him. Funny how he defends Seth for his shitty actions because he understands him...and yet when given the same choice, Kassam has chosen again and again to have my back and defend me. He stood up to Lachesis and Seth on Margo's behalf, not because he cared about Margo, but because it mattered to me. "Thank you," I say softly. "You said a lot of nice things back there when Lachesis and Seth were trying to rush us."

"I made a promise to you, Carly. I intend to keep it." He watches me carefully. "You are my wife. I have never had a bond like that before and I am curious to explore it."

Is that what this is to him? A new experience after all this time? Well, it doesn't matter. He's not the only one "curious" to explore. I sit up and lean over him, brushing my lips against his. "I can still thank you."

He looks up at me as I hover over him, heat in his gaze. He watches my mouth, curious. "You kissed me. You said you would not."

"I said they weren't part of the deal, because there had to be affection between us."

Kassam looks up at me. "And are you feeling affectionate toward me right now?"

"Very much so." I put a hand on his chest and give him a sultry smile. I press lightly, indicating he should fall back, and when he does, I lean over him once more and begin to kiss my way down his abdomen. "Let me show you my thanks."

He groans with pleasure, his hand dragging through my hair as he closes his eyes and relaxes. "You're thanking me for intervening with one foolish mortal who should have known better than to make a verbal agreement with a stranger?"

"I'm thanking you for treating me like I matter."

"You matter to me."

"And for that, you get a blow job," I agree, letting my mouth trail lower on his abdomen. "Though, really, it's for me as much as it is for you."

He's silent, and then finally chuckles. "You may blow on my cock all you like, my pretty Carly, but I will like it even more if you put it in your mouth."

I blink, and it takes everything I have not to break into giggles. Does he really think I'm going to bend down and just... blow on his cock like it's a dandelion? Like a flute? My mouth quivers with the urge to laugh, and I'm tempted to lean in and fan my breath over him just to be a shit. But I'm not about to deprive myself.

So I smile at him, curl my hand around his shaft, and lower my head to taste the tip of him.

30

I moan at the taste of him. It's such a cliché to think that he tastes like sunshine and warm skin, but he does. Of course he does. He's a god of nature here, even if he's been stripped of his powers. That first musky taste of him only makes me hungry for more, though. Greedy, I explore him with my fingers, learning him by touch as my mouth closes over the head of his cock. He's thick and uncircumcised, and even though this isn't a surprise for me, I've never really explored him at my leisure or taken control. It's always been about scratching the itch, feeding the need as quickly as possible.

But oh, I'm enjoying this. I love the way his body twitches in response the moment I swirl my tongue under the head of his cock. I love the hiss of his breath when my exploring fingers brush over the seam of his sac. I love the way he tastes and how he subtly pushes against my tongue when I take him deeper into my mouth, how his fingers tighten in my hair. I love all of it.

"That mouth of yours is so sweet," he murmurs as I lick him. "I much prefer this to blowing."

This time, I do chuckle. "It's an expression, silly. I always intended to put my mouth all over your cock." I lean in to lick the base and then move all the way up to the tip, trailing my tongue along the underside. "Kinda feel as if I've been depriving myself considering we haven't done this before."

"Then please, do not let me deprive you, my little light." He flexes his hips, pushing his cock forward as I kiss the tip again. "Take as much of me as you like."

He still sounds as if he's in control, which is slightly annoying. I want him to get lost in this moment. I want him to realize that I'm the one in charge. I want to take over and blow his damn mind. So I lift my head and give him a completely lascivious lick, swirling my tongue over the tip. "Quiet. I need to concentrate. You're only allowed to speak if you call me by my name."

One of those brows goes up and he chuckles, amused at my bossiness. "What if I call you 'wife'?"

"I'll accept it." I lap at the head of his cock.

"What if I call you 'mortal woman'?"

"I'll use my teeth."

Kassam laughs, the sound full of delight. "What if—"

I suck the head of him into my mouth again to shut him up, slowly stroking his cock. I grasp him loosely, using his foreskin to provide the movement, and keep my hand steadily pumping as I pull him deeper into my mouth. He grunts, his hand tightening in my hair, and finally shuts up. Good.

I stroke his cock as I take as much of him as I can into my mouth, until my fingers meet my lips and I'm deep throating him. He groans, shuttling his hips slightly in an effort to push deeper, and so I grip his thigh and concentrate on keeping my mouth as loose as possible while he fucks my face. It feels good, and I love that he's using me, but at the same time, I mourn that I lost control again. Maybe I just can't keep control when I'm in bed with a god. Maybe it's foolish to even try.

"Carly," he groans. "Your mouth. Incredible. You're taking me so deep, little light."

I caress his sac, nuzzling deeper against his skin as he pounds against the back of my throat. I breathe deep, doing my best not to gag as I fondle the heavy weight of his balls. A tiny, naughty idea occurs to me and I wonder if I'm brave enough to do it.

Then I decide…fuck it. If you can't finger the prostate of a god, whose prostate *can* you finger?

I lift my mouth off his cock, panting, and go back to tonguing his shaft and foreskin. I glance up at him to see if he's paying attention, but his eyes are closed, his face tight with pleasure. Perfect. With one hand, I work his shaft. With the other, I lick my finger, coating it liberally with my saliva before I bend down to take the head of his cock into my mouth again.

As he groans, lifting his hips, I dive. I trace his sac with my pinky, then gently tease until I'm toying with the underside. A moment later, I go for the butthole. I push lightly, then with a bit more force, sinking my finger in as Kassam sucks in a deep breath, arching against me. Once my finger is in deep, I search for his prostate. Maybe a god doesn't have one. Maybe—

The moment I rub my finger against it, Kassam's breath hisses out from between his teeth. His entire body jerks, and I'm delighted by the response. I continue rubbing as he pumps into my mouth, his movements frantic and wild. His body bows and his hooves smack against the ground as he clenches. A hot spurt of release hits my tongue, the first warning that he's about to explode. Then, Kassam erupts with a low cry, his bottom tight around my finger as I tease his prostate even as he fills my mouth with his release. He floods my tongue and down my throat, and when I pull back, he continues to come, spilling over my cheeks and chin. Carefully, I slip my finger back out and try not to look too smug as I sit up.

I've only done that once before, and the results were not

nearly as satisfying as this time. Kassam's head is thrown back and he pants wildly, as if he can't find enough air to breathe.

"I'm just going to go clean up," I purr, feeling rather proud of myself. I'm still turned on to an insane degree, but I like that I made him lose his mind. Pleased, I move back to the water's edge and wash my hands and face. My jeans are wet and feel too abrasive against my sensitized skin, so I peel them (and my soaked boots) off at the water's edge, sighing with pleasure when I'm in nothing but my panties.

A big arm wraps around my waist as I bend over. "Not so fast," Kassam murmurs as I yelp in surprise. "You deserve to have your itches scratched as well."

My heart sinks when he says that. Is that all this is to him, still? Scratching an itch? Why did I expect anything more? But then he pulls me down onto my hands and knees, and his warm breath fans over my wet panties. "That finger…that was a surprise."

"Gotta keep you on your toes," I say, breathless. "I need to represent for all mortals out there."

He chuckles. "Trust me, Carly, you are not like any mortal I know."

I decide I'm going to take that as a compliment. And when he slides the fabric of my panties aside and puts his mouth on my pussy, I don't think of anything at all. I just close my eyes and enjoy.

∼

A SHORT TIME LATER, after we're both sated, my stomach growls again and I rub it absently as I spread my jeans out on the rocks to dry. "So where are we, exactly? You said you knew?"

Kassam shrugs, petting an eagle that showed up while I was gasping for air after my fourth tongue-induced orgasm. He gazes at it thoughtfully. "The Wildlands. This place is sacred to me. Or rather, it was a thousand years ago. I'm pleased it remains the same."

"Huh," is all I say. I don't know anything about his world, and I have to admit, I'm a little worried about how...wild it is. Which is stupid. Kassam is a nature god. Of course he's going to want to hang out where there's nothing but trees and animals. It's just that...I'm a city girl. I'm already a little worried about the lack of plumbing and accessible food. Beds. Paths. Things like that. I expected us to be starting fresh when we came over to his world. I just didn't realize we'd be starting with nothing at all. I'm suddenly glad I packed my enormous bag. I move over to it, unzipping and pulling out fresh clothes and shoes. I find a protein bar and unwrap it, chewing as Kassam strokes the eagle's feathers. He's got a huge frown on his face. "What's wrong?"

He glances over at me. "My friend tells me there is a city not far from here. A day's flight, maybe a bit more. I don't like that."

"Why not?"

"Because there should be no city here. These lands are supposed to remain wild. They are my lands."

I don't point out that he's been gone for a thousand years, or that the world can change a lot in a hundred years, much less a thousand. He knows this, of course. Me, personally, I'm rather thrilled there's a city. I like the woods, but if we're going to find Seth and Margo, we'll find them near a city. Seth is absolutely not a nature god. I study him and the eagle instead. "He told you that?"

Kassam shrugs. "I see it in his thoughts."

"Should you be doing that? Am I going to have another nosebleed again?"

His mouth pulls into a frown and he glances over at me. "I... do not know." With a flick of his wrist, the eagle flies away, soaring once more. "Are you in pain?"

"No, I just want to be careful, that's all."

Kassam's expression grows pained. "I do not know how to stop reading their thoughts. They speak to me, as easily as you or I." Worried, he looks at the squirrels at his feet. "Even now, they tell me where they keep their food, and who stalks these woods at night."

I rub my forehead, but it doesn't hurt. "Maybe that's all right, then. But if I start to hurt, I'm going to need you to stop unless you want to carry me all the way to the nearest city."

He makes a grimace of disgust. "Cities. Pah."

I gesture at the pastoral scene around us. "You think Seth is somewhere around here?"

"No." Kassam looks thoughtful. "He will have directed Lachesis to send him toward the nearest settlement. We will find him there."

"Okay then, so what's the plan?" I cross my legs in the grass, and it feels cool under my bare legs and ass. I'm naked except for my bra, but I don't feel uncomfortable like this. Kassam is so easy in his own skin that it makes me relax. "How do we move forward?"

31

He is quiet for a long moment, the only movement that of his thick hair waving in the breeze. Then, he gives a fond look to the trees at the edge of the clearing, infested with birds and squirrels. The deer hover nearby, seemingly waiting for his answer as well. "We let the gods know I have returned. We gather my army, and we join Seth." Kassam clenches a fist, a surprisingly cruel grin on his face. "Then, we go after Riekki."

I'm a little concerned about that to-do list, because the expression on Kassam's face is distinctly vengeful, and it doesn't match the man—er, god—I've come to know. "Okay, let's think about this. How are you going to let the gods know you've returned if they're all here in the mortal realm?"

He crosses his arms over his chest. "I thought a show of my might. Uproot the trees from the land itself and make them walk. Wither the crops. Make the animals attack anyone that comes near. Show how angry the very earth is that I have been wronged."

I raise a finger in the air. "Hold up."

Kassam frowns at me. "What?"

"How are you going to make that happen? You're going to squeeze your anchor—that's me, by the way—so hard that when my head pops off from all the magic you're using, you'll be happy? You think a few dancing trees and rabid dogs are going to show them anything?"

His mouth pulls down, slightly sulky. "I...forgot it hurts you."

"Which is why I'm here to remind you," I say gently. "You were sent to the human world to learn a lesson, right?"

"That I am supposed to care more for humans."

Well, that's a lesson that clearly needs a bit of reminding here and there. "Okay, so let's table the whole marching trees and rabid army thing for now. We don't have the resources—as in, the magic. So what can we do to show people that you're back and ready to kick ass and take names?"

Kassam gives me a curious look. "Why would I take their names?"

I wave a hand in the air. "Just a saying. Focus, Kassam. How do we go about showing people that you're back and you mean business without killing me?"

I expect Kassam to think about it for a moment. Instead, he beams at me and moves to my side, offering a hand. I take it and get to my feet, and he cups my face and kisses my forehead. "Do you know, I think I have learned to care about humans a tiny bit? Because you mentioned that my magic might kill you, and I did not like that realization."

He looks proud of himself. "Great?"

"It would make me sad if you were to die." His smile grows wider. "Fascinating. I do not think I have ever felt this before. I wonder what it would feel like if you did die? Would I feel grief?" He looks mystified and intrigued. "I do not think I have ever felt grief before."

I pull his hands away from my face, because he's making me feel a bit like a bug that he can't decide if he wants to squash or not. "You've felt grief," I offer. "When you were trapped in my world and thought you might never make it back here. When you realized you'd been gone for a thousand years and everyone had forgotten you. That feeling is grief."

His expression falls. "It's not a good feeling."

I shake my head. "Not my favorite, no."

Just as quickly, Kassam's face brightens once more. "Which is why I have you as my anchor. So you can guide me."

I don't feel much like a guide right now. I feel completely out of my depth and I know nothing about this world, but I know how to "human" at least. "Okay, so let's focus. We find Seth, yes?"

He nods, antlers bobbing. "Once we gather my army."

"And how is it we manage that?" I pat his chest. "Keeping in mind my limitations?"

Kassam tilts his head toward the trees. "Look upon them." When I glance over, I see deer and squirrels, just like before. "They felt my return and came to me. Others will do the same, from far away. We will wait for the fiercest of creatures to come to my side, and we will ride them into the city that some fool has thought to build near my wildlands."

I regard the deer, who even now look as if they're waiting for Kassam to put a hand out so they can join him at his side again. Nothing hurts, so maybe he's right and his presence just attracts them. If so, I guess we can build an army easily enough, though I'm a little worried at what's going to come out of the woodwork. "So we wait for a few days? Is that what you're saying?"

He nods.

"I guess we can hang out for a bit. It probably makes sense to bring an army." I glance up at him. "You're sure that army won't eat me, by the way?"

"They will smell me on you and know that you are claimed."

His look grows positively feral and he tugs me into his arms again.

I can guess how we're going to spend the time waiting for his army to arrive.

～

For the next two days, I eat my weight in fruit and raw vegetables, make love with Kassam at least once an hour, and sleep. So much sleeping and eating. It's like now that we're back in his world, the anchor-bond is magnified a dozen times, and I'm always stuffing my face with either food or his cock.

Hedonism is exhausting. Fun, but exhausting.

I think it even wears Kassam out. He says he doesn't need to sleep—and I don't think I've ever seen him do so—but every now and then, he wanders off into the woods by himself and just "breathes in his surroundings." It might be a form of meditation. It might be him just appreciating being back...or it might be him needing a break from me for an hour or two.

I totally get it. Even though I love having sex with him, sometimes it's nice to take a moment to breathe.

After about four days of waiting, the glade and all its surroundings are teeming with animals of every kind and shape imaginable. There are foxes and badgers and mice, and some other small creatures I don't recognize. The deer that appear grow bigger in size by the day, some with shaggy hides and enormous racks of antlers. Kassam says they're a mountain breed. There's also a creature called a woale, which looks like a cross between a hippo and a rhino with no horns. There are goats, and sheep, and antelope, and a type of horned elk so tall that it can eat the highest branches. There are birds of every kind, from songbirds to enormous eagles that are so large the branches of the trees dip underneath their weight.

There are predators, too. I try to keep my distance from

them because I'm skittish and afraid something will eat me, but they lurk at the edges of the clearing. Enormous wildcats with shaggy manes and dangerous fangs approach in entire prides, and wolf packs appear by the dozens. There are snakes and lizards, both big enough that they terrify me on sight. And there are some creatures straight out of a fairy tale that I've never seen before. Flying birds the size of houses that fly overhead and cast obscenely large shadows. Ground-prowling things with eagle-like heads and lionlike bodies. Gigantic worms with multiple heads and feelers that wreck the trees and pick fights with the gargantuan birds. I'm pretty sure I saw a centaur or two, but they keep their distance from me.

No dragons appear, which disappoints Kassam. "This world was once full of dragon-kind," he tells me as he regards his growing army, sprawling through the woods as far as the eye can see. "Perhaps if any live, they are ignoring my presence, like the clans are."

"Clans?" I ask.

"Ogres and goblins. Troll clans. If they yet exist, they are not answering the call." He shrugs. "It is just as well."

I want to tell him to send the gigantic worms and more monstrous things away, too, but I guess if we're making an army, we need the scariest creatures more than the deer. So I do my best to ignore them and they ignore me, too.

"When will we be ready to go?" I ask Kassam at one point.

"Soon," is all he says.

∼

AFTER A WEEK OF THIS, I watch one of the eagles tear apart a songbird that just laid there for them, and decide I need to get away for a bit. The wild is sometimes a bit "much" for me. Shoving my boots on, I glance around for Kassam. I find him near the edge of the pool, his eyes closed as birds rest in his antlers and a fox cradles between his thighs. Rabbits curl up against him, quivering at the sight of me, and I decide not to disturb him. He's having his "me" time and I want some of my own.

I turn around and head off into the trees.

The animals of all kinds part as I approach, making room for me. I take a few steps into the woods, and when they continue to trail behind me, I stop. "No, guys. This is break time. Potty time."

One of the deer watches me with dark, sweet eyes, an ear flicking. That face is so beautiful that it just reinforces that I need to get away for a bit. I have issues watching the gentler animals just lie down so the carnivores can eat them. Kassam says it's all part of the wild, and I know it's the circle of life and yadda yadda, but it's so hard for me to watch. I've been thinking of them like pets, but they're not pets. They're wild animals gathered into a very small area and my sheltered human brain is having a difficult time processing it.

"No one follow me," I say again, and when I take a few more steps into the woods, I'm relieved that the train of animals seems to be listening. I step away from the deer, and the big-as-tigers wildcats, and the griffins and everything else. I keep walking through the trees until the clustered animal "army" thins out and then there's just nothing but quiet trees around me, the only sound the rustle of leaves.

I feel like I can breathe. The tug of the bond between myself and Kassam is starting to pull, like a tight muscle, but it's not so bad. I'm farther from him than I've ever been before, but I'm not actually trying to *leave* him and so I think it's giving me a bit of leeway. I just need a few moments to myself, to gather my thoughts. So I walk through the woods, and when the bond starts to tug too hard, I turn back just enough for it to stop pulling and keep wandering. I'm not being foolish by heading away from camp—none of the creatures there will harm me, no matter how fierce they look, and there are no cities near here. It's just me catching my breath, because the realities of what a "wild army" is sometimes gets to me. I know griffins and bears have to eat. I just wish they wouldn't eat the sad-eyed deer, and right in front of me.

I'm thinking about those sad-eyed deer as I brush my fingers over a leafy fern, bright with flowers. Everything in the vicinity is in full bloom and flowering, as if simply being near Kassam is making the entire forest vibrant with health. It means plenty of fruit to eat, even if it doesn't fill me up much. After the last week spent watching the army gather, I'm not sure I could ever eat a steak again. I've watched too many meat-eaters relish their meals recently.

A twig snaps somewhere nearby.

The small hairs on the back of my neck stand up and I glance around. I see nothing, but that doesn't mean anything at all. It could be one of the deer, who camouflage well, or one of the snakes, climbing up a tree for...snake business. I actually don't know what snakes do, now that I think of it. I look for a face, or horns, or something that will indicate to me who or what is approaching, but I see nothing but greenery. Frowning, I turn around again to head back—

—and hear growling.

Growling coming from a very, very large creature. My skin prickles with fear, and I know something's wrong. There are wolves at camp—there have been wolves at camp for days. Huge ones, with thick, shaggy fur and pointed ears. They're ferocious and terrifying looking, but the ones at camp ignore me. As do the bears, the lions, and even the horrible worm-creatures with multiple heads that Kassam calls dustwyrms. No one growls at me.

So...now I have a problem.

I pat my hands on my muddy, stiff jeans, but I've got no weapon with me. I haven't needed one, and now I'm regretting that bitterly. My Styx T-shirt won't do anything for me, either, but I'm wearing my belt. Slowly, I unbuckle it and pull it free from the loops. "Who's out there?"

More growling. It sounds deep and ominous and my heart races with terror.

Something moves up ahead. I turn, and watch, terrified, as a gargantuan wolf of midnight black melts out of the shadows and takes a step toward me. The eyes are a glowing, feral yellow. He's enormous, as big as the other wolves that make up part of Kassam's army, but where those just seem wild, this one seems...sinister. Like night and anger personified. He takes a step forward, baring white teeth, and I catch a glint of gold against his black nose.

He keeps growling, even as he prowls toward me.

I take a step backward, clutching my belt against my chest. "In case you can't smell it, I'm Kassam's anchor," I call out. "Maybe you've forgotten, but you're not supposed to attack me. It's cool. I won't hold a grudge."

The wolf's lips curl back, the snarl growing deeper.

Another snarl picks up behind me.

Then to the side.

I look over to my left and then to my right as more of those creepy, shadowy wolves appear, stalking toward me. Each one is midnight black, and as I gasp and take another step backward, I notice the one closest to me has a ring in his nose also. They all do. "If you guys are someone's pets, you should know—"

One lunges for me before I can finish my sentence.

I scream. Using my belt as a whip, I strike the closest wolf across the nose. Another one lunges at me, but there's no time for me to strike it. It shoves me into the dirt and my chin hits a root. I sprawl on my stomach, the wind knocked out of me. Dimly, I'm aware that I'm about to die, and I think of Kassam. He's going to be so upset...

Jaws latch around my arm, and the wolf shakes it wildly. My belt goes flying, and I cry out in pain.

A heavy weight sprawls on top of me and I realize another one of the wolves is lying over me. He growls and I go still, terrified. But the other wolf drops my arm and I snatch it under my body protectively. My skin is torn to shreds and hurts like hell, and I brace myself, eyes closed and face scrunched up, as I wait for the end.

Nothing attacks me. There's an animalistic snort, almost disgusted, and then teeth scrape against my back. I freeze. In the next moment, the wolf hauls me up by my T-shirt, the collar chokingly tight, and drags me.

Oh. Clutching my wounded arm, I remain limp, watching as the others file in next to the leader—the one that has me—and move at his side. "Hey," I try again, since they don't seem to be attacking me. One of the wolves walking close by has that glint of gold in his nose, and the sight of it reminds me that they might be someone's pets. "Good doggy. Put me down?"

The wolves ignore me. If they're someone's pet, they're not friendly pets.

Okay then, time for a new plan. The wolf dragging me is easily the size of a Clydesdale, so I suspect he can drag my ass all over this forest without getting tired. Something tells me he's not going to stop, either. I clutch my bleeding arm, and when the collar of my T-shirt cuts into my neck, it gives me an idea.

I go limp, throwing my arms up. In the next moment, I slide out of my overstretched T-shirt and tumble onto the ground. The moment I hit dirt, I scramble to my feet, grabbing the nearest plant to brace myself. I run—

Only to have one of the wolves tackle me and drop me into the dirt again. Immediately, I'm surrounded by the snarling pack, and I curl up in a ball as they loom over me.

Teeth grab the leg of my jeans and there's a deep warning

snarl. I can just imagine what it's saying. Don't fucking try that again, human. "I get the picture," I whisper, cradling my hurt arm protectively against my breasts. "Message received."

My head bounces off of a root as they yank me along, and I groan with pain. This is going to be a rough ride. I twist in my jeans, but one of the wolves lunges at me, snarling, and I yelp, curling up again protectively. Maybe they're taking me back to camp. Maybe—

The tether between myself and Kassam stretches, pulls tight. I let out a whimper as pain washes over me. "Stop," I call out. "I can't leave. Stop!"

The wolves ignore me. One growls, a low warning, but to the rest, my pain is insignificant.

The tether grows painful, and I cry out, twisting wildly. "Stop! Stop!"

They never stop, though, and it wracks my body, worse than anything I've ever experienced before. It feels as if I'm being pulled apart from inside, and I scream, and scream, and scream. The wolves never let me go, and no matter how much I twist and struggle to break free, they don't release me, either.

The pain just keeps coming, and I drown inside it, utterly lost.

32

The throb of my injured arm wakes me from my sleep. Carefully, I keep my eyes closed and pretend to be sleeping, remembering the pack of unearthly wolves that dragged me away. My skin feels scratched up all over my back and stomach, and my bra is pushed up past my breasts and around my neck. Terrified of what that means, I mentally assess my body. My jeans are still on, so I don't think anyone has molested me. I tug my bra back down to cover my tits, and as I do, grass, leaves and dirt fall out of it. Okay, it must have crawled up my body when the wolves dragged me. It occurs to me that other than being banged up and my arm throbbing, I'm not in pain. The horrible, excruciating pain that comes with the tether between myself and Kassam being stretched past its limits.

That means he must be nearby. He's come for me. Exhaling in relief, I look around.

I'm in some ancient stone building. Or maybe it was a building once, but there's no roof. There's only broken pillars framing a thick stone floor, and I'm reminded of the Greek ruins of the Parthenon. Grass pushes its way between the enormous flagstones that make up the floor, and between the crumbled pillars, there are enormous, heavy pots with withered plants inside them. Everything's covered in dust and detritus from neglect. The wolves are nowhere to be seen. They must have brought me here and dumped me.

As I sit up, I notice that I'm at the top of a set of five heavy stone steps that lead up to a dais. Getting to my feet, I dust off my filthy jeans (a useless action) and look behind me. I've been left at the base of an altar.

Not just any altar. A pair of carved antlers that loom over the slab of weathered stone make it very clear whose altar it is. My mouth goes dry at the realization, and I stare at the dead flowers, animal skulls, and pelts that cover every inch of the surface. They're all ancient and faded, as if the people who left the offerings gave up long ago. All of this has been abandoned for a very, very long time. I turn, gazing out past the pillars. I can see the thick forest in the distance, but around the broken temple is nothing but knee-high, waving grasses. There are no roads, no homes, no nothing. Just an abandoned temple in the middle of nowhere.

I'm positive I was brought here to send a message, and my skin prickles with the realization.

"CARLY!"

It's Kassam. He's somewhere in the distance, shouting my name. I race down the steps—

—only to have one of the gargantuan shadow wolves appear, blocking my path. It looks at me as I skid to a halt and growls.

Okay, then. I get the picture. I cup my hands to my mouth. "I'm here!"

"Carly!" I watch as a tall form emerges from the trees and races toward the temple, toward me. I remain where I am, bouncing on my toes, because I can't wait for him to come and get me. I feel safe at his side. Protected. And right now, I need to feel safe desperately.

More wolves slink out of the shadows, until the temple has at least a dozen of them lurking in wait. "Be careful," I shout. "There are wolves everywhere!"

I watch as he approaches, moving with speed, and then his steps slow the closer he gets to the temple. He regards my surroundings with a grim expression, and that grim expression turns to dismay as he sees the wolves. I could swear that he pales underneath his sun-kissed tan, and that worries me.

"Are you okay?" I call out. "Will they hurt you?"

"They will not," he says, voice oddly stilted as he takes a step into the temple, toward me. "They are sending me a message." He gazes at the nearest one for so long that I worry he's been put under a spell of some kind. I try to move toward him, but one of the wolves blocks me, moving subtly into my path. It's clear that they want him to come to me and not the other way around. He tears his gaze away from the wolves and focuses on me. His expression darkens at the sight of my bloody arm. "They hurt you?"

Something about this feels off. Odd. They could have torn me to shreds a dozen times over but all they did was force me to put down the belt I was using as a weapon. "I'm a little banged up, but I'm all right. Are you okay?"

He looks awfully pale, his expression tight as he moves to my side and runs his hands over my bare arms, frowning at my scratches and especially at the bite on my arm. "I don't like this."

"It'll heal. I don't think they were trying to hurt me. Just scare me."

Kassam continues to touch me all over, as if he has to determine for himself that I truly am all right. His mouth remains a flat, unhappy line, and when he's satisfied that I'm not in danger, he pulls me against him and wraps his arms around me, tucking me against his chest.

"Wh-what are you doing?" I manage.

"I am hugging you. You like hugs. Now hush."

I'm not sure if I'm the one that needs comforting right now or if it's him. Kassam continues to hold me tight, his chin resting atop my head as he strokes my head and then my back. Leaves and debris rain out of my shoulder-length hair, and I can only imagine how rough I look right now. He's right, though—the hug does feel good. It's soothing some deep, worried kernel deep inside me. "Thank you for coming after me."

"I will always come after you," he vows, surprisingly fervent.

"Right, because of the bond."

"Because you belong to me," Kassam corrects. "You are my wife."

I'd forgotten.

He is quiet for a long moment and then says, in a ragged voice, "This is one of my temples."

"I noticed."

"The offerings..." He turns his head slightly, his chin rubbing against the top of my head, and I know he's gazing at the altar. "They came here. They prayed to me even when I was gone, and it did them no good. They still hoped I would be here to answer them, and I could not." His grip tightens on me as he squeezes me against him. "I am feeling grief again, Carly, and I do not like it. How do I make it stop?"

"You can't," I say softly. "The only thing you can do is learn how to live with it. To find enough pleasure in other things that it takes the edge off the grief."

"I do not like it," he says again, his voice rough as he holds me even tighter. "A god cursed with hedonism should not have to feel grief."

It's my turn to comfort. We're still hugging, so I rub his back gently and snuggle against his chest. He smells like the woods, earthy and full of fresh air and grass, and I find it instantly soothing. "I think part of the reason you're here is so you do feel those things," I point out. "So you learn what it's like to care."

He grunts. When I pull back to look up at him, his gaze is glued to that altar. "I wonder how long it took for them to realize they had been abandoned."

"Don't think like that," I protest. "You're not being fair to yourself. It's not as if you planned for Riekki to betray you. You're not to blame for your followers leaving."

He frowns down at me, and his gaze goes to my arm. He gently takes my wrist in his grip and shakes his head. "And I am so powerless I cannot even heal this. Truly, the High Father aims to humble his sons." Kassam rubs his thumb over the inside of my wrist. "Does it pain you much?"

"It's okay," I say, deciding not to go into too much detail. I don't want him feeling worse than he already does. "Give it a day and it'll feel good as new." Unless I contract rabies, but I decide not to point that out.

"I should clean them for you," Kassam declares. "I will carry you back to our waterfall and I will tend to your wounds, and then I will lick your cunt until you forget all about this place."

Something tells me I'm not the one that needs to forget about this place, but if Kassam wants to lose himself in hedonism for a bit to ease the pain, I get it. And if I get a few hours of mind-blowing oral sex out of it? I'd be a madwoman to complain. "It'll make me feel better," I admit. "But what about the wolves?"

To my surprise, he rolls his eyes. "The *conmac*. Always with the power plays." His expression hardens and he glances over his shoulder. "You've proved your point. You've shown me the temple and she is appropriately scared. Good job. Hopefully you are satisfied now."

One of the wolves moves forward, growling low in his

throat. He stalks a short distance away from us, circling, as the others watch from the shadows.

I'm still a little thrown by his words. "*Conmac*? These are your wolf sons? The ones you forced to defend your forests?" No wonder they don't seem pleased to see him. Somewhere under those shiny midnight coats and glowing yellow eyes are people. Fae people, but people nevertheless.

"I cannot read their thoughts like the birds," Kassam says, a frown on his face. "They are not truly wild, despite their forms. They are choosing to be nature's creatures, even though the fae were born in Belara's realm." He lifts his chin, indicating the wolves. "You have proved your point. Change back so we may speak on this."

The wolf in front of us sits down on his haunches. I could almost swear he's displeased. Another rubs his nose, the golden ring flashing.

Kassam sucks in a breath. He clutches my shoulder tightly, and his body goes stiff.

"Are you okay?"

"I am feeling more grief, Carly." There is a panicked note in his voice. "I need it to stop."

"Why? What's wrong?" I glance at him, then at the wolves that watch him so very patiently. I can't recall everything he told me about them, just that he gave them wolf-skins so they could run through the forests and...I watch as another rubs his nose with one large, dangerous-looking paw, the ring glinting in the late afternoon sunlight. A new idea occurs to me. "They can't change back, can they?"

Kassam stares out at the wolves, his expression hollow. "I told you that I forced them to guard the forests, yes?"

I nod.

"They did not wish to serve. They refused, and I grew angry that they were being selfish. So I...forced them into their skins. Locked them into their wolf forms with a magic ring that I promised to remove once the Anticipation was over." His jaw clenches. "They are...still waiting. They have been waiting all this time."

Oh. Oh god. "They've been wolves—"

"All this time. Yes. And even now, I cannot free them. Because the magic I used to bind them into their forms is only available to me—"

"—when you return. Which means I need to die."

The look he gives me is fierce. "You're not going to die. We're going to figure a way around it, *wife.*"

The way he says "wife" is utterly charged, as if daring me to dispute him. "Okay," I say softly, sensing he's fraying a bit at the edges. "We'll add this to our to-do list. We take down Riekki, get you home, and free the wolves."

"The *conmac.*" Kassam suddenly looks very, very tired. "I have done you wrong, my wolf sons. I swear I will make it up to you. Somehow."

The wolves merely blink their glowing yellow eyes at us.

33

"They hate me," Kassam says dully as I place sticks in the makeshift fire pit we've created.

I'm not entirely sure what to say to that. Being trapped as a wolf for a thousand-plus years? Yeah, I could definitely see them hating him. But Kassam doesn't seem to be handling this well, so I try to gentle my response. "I'm sure they're unhappy, but we're doing everything we can. They've waited this long, they can wait a few more weeks."

"It is their right to hate me." Kassam picks up one of the twigs out of the fire pit I'm carefully arranging and tosses it away in frustration. "I was selfish and trapped them. I never thought anything would happen to me. I was foolish and arrogant."

When he reaches for another stick, I smack his hand, earning myself a scowl. "I'm trying to build a fire here."

"Why?" he asks, sulky.

I gesture at the skies. "Because it's going to rain. There's a storm coming in." I add a few more of the twigs and sticks I carefully gathered on our silent walk back to the glade, trying not to lose my temper. It's been a shitty day for me, too, what with being attacked and all, and now it's getting cold. It's almost dark, the temperature is dropping, and we have no shelter. The magic wolves, the *conmac*, have followed us back to the glade and are even now snarling their anger from the shadows.

And now Kassam is upset and taking it out on me, because there's no one else to take it out on.

At my mention of the weather, though, he turns his face to the heavens. When rolling thunder crackles overhead, his expression becomes even more downcast. "Do you hear that? Aron, Lord of Storms, is back in his domain." He glares at the skies. "I am trapped here, and my brothers return to their rightful homes."

"That means that his anchor is dead," I shoot back. "Do you really want that?"

"You know I do not!" Kassam gets to his feet, storming away. "I do not want to feel this guilt, either. Or this grief. I am tired of these human emotions, Carly. I do not like it!"

I give up on the fire. It's not like I know how to make a flame anyhow. Tossing down the sticks, I trail after Kassam. The deer follow me, licking at my hand and nibbling at my jeans and making cute nuisances of themselves. He is by the water, his arms crossed over his chest, absolutely glowering. I move to his side and rub his back, trying to think of the words to comfort him. What exactly do you say to someone that fucked over a bunch of people for a thousand years?

I decide a distraction is the best medicine. Patting his back, I offer, "Do you want a finger in your ass to make you feel better?"

"Do not make me laugh, Carly. I am upset. Truly." He struggles to keep his face straight, and I can tell that Kassam is pleased that I made a joke, but he's still punishing himself. "I have disappointed the *conmac*. I have abandoned the faithful." He shakes his head. "I dreamed of returning for so long, and I did not realize I would be coming back to"—he gestures at his surroundings—"this."

"A glade full of friendly deer and pissy wolves?"

He scowls at me. "Ruined temples. Furious *conmac*." His jaw clenches. "I feel very, very guilty, and it is not something I have expected to feel." Kassam leans closer to me. "I can feel them all watching me. They stare at me as if they are waiting for me to disappear again. I know this, and I know they have a reason to fear it, and it still makes me feel...very, very bad."

I take his hand in mine, lacing my fingers with his. "Don't you think that's maybe the point?" At Kassam's glare, I continue. "You were sent to the mortal realm for a reason, remember? You told me the High Father cast out the gods when he felt they needed to learn a lesson. I'm guessing this is part of the lesson you're supposed to learn."

"What guilt feels like?" he grumbles.

"Not just that. Maybe you're supposed to realize that actions have consequences. That you can't always push to get your way and expect everyone to be happy with it. Maybe you're supposed to realize that if you want your followers to love you—the human ones," I correct, gently nudging my hip against a too-friendly doe. "If you want them to love you, you need to be there for them. You need to appreciate them."

"I do not like learning lessons," he admits, his tone sullen. "It does not feel good."

"It never does, but it's valuable to learn so you won't do it again in the future." I give his hand a squeeze. "So you need to acknowledge the guilt, and the sadness, and remember this so you can be a better god of the wild when you return to your home. Understand?"

Kassam looks over at me, and his expression is bleak as he searches my face. "They could have killed you to send me home. I realized that when I saw you in the temple, covered in blood. They could have killed you and I would have been powerless to stop it. That terrifies me."

I'm stunned at his words. He was worried about me? That's why he's in such a shitty mood? It's not just guilt driving him—it's realizing that I was in very real danger and he would have been too late to do anything about it. My sunshine nature god is realizing that this is a big deal, finally. That this isn't just a fun, hedonistic lark through the woods. That I could die, and the *conmac* could be cursed forever, and that there are real consequences.

I feel a little sorry for him, but I'm also glad he's figuring this out. "If it makes you feel any better, I don't think they would have killed me. They know I belong to you and if they want you to turn them back, they probably don't want to piss you off."

"Or they're too lost in their wolf minds to think about such things, and I arrived just in time before instinct told them to eat a very tasty prize," he grumbles.

I'm pretty sure the *conmac* are more "there" than he's giving them credit for. When I look at them, I see wolves, true, but I also see an otherworldly intelligence. I think about how the one bit me just enough to make me release my belt. There's still a human mind in there.

Or wait, fae.

Kassam looks so glum that it makes me ache. Impulsively, I stand on my tiptoes and tug him down, just enough to kiss his cheek.

He gives me a surprised look. "Why did you do that?"

"Because you're sweet. And because you seemed to need it."

He thinks for a long moment and then asks, "Can I have a hug?"

My heart melts. I know he's joked a dozen times that gods don't feel anything for mortals, but this mortal is definitely starting to catch some feelings for this god. I release his hand and hold my arms out. "Of course you can have a hug."

Kassam moves into my embrace, hugging me tightly and wrapping his big arms around me. He's naked—always naked—and for a moment I think it might be a come on, that he's just pulling me in close because he wants to get me naked. But then he sighs with contentment, his head dropping to rest against mine and he just...holds me.

And I hold him.

And...it's lovely. It's nice to just hug one another, to just breathe in each other's skin and share space, comforting with simple touches. I rub my hands up and down his back, murmuring soft words. I tell him that it'll be okay. That everything will work out. That I'm right here at his side.

"I am home, but I still feel lost," he confesses, his breath teasing my hair.

I run my hand up his spine. "I'm here with you. We'll figure this out together, I promise. You're not alone in this."

Kassam pulls out of the hug, his arms still around me. He gazes down at me, and his normally laughing face is somber. "I would be lost without you, little light."

"You'd be fine," I say automatically. "Anyone would be willing to be your anchor. I hear the benefits are pretty good."

He shakes his head, not amused by my joke. "I would be lost without you, my Carly. You have been strong and determined through all of this. I have had anchors in the past, but I do not remember any of them. They are faceless."

"Old memories—"

"No. Even when they were at my side, they were faceless. I did not care about them. I did not care if they lived or died, if they were happy or sad. I did not care if they abandoned their families to join me. But with you...I care." He strokes my cheek gently. "I will remember you, always."

A strange knot forms in my throat, and I don't know how to

respond to that. He's obviously forgotten that I'm Carly the unfinisher, the woman who never sees anything through. Even right now, the urge to run away from his heartfelt words is strong. I'm not good at relationships. I'm not good at forever. But Kassam has never promised me forever, and that steadies me a little. I give him a saucy wink. "You're just saying that because I gave your prostate a tickle."

Kassam chuckles, his thumb moving across my skin to tease my lower lip. "You are very proud of yourself for that, you know."

"I should be. You're a god. I have to figure out how to one-up you when you go all hedonism on me. I can't have you bored."

He shakes his head. "I'm never bored with you. It's strange to realize that, but even in the quiet moments, when we are not touching, I like your company." He strokes my lip again, his expression thoughtful. "Do you still not want me to kiss you? On the lips?"

Oh. Are we going there?

My heart flutters. "It's just...I know we're in this to scratch each other's itches. But for me, if we add kisses, it has to mean something. It has to be more than just responding to a base need. Does that make sense?"

"And if I tell you I still want to kiss you, my wife?" His eyes are molten silver.

Heat blooms through my body, and I feel...warm. Happy. Today has been absolute shit but I forget all of it in this moment. I gaze up at him, and then nod, almost shy. "Then we can kiss."

Kassam leans in, and his lips graze mine in the lightest caress. As kisses go, it's just a tease, and I decide that if that's all I get, I'm going to riot. He can't say things like that and then just butterfly-peck me. He—

The god captures my chin, angling my mouth, and then *consumes* me. His mouth devours mine, hungry and seeking and desperate. I meet him with equal urgency, desperate to lose myself in the pleasure of his embrace. His tongue strokes against mine, deep and certain and ravenous. This is familiar, this utterly consuming hedonism, and I moan against him.

"No," Kassam murmurs, and pulls away slightly to gaze down at me. "No, I am going to savor this today. This is not hedonism. This is Kassam and his wife, Carly."

I gaze at him, surprised. He pulls me against him once more and then tugs me down onto the soft grass. As he does, the deer nearby move away, and we're alone—or as alone as one can be in a clearing full of magically called wild animals of all kinds. He holds me against him, searching my face before he leans in to carefully kiss me again. Instead of the frantic, desperate need of before, this kiss is soft. Tender. It's like he realizes I'm not going anywhere, and he can slow down and enjoy. The kiss changes, and he licks at my mouth as if I'm a delicious treat that must be savored. I whimper against his mouth, digging my hands into his tangled, thick hair.

"My wife," he breathes against my lips, and it's the sexiest thing I've ever heard.

He caresses my breast through the cup of my bra, teasing my nipple until I'm pressing up against him with hunger. I forget about the wolves, the shitty day we've had, my endlessly growling stomach, everything in light of his touch. When he undresses me, it's with reverent fingers, as if he's seeing me for the first time. He touches me all over, skimming his hands along my flesh and watching me with such awe that everything feels different. When he touches me between my thighs, I gasp and cling to his neck, our gazes locked as I ride his hand until he makes me come. As I shudder with my release, he works me with delicate touches, whispering about how beautiful I am, how special, and that I belong to him and no one else. It's a bit of possessiveness tangled with the sweet, and it absolutely makes me hot.

When he pulls me into his lap and seats me atop his cock, it means that we're making love facing each other. There's no getting away from looking at him, not like when we're in missionary style and I can just close my eyes and lose myself to the feelings. This feels ten times more intimate, and I cup his face and kiss him as he rocks his hips in time with me moving over him. Kassam gazes at me the entire time, not breaking eye contact once, and just the intensity of his stare adds another level of arousal. I come again, lost in his eyes, and then come a third time before he comes.

I collapse against his chest, sweaty and sated, even as I'm still speared atop him. He presses delicate kisses to my face and murmurs my name over and over again, and I don't think I've ever felt more cherished or more seen in a relationship.

It's absolutely wonderful...and absolutely terrifying.

I know this thing with Kassam isn't going to last. I'm his "little light," his expendable human sidekick. For all that he's feeling things right now, it's not going to last. He's said himself he's had plenty of anchors before and he can't remember their faces. He probably won't remember mine once this is over, and I resign myself to that fact. He can call me "wife" all he wants, but the reality is, he's a god and I'm a mortal. Meeting Seth made me start to realize just how vast that gap can be.

But that's something to worry about tomorrow. For now I cuddle against Kassam and run my hands over his skin. "I'm here," I whisper. "I'm here." He needs me right now. Maybe he won't in the future, but at least I can be there for him right now.

34

I wake up the next morning to the sound of the griffins screaming.

I jerk upright, terrified as two of the largest griffins settle in the clearing, clawing at one another with their oversized eagle-like beaks. Nearby, Kassam watches with an almost bored expression that turns to a smile at the sight of me. "My little light," Kassam declares. "You are awake."

"I don't think anyone could sleep through that," I point out, moving to his side and carefully avoiding the griffins that circle and snap at one another. They won't attack me—they're obedient, unlike the *conmac*—but it doesn't mean I can't be accidentally trampled by a clawed foot. "I've never heard anything so damn loud."

Kassam just chuckles and slings an arm around my shoulders, pressing a kiss to my temples. "I seem to recall someone crying out just as loud last night as she rode my lap—"

I smack him lightly to silence him, blushing. Okay, so I get a little loud during sex. But it's not griffin-loud. The griffins are screaming at the top of their lungs, and they sound like cats in heat—or cats that have been stepped on—but with megaphones strapped to their faces. I've never heard anything like it, and it's completely jarring. "Why are they so mad?"

"They are not mad. They are vying for who will have the honor of carrying us as we lead our army."

Oh. "Are we going then?"

Kassam nods. "Today. With the return of the *conmac*, I have realized that there is no point in waiting. If someone wishes to join us, they will have done so. We cannot wait forever for my glorious return. I am needed back in my realm, where I can make a difference. I am stranded here, powerless and weak, and I hate it."

"You make it sound terrible," I say lightly, trying not to feel hurt. It's stupid to feel hurt. Of course he hates being stuck in the mortal realm.

"It is terrible," he agrees, then looks over at me as I slip out from under his arm. "You are the only thing that makes this bearable, my Carly, but I plan on having you at my side when I return, so why waste time?"

Why indeed. He says it so flippantly, despite the fact that we still haven't figured out the whole "the anchor needs to die" part of his return. He swears we will, but I haven't yet heard a solution. I'm trying not to worry because Kassam *promised* me. Even so…I can't help but think about it. "I see. So where are we taking the army again?"

"The birds whisper that there is a city of some size to the west of my resting place."

"Resting place?"

His sunny expression darkens. "The Blood Glacier."

Shit. Right. "Ah."

"I am not happy there is a city so near the mountains," he continues on as the griffins scream at one another again, and I wince, instinctively drawing closer to Kassam again. He pulls me against him automatically. "These lands are supposed to be wild. But I suppose I cannot fault those that settled in my territory when I was silent." He glances down at me. "If Lachesis has left Seth nearby, he will be there."

"So we take our army." I gesture at the animals that teem in the clearing and spread into the woods beyond. "And then what?"

His eyes gleam cruelly, and for a moment, he no longer looks like my cheery Kassam, but like a vengeful god. "Then we find Riekki and make her pay."

~

TRAVELING AT THE HEAD OF A "WILD" army is...unlike anything I've ever experienced before. As we move out, the noise is deafening—birds calling, wolves howling, lions roaring, mountain goats bleating—it all rises into an endless cacophony that probably announces our presence before we come into sight. It's a slow-moving army, because even the animals with the shortest legs are valued as part of the "team" and so our army stretches out as far as the eye can see, across the rolling plains toward the snow-capped mountains in the west. The griffins finally settle on who is going to be Kassam's mount, and since our army is mostly ground-based, Kassam insists upon riding at the front instead of flying.

Because I'm an absolute weenie and not a horsewoman, I spend my time clinging to Kassam's back as we ride atop the largest griffin with no saddle of any kind. Sometimes he rides at the front, and sometimes the griffin flies along the winding path of the army, as if encouraging the back end to catch up. I'm amazed at the sheer number of animals that make up the barking, chirping, screeching, howling, hissing army.

The *conmac* slither in and out of the woods like shadows, darting amongst the trees at the edges of the army and appearing only long enough to remind us that they're still with us. Sometimes they're out of sight for so long that I start to wonder if they've gone, but then they appear once more. The message is clear—they're as reluctant to be part of this now as they were a thousand years ago.

We march onward, and as the zoo of an army trickles across the plains and toward the mountains, we leave a path of destruction in our wake. The grasses are trampled, the trees are stripped of their leaves from the herbivores, and skeletons line the edges of the path as the carnivores eat part of the army that marches toward the setting sun. When we fly overhead to supervise, it looks like a black stain moving over the countryside, and Kassam only clucks his tongue when I point out what sort of destruction he's causing. "They know it is my right to avenge myself against Riekki," is all he says. "They give their lives for me. Every tree, every rodent, every buck that dies in this fashion does so in my name, and they will be honored."

As I watch the *conmac* take down a bawling antelope, I don't know that I agree. This seems like…a lot. And Kassam isn't supposed to be a god of vengeance or of war. He's supposed to be a lover, not a fighter. I don't get it.

When we reach the Blood Glacier, though…I absolutely get it.

For some reason, I thought the glacier would be a "past tense" sort of thing. After all, Kassam is free and in my arms, and I thought it would just…disappear. But as we get closer to the mountains, a coppery, salty smell tinges the air and I see what looks like a dark blot against the horizon. As we get closer, it looks like a giant, dark red carpet spreading between the craggy rocks, and I realize what I'm looking at.

Oh god.

There's so much of it.

I'm staggered as the army approaches the Blood Glacier. I don't know what I expected, but not this. Not to see Kassam's frozen blood for as far as the eye can see. Not to smell the thick, awful reek of it hanging in the air, or to see animals feasting on the meltwater. The flies that buzz around it, or the fact that the grasses are dead the closer we approach.

It's enormous. And this all came from Kassam, who was abandoned, left bleeding and stuck between worlds.

It only takes half a day to cross it, but it feels like forever. As the wild army trudges over the groaning ice, the smell of it gags me, as does the sight of the blood staining the legs of the crossing animals. Kassam is utterly silent, and I touch him to let him know that I'm here, that I'm with him, that he's no longer trapped. It doesn't help his mood, though, and I don't blame him.

For the first time, I get it. I get why he's so furious at Riekki. All this because Kassam wouldn't marry her? She caused him a thousand years of misery all because he turned her down? It's because of her that he lost all his followers. It's because of her selfish, petty actions that the *conmac* were trapped just as much as Kassam was.

There's nothing I can say to him that will make this better. There's nothing I can say, nothing I can do that will make this pain go away for him. It doesn't matter that he's cursed with hedonism—some things are deeper than pleasure. So when we camp that night, and Kassam takes me in his arms and fucks me like a demon, I get it. I cling to him as I come, and I whisper only one thing in his ear.

"We're going to make her pay," I promise my husband.

With a growl, he comes inside me, and I hold him as he quakes with the force of his release. It doesn't matter that he ejaculates inside me. We're long past condoms, just like we're long past forgiveness.

We're in this until the bitter end.

35

It feels like I'm the only one in the army that has to sleep. Kassam doesn't, and the rest of the animals are a honking, braying, snarling mess. Because of that, and because we're always moving, I insist that we keep moving. We stop every now and then for bodily functions and for me to eat some fruit or vegetables that Kassam forages for me. When food is scarce for me as well as his army, he pulls on his magic and I end up with a nasty nosebleed and a migraine, but I bear them as stoically as I can. This is bigger than a headache, I remind myself.

But sleep is the tough one. I finally figure out how to catnap with my cheek pressed to Kassam's back, my hands tied around his waist so I don't slide off the back of the griffin. Fatigue makes it difficult for me to keep track of where we are, and after we pass the glacier, I lose any sense of where we're going. Between naps, I see the mountains receding and a thick, endless forest in the distance. Then we're closer to the forest, and when I wake again, we're deep in its branches. Sometime in the middle of the night, I rouse again and lift my head to look at our surroundings. The stars overhead are brilliant, but I see more lights in the distance. It takes me a moment to realize that I'm seeing a settlement at the edge of the horizon. "Is that..."

"The city," Kassam agrees. "It must be. Those are human lights."

"We'll be there soon, then?"

"Some time tomorrow. Rest for now." He pats my arm gently. "I have you."

The city, I realize. The city that Seth should be in. I don't know if I'm excited or a little scared to go face to face with him again. My injured arm throbs as I squeeze Kassam's sides. Holding tight to him makes me feel better, and we ride on through the night and onto the morning. As it grows light outside, I get a better look at the city we approach. There are farms scattered across the countryside, small and rough with tiny houses. The griffin that leads the army with us on his back walks regally along a rutted, wide dirt road that winds through the farmlands, leading toward the distant city atop a hill. From far away, I can see walls encircling the base of the broad hill, and farther up, a tighter set of walls around the city, protecting what look like low square buildings made of stone. We're still too far away to make out many of the features of the city, but I spot dark blobs moving around, so those must be people or domesticated animals.

"My lord Kassam!" cries out a reedy voice. I jerk, startled, and turn to see an elderly woman hobbling across fields, followed by a wide-eyed younger man that must be her son. The woman raises her arms at the sight of Kassam, a look of pure bliss on her face. Tears course down her lined face. "My lord! You have returned to us! I have always prayed to you. Always. You are not forgotten in Chandrilhar."

Kassam tenses under my hands and then nods at the woman. "I will remember."

She drops to her knees, her son following suit, and clasps

her hands over her heart. "He has returned," she says, over and over again. "He has returned."

My skin prickles at the blissful look on her face. She's rapturous as she watches us move past, the mess of Kassam's howling, bleating wild army following behind us. "That was amazing."

He grunts. "I am pleased, yes."

"I...aren't you going to say anything to her?" I whisper to him. "She's been waiting for your return. She's been faithful. And you're just going to nod?"

"What would you have me do?" Kassam glances over his shoulder at me.

I can't believe no one has given the gods PR advice in all this time. "Get down from here. Go shake her hand. Make a real connection. Think of what a difference it will make to her if she gets to actually meet a god instead of just watching him stroll past. A person like that will tell others of her experience." I poke him in the ribs. "Try doing things differently this time and maybe there won't be a next time."

He glares down at me but then considers the woman and her son, prostrate in the dirt as the wild army soldiers past. They both quiver, no doubt scared out of their minds at the sight of both Kassam and the animal madness he's at the head of. When I poke him again, he shoots me an irritated look and then slides off the side of the griffin. I remain atop it, because no one cares if I say hello to the locals.

Kassam approaches the woman, and I inwardly wince at the sight of his bare ass. Maybe I should have suggested pants.

The woman sits up on her knees, trembling as Kassam approaches. He holds a hand out to her and she takes it, reverent, and presses it to her brow. He murmurs something to her and her son, and there's a look of complete rapture on her face as she gazes at him, so earnest that it's almost painful to watch. He brushes his fingers over her face lightly, and then that of her son, and walks back toward the pawing griffin I sit atop. He walks alongside it, his hand on the griffin's flank.

"Well?" I prompt when we're out of earshot. "How'd it go?"

The look on Kassam's face is thoughtful. "She said such nice things. It made me feel good. Not forgotten." He glances up at me. "Your advice was wise."

"I'm your anchor. That's my job, right?" I smile down at him, pleased and a little proud that I was able to help.

"More than that. You are my wife." He reaches up and brushes a hand possessively down my leg, sending a flare of desire rushing through me. It's been hours since we last stopped to have sex and eat, and I'm feeling the hedonism beast inside me needing to be fed again. "Are you all right up there?" he asks. "I think I shall walk and greet the mortals as we arrive. I...like seeing their faces."

I'm pleased at his words. He's taking this seriously, which is good. Maybe this is another thing that will help him return to power that much quicker, and I'm glad I said something. "I'm fine. But if I can offer a suggestion..."

He gives me a heated look. "All of your suggestions have been wise so far, my little light. Speak freely."

"Pants."

Kassam blinks up at me—and then laughs. "Pants?"

"I'm just saying, godlike junk might be in a lot of faces if everyone drops to their knees." I wrinkle my nose. "At the very least, maybe a nice towel wrap around the hips."

Kassam just laughs and laughs.

∽

IN THE END, Kassam goes with one of the plain white shirts I packed for him, torn into a long piece and knotted with vine at his hip. Between the hooves and antlers, the silvery eyes and the tangled hair that never seems to stay in one place, he looks absolutely wild and godlike. If I wasn't already completely messed up over him, I'd probably be as besotted as the farmers that come out in droves to see him.

Because they do come out in droves to see him. The farmer and her son are just the beginning. As we approach the city, more farmers and travelers come to a halt in front of us, dropping to their knees in front of Kassam. Many cry at the sight of him, women hold their babies out to him, and horses and cattle from the farmers leave the fields and join our ragtag army.

Everyone knows Kassam's name. He's not been all that forgotten, it seems, because they chant and whisper about him. They follow him towards the city atop the hill—Chandrilhar—and cry with pure joy when he touches them. They flock at his side, gazing at him adoringly, and I think it does wonders for his bruised god-ego. He's worried so much about being completely forgotten, but it's obvious that even back in the day, people loved him. That they remember him with fondness and they're genuinely thrilled to see his return.

I bet Seth can't say the same, and the thought makes me a little smug.

By the time we get to the lower set of walls around the city, there's a parade around Kassam. People have abandoned their farms to walk at his side, clutching children and gazing at him with adoration as he speaks. He tells the story of Riekki's betrayal over and over again, and I'd swear the mob is ready to destroy her on his behalf. They seem furious that one god would sabotage another, and vow vengeance on his behalf. The hedonism affects them, and they touch Kassam all over, shooting him lascivious, hungry looks before turning on each other. A lot of people make it to the bushes nearby to sate their needs. Quite a few of them don't.

More than one of Kassam's devotees shoot looks in my direction, and it makes me more than a little wary.

"Shall we kill your anchor for you, my lord Kassam?" someone cries out.

I'm suddenly glad I'm atop a mean-looking griffin instead of on the ground, in the midst of the parade next to Kassam. I shoot him a worried look.

"My friends," Kassam says in that rich, honeyed voice of his. "This is Carly. She is my anchor and has traveled from another world to serve at my side. She is also my wife and my chosen mate. I know that an anchor must die to free the god they are bound to, but I would keep Carly alive and unharmed. Once we have taken care of the evil Riekki, we will journey to the Spidae and beg for their help to keep her safe."

"Is it love?" a woman asks, reaching out to touch Kassam's arm.

He takes the woman's hand and kisses her knuckles. "It is. I have fallen for a mortal female. Protect and cherish her as you would protect and cherish me."

I gape at Kassam. Is he...lying? Or is it the truth? Why is my heart fluttering like mad at the thought? I have a lot of feelings for him myself, but I haven't unpacked them. If anything, I've deliberately avoided thinking about my feelings lately because the thought of love generally makes me want to run for the hills. It's just another one of those things that I'm terrible at.

But Kassam smiles up at me, all cheer once more.

I don't smile back. I don't know what to think. Part of me wants to steer this griffin back toward the mountains, because at least there, I didn't have to worry about well-meaning people eagerly asking if they can kill me. It's not the only reason, of course. The bigger part of me wants to run because of Kassam's declaration. If it's the truth, it's just going to cause us both misery. If he's lying...well, my feelings are still hurt, stupidly enough.

The pull of hedonism starts to get to the people around us, and Kassam's parade turns into a traveling orgy. They pull at his minuscule clothing, and when that doesn't work, they pull at him, trying to get him to join them. I try not to judge. I really do. Kassam affects everyone like that. But each time a strange woman touches his hair, or a man runs his hand down Kassam's well-muscled arm, I feel a surge of jealousy. Stupid, petty jealousy.

Here I am sitting atop the world's angriest bird-lion and people are touching my man.

And then I get mad at myself because I think of him as my man. He's not mine, and he's not a man, as he's reminded me many times before. Here I am dripping with crystals to keep my sanity and…why? So someone else can paw him? So they can all flock around him and make goo-goo eyes at him and threaten to kill me just to please him? Not for the first time, I wonder why I agreed to this.

But then Kassam glances up at me and gives me a rueful smile as if to say "Look at this mess" and my heart skips a beat.

Because I know why I'm here. I know why I went through all of this. I know why I'm at his side even if it's dangerous and people want to kill me. It's because of Kassam. Kassam with his laughing, affectionate nature and his eager drive to set things right. It's the way he smiles at me and looks at me. It's the way he's possessive of me, and how he gazes at me with so much pride when I speak. He's everything I'd want in a partner, and I'm probably falling in love with him.

It's typical Carly Randall. If I'm not the one sabotaging my relationship, it's because I'm in love with someone unattainable. I'm sure some of that is the hedonism leaking into my brain and making me look at him with heart-eyes, but even when I'm covered in crystals to thwart his appeal, I still…like him. He still makes me smile and hope for a better future. He makes me feel like I'm worthwhile.

Falling in love with him might be the most dangerous part of this journey after all.

36

Once word hits the city that a god has returned, even more people flood the streets. Kassam's expression changes from benevolent to impatient, especially when people start to jostle my griffin, trying to get closer to me, and another brings up the idea of killing me once more. The wild army encircles the outer wall, the animals not going into the city proper, and it becomes chaos as the townsfolk, drugged with the proximity of Kassam's hedonism, try to touch the creatures.

It's going to get ugly soon, and as Kassam's frown deepens, I decide it's time to play the wife card.

"Kassam, my lord," I call out from atop the prancing, agitated griffin I haven't dared to get off of. "A word with you, please?"

He pushes away a few of the more eager people clustered around him, wading through the unruly crowd to get to me. The moment he touches the griffin, it calms, feathers smoothing, but the crowd seems to get even more agitated. It's like they're jealous of any time he spends with the animals...or me. And that's going to be a problem. "What is it, little light?" Kassam asks, touching my leg.

I project my voice so the people crowding around can hear, even though I keep my attention focused solely on Kassam. "I'm very tired after such a long journey, my Lord of the Wild. If I'm to be your fuel for the coming weeks, I need rest and food. Please, let me do what I can to make your stay as comfortable as possible. I don't want to fail you, but I am only mortal." I do my best to look as helpless and tired as I can, and when Kassam's brows furrow together, I shoot him a meaningful look.

It finally dawns on him that I'm acting. "Of course, my anchor." He turns to the crowd, and they go silent, watching him with bated breath. "My fragile human anchor needs sleep and food if she is to see to my needs. Where can she rest in comfort?"

A few people offer their beds—big yikes—but one fat, well-dressed man steps forward, giving Kassam an adoring look. "It would be an honor to serve you both at my inn," the merchant says. "You shall have the finest rooms and the best meals."

Another man steps forward, this one tall and lean, with a pinched-looking face. "He should be established in the palace, just as the new god of knowledge." His face grows bright. "Chandrilhar shall boast two gods! Truly it is a blessed omen to be of such service in the Anticipation."

I nudge Kassam with my foot. "God of knowledge? He's here?"

The thin man overhears me, his gaze sharp as it roams over my form. "You know of him?"

"We come from the same world," I offer. "He came here to help Kassam avenge himself against Riekki." I don't point out that Seth is serving himself before anyone else, and that he's not exactly a god of knowledge. It seems wrong to deceive, but if these people have to choose between Seth or Riekki as a god, they're kind of fucked anyhow.

That seems to settle it. The fat merchant bows. "We will of

course house the gods together, in the finest of dwellings in Chandrilhar. But allow my cooks to bring you the finest meal possible."

My mouth waters at the thought. "Vegetarian, please. I don't eat meat." And I gesture at the animals around me.

"One would expect no less from the anchor of the god of the wild," the merchant says with a smile, and I feel I've done something right, at least.

∽

CHANDRILHAR, for all of its cluster of walls and houses, isn't the richest of places. The homes we pass are crowded and in disrepair, the streets hard-packed dirt instead of stone. Everyone looks happy and healthy, though, so I guess it could be worse. There are vendors with goods spread out on small blankets in front of various buildings, and we pass a butcher with a table out in the open, covered in flies, which makes me glad I insisted on being vegetarian.

Once we get out of the main section of the city, the streets open up a bit more, the houses becoming two-level, and they're not made of stone at all but some sort of brick, just like the walls. The brick houses are covered in flowering vines, and people stand on the roofs and wave down at Kassam as he walks through the streets, me still on the lone griffin (the rest of the army having been left outside the walls). At the top of the hill, with the best views, must be the palace. It's a long, expansive building with a second floor, the vines neatly covering the white-painted brick walls and there are even pretty stained-glass windows that make the place look colorful and attractive. A long train of stone steps wind up the side of the hill leading up to the palace, so I finally dismount from the griffin, who immediately flies away, and move to Kassam's side.

I'm sticking to him like glue.

The tall, thin man escorts us up the stairs. "I will issue my apologies on behalf of the prince himself. He is visiting his wife's family in Glistentide and will not return for many weeks. He will be thrilled for you to make use of his home and servants, however. Will you be staying for some time?"

Kassam shakes his head. "We ride on once Seth's army is ready."

"Then my prince will be very sad indeed to have missed you, Lord of the Wild. They will be singing songs of your return for generations to come." The smile that creases his face is genuine. "We are so honored you are here."

Indeed, everyone seems to be awed at the sight of Kassam. There are guards posted at each of the doors to the palace, and they gape openly at Kassam's figure. I mean, the guy is splendid to look at, from his hooves to the horns in his thick hair, to the vines that curl at his waist and trail up one arm, to the delectable brown skin that makes me want to lick him all over—

I rub my crystals, frowning. When was the last time we had sex? This morning? Yeah, he's about due for a hedonism recharge, and so am I. My stomach growls, reminding me that I need to eat, too.

The interior of the palace is cool and delightful. The floors are a beautiful painted tile, and even though the interior is dark, it's spacious and open. Rich, fluttery wall-hangings covered in beads clink as we walk past, stirring them, and there are leafy plants potted amidst the delicate furniture, made from shaped metal with a woven mat for a seat. There are statues lining the walls, and Kassam pauses in front of them, noting the bowls of oils and incense before each one. "You pray to all the gods here?"

"All of them," the tall man says happily. "My prince's family is quite traditional." He gestures down the line of statues, and sure enough, there's one with a pair of curling ram horns. It's not quite the same horns that he's wearing right now, but Kassam looks pleased that his altar has fresh flowers on it. As we walk, I notice that one of the statues is missing a head, and the marble form seems to have been covered by a black cloth. The man gestures at it, saying, "The god Seth insisted upon Riekki's removal. We have not yet had our statue of him returned to us yet, but the sculptors are hard at work already."

Kassam grunts, then glances down another hall where servants scurry past. "I see oracles here. They serve the prince?"

Oracles? I try to peer down the hall, but I didn't pay attention. Everyone here wears flapping robes of various colors—except for Kassam, of course, who is touchably almost-naked. To me, they all look the same, but maybe they feel different to Kassam. "What's an oracle?" I whisper, using this moment as an excuse to lean in close to him...and maybe press my mouth against his skin, just a little.

He pulls me in under his arm, and the warmth of him is like a blanket. His scent envelops me, and I have a hard time concentrating as he explains, "Oracles serve the gods. They pray on behalf of the people and are keepers of lore. Many choose to serve one god alone, but there are some that serve all, choosing to be of service to mortal man instead of seeking the love of one particular god. If they are not dedicated, they will not receive prophecies."

Right. Because the gods stick their hands into things here and go to war with each other. "Are you going to give out any prophecies while we're here?"

"Shall I just whisper naughty things in their ears, then?" he teases, looking down at me. "As I do you?"

My breath stutters at those laughing silver eyes. Heat floods through my body and I place my hand on one firm pectoral, brushing my thumb over his nipple. "Save your naughty things for me and me alone."

Kassam returns my heated look with one of his own.

Servants race down the halls ahead of us as the tall man—the vizier to Prince Rahim—gives us an aggravatingly leisurely tour of the palace. These are the family's personal shrines to the gods. These are the tapestries brought here as a wedding gift from Rahim's mother's people. These are the finely made chairs that show off the metalwork that Chandrilhar is famous for. This is the library, full of ancient books (and oracles hard at work reading and taking notes).

I try not to seem impatient, but I'm exhausted and grimy and starving. I just want to sleep and eat, in either order.

We're finally shown to the suite of apartments that will be ours. It's three rooms, and the entirety of them is as big as my apartment back in Chicago. There's a sitting area full of small chairs, cushions, and what looks like some sort of stringed musical instrument in one corner. The next room is the bedroom, comprised of a low-slung metal-postered bed and an extremely wide, flat mattress covered in dozens of pillows. The final room looks like bathing implements, with a beaten metal tub, a cloudy, ornate mirror on the wall, and a table with various cosmetics on it.

The bed looks like heaven to me, and I sit on the edge, kicking off my boots as I do.

"My Lord of Knowledge, Seth, has asked not to be disturbed for any reason," the vizier says, watching me as I pull off my shoes. "I would introduce you to him, but until he sends for us..."

Kassam waves a hand idly. "It is fine. There will be time enough to see him again. My anchor needs to rest."

"Of course she does," the vizier says smoothly. "There are servants assigned to these quarters, and they will bring food and fresh clothes, and will play music for you to soothe you as you rest. I will bring footmen to fan you as you rest, and they will also draw you a bath—"

I raise a hand, weary. "All of that sounds awesome, but I just want to sleep. I don't need music or fanning."

Kassam strokes my cheek with a gentle finger. "Then you will rest, my little light." He turns toward the vizier. "But I have a few requests. What kind of sweets do you have?"

"Sweets?" the vizier echoes, clearly confused.

"To feed his hedonism," I say with a tired smile. The blankets look soft and appealing, and even though I'm covered in travel dust, I pull up one corner and slide underneath, shoving aside a dozen pillows.

The vizier's expression turns knowing. "Of course, of course. We have one of the finest cooks in all the land who would be happy to make anything you like. Tell me. Do you prefer nuts or fruit in your baked goods?"

"I like both," Kassam says, straightening as I fluff a pillow under my head. God, it feels good to lie down. I'm in heaven.

"And nose spices?" the vizier inquires. "Shall I—"

"No nose spices," Kassam says, and looks over at me. "But I will taste all your beers and wines." He picks up one of the decorative pillows from the bed and sniffs it. "This smells like fruit?"

"Do you like perfumes?" the vizier asks. "I can show you those, as well."

I smile sleepily at Kassam as he gives me one last look and then follows the vizier out of the room. I wait for the dangerous, pulling feeling of the bond, but it's gentle, and I realize they must not be going far. Closing my eyes, I start to drift off—

—when I hear something moving in my room.

I open my eyes, my senses immediately on alert. I'm an idiot, I realize. I just hopped into bed in a strange place and assumed I was safe. What if someone's come to assassinate me because they think they're doing Kassam a favor? Terrified, I clutch one of the stupid pillows on the bed to use as the saddest weapon ever and peer over the edge.

One of the *conmac* settles on the floor on the far side of my bed. His long, wolven body stretches out and he lowers his enormous head onto one leg, giving me a reproachful look with his bright yellow eyes. As I relax, another *conmac* wolf slips in and settles on the other side of my bed, practically glaring at me.

They must have followed us through the city, and now they're settling themselves down next to my bed, guarding me. They want me alive because—I'm guessing—they suspect Kassam won't follow through with his promise to free them if something happens to me.

"I know," I say. "I know. I should have thought it through. Being a target is kinda new to me."

One of the *conmac* yawns, as if my excuses are tiresome.

"Point taken. Thank you anyhow. I owe you guys one." I settle down into the bed again, and this time when I drift off, no one interrupts.

37

When I wake up again, it's dark in the bedroom, no afternoon light flooding through the pretty stained-glass windows. The *conmac* are no longer next to the bed, and when I close my eyes and mentally "feel" for the bond I share with Kassam, there's no pulling at all. He must be back.

Yawning, I pad to the bathroom area and use a chamber pot (which beats the bushes I've been using for the last while) and then splash myself clean with a bit of water and soap left by the mirror. When I feel marginally fresher, I head out of the bedroom and towards the sitting room, opening the fancy beaten-metal double doors.

Kassam sits in a plush chair, petting a golden-feathered falcon as he pops something that looks like a cookie into his mouth. There's a tray with no less than eight wine goblets on a table near him, and two servants hover a short distance away, both of them armed with what look like masses of pastries.

"My light!" Kassam declares as I step inside, feeling about as fresh as roadkill. He gives me a cheery look. "You are finally awake. Do you feel better?"

I thump down into the chair across from him and steal one

of his pastries. It melts into my mouth, a sugary-sweet concoction filled with fruit and flaky pastry, and I moan at how delicious it is. "I'm starving," I admit. "Have you been waiting long?"

He shrugs, petting the falcon. "What is time when you are endless?"

Okay, fair point. I smile my thanks at the women as they set another tray on the table nearest to me and fill it up with food —all vegetarian from the looks of it. There's a thick bean-like paste, chopped vegetables, bowls of nuts, crackers, breads of all kinds, and so many different sweets that it makes my head spin. I shove some of the bean paste onto a cracker and bite down. It's heavily spiced and salty and delicious and I immediately want to eat the whole bowl. "What happened while I was asleep?"

"Not much. I did not stray far because I did not wish to pain you. You needed your rest." He watches as the two servants leave and we're alone. Kassam gets to his feet and opens one of the windows, murmurs something to the falcon, and then watches as it flies out into the night. "It is barely past sunset, so you did not sleep for too long."

I yawn between bites, then steal one of his goblets of wine. "I'll be honest, I could sleep again." Oh man, the wine is delicious, too. I chug it, then stuff a cut length of raw vegetable into the paste and eat it next. "Any sign of our good buddy Seth or Margo?"

Kassam shuts the window, giving me a curious look. "He is not my good buddy. And no. I did not look for him, and I imagine he is hiding her for his own protection. If Riekki has faithful here in this city, they will quietly go after him for daring to challenge her for her position."

Makes sense. I pick up another goblet of wine—different blend, equally delicious—and glance up at him. "So what's the plan, then?"

He shrugs, moving to my side. He pulls my hair over to one

shoulder and then leans in, kissing my neck as I stuff my face. "There is a celebration tonight in my honor."

I groan at the thought. A party. I'm sure he wants to go—he's thrilled at all the attention after being forgotten for so long—but I kind of just want to crawl back into bed with a plate of pastries and call it a day.

Kassam chuckles, grazing his teeth over my neck in a way that sends prickles of awareness through my body. "It is probably wisest if you hide away."

"Awesome. I love that idea." I tilt my neck a little more, setting down the food to focus on him. I'm suddenly less hungry for pastries and feeling a different sort of craving. "Are you...going to stay in bed with me?"

He nips at my ear, sending shivers up my spine. "Alas, I must go. But the *conmac* will remain at your side. I shall keep you safe and protected, never fear." He presses another kiss to my neck. "Perhaps Seth has the right of it, hiding Margo away in his bed and not letting anyone gaze upon her. Letting her serve him and only him."

I moan, because this is sounding less like we're talking about Margo by the minute. "Is that what you want to do? Have me in your bed, waiting to serve you?"

He chuckles, the sound low and sending aching pulses through my body. "Among other things. Can...I kiss you, my little light?"

As long as you don't call me your "little light," I want to grumble, but I don't bring it up. Just like I don't bring up the whole declaration of love he made in the courtyard. I'm almost positive he was lying to make people feel better about my presence. He's told me before that gods don't feel things that mortals do. But...I also don't ask about it, because I don't want to know the truth. I'm going to bask in the lies for a little while longer. "You can kiss me as long as it means something to you."

He takes my hand and pulls me out of my chair, and when I

face him, he's smiling. Kassam has been so filled with joy all day long that it makes me ache to see him so happy. It's like being back here is filling all the hollow parts inside him and making him who he was meant to be all along. And I love it, because I love it for him. I want this to go perfectly for him. I want people feasting his return and celebrating for days that someone as awesome as Kassam has returned. Because in my eyes, he deserves the world.

I'm falling for him, which might be the stupidest thing ever. This time, it won't be me pulling the plug on the relationship. It'll be the gods themselves, either sending me home or severing the bond between us and sending us on our separate ways. But until then...he's mine.

The thought makes me so desperate that I'm the one that crosses the short distance between us. I kiss him fiercely, holding onto him so tightly that I dig my nails into his skin. I want to leave my mark on him somewhere, somehow, so after I'm gone, he'll be able to remember me. Did all his anchors feel like this, I wonder? Desperate for his love and knowing it'll always be out of reach because of who and what he is?

"Mmm." He runs his hands over me as I kiss him, my mouth frantic on his. "I see you missed me."

"Nah," I lie, and I don't even sound convincing to my own ears. "Maybe I just woke up horny."

Kassam's eyes flare at that, and he grins down at me. "Good, because I want to play for a bit."

Play? I blink at him, surprised. "Okay?"

"I asked for a few things to be brought up to our rooms," Kassam tells me, hiking me into his arms and sliding a hand under my butt. I put my legs around his waist, and he carries me back into the bedroom, toward the bed. "And since we have time before my feast tonight, this seems like the perfect opportunity."

He settles me gently down onto the bed again, then flings

off the tiny scrap of loincloth he's been wearing. He's bare to my gaze once more, his cock hard and as breathtaking as ever. I automatically reach for it—and him—only to have Kassam grab my hands in his. He kisses my palms and then grins down at me. "Are you ready?"

"For?"

"For a one-up, as you call it." He leans in and gives my palm a lascivious lick and then moves back into the sitting room.

Oh god. A one-up. He's thought of a suitable payback for me putting a finger in his ass. Hot arousal floods through me, and I clench my thighs together tightly, waiting to see what he went to get. Another type of food to share? More wine? Something sexy to wear?

Kassam re-enters with a lacquered box, about the size of a large jewelry box. More quartz, I wonder? Is that the goal—to cover me in crystals and turn me on without his hedonism? He sets the box down on the table beside the bed and pulls out a long, silk length of fabric. "Give me your hand."

Oh. Bondage. I've never done it before, but I'm game. I hold my wrist out to him obediently. "Do I get a safe word?"

"What is a safe word?"

I watch as he ties my wrist to one post of the bed, then pulls another length of silk out and moves to tie the other to the opposite post. "It's where I have a word that I can say, and if I use it, then you'll stop. It's like if it gets to be too much for me."

The god gives me an arch look. "I will make sure it's not too much for you."

"I still want a safe word. Let's use 'pineapple.'"

He finishes tying my other wrist and then my arms are spread wide, my quivering thighs clenched together. Kassam leans in and kisses me. "Or you could simply ask me to stop."

"Sometimes 'stop' means 'keep going,'" I point out, settling back against the pillows. "Especially if it feels really intense."

"Mmm, this should be intense," he agrees. "Very well. Say your word for me again?"

"Pineapple!"

He grins, inclining his head to indicate he heard me. "And are you comfortable?"

"Comfortable enough?" I give a little wiggle on the bed. "But I'm still wearing my clothes. Or is that part of the plan?"

Kassam shakes his head. "It is not. Your clothes are filthy and should be discarded anyhow." He pulls a knife out of the box and reaches for the front of my t-shirt.

"Don't you dare—" He cuts into my shirt, slicing right up the front. Either the knife is extremely sharp or my shirt is extremely worn, but it falls apart like butter and I make an utterly outraged sound, wrestling against the silken bonds at my wrists. "Kassam! You fucker! I don't have an infinite supply of those!"

"I have new clothes for you," he purrs, undeterred as he slices the remnants of my shirt off.

I scowl at him.

He offers me a wink and then snaps the thin bit of fabric that holds my bra together.

"You suck," I tell him, as he cuts the last bits of my upper clothing off and then the knife travels down my belly, toward my jeans. Oh no. "Wait, wait, pineapple," I tell him. "Don't you dare cut my jeans."

Undeterred at my anger, he puts the knife between his teeth and slips my jeans and panties off my legs the traditional way. When I'm naked, he runs his hands up and down my legs, stroking me. "I like you like this," he murmurs. "Soft and willing."

"Willing?" I chuckle at that. "I'm tied up, Kassam."

"Yes, but you're quivering with excitement. And your cunt is already wet for me." He leans in and presses a kiss to the top of my mound. "I bet if I finger you, I find you hot and juicy and ripe for my cock, won't I?"

I whimper, my breasts peaking at his words. He's not wrong. My pulse is racing with anticipation, and I can't wait to see what he does to me now that I'm tied up. As one-ups go, this is a little tame, but I don't mind. I'm enjoying the play between us.

"So beautiful," Kassam murmurs, his hand gliding over my belly. "You know what would make you even more beautiful?"

"What?"

He gets off the bed and strides over to the tableside once more. I'm frustrated and helpless, twisting my hands in the silk bonds as his gorgeous, prominent cock bobs just out of reach. Really, that's unfair of him to put that so close to my face and not let me lick it. I whimper a protest, but he ignores me. I don't think I've ever viscerally reacted to a man like I do to Kassam, and I'm not sure all of it is because of hedonism. He's a god, and so of course he's got a perfect, golden-brown ass that's the right level of muscle and cushion. Of course he's got tight, tapered hips and obliques so sharp they could cut you. Of course a god would have massive, muscular thighs and the perfect thickness to his chest with a six-pack and square pectorals.

Of course a god would have a fat, nine-inch cock. It's just science.

But when he looks over at me and gives me that roguish, naughty grin, I realize it's not just his appearance—it's not his body or his face. His personality makes me laugh. I love how he likes to tease me about everything. I love how he has made it through some awful shit and still finds time to smile. I love how he accepts when things are new to him, and I love how upset he gets when he feels something he's never experienced before. He never bores me. He never makes me feel ugly, or foolish when I'm in bed with him. If anything, he makes me feel like I'm the sexiest thing he's ever seen, and that's a big ego boost considering he's a god.

I've never been more compatible with someone, both in personality and physically.

It's that naughty look that makes me jingle my quartz bracelet at him. "Should you take my crystals off?" The sex is really good with the crystals on, but it's a new kind of mindless wild when I get the full force of his hedonism.

I'm a little surprised when he shakes his head, though. "I want you to be in your mind when we do this. I want you to tell me how it feels."

"Oh, okay." I blink up at him, trying desperately not to squirm on the bed like a needy, needy tramp. "How what feels?"

Kassam pulls out a crystal decanter and holds it up to the light.

"Body oil?" I guess.

"A lubricant," he agrees. "You'll need it for this."

And then he pulls out the biggest fucking dildo I've ever seen.

38

I stare.

And stare.

"What the fuck, Kassam?" I finally manage, blinking rapidly as I take in the sight of the thing. It must be made of marble or ivory, because it's a pale, ghostly white, and veiny as all get-out. It's bigger than his already-impressive cock, and he waves it in front of my face with a smug smile. "Where the hell did you get that?"

The god shrugs. "They wished to please me. Said I could ask for anything. So I asked for this and oil to grease your pretty little cunt with." He studies it with a curious expression. "It's quite large, isn't it?"

I wonder if the floor will swallow me up if I ask nicely. "I can't believe we've been here for less than a day and you're demanding dildos from these people."

He snorts. "You worry too much, little light. They're probably just curious as to why I haven't had you sucking off half the town just to please me."

I straighten up in bed, at least as much as I can, considering my hands are tied, and give him a horrified look. "Is that what happens with other hedonism aspects?" I lower my voice, since it's getting louder by the moment. "Is that what they *do*?"

"They do anything and everything to please their god," he says, sitting down on the edge of the bed. "But I find the longer I'm with you, the less I like the idea of sharing you." The look he shoots me is both devouring and possessive. "You're my wife, and I'm not sharing you with anyone."

"Oh, good," I say, laughing nervously. "Because I don't want to be shared. And the same goes for you."

"I do not want anyone else." He brandishes the dildo, eyeing the impressive length before giving me a cat-that-just-ate-the-cream smile. "Just you."

"And that thing?" I nod at the dildo.

Kassam grins widely. "I was sad I did not get to use your toys on you. I have been thinking about it for many, many days."

Even though I'm feeling a little out of my depth at the moment, hearing that from him makes my body pulse with hunger. "Have you?"

"Constantly," he purrs at me, and then runs the tip of the thing down my belly. "You have your word. Are you going to use it?"

I bite back a whimper, squirming against the silk ties. "No."

"My perfect little light," Kassam murmurs. "You have no idea how much that pleases me."

"Will you kiss me first?" I ask, breathless. He looks thrilled at my request, tossing the dildo down on the bed beside me and leaning over my body. His mouth brushes over mine, and I moan when his tongue slicks into my mouth. God, he kisses like a dream. His tongue dances against mine, tasting, teasing, and sending little flares of pleasure all through my body. His weight is heavy against mine, but I like it, and I like that his scent is everywhere—he smells like sunshine and outdoors and sun-kissed skin, and I'm obsessed with it.

Kassam gives me another hungry kiss, then gently bites my

lower lip. At my whimper, he grins and kisses lower, then cups my aching breasts. I tug at my wrists, practically sobbing my need when he teases both nipples at the same time, massaging the rounded weight of each breast before returning to the tips to torment them. Nothing has ever felt so good, and the fact that I'm helpless to push him away or to touch him anywhere just adds to the pleasure of it. By the time he squeezes one breast to feed the nipple into his mouth, I'm whining like a madwoman, making frantic little keening noises as he laps at my skin.

I need it.

Need *him*.

So, so badly. "Kassam!" I cry out as he scrapes his teeth over one breast. "Please, let me touch you. Please, please."

"Later," he says, nuzzling at the tip in a way that makes my pussy clench in response. "Are you ready for the oil?"

"No," I whine, wriggling against his touch.

"Then use your word," he commands, flicking a finger against my quartz necklace.

I squirm against the bonds, aroused and panting. I don't want to ask, but I also don't want to stop. "Fine, you fucker," I explode. "Give me the oil. Just make me come."

He laughs at my angry response. "So furious when all I want to do is pleasure you." With a grin, he flicks his tongue over one nipple and then sits up. "You are welcome to use your word at any time if you wish this to stop. If you do not, I will assume it is all delicious. Like you said, sometimes no means yes."

I hate that he's tossing my words into my face, and even more, that they're turning me on. I watch, breathless, as he pours a good bit of oil into his hand, the contents slopping over his fingers and down his arm. He gives me a burning look and then rubs his hands together, oiling them both. "Ready?"

God, is he going to make me beg for every step of the way? "Yes!"

He slicks one warm hand over my breast, teasing and plucking at the nipple. I gasp, because the oil adds an entirely new dimension to the feel of his skin against mine, and it's incredible. He greases up both of my breasts and toys with them for a time, then moves between my thighs. "Spread for me, little light."

Shamelessly, I do so, and he slides those slick fingers up and down my folds, circling my clit and making me arch up on the bed. His hands are so slick that his fingers feel like silk over my skin, and my lips part in a wordless cry as he rubs my clit back and forth, bringing me toward climax—

—only to stop when I'm at the edge. Legs trembling, I shoot him a glare.

He gives me a slow, teasing grin and moves one slippery finger to the entrance of my body, pushing in and then skating back out again. I whimper a protest, and he pushes two fingers into me, then three, fucking me with lazy, unhurried movements. "We need to make sure you can take it," he murmurs. "It's a very big toy, much bigger than your little one."

I moan, rocking against his hand as he works me. I'm so close again. "Yes," I pant. "Yes, yes, please."

My eyes are closed, and I'm not paying attention to anything except for his fingers pushing in and out of me, and the wet sounds my body makes. Something wet and cool slicks over my pussy and I writhe in surprise as he works more oil over my folds and then dips down to my backside. "You'll need this good and slick, too, little light."

He presses a fingertip against the entrance to my body there and I shift, not entirely sure if I like it or not. "Why?" I pant. "I thought—"

"Because I have a little something for you there, too." The smile he gives me is pure evil.

"Oh no," I moan.

"Use your word," he says cheerfully, pulling something new

out of that hateful, hateful box. Sure enough, it's a matching plug for my backside. It's the same sort of marble, with a T-shaped handle on one end. The plug is tapered at the tip and wider at the base like a teardrop, and even though it's not that big, I shudder at the sight of it. Kassam waves it in front of my face. "Unless you say something, we'll go with this first."

"Kassam," I pant, squirming as he rubs the head of the plug through my folds. "I don't know—"

"I do. You wished to one-up, did you not? I can play this game, too." And he pushes the plug against the entrance to my backside.

I go still, moaning at the invasion.

"Relax," he tells me in a gentle voice, one big hand on my stomach. "Relax and let your body take it."

It feels like too much. I've never done this, and I'm not sure I like it. But Kassam watches me with those gorgeous silver eyes and murmurs how beautiful I am, and how much he likes playing this game with me, and then before I know it, the plug is entirely in. I wriggle on the bed, frowning to myself as I try to get used to the sensation. I'm not entirely sure I like it. It's...a lot. It didn't look very big outside of my body, but inside it feels, well, like an immovable object has been stuffed in a place it doesn't belong, and no amount of wriggling is going to free it.

Kassam reaches between my thighs and gives my slippery clit a caress, and everything inside me jolts to awareness. I suck in a breath, because the reflexive clench of my body made that plug feel...intense. "Are you all right, little light? Do you want to stop playing and acknowledge that I have won our game?"

I glare at him, jerking my hands ineffectively against the bonds. "You haven't won squat."

His eyes gleam, predatory, and he gives my clit a very slow, tantalizing circle that makes my pussy clench around nothing at all. "Does that mean we are still playing?"

I pant, lifting my chin defiantly.

"Ah, my sweet, beautiful Carly," he says with a chuckle. "How I love that you are my anchor. I would rather do this with no one else."

As declarations of love go, it kinda stinks, but I still preen at his praise. I love feeling special to him, which is silly, but I can't help myself. I'm in deep and going deeper by the minute. "I'm your wife," I choke out, and practically orgasm when he gives me that satisfied smile.

"Yes," he purrs. "Yes you are."

And then the asshole picks up the dildo.

Kassam runs one oil-slick hand over the shaft of the damned thing, then pours a little more oil on it and works his palm along the length. "You're such a good girl for me," he murmurs. "Even though you're trembling, you still want to do this, don't you?"

I'm trembling? I whimper a response, because I guess I am. I just need him to touch me desperately, and I'm so aroused I can't stand it. I feel like a bomb ready to go off, just waiting for my fuse to be lit. "Kassam," I plead. "Touch me. I'm so close."

"I've got you, little light," he murmurs, and teases the head of the thing around one of my gleaming nipples. I bite my lip, because it feels good, of course, but it's also exactly the wrong end of the body I want him teasing. "So pretty. I don't think I've ever seen something prettier than you like this, eager for me, my Carly." He trails the head of the dildo down my belly, to my navel. "Do you need to come?"

"*Yes.*"

"Did you want to use your word?"

"Fuck no," I blurt out, arching my hips, my hands pulling at the restraints. "Please. Just touch me."

With a wicked grin, he trails it lower, rubbing it over my mound and then using it to part the folds of my sex. He rubs the head of it back and forth against my clit, and I cry out, so close to the edge that I can taste it, only for him to skim away once more. "I tied you up so I could play with you," Kassam says in a light voice. "Aren't you having fun?"

"Fuck you," I wheeze as he dips the head of it to the entrance of my core. It feels so good there that I arch up—only for him to tease it away again. "Kassam!"

"Ask me nicely, wife."

I want to kiss the hell out of him—or tear his head off.

When I don't comply, he tsks as if displeased, but his grin widens and I know he's loving this. Like the tormentor he is, Kassam uses the dildo on me everywhere except where I need it. He teases my clit, circles the entrance to my core but never dips in, and all the while whispers filthy, delicious things to me. He plays me like a violin, watching me from the edge of the bed with that hungry look on his face, and I know he's drinking in every whiny noise I make, every twist in the silken bonds, every time my hips jerk frantically.

"*Please*," I beg, finally breaking. "Please, Kassam. Please fuck me."

"I'll consider it."

"I asked nicely," I cry, nearly at tears. I'm so turned on that it's making me crazy. "Please, Kassam. I asked so nicely. Please, please."

He caresses my face with one oil-slick hand and I turn, pressing my cheek toward his touch. I'm so desperate and needy, and when his finger skims over my lip, I capture the tip in my mouth and suck on it, trying to entice him. The oil has a slightly herbal taste to it, but I don't care if it's edible or not. All that matters is Kassam.

"My pretty little wife," he murmurs, watching as I suck frantically on his finger. "I love seeing you need me as much as I need you."

Need him as much as he needs me? What—

Kassam pushes the dildo home, pumping it into me.

I make an obscene cawing noise when it finally sinks in,

and my entire body quivers and spasms. A hard orgasm rips through me, because the dildo—along with the plug—makes for a tight fit, and it's sending sparks of sensation all through my body in all the right places. It feels like nothing I've experienced before, and I quake with the intensity of my climax.

Before I can catch my breath, though, Kassam is there again. He cups me by the back of my neck and hovers his mouth over mine, an intense look on his face as he works the dildo in and out of my cunt. "Can I kiss you?"

"Always," I breathe, and then his mouth is on mine, and he's kissing me hard and fast and needy, and all the while he fucks me with the dildo, the strokes quick and certain. Another orgasm rockets through me, and I clench hard around the dildo even as he drives it into my body over and over again as his lips caress me.

"Do it for me again," he whispers between kisses. "I love watching you come."

I breathe his name against his lips, arching as he changes the angle of the dildo, and then suddenly it's all pressure and tightness, stroking against that perfect spot inside me even as the plug in my ass adds to the intensity. I'm sweating as he frantically drives me up towards another climax, and this time, when I come, I scream as if I'm coming apart at the seams.

He hovers over me, drinking in my responses from inches away, his gaze moving over my face. "Mine," he finally whispers, and grazes his teeth along the line of my jaw. "My sweet little wife."

Orgasm-drunk, I sag in the bonds. I tilt my head so he can kiss my neck, but I'm too tired to do anything else. Tired, but the lower half of me is still throbbing with awareness of that enormous dildo lodged inside me, along with the plug. I shift a little as Kassam rubs his cheek to mine, like a cat in heat. Only one of us has come, I realize, and this isn't over yet. My body quivers at the realization, and I moan as Kassam reaches down between us and teases my clit, my channel clenching around the invasive shaft inside me.

"Should I make you come again?" Kassam whispers, his gaze tender as he lifts his head, watching me. "Or do you finally need your word?"

I cry out, shuddering against him as he circles my clit, everything in me tightening up again. "Can...can you die from orgasms?" I wheeze. "Because if so, I'm close."

He chuckles, moving in to kiss me again. "Remember, I like you alive."

Oh, I can't forget. Just like I can't forget the plug inside me, or the dildo that I'm even now clenching around helplessly as he rubs my clit and makes me come again. The orgasm he wrings out of me is hard and messy, and I whimper when the quaking in my body subsides and I can breathe once more.

Before I have time to process what he's doing, Kassam pulls the bigger toy free from my body and moves over me. "My wife," he says, sounding possessive as hell. "My anchor. My Carly." He sinks into me, and he feels bigger than ever, thanks to the plug still in my ass. I gasp, then lift my trembling, exhausted legs around his hips as he fucks me brutally, driving into me with a ferocious intensity that takes my breath away. "Mine alone."

And as I spiral into yet another orgasm, I'm dimly aware of how possessive Kassam is...and how much I love it. I don't think anyone expected him to be so feral and possessive when it comes to me, least of all him. Here I thought our marriage would be a sham.

I'm starting to realize that when Kassam promised forever, he meant it.

39

Sometime later, when Kassam is finished with me, the plug is removed from my backside and he releases my wrists and gives me a sponge bath. He kisses and cuddles me for a while, stroking my hair and snuggling as I drift in post-orgasmic bliss. He kisses me one last time and then tucks the blankets carefully around me before heading down to the feast in his honor. He's all energy, but I'm wrecked and exhausted. I doze off in a nest of pillows, sore but sated.

A heavy weight sitting on the edge of the bed wakes me up from deep sleep. I groan, rolling over on my side. "Back already?"

"I'm afraid not," says a voice that's not Kassam's. "He's supervising the orgy downstairs."

I open my eyes a crack, and glare at Seth, who is sitting inches away from me on the bed. I hug the blankets closer to my naked body. "How did you get in here? And did you say orgy?"

Seth laughs, the sound tight and humorless. "If you're worried, he's not participating."

"I'm not worried." I yawn and rise up on one elbow, trying

not to wince at how sore my lower half is. Feels awesome, but sore. My face will probably be permanently red every time I think about what Kassam and I did earlier, but I decide it's just the price I'll have to pay. "How's Margo?"

"Safe." A look of annoyance crosses his handsome face. "A pain in my ass, but safe."

Good. I eye him. He's wearing long, sweeping white robes covered in expensive-looking embroidery of a deep blue shade, and I wonder briefly if those are his colors or Riekki's. His dark, short hair looks the same, right down to the rakish lock of hair over his brow, and he's wearing a metal circlet across his brow. He looks regal enough, though I don't know if he looks as godlike here as he did back home. "When did you get to Chandrilhar?"

"Lachesis dropped me here. You're full of questions, aren't you?" He smirks at me.

"Considering you've been hiding out, yeah. You're avoiding us."

Seth rolls his eyes. "Not avoiding. I was busy. And when I had time this afternoon, you and Kassam were here, holed up in your rooms and he was making you shriek like a banshee. Forgive me if I didn't barge in and interrupt."

Oh god. Are the walls thin here? Was I that loud? How humiliating. I grimace. "Point taken." He looks so irritated that I assume he's not afflicted by hedonism like Kassam is, or he'd be downstairs directing (or participating in) the orgy. "So which Aspect are you?" At his sharp look, I continue. "Kassam said that when the gods are walking the mortal realm they're cast into four different Aspects—hedonism, apathy, arrogance and lies. Which one are you? Not Hedonism, clearly."

"Not all the rules apply to me," he says vaguely. "I have an anchor, but I have not been split. Perhaps because I have not yet offended the High Father?"

"Give it time," I quip. "I'm sure he'll find you offensive at some point."

The look Seth gives me is withering. Oddly enough though, I'm not afraid of him. Maybe I should be, given that he's crept into my bedroom while I'm naked, but it's clear he's not interested in me physically. He looks at me like I'm a worm he has to tolerate. "Well," I say, fighting a yawn. "Kassam should be back in a little while, I'm sure. You guys can discuss plans when he returns. He's got plenty of them."

"Thank you for the reminder," Seth says, and I realize he's serious. He gazes down at me, thoughtful. "I admit, I came in here to satisfy my curiosity."

"About what?" God, this guy loves the smell of his own farts. Why is he still talking to me? I'm a worm in his eyes, barely worth noticing.

Seth continues to study me, his dark eyes glittering in the shadows. "Why he's so obsessed with you. Why he *married* you. Why he pretends that you're his equal." His lip curls slightly. "I have known many a fascinating human and you are not one. So I am trying to determine what it is about you that makes you so special in his eyes."

Now that's just rude. Why does he think it's okay to sneak into my bedroom and insult me? "Maybe you're wrong and you're the Arrogance aspect after all," I snipe. "Because you're kind of an asshole."

He gives me a toothy smile. Here, his teeth aren't sharp fangs like they were back on Earth. It's a perfect grin—almost too perfect—and I suspect it's all part of his plan to steal Riekki's spot as the god of knowledge. Can't look too evil, after all. Wouldn't want anyone to think you're up to something. "You're making this easier for me all the time, mortal. But I do hope you won't take this personally." He gets to his feet, adjusting his clothes as he gazes down at me. "I just need a god on my side, and you're in the way."

Making this easier...in the way...?

A pillow slams down over my face, muffling my shriek of surprise. I flail, and in the next moment, it feels like he punches me in the chest. He punches me again, and water sprays across my belly and my skin. Something hard and cold and painful lodges in my chest, pinning me down. I let out a gurgled squawk of surprise and my hands flutter, reaching for that strange thing pinning me to the bed—and my hands encounter a knife.

The knife is seated deep between my breasts. It's not water I'm feeling coursing down my skin, it's my blood.

He's stabbed me.

"Like I said," Seth calls, his voice muffled through the pillow over my face. "It's nothing personal. But I need Kassam at his full power if we're to take down the goddess, and you're just a mortal."

Oh god. Something wet bubbles up in my mouth and I can feel it spilling over my breasts, my skin. That hot spear remains lodged in my heart, and I can't breathe. I'm dying. When Seth lifts the pillow off my face, I still can't breathe. It's like my lungs have flattened. He stares down at me, his expressionless, cold face blurry. Blackness claims me. I sink into death...

...and wait.

40

Nothing happens.

I realize it at the same time Seth does, my eyes fluttering open to see him frowning down at me. He grabs the knife shoved in my chest and gives it a vicious twist that sends a rippling chill up my body, and I automatically reach out and slap at him.

"Ow," I manage.

Seth snarls. "No." He shoves the knife in deeper, and all it results in is a bubble of blood pushing out from my lips. My lungs feel like they're flooded, yet somehow I'm still...here? When I shove a hand at his face, he slaps it away. "Die already!"

"Fuck...you," I manage, and shove a middle finger at him. I don't know why I'm not dying— clearly my body wants to—but somehow I'm sticking around. Is this how it normally works? I don't understand. My slippery hands flutter again and find the knife lodged deep between my breasts. I grab it, and it takes a few tries before I'm able to tug it free. More blood gushes onto the bed.

Really, I had no idea I had so much damn blood.

Seth rakes a blood-spattered hand through his hair,

jumping up from the bed and starting to pace. "That sneaky female...she burned me." He lets out a hard laugh. "Lachesis, you absolute bitch." He shakes a finger at me. "She's doing this on purpose."

"What?" I manage, trying to sit up. It feels like I have a pulled muscle in the middle of my chest, but I don't want to lie in bed and just...bleed everywhere. It feels important to sit up, and I'm shocked when I manage to do so. "Fffuuuucckkk."

"You can't die," Seth says bitterly. "Lachesis promised not to pull your thread, remember? I killed you, but you won't die, and now we're both fucked."

I touch my chest, at the brand-new, deep wound there, and...I don't know what to do. I'm too numb to be hysterical, even though I probably should be. There's a gaping hole where my heart should be, and fresh blood just keeps gushing out. I grab the blanket, now sodden with my blood, and push it against my skin, trying to stem the tide. It takes a moment for Seth's angry words to sink in.

Lachesis won't pull my thread. Is that what she promised Kassam? I don't remember the wording, but she did promise not to pull me early. Maybe she's getting back at Seth for leaving me here.

Fucking Seth. I turn my hostile glare toward him. "You betrayed us!"

"No, you little fool." He pauses, pinching the bridge of his nose as if a headache is forming. "I betrayed you, not him. Him, I'm trying to help. You think we can waltz in, as powerless as we are like this, and conquer anything? We're little better than mortals right now." He gestures at me. "If you die, Kassam returns to his full glory, since you're the only thing holding him back. Then, we'd have the full force of the nature god on our side...but Lachesis has decided to send me one last 'fuck you.'" He shakes his head, as if he's the injured party here. "Try and soothe his anger when he comes back. He'll need me if he wants to take down Riekki. Only together can we hope to bring down any sort of army she has created."

With that, he leaves the room, abandoning me.

I make a wordless sound, still beyond stunned at what just happened.

Seth killed me. Or tried to, except I didn't die. All because he wants Kassam back at his full powers, and he figures I won't be missed. I'm just the mortal part of the equation. The expendable part. And I have no idea how to stop a mortal wound from bleeding, or even what I do now that I'm...what, a zombie?

I don't know what I am. I put a finger to my wrist, feeling for my pulse, but it's not there. I feel at my neck for the same, too, and I can't find anything. Doesn't mean shit, I remind myself. You're not a nurse. You probably couldn't find it anyhow. There's too much blood everywhere, maybe. Gingerly, I get to my feet and find a fresh towel to push against the wound on my chest, and then wince at the sight of my gore-covered skin in the mirror. I pour a bit of water into the washbasin, my hands trembling, and I try to scrub at my face with one hand, the other holding the towel to my wound.

What happens when I run out of blood? Can my wound get infected? What happens to me if Lachesis changes her mind and just yanks my thread after all? I'm shaking as I wipe at my hands, feeling very alone and terrified. Kassam said he wanted to ask the Fates to keep me at his side—does this change things if I'm the walking dead? But...maybe I'm not dead. Maybe he missed my heart and I'm fine. I glance down at the bright red water basin in front of me and then back at the bed.

No way. There's far too much blood. No one can live after losing that much blood.

Numb, I clutch the towel to my chest and move to the bed once more. It's a mess, so I sink into one of the chairs nearby, dazed. My head gets foggy—probably blood loss—and I lose track of how long I sit in the chair. I try to think things through. Kassam—how is he going to take this? Is he going to be mad that he was betrayed? Is Seth right that we still need him to go forward? I worry that he's right. I don't know Riekki or anything about her except what Kassam has told me, but if she was strong enough to imprison him for a thousand years, how strong is she now that she's had that millennium to get even stronger?

And what happens to me now? Is my body going to rot and I'm stuck in it? I'm horrified at the thought, but I don't know what to do. Lachesis promised Kassam she wouldn't touch me, and I don't think we thought that promise through. Seth certainly didn't.

The door to our suite opens and Kassam enters in a flourish, holding a bottle of wine. "Little light! I brought you a present—"

I watch him as he chokes on the words, as his gaze slides from the bloody bed to where I sit on the chair a few paces away, equally bloody towel clutched to my chest.

"No," he breathes, tossing aside the wine. It falls to the floor with a crash, spilling its contents on the stone. Kassam doesn't even look. He drops to his knees at my side, horror in his gaze. Gently, he touches my cheek even as his gaze moves over my body. "No, no. Carly, my light. Don't leave me."

"I...don't think I can," I manage, and a watery, horrible giggle escapes me.

With delicate fingers, he peels the towel from my chest and makes a ragged sound of agony at the sight of the wound between my breasts. "Who did this to you."

I think about Seth's words. About how Kassam needs him if he wants his vengeance, if he wants to be free of Riekki. I clutch at his hand. "I don't think I can die, Kassam. I...I should be dead but I'm not. I think Lachesis won't pull my thread." I squeeze his hand, my body still feeling curiously floaty. "What happens if she doesn't pull my thread?"

"I do not know, my heart. The thread is pulled by the Fates, but it is Death who receives the spirit. I do not know what happens when one conflicts with another." The look he gives me is anguished. "Are you...in pain?"

I shake my head. "I feel strange," I whisper. "But it doesn't hurt."

"What can I do?" He takes my hand and lifts it to his mouth, pressing a kiss to my palm. "How can I help?"

I lick my dry lips, and my entire mouth feels like a desert, actually. "Can you help me wash the blood off?"

He gazes down at me, and Kassam suddenly looks furious as he scoops me into his arms and carries me across the room. "I am going to clean you," he states in an icy voice. "And I am going to take care of you. I will never leave your side again. It is my fault this happened. I should have known someone would try to take you from me. I should have known that they would grow jealous of my anchor and seek to return me to the heavens. They think they are helping, but you are my *wife*." His voice grows more ragged by the moment. "It destroys me to think of you being hurt."

Oh so carefully, he sets me down in the beaten copper tub, and when a fresh stream of blood rolls out of my chest, he flinches, his eyes tormented. "I'm okay," I manage. His pain is tearing me apart. It actually hurts more to see him so upset than my wound does. "Really."

"You are not okay," he growls back, even as he tenderly pours water over my shoulder. "I let this happen to you. I am your husband and I promised before the gods—before your mother—that I would watch over you and keep you safe. I have failed you." His eyes widen and he looks around. "Where are the *conmac*?"

Is he looking for someone to blame? The thought makes me

tired. I know Kassam doesn't like dealing with his feelings. "You sent them away earlier, remember? When we were in bed together."

He looks stricken. "I did not call them back." He clenches the water jug in his hand, his jaw working silently. "I hate this. I hate all of this, Carly."

"It's not my favorite either," I point out. "But it's done. Just help me clean up, all right?"

Kassam makes another unhappy sound, but he helps me wash up, avoiding the wound in the center of my chest. I'm not sure what to do with it either, but it keeps bleeding. When he takes a fresh hand towel and places it over it, I shove it inside the gash and then laugh hysterically as tears bubble up.

"Please don't cry, little light," Kassam whispers, brushing a finger over my cheek. "I hate the anger I am feeling, and the grief, but more than anything, I hate the way it feels when you are sad. Please don't." He leans in and presses a kiss to my cheek and then just wraps himself around me, hugging me. "We will figure this out. It changes nothing. We will still go to the gods and ask them to leave you at my side, always. You are still my wife and my anchor. Do you hear me? *This changes nothing.*"

He squeezes me tightly, and I don't know if he's trying to convince himself or me. Easy for him to say it changes nothing when he's whole and I have a gaping hole in my chest and I've lost more blood than I thought was in the human body.

41

"Who did this to you?" Kassam demands.

I shake my head, too tired to answer, and push against the wound between my breasts as if somehow I can close it shut with sheer determination. He doesn't press me for an answer, but I know he's not going to let it go.

For the next while, Kassam fusses over me. He bathes me with tender motions and sets me gently back into my chair again, wrapped in a fluffy towel. The god strips the sheets off the bed, and when he sees the pool of blood that's soaked through on the other side of the mattress, it snaps something inside him. Gone is the easygoing, smiling Kassam. In his place is a god full of rage and fury. He calls for the vizier and the servants and bellows at them.

The vizier, he yells at for allowing an assassin to make an "attempt" on my life (it was not attempted, it was succeeded).

The servants, he snarls at because he wants fresh blankets and food for me *yesterday* and everyone's still half-drunk from the orgy-slash-party downstairs. They stumble through the room, eager to please Kassam, bringing fresh linens and trying (unsuccessfully) not to stare at me. Two of the *conmac* slink into the room, shooting us reproachful looks as they settle on either side of my chair.

"No one is to get near my wife," Kassam growls at the quaking vizier. "If I so much as get a hint that her life is in danger again, I will raze this city to the ground and let my army devour its inhabitants. Do you understand?" He paces angrily, his movements jerking with the fury that boils through him. "Now, where is the healer I asked for?"

"Of course, my Lord Kassam." The vizier looks visibly distressed, glancing back and forth between myself and Kassam. "We are ashamed such a thing would occur here, when we have welcomed you with our arms open. We beg your forgiveness—"

"Just get the healer," Kassam bellows, looming over him. "She is yet bleeding, you fool!"

The vizier drops to his knees. "Of course, my lord. Of course."

When Kassam gestures at the door, the vizier scurries for it, and Kassam storms back to my side. The moment he's near me, his movements change to gentle, courteous. He pulls my damp hair back off my shoulders and strokes my arm. "Hurting?"

"Not at all," I lie. Truth is, my chest feels hollow and cold and awfully, awfully still. Like something vital is missing, but I don't want to worry him more than he already is, since I seem to be (mostly) fine.

"Hungry?" he asks.

I shake my head. The urge to eat is gone, along with the incessant thirst that accompanied being his anchor, and that's worrying to me. Hell, who am I kidding? It's all worrying and I've got a fucking gaping wound in my chest. Nothing's going to be normal anymore.

The healer arrives, a young woman in a simple brown dress, a belt covered with pouches, and her hair pulled back in a hood. She bows to Kassam and then to me, then pulls up a stool beside my chair and inspects my wound, saying nothing. Finally, she presses the towels back against it and gives me a long, knowing look. "Your heart has been pierced. Twice."

"I know." I lick my lips again, but they're bone dry.

"I can wash and sew up the wound and pad it to prevent more bleeding, but that's about all I can do." She pulls a pouch onto her lap and produces a needle and some bright red thread. Then she bows her head. "If this pleases my Lord Kassam, I will get to work."

Kassam gives me a jerky nod, and when the girl reaches for her needle again, he growls and turns away.

She hesitates.

"It's okay," I whisper. "I don't think he likes seeing me hurt." Which...I don't like being hurt, either, but it's nice to see how concerned Kassam is. He's fussed over me and made everything about me and my injuries, not about how it affects him and his plans. It's like I'm really his wife and he's frantic for my well-being. I watch the girl as she wipes my skin down and then carefully inserts the needle, beginning to stitch. It doesn't hurt, but I can feel the cold needle moving in and out of my skin, and the tug of the thread, and that freaks me out, so I focus on her face. She's young, no more than a teenager, but she seems to know what she's doing. "How come you're not freaking out?" I ask, curious.

"I have stitched up many wounds in my time," she replies smoothly, not looking up from her work.

"To people with pierced hearts?"

That gets her attention. She gives me an uneasy look, then returns to her stitching. "The Anticipation has brought with it many strange happenings," the healer says, her voice low. "I have been called to many houses where people were dead but did not die. Their bodies continued to move, their eyes watched all, even when the head was removed from the neck."

I gasp. What the fuck?

She purses her lips, then nods and continues. "Lord Rhagos was not in his realm to receive the fallen. Thank the gods he has returned, and the dead no longer scratch at their coffins, crying for release."

I swallow hard. Okay, so Death is now back home, and I'm still here because Lachesis decided to creatively interpret the rules. "So...what happens when Death finds out I'm an overdue delivery?"

"Nothing," Kassam says in a fervent voice, interrupting. He moves to my side and takes my hand in his, kissing my knuckles. "You remain with me. Rhagos will not touch you. I will not let him." His silver eyes glitter with such intensity that they take my breath away. "He would not dare to take my wife. Do you understand me, Carly?"

I nod.

"Good." Those gorgeous silver eyes narrow. "Now tell me who did this to you so I can feed them to the griffins." He pauses and then adds, "In very small pieces."

I hesitate. On one hand, I worry that Kassam is going to go after Seth. And while Seth himself can die in a fire for all I care, Margo is blameless. Margo also can't die, like me, so there's no point. Punching a few holes in Margo won't solve anything or make Seth go away...and what if Seth is right and we need him? I don't want to protect him, but I've also never seen Kassam so enraged. "I'm tired," I say. "Let's talk about this tomorrow."

"Do you not wish me to avenge you?" Kassam asks, frowning darkly.

It's entirely possible that vengeance is what got him exiled in the first place, and it might be a bad idea to encourage that. "I just want to get stitched up," I say, giving an awkward smile to the girl working on my wounds.

Kassam makes an annoyed sound but continues to hold my hand as she finishes up. She bows to us both, hesitates, and then looks at me. "No sudden movements lest you tear your stitches for at least a week...maybe longer." Her pained smile tells me that the "longer" is more likely. She gathers her things and leaves, and then I'm alone with a cranky, glowering god and two *conmac* who watch us both with remote yellow eyes. Something tells me I'm never going to have a moment to myself again, and the thought doesn't fill me with as much irritation as it should.

"We are alone now," Kassam finally says. "Speak to me, Carly."

"Kassam," I sigh.

"I want to know who dared to attack my wife. Who dared to touch what is *mine*."

I rub my brow. "So that's it? Someone touched your toys and you're mad?"

Kassam's grip tightens on my hand. "No, I am not *mad* because someone touched my toys, as you put it. I am furious that someone hurt you. I am beside myself with anger that someone attacked you and it was my own foolishness that left you unguarded. I am upset that because of this stupid curse, I was in the dining hall, watching strangers fuck, while someone crept into our rooms and stabbed you." Self-loathing fills his voice. "I am upset that I cannot be a better husband to you. That I made a promise I did not keep and you were hurt as a result." He turns those furious silver eyes on me. "So let me fix this by claiming vengeance on the one who did this to you."

Oh. I reach out and touch his cheek. "You can't help your curse, so don't beat yourself up. But...thank you for being so sweet. It makes me feel a little better."

"Still you will not speak the name? Why?"

I'm not as good at deflecting as I'd hoped. "Because you're going to attack them and I hate to say it, but we probably need them."

His face darkens. I can see the exact moment he realizes what I mean, and he fairly bristles with fury. "Was it Seth?"

I give him an exasperated look. "Even if it was, what can you do?"

"I can do a lot," Kassam growls, danger written all over his face. "I can make him pay—"

"No," I say sharply. "You can make Margo pay. Because Seth is a god, and she's the only way he's vulnerable. Would you do this to her?" I gesture at my stitched-up chest. "Knowing that she's innocent? That she was pulled into this because he manipulated her? He knows you can't do anything to him." I shake my head. "I know you want to avenge me, but we have to think this through. It's not black and white." Squeezing Kassam's hand in my grip, I continue. "I hate the guy. You know I do. I don't trust him. Never have, never will. But he needs you and you need him if you're going to take down Riekki. That's why he did this—he thought you'd be able to do more as a full-blown god instead of trapped here in a mortal form."

Kassam looks furious. "He touched you—"

"He killed me," I correct. "But you've said yourself, gods don't feel anything for mortals. We're nobody and nothing. Why would you think him killing me would mean anything? He probably thinks he's doing you a favor."

That flummoxes him. "You are not nothing to me," he says after a moment. "You are my wife."

I pat his hand. "And if I wasn't, would you care? Did you care when your other anchors died?" I can tell I've made a point then, because his expression grows mulish. "Look, I'm just as upset as anyone else over this." I try to keep my tone light, but there's a hard knot in my throat. "But I'm trying to not take it personally."

Not take my own murder personally. Jesus.

"The point is," I continue, rubbing his hand, "Seth doesn't know or doesn't understand how you feel about me. To him, I'm just another Margo—a pain in the ass you have to drag along with you. To him, getting rid of me probably means nothing more than squashing a bug. You've told me a dozen times that gods don't think like mortals do. So let's look at this from a god's perspective. You still need him to take down Riekki. Two heads are better than one. Seth has shown he's not afraid to do dirty work, so don't make an enemy out of him...yet."

"Yet?" Kassam's expression perks up.

"Oh yeah." I manage a faint smile. "After we take care of this Riekki business and you're back to your full power? Burn the asshole for all I care. But let's get our vengeance on her before we take him out."

Kassam studies me, his expression thoughtful. "Delaying our revenge on him will be difficult. I want nothing more than to find him and tear his tongue out. But...perhaps you are wise. Perhaps I am not considering this as I should." He rubs my knuckles thoughtfully, gazing down at them. "I have said many times that gods do not think much of mortals."

"Many, many times," I point out.

He glances up at me, silvery eyes unreadable. "I hope you realize that you are different. That the way I feel about you is...different."

"Different...how?"

He brushes his lips over my knuckles in an almost-kiss, watching me as he does. "I love you."

I'm shocked at his confession. Shocked, and a little flummoxed. "You...love me? How do you figure?"

"We have gone through much together. And I am experiencing all kinds of new feelings around you. Some are not good—like guilt and grief. But when I am with you, the happy times are much...happier. The sex is better. Everything is better when I see you smile. Is that not love?"

Is it? Or is it just him misreading his emotions because they're new to him? "I'm not sure, Kassam. I mean...we've been pulled one way or another this entire time. We're barely friends. I'm not sure you can be in love with me. I haven't done anything."

"You wish to become friends before I declare love again? Very well." A hint of his normal impish personality returns. "We will become very good friends, and next time I declare my love, you will believe it."

"Is that a command?"

"It might be." He gazes down at my chest, at the red stitching there, and his expression grows murderous again. "Remind me that our vengeance must be delayed."

"Don't touch him until we get what we want," I say softly. "It'll be better in the long run if he doesn't see it coming."

Kassam sighs. "Is that a command?"

"It might be," I echo back to him. "You've waited a thousand years for Riekki. Let's not wait any longer."

And just like that, I somehow convince my lover not to kill my murderer. I must be an idiot.

42

I can't sleep.

It's weird, to lie in bed, running my fingers up and down the stitches between my breasts, and not hear my pulse in my ears, or need to breathe, or anything like that. I'm dead, but I'm not. It frightens me a little, so I lie in bed, determined to try and feign sleep even if real sleep won't come. Kassam sits across the room, sticking to his vow to stay at my side. The window is open, eagles and falcons and even pigeons flying in to report to him, only to turn around and leave after they've shared their thoughts. The *conmac* lie at the foot of my bed, silent as ghosts.

Despite the crowd in my room, I still feel alone. I wish Kassam would come and lie next to me, but he has to communicate with his army. We're leaving first thing in the morning, and he's sent a message to Seth to let him know. If Seth still wants to work with us, he'll meet us at dawn. If not, we go on alone.

He'll meet us. He's put too much on the line not to.

I rub the stitches on my chest again, my eyes closed as I try fervently to sleep. If I sleep, it means my body is back to normal. If I sleep, it means all the other bodily functions will kick in again soon. It'll mean that I'm not really dead.

But I lie there, and lie there, and sleep, which has always been easy to come by, eludes me. Hours pass and I lie in the bed, silent and still, waiting. I close my eyes again—

—and when I open them, I'm no longer in our rooms at the palace. I stare up at open sky, an aurora rippling through it. The stars dance and move in front of my disbelieving gaze, like fireflies moving through a forest. Startled, I sit up and realize I'm no longer in a bed, either. I'm naked and there's no ground beneath my feet, nothing but more stars. I reach a hand out in front of me, trying to touch the green, shimmering aurora, only to have it snake away again. "Kassam?" I call. "Are you here?"

"Are you one of the Faithful?" a strange, low voice asks. It's not Kassam's voice. This one is low and smoky and urgent, without a hint of the laughter that seems to permeate Kassam's personality. The voice is also rich with power, reverberating through my surroundings.

I look around, but I don't see a face or a form to put with that voice. There's nothing but darkness and stars. "Hello? Who's there?"

A figure strides out of the shadows, with dark hair and piercing green eyes, and features that seem too large for his strange face. He's tall and ominous looking, dressed all in black and a scar going up one side of his face. He gazes at me as if he's trying to figure me out, circling around me, and even though I'm naked, I don't feel objectified. If anything, I feel oddly disconnected.

"Are you one of Kassam's faithful?" he prompts again. "Your soul is trapped, mortal. I am intervening and I must know where to send you."

Oh. This must be the god of death, the one that's returned to his home. He knows I'm some weird quasi-zombie and he's come to fetch me. "I don't know if I'm his faithful? I'm actually his wife..."

"Wife?" That makes Death stop his circling around me. He studies me closely, peering at my face. "You are not from our world, are you? You are from the other web, like my Max."

"Who's Max?"

He brushes aside my question as if it's unimportant. "You are from another world?" he prompts again. "Do you serve here?"

"I'm Kassam's anchor, if that's what you're asking." I touch the skin between my breasts. Even here, in this dreamscape, the stitches are still there. Damn it. "Are you taking me from him?"

"If you like." He tilts his head, gazing down a too-long nose at me. "How is Kassam? Is he returning?"

"Sort of?" I launch into a quick run-down of what we're doing, the army we've gathered, Seth joining us in this world, all so we can head after Riekki and take her down for what she did to Kassam. He asks more questions about how we traveled over from the other world, which is when I bring up Lachesis and her comment about not pulling my thread.

The god of death nods, as if this makes sense. "The dead drift into my realm when they pass, like stones sinking to the bottom of a pond. You, however, have not. I can feel it at the edge of my senses." His hand drifts up to his thick, tumbled black hair. "You are caught in the mortal realm."

"So what do we do? How do we fix that?"

Death rubs his chin. "Kassam is a friend. I can approach the Fates and ask them to tug your thread back into your realm. If I do it now, though, you will die immediately." He gestures at the stitches between my breasts, and I scratch at them absently. "So that will not do. Instead, I can ask them to tug your thread earlier, separating you from Kassam before you ever cross over into this world."

"Before? What happens to Kassam? His army?"

Those green eyes focus on me. "Does it matter?"

"It matters to me."

He shrugs, the movement seeming to ripple the darkness around him. "Kassam will return to his rightful place amongst the gods. He will cross over without an anchor, and return to his immortal life. You will return to your mortal one and recall nothing of meeting him."

Oh. The thought makes me ache. No Kassam...at all? "Will he remember me?"

Death nods.

"And what about Riekki? Will he be able to go after her?"

The smile he gives me is faint. "Not unless he wishes to risk the High Father's wrath. When we are amongst the mortals, we are expected to participate in their petty squabbles and wars. When we are in the higher realms, we are expected to be better. He will be forced to put aside his quest and hope that the High Father will somehow punish her."

"And do you think that's going to happen?"

"He spent a thousand years inside that glacier, mortal. You tell me."

I flinch. Of course it's not going to happen. If the gods turned a blind eye for a thousand years to the fact that Kassam was missing, they're not going to do squat when it comes to punishing Riekki. Kassam only has one chance for vengeance, and it's if he gets it before he returns to being a god. I can go home, but if I go home, I screw over all of Kassam's plans and a revenge he's probably waited a thousand years for. "I can't go right now," I confess to the death god. "Kassam needs me. He needs to take out Riekki or she could do this again."

The thought's a terrifying one, and something that I just realized. There's no guarantee of Kassam's safety if I turn my back. Riekki sidelined him before, what's to stop her from doing so again? The moment she returns to her full goddess-hood, what's to stop the evil bitch from sending him right back to that glacier and hiding the information for another thousand years once more?

I can't let that happen. I can't.

"Mortal, you do not understand. If you do not go back now, I cannot send you back later." He gives me a look that practically screams "you're being stupid." "I do not normally see the threads of the dying as they are culled from the webs, but I can see yours. It is pulled taut, with so many forces pulling on it from all sides. Soon it will start to fray, and if it snaps, there is no returning you. Do you understand?"

I swallow hard. "I get it." If I don't go now, I don't go ever. I have to choose between Kassam and my own security. There's no guarantee that the Fates will help me, either. We could get to the end of this and they could decide that I need to stay dead. Or this could go on for years and years, and what happens to me then? Do I stay trapped inside my body? Do I rot? Shuddering at the thought, I try to weigh both sides equally...but I can't.

I can't abandon Kassam. Carly, the great un-finisher, is finally going to finish something. God, my mother would be proud.

I choke on a sob. My mother. I don't know if I'll ever see her again. More than anything, I want to hug her in this moment, more than anything. I want to tell her that I love her and that she's amazing and my best friend. I want to tell her that she's strong, and smart, and beautiful, and my father was a liar. That she deserved better. But Ma is strong and can handle herself.

Kassam needs me. "I have to stay."

"You realize—"

"I know," I say softly. "I know what it means. But Kassam needs this, and he needs me. I can't abandon him to save myself. Not when it could destroy him all over again." I manage a smile. "So I'm staying."

He gives me a thoughtful look, his strong features somber.

Finally, he nods. "It is a brave choice. A foolish one, perhaps, but I am glad for Kassam that he has such a friend at his side." The death god studies me for a moment longer. "If you do end up in my realm, know that there will be a place for you. My anchor—my Max—would see you are taken care of." Warmth edges into his deep, unearthly voice. "You need not fear death. It will be kind to you."

"Thank you." I suspect it's not an offer that's made often, if ever. "Something tells me we'll be seeing each other soon."

"Have Faith," he says.

Then, a hard jolt shifts through my body, and I awaken with a gasp, sucking in deep lungfuls of air. I'm no longer in a starless void, I realize. I'm in my room in Chandrilhar. I'm in bed. I touch the stitches between my breasts.

I'm still the living dead.

"Carly?" Kassam calls my voice from across the room, and I look over at him. His normally laughing face seems to be lined with worry, and he brushes an eagle off his shoulder and gets to his feet. "What's wrong?"

I scrub a hand over my face, fighting the urge to cry. "Nothing. It's okay." I know if I explain to him that I just had a dream in which I talked with Death, he'd understand it. Hell, he'd probably ask me to send a message along to an old pal the next time I sleep. If anyone would get it, it's Kassam. But I don't want to tell him about what Death said to me. That I'm risking my life if I stay, because my thread might be too frayed for me to recover from. Kassam would bluster and insist I go home. That he'd figure it out somehow without me.

He'd be lying. He needs me at his side. Needs me to support this quest for vengeance. It's not about Seth, or about a pissing war for a spot amongst the gods. It's about a thousand years of pain, of being forgotten, and how that's the worst thing that can be done to someone who relies on the worship of others. It's about making sure that Riekki doesn't do that to anyone else.

It's about making sure Kassam returns to his rightful spot amongst the heavens, for the people that have waited so long for him to return.

It's more than one silly mortal life, even if it is mine.

"Are you well, little light?" Kassam asks, holding a hand out to me. At his side, one of the *conmac* sits up, giving me another one of those watchful stares.

"Can I have a hug?" I ask hoarsely, getting to my feet and moving toward him.

He pulls me forward, tugging me into his arms and seating me on his lap. His big arms go around me and I lean against him, and the urge to cry fades slowly. Strangely enough, I feel like I'm home.

43

It feels as if the entire city has decided to send us off at the crack of dawn. I'm surprised when we emerge from the palace with trunks of supplies, only to be greeted by the cheering of a thousand voices. People crowd the streets, crying out Kassam's name, and he waves at them. I half-expect him to surge forward and hang out with the crowd, but instead, he moves closer to me, tucking my cloak carefully around my face. "Can you walk, little light?"

I nod, holding onto his arm. It's weird—I feel as strong as ever, but...hollow. Brittle. Like a strong gust of wind will blow me away. It's almost like my body has turned into a house of cards, ready to topple at any moment. I still haven't eaten, or slept, and though my mouth is dry, I'm not thirsty, either.

I also haven't felt the pull of Kassam's hedonism. That worries me more than eating or drinking. Does that mean our bond is severed? Or is it just muted? I decide it must be muted, since Kassam is still here.

The people closest to us bow and cry when Kassam passes by, and people grab at my cloak, trying to pull me away from him. Kassam growls protectively and tucks me behind him. "*No one* touches Carly but me!" There's a wild-eyed look on his face. "Stay back! All of you!"

"It's okay," I tell him, touching his arm. "Really, Kassam. They're just excited."

"I will *not* put you in danger again," he seethes. "Where are the *conmac*? Why are they not guarding you?" He glares at our surroundings as if the magic wolves are somehow to blame for things. "What purpose do they serve if not to guard you when you are vulnerable?"

He roars the last, and I worry that he's backsliding. All those lessons the High Father sent him to the mortal realm to learn are going to vanish in the wind because he's feeling protective of me. I need to nip this in the bud, so I move in front of him and place my (alarmingly cold) hands on his cheeks. "Kassam. Calm down. Deep breaths. The *conmac* are here, okay? I'm here. No one's going to harm me. We're just heading for your army." I keep my voice smooth and sweet. "Deep breaths, my husband. You want to wear your game face when you see Seth, don't you?"

Like a petulant child, Kassam clenches his jaw, his nostrils flaring. He leans in to me, muttering, "I want to wear *Seth's* face. I want to rip it off his smug, lying head and wear it like a trophy."

"Let's put a pin in that for now." Threatening violence against the man that stabbed me should not be nearly as sexy as it is, but damn. It revs my stalled engine, all right. I straighten the ornate green traveling cloak he's wearing (a gift from the vizier) and smile up at him. "We're going to wave to people, and smile, and we're going to mount the meanest-looking griffin and head off to find the goddess. If Seth approaches us, we'll work with him, but we won't trust him. Understand? We're in control here."

"I will not have you hurt again," Kassam grits, tugging me against his chest. "The thought tears me apart."

In the end, the *conmac* come to the rescue. They surge forward, two dozen of the shadow wolves appearing from the midst of the crowd, and it makes me wonder if they have some sort of magic to make them unnoticed until they choose to be noticed. The sight of them makes people scatter with shrieks of alarm, and they file in close around Kassam and myself, establishing themselves as guards. In this manner, we're able to go through the rest of the city out to the walls, the retainers with our supplies following close behind.

Before we even get outside the city, I can see a mass of people waiting outside the walls, dressed in white cloaks and carrying shields. Seth's army is there to greet us, and at the front of the ranks of men sits the hated asshole himself, atop a silks-draped palanquin on the back of one of the large land-hippos. It's surrounded by cloaked women and armed soldiers, and I don't see Margo anywhere as I scan faces, looking for her desperately. He has to keep her with him, right? Those are the rules and—

I almost miss the tiny wave one of the cloaked women gives me. She pulls back her hood just long enough to let me see her face and then drops it again. Margo. She looks like she's having fun, at least, and had a smile on her face. Ten bucks says Seth didn't tell her about him trying to kill my ass.

The god rides forward slowly on his palanquin, clutching the arms of his throne.

The moment we come into sight, Kassam's animal army starts screaming and howling, drowning out anything Seth might have said. I love that annoyance flicks over his face, and I squeeze Kassam's arm to remind him that we need to play this cool. That we wait to claim our revenge. Seth has showed his hand already. We know he can't be trusted. And right now, he *needs* us. So we wait.

Kassam shoots a dismissive look to Seth as he rides forward, and ignores the god's upraised hand, as if he wishes to speak to us. The howling of the animal army continues, and Kassam ushers me toward the fiercest, meanest, largest griffin who waits near the walls for us. He helps me climb aboard the creature's back, and I give the feathers a pat. I tense a little as Seth continues to approach, half expecting Kassam to turn and attack him. Instead, the god of the wild seats himself behind me and whistles at the griffin, who lurches into action.

"Not going to talk to Seth?" I ask from the safety of Kassam's arms.

"No," he says flatly. "He knows what we plan. He can choose to join us, or not, but if I move any closer to him, my fist will encounter his face. Repeatedly."

Fair enough. I love the look of angry frustration on Seth's face as we ride away.

∞

THE TWO ARMIES move slowly westward, and the cold war between Kassam and Seth continues. After two days of being ignored, Seth finally sends over emissaries to speak with Kassam. A vague sort of deal is hammered out—Kassam and Seth will avoid each other but share information. The wild army will ride ahead, and the human army will follow. Seth's army is impressively uniformed, but much smaller than Kassam's mass of wild creatures. Still, more people trickle in to join with us every day that we travel, every village we pass. At night, when we settle down to rest, I can hear Seth making important-sounding speeches, his voice carrying on the wind. Kassam looks less thrilled, but I point out that a big army for Seth equals good news for us.

I think it would soothe Kassam's wounded feelings if Seth had no army, but I'm not surprised. Con men are always good at talking.

Seth's spies find out that Riekki has an Aspect living openly in a tree city called Hrit Svala. It's conveniently close, and so the slow-moving dual armies head toward the forest. There, more creatures join Kassam's ranks, and there's no sneaking up on anyone. It's going to be obvious for miles and miles around that we're on our way. In a way, that's probably a good thing, because by the time we reach the forests of Hrit Svala, our wild army has doubled in size, though most of the creatures are less impressive than the griffins and mighty wyrms from the deep wildlands. It's deer, and wolves, and woales, and so many birds that they darken the skies as we approach. I try not to wince when I see a deer taken down by a predator, because it's part of the natural circle and I know we need that predator for the upcoming battle. Even so, it's hard on my soft heart.

The moment the first trees of the city come into sight at twilight, Kassam raises a hand in the air, and our army stops. One of the outriders for Seth's army immediately rides back to inform them that we're stopping, and I watch as the army marching parallel to ours ripples to a halt. I glance up at the trees. Spies that run back and forth through our camps have told us that Hrit Svala is a tree city, and I'm not sure what I expected. It wasn't for the trees to be bigger than any redwood, the branches lined with so many bridges and pulleys that it looks a spiderweb amongst the leaves. High up off the ground by several stories, I can see a wide wooden platform twining around the thick trunk, like a frill, and above that, I can see a few small lights, no doubt from houses far above and impossible to see from below.

As I watch, those lights wink out.

"They know we're here," I murmur to Kassam as I clutch at his waist.

"They would have to be without ears or eyes to miss us," he agrees. "But that is not why we are stopping."

"Nighttime rest?" I guess, watching him. Even though I don't need to sleep now (a fact which still wigs me out), Kassam insists on stopping each and every night so he can fuss over me. "I promise I'm fine if you want to keep going."

He shakes his head. "We stop because we are going to make Riekki wonder." A hard smile curves his mouth. "She is going to get word of our army camped outside her domain, and she will fret and worry and wonder what it is we are up to. If we are friends or foes." He puts a hand over mine on his waist even as one of Seth's riders approaches on a snorting, nervous horse, waiting for orders to convey back to his leader. "We will attack at dawn. Until then, we rest."

It's not the worst idea. I'm not sure if I like the concept of waiting to attack, because it gives Riekki time to prepare instead of a surprise. But this is Kassam's revenge, so I'm not going to spoil it for him. I'm going to support him every step of the way, just like he's done with me.

And just like we've done every night we've traveled, Kassam hops down from the griffin, pets its feathers and murmurs gentle words to it, and then extends a hand up to me to help me down. I slide off the griffin's back and into his arms, and he immediately kisses me. "We are near the end, my little light. Can you feel it?"

I skip the zombie-kissing joke I had bubbling and just clutch at his arms, smiling up at him. "You're practically vibrating with excitement."

"I have waited a thousand years for this moment." He gazes up at the trees, full of shadows now that all the lights have gone out. "Tomorrow will be the culmination of my dreams." Kassam's silver eyes practically blaze with excitement. "We will burn her tree city to the ground and leave her nowhere to hide."

Did I just tell myself I wasn't going to get involved? Because I'm going to get involved. I take his hand in mine and tug him forward. "Come on, let's take a walk. I need to stretch my legs."

That immediately grabs his attention. "Do they pain you? Do I need to rub them?"

"I'm okay," I promise him. "I just want to walk it out." I lean on his arm, though, to make sure he stays at my side. Have I been pulling the "slightly weaker than usual" card out when needed? Absolutely. Ever since my stabbing, Kassam has been hovering over me like an attentive husband, which is nice. Even so, sometimes he gets distracted. A glimpse of Seth at the head of his army makes him stiffen with rage, or when one of the poor messengers comes by with one of Seth's always ill-timed updates. He's a bit of a braggart, our buddy Seth, and feels the need to constantly update us with how big his army has swelled, or what news he's found out. He always invites Kassam and me over for a "summit" and we always turn him down. I suspect if Kassam ends up in the same room with him, Seth is going to find himself torn to shreds.

So sometimes I pretend to be a little needy and helpless.

Mostly though, I feel surprisingly well. Other than the gigantic, stitched-up hole in my chest, I feel mostly normal. A little too silent, my fingers and toes a little too cold, and my mouth a little too dry, but otherwise I feel as human as ever. I haven't needed to eat, to sleep, or any other bodily functions that a normal person would, though. And while I'm glad I don't have to constantly poop under a bush while the army crawls relentlessly forward, I worry what it's going to mean when I'm brought back to life.

If I'm brought back to life. I'm trying not to think about that possibility right now, but it's a very real one. Even Death said he couldn't do much for me if I refused him.

I...still haven't told Kassam about that. He's got enough to worry about right now.

And worry, he is. Kassam walks at my side, cradling me gently against him when we need to step over a particularly large tree root or if there's a muddy puddle that needs avoiding. Normally he fusses, making sure my hair is braided back and hasn't fallen loose, or checks my boots to ensure there's no holes. He offers to help me bathe. He offers to get me snacks. He offers to fuck me silly.

I somehow manage to avoid all of them. Not that I don't want snacks, or sex, but...my body doesn't need them. I'm not sure how it'll go if Kassam fucks me when I'm a zombie, so I've asked him to wait if he can, for me to be healed. It means we're feeding his hedonism less, but instead of all-night fuck-a-thons, it's turned into Kassam eating and drinking, and cuddle sessions when we stop.

Cuddling feeds the hedonism, he tells me, because it's pleasure. And it's less exciting than sex, of course, but it still works.

As for me, I kind of love an all-night cuddle-fest. So when we pick through the trees as I "stretch" my legs, I know we're going to find a spot to hunker down and have our nightly snuggle. We walk amongst the massive trees, and I try not to marvel at them too much. I don't want to seem entranced with Riekki's location. I should hate it, right? I should hate it out of sheer solidarity. But the forest is large and peaceful and pretty. The birds settle in around us, their nighttime songs filling the air. The homes are so high up and distant that it feels safe to wander about—

—at least it does until we run across a road that winds through the trees, and across the road, a crowded little lot.

At first, I think I'm looking at scarecrows. It strikes me as an odd place to set up a patch of vegetables, in the shade by the side of the road. It also seems odd to cluster so many scarecrows together...and then I smell it.

I raise a hand to my nose in horror. "Kassam, is that—"

"I smell it," he says, and takes a few steps forward, toward the dead people on spikes.

44

I'm horrified at the sight, but I don't know why. Of course Riekki is evil. Of course she'd be shoving stakes into people and leaving their bodies to rot. Of course we'd run across it. I swallow hard, trying not to look too closely. "Do you...think they impaled them because they couldn't bury them? Because the death god was missing? That maybe they were all dead?"

Kassam snorts. "No. I think she impaled them because she was displeased with them. I recognize this one." He gestures at one of the fresher looking corpses at the front.

"You...do?"

Kassam nods, gazing at what's left of the man's body, the robes tattered. "Riekki sent him with Rhagos and his anchor. I saw him when I awoke, moments before I arrived in your world. I am guessing she was angry he did not return with me." He moves back to my side, stepping in front of the sight. "Come, little light. It is not something for your eyes this night. We will find somewhere else to spend time together."

I swallow hard. "Should we take them down? It seems awful to leave them like that."

"Once the city is ours, I will have them buried properly, if it would please you, my soft one." His smile is teasing as he slides a guiding arm around my shoulders and steers me away.

"It would," I say. "And that's not the only thing I want, if you're offering."

"Ask." Kassam's voice is low and easy, a playful note in there, as if his mood is on the upswing despite the horrible sight of all those bodies. And why wouldn't it be? We're about to take down his enemy with an army. Of course he's in a good mood. Tomorrow, the goddess who destroyed his life for the last thousand years gets taken down...hopefully. He should be giddy.

I hope I don't stomp on his parade. "There are probably a lot of innocent people up there," I say carefully. "Since we're not going to take her by surprise, could we, I don't know, send a message to the city telling everyone that they need to get out? That Kassam the badass god of the wild is here to kick butt and take names, and unless they want to fight, they need to leave peacefully? We could give them another day, give them a chance to flee. It'll make you seem like a nice guy, and it'll probably hurt Riekki's pride if everyone in the city starts running for their lives."

Kassam looks thoughtful as we move through the forest, away from the pike-strewn impalement graveyard.

"I know I'm asking you to avoid your vengeance for another day, and I'm not saying you shouldn't absolutely destroy Riekki if given the chance," I continue on, breathless. "But think of the people that are in the city. If you give them safe passage to leave because your quarrel is with the goddess and not them, you'll be seen as a kind, benevolent returning god instead of a vengeful, angry one. These people don't know that Riekki is responsible for your disappearance. All they know is that you've been gone. You don't want the only thing people know about your return to be that you showed up with that asshole Seth and slaughtered an entire city."

He looks down at me, silent.

"It's just a thought," I say quickly.

"It is a good thought," Kassam replies. "You are right. The people here do not know me. They do not know what she has done to me. They think only of the goddess in their midst, not realizing the evil behind her lovely facade." He lightly runs his knuckles along my cheek. "Very wise, my Carly. Again and again, you prove that I am better with you at my side."

That makes me blush. "That's sweet of you, but I'm no goddess."

"Yes, which is a good thing. You see how the goddess acts." He picks a tree and leans back against one of the enormous roots, then tugs me into his arms. Kassam wraps himself around me, my back pressed to his front, and just...holds me.

Sex with him is amazing, but the cuddling...the cuddling might break me. Because I love this more than anything. The times when he holds me and just talks to me? It makes me feel like the most special woman in the world. Heck, in two worlds. I lean back against him, trying not to feel weird that a five-minute walk away, there's a bunch of piked dead guys, and five minutes farther, there's a tree city we're about to attack.

Kassam nuzzles at my neck, brushing gentle kisses over my skin. "If you were a goddess, you would not have the heart that you do. You would not care that people are in danger, or that my wolves must eat my deer in order to survive. You would care about nothing except for your own selfish wishes. So I am very, very glad that you are just my Carly."

I tilt my head so he can better kiss my neck, my eyes drifting closed. "Are you saying that you're selfish, too, oh god of the wild?"

"Yes," he answers promptly. "But I am starting to understand why the High Father has sent us down as he does. Why he forces us to take mortal anchors. It is not just because we must be tied here to the mortal plane. We must learn from you, too."

I chuckle. "This all sounds like flattery."

"Why should I not flatter my wife?" He slides a hand into my hair and twines his fingers in it, forcing my head to one side even more as he nips at my neck. All right, so I'm not completely dead to things as a zombie. I'm definitely feeling the pulse of desire racing through my body at that touch, even if it's muted. "Have I not told you how special you are to me?"

"Mmm, once or twice. But you can always say so again. I don't mind hearing it." My gaze lands on a remote light in the distant trees, and as I watch, it winks out. That reminds me—while I'm sitting here cuddling with Kassam, there are people worried for their lives. Reluctantly, I slide out of his arms. "I should probably contact one of Seth's runners and see if we can get someone to write up warnings to take into the city. Maybe we can have eagles drop them or something?"

He pulls me back into his grip. "That can wait a bit longer. I wish you to look at the stars with me."

The...stars? I blink up at the sky and sure enough, the branches of the tree seem to shift imperceptibly, just enough to give us a glimpse of the starry sky above. Every night when we stop, it's a different excuse to spend time alone together, wrapped around one another. Last night, he told me he was tired of the birds chirping and wanted to get away. The night before, he wanted to relax among the tall grasses of a nearby meadow because it "reminded him of home." Each time, he insists I come with him, and we end up snuggling for hours on end. It's no chore, but I'm a little amused that he's resorting to the stars. He tightens a big arm around my waist and I hug him against me. "You make it sound like we don't spend every day, every hour together."

"Tomorrow will be different."

I frown to myself. "It...will? How?"

"You will be in the skies with the griffins, far away from the fight. I will not have you put in danger, from our army or from

Riekki's." His voice grows hard, his arms tightening around me. "The only ones I trust to keep you safe are those I can command."

"Oh." It makes sense. I can't fault the logic of it—he's immortal unless I get taken down—but I hate the thought that I don't get to be anywhere close to him as the battle rages. Riekki attacked him once before when he was in an Anticipation, and I worry she'll have some new sneaky way to hurt him. "How will I know if you're safe?"

Kassam hesitates. "If I am gone, my griffins will no longer be tame. They will not like having a passenger."

"So basically if I get dumped out of the skies, I'll know things are fucked?" I wince. "I guess it's a good thing I'm already dead."

"Do not say that," he growls.

"Walking dead? Zombie girlfriend?" I offer, trailing my fingers up his arm in a teasing touch. "Undead and probably underestimated?" He doesn't laugh at my jokes. Kassam really doesn't have a sense of humor about my un-living situation. I'm trying to look on the bright side, but when he remains silent, I snuggle back against him and pat his arm. "I'm sorry, Kassam. It's not funny. I'm just trying to cope with it."

"I don't like that you were hurt," he says stiffly. "I blame myself. I should have realized—"

I turn in his arms, because he's been beating himself up for days now. "You've done everything you can. You can't be everywhere."

"I could before," he says darkly. "A god would have been aware of the danger you were in."

"Consider this another lesson the High Father is having you learn," I say. I just hope it ends up all right for me. I try not to think about my thread, pulled between worlds and fraying like Death said. Forcing a bright smile to my face, I tap a finger on his chin. "So when you win against Riekki, does that mean you're more or less done with your Anticipation? What happens then?"

His gaze is locked on my face. "We ride to the Tower of the Spidae and we tell them of Seth's betrayal. I demand that they fix you. Then I return to my home with you at my side." He thinks for a moment. "And of course, we will retrieve your mother."

That sounds like a whole lot of "asks" from the Fates. Big, big asks. But I've followed him this far, and I'll follow him into hell if need be. I cup his face in my chilly hands. "I'm with you every step of the way. You know that, right?" When he nods, I lean in and lightly kiss his lips. "Once this is done, we celebrate."

Kassam gives me one of his wicked smiles. "Celebrating is one of the things I do best."

"How did you celebrate in the past?" I twine my arms around his neck, leaning in. "Come to think of it, how many Anticipations is that for you?"

He shrugs. "Three or four. They are a blur to me."

Again, kinda seeing why the High Father sends them down over and over again. "Do you think you learned your lessons before?" When he shrugs again, I bite back a smile of affection. He can't help who he is. Kassam is someone that lives in the moment, someone addicted to pleasure. And while some of that is hedonism, I'd bet money that his real personality isn't all that far off from things. "Which Aspects win for you most often? I bet it's hedonism, isn't it? You strike me as heavy hedonism with a dash of arrogance in there."

His grin grows wider. "You think I'm arrogant?"

I scoff. "God, yeah. You're so fucking proud of yourself every time we climb into bed together." I scrunch up my face and deepen my voice, mimicking him. "Look at me, I'm Kassam of the Wild. I've got a big dildo to use on my woman. I like a finger in my butt. Hurr hurr."

He throws his head back and laughs, bright peals carrying through the nighttime forest. "You think I sound like that?"

"Oh, absolutely."

"Are we talking about how you sound, then, my pretty wife?" He kisses the tip of my nose. "Shall I point out how much you liked my dildo? How much you screamed your pleasure when I filled both your holes with toys? Shall I bring up how loudly you cry out my name when my mouth is on your sweet little clit—"

His words cut off when I press my fingers to his lips. He grins behind my fingertips, nipping at them. "Everyone's going to hear you," I whisper, biting back my laughter. "Keep it down."

"Shall I put my mouth on your sweet little clit right now?" he purrs, giving me a heated look.

I bite my lip, because I'm not sure how I feel about zombie sex. Is it...necrophilia? What if I can't get wet for him? My mouth is constantly dry as it is, and I don't know if the rest of me is drying out as well. It's a weird, weird thing to worry about. But...I still want him. And if he's right that tomorrow changes everything... I study him, my conflicting feelings surging through me. "Promise me you'll be safe tomorrow."

"I can promise nothing." He gives me a faint smile. "Only that this is something I must do."

Fair enough. I reach for him, pressing my ear to his chest, and for the first time, I notice his heart doesn't beat. Huh. Seems a weird thing to miss out on up until now, but maybe it's because I've become exceedingly aware of my own silent chest. I hug him tightly. "You're going to do amazing tomorrow. You'll kick her ass up one tree and down the next."

He rubs my back, a faint laugh escaping him. "I do not know about that, but I will not rest until she is defeated."

I nod against his chest, not wanting to move just yet. "Any regrets?"

"What would I possibly regret?" His voice is too light, too

airy. Oh, there are some regrets there. My pleasure-loving god just doesn't want to admit them.

So I snuggle closer, my heart brimming with love for him and his soft, vulnerable parts that he hides behind a smile. "You don't have to say anything. Just hold me." I give his ribs a teasing poke. "Gods probably don't have regrets anyhow, just like they don't have real feelings."

He does, his big hand trailing up and down my dress, one given to me back in Chandrilhar. He's silent for so long that I hear the birds chirping and the distant howl of the wolves back with the army. We should probably get back soon, I realize. I've got to get one of Seth's messengers to start drafting the communications to go to the people of the city, and then they've got to be delivered, and—

"I have a few," Kassam finally admits, his tone achingly soft and gentle. "I regret that I did not realize how far Riekki would go when she was spurned. I should have been more careful with my words. I regret that I demanded that the *conmac* serve me, and when they would not do so willingly, I forced them to my will. I regret that every time I see those gold rings in their noses. I hate every time they look at me with their accusing yellow eyes. So yes, I have regrets."

Oh. "Kassam—"

"But most of all, I regret that I could not protect you when I should have." He squeezes me against his chest, even tighter. "I regret I am not the husband I should have been. So yes, my Carly, even a god has regrets." His hand pauses in the middle of my back and then strokes down my spine again.

I notice he doesn't bring up the real feelings, but too much has already been said.

45

We linger in the trees, talking about nothing and everything, for what feels like hours. It's hard to tell time in this unfamiliar place, but the big red moon eventually rises and disappears into the trees once more, and we remain where we're at. Kassam tells me stories, like he does every night. He tells me about the other gods, about Aron of the Cleaver, who was a butcher in a town long, long ago and was so bloodthirsty and fierce that the High Father raised him to become the battle god. He tells me about Tadekha, the Lady of Magic, who is obsessed with her own importance and created all kinds of complicated rules for magic users to limit who could receive her blessings. He tells me of the Fates, who are either represented by spiders (or are spiders, it's hard to tell) and how they choose to live on the mortal plane when the other gods reside in their own secret planes. He tells me of the Great Endless Forest, his home, and when he opened it to the fae. He tells me of the *conmac* leader, an arrogant-sounding asshole who took every impossible task that Kassam assigned him and completed it, earning his wolf-skin.

My own stories feel small and stupid in comparison, but I

share them anyhow. He especially likes the story about the time my mom went to a psychic fair and stormed away, angry, because she realized they were not all psychics. He enjoys my bartending tales, but when I mention my endless projects that I've bailed out on or the relationships I abandoned, he simply tsks at me. "Do not sell yourself short, my Carly. Just because you did not finish these unimportant things, it does not mean you are worthless. You will finish the job when the time is right."

And that makes me go quiet, because I think about the death god again, and my thread, fraying beyond all repair. That's a problem for Tomorrow-Carly, though. Tonight-Carly just wants to linger in Kassam's arms for a little longer. Eventually, though, even the birds settle down to sleep and it grows chilly. I tap Kassam's hand. "I should get back. If you're attacking tomorrow, I need to get those messages drafted and give people time to leave. If they have kids they might need more time, or livestock..."

"Stay a while," Kassam tells me, resting his chin atop my head as he hugs me close. "We can delay one more day. It will give our armies time to rest up, the innocent time to flee, and time for Riekki to sweat. One more day will not matter."

He's delaying this just so we can gaze up at the stars a bit longer? That secret romantic side to Kassam is strong indeed. So I relax in his arms. "Being together like this is my favorite time of day," I admit. "I don't mind staying a little longer."

Kassam chuckles, rubbing his hands up and down my arms. "It is strange, I thought that hedonism would need to be fed as it has in the past—with parties, wine, and partners." He pauses. "Many, many partners—"

"Okay now," I cut in. Not sure I want to hear about all the people he's fucked over millennia.

"—but I find my soul is quietest when I am here with you, just talking and surrounded by the trees." He wraps me in another hug. "Strange, because I have never thought of myself as lonely, but having you with me just feels...whole. Does that make sense?"

In a way, it does. It makes me feel good to hear that just being with me brings him happiness. I don't think anyone (other than my mother) has said the same. I try to imagine what it's going to be like for me, if the gods won't let me stay. If I go back home to Mom, she'll be thrilled. And I'll be...without Kassam. Returning to a gray, gray world without a laughing hedonism god.

I try not to think about that too hard. Kassam wants me to stay, after all. And if my thread frays...

Kassam shifts his weight, smoothly pulling me behind him in a single move. "Someone approaches."

"Oh?" I blanch as a horrid thought occurs to me. "Not Seth, I hope? I'm not ready to see his ass again."

He lifts his head, sniffing the air like one of the *conmac*. "Not Seth. Female."

"Hellooooo," calls out a voice. "I come in peace!"

Margo. How she managed to get out of Seth's clutches is surprising to me, but I don't move from my spot hidden behind Kassam. If Margo is working with Seth, I could be in just as much danger from her as from him. All the trust I had in the world kinda died the moment I did, and I touch the stitches in my chest that are a constant reminder that I'm not safe here. "What does she want?"

"We will know soon enough, little light. I won't let any harm come to you." He keeps me tucked behind him and reaches back to give me a reassuring pat...that lands right on my ass. I shouldn't be surprised at that. "Stay back and let me deal with her."

He doesn't have to tell me twice. I remain hidden behind him, watching as a white-cloaked figure tromps through the forest to get to us. I wince at every twig breaking, at every rustle of leaves, at every crunch of footsteps on the ground. Margo does not know how to be stealthy in the slightest…or Kassam is making things difficult for her. As I watch a vine catch on her cloak and she pauses to pull it free, I suspect it's a little of both.

The moment Margo notices us, she lowers her hood and gives us a bright smile. She looks a little different than when I saw her last. A little more disheveled, a little more windblown. Her hair is a mess and she isn't wearing a stitch of makeup, but her smile is bright with enthusiasm as she looks at the two of us. "Hi there! How are things?"

"What do you want?" Kassam asks, glaring at her as she tries to peek around his shoulder to see me.

"Um, I wanted to say hi to Carly." Her brows draw together at Kassam, and then she looks at me, grinning in bizarre solidarity. "This guy, am I right?" She finds the nearest waist-high root and awkwardly hops up on it, then swings her legs as she looks at us. "I thought I'd come over and say hi since tomorrow's the big day and all?"

"The day after," Kassam corrects. "Carly wishes to save all the innocent from the city. We need one of Seth's messengers to spread the word."

Margo looks surprised. She leans heavily in an obvious effort to peer in my direction. "Carly can't speak for herself?"

"It depends," I interject. "Am I going to get stabbed again?"

She grimaces, toying with her cloak and straightening her bright purple skirt. Her boots look sturdy, her clothes of a good make despite the fact that they're travel-stained. Clearly she's not suffering by traveling with Seth. "So that was him being shitty, I totally agree. I had nothing to do with it, though."

"But you still serve," Kassam points out.

Margo gives me an entreating, helpless look. "What am I supposed to do? I have to if I want to go home again."

She's got a point. I pat Kassam's protective arms and step out from behind him. "Just tell us what you want, Margo."

For a moment, a desolate look crosses her face. "I wanted to chat with you, actually. Sometimes it gets lonely being surrounded by a bunch of religious zealots who have never heard of Earth. I figured you and me, we're kinda in this together. We could commiserate."

Maybe I'm an idiot, but I believe her. "It's okay, Kassam," I whisper, even as he glares at her. "We'll talk for a few minutes and then we can send her back to Seth's camp with our plans. We had to talk to someone over there anyhow, right?"

Kassam smooths my hair back from my face, brushing his fingers over my cheek. "I do not like it." He leans in. "Shall I do the same to her that he did to you?"

I shake my head. "We're not sinking to his level, and she could be innocent." I reach up and pat his cheek. "Maybe bring us some snacks? She's bound to be hungry."

He arches a brow at me. "And leave you unprotected?"

"Well...if I get stabbed again, you're allowed to tell me 'I told you so.'"

Kassam grunts, clearly displeased. He turns and gives Margo a withering glare. "Do not touch one hair on her head or I will ensure your innards are chewed upon by rats for all eternity." With that, he pulls me close, plants a hard kiss on my mouth, and stomps away into the forest.

Margo looks pale as a sheet. "Damn," she says after he leaves. "He's in a mood."

Secretly, I kinda love his mood. "He's been a little bit Papa Bear over me since Seth killed me. You'll have to forgive him for being a tiny bit upset."

She blanches. "I get it. He has every right to be upset. You do, too." Her gaze locks onto me and she bites her lip. "I didn't know, you know. Seth has a million plans and he doesn't share them with anyone. If he'd have told me, I'd have said for him to leave you alone, but...he didn't. I'm so sorry."

I shrug. "Nothing to do but hope that it can be reversed, I

guess." I cross my arms under my breasts and lean against the root, not stepping toward her. I've learned my lesson about being trusting, and we've got ten feet between us. My bond with Kassam doesn't feel tight, so I suspect he's lurking nearby. "Did Seth send you over to apologize?"

"No, actually, he doesn't know that I'm here." She fusses with her skirt, folding and unfolding the same ripple of fabric over and over again. "He'd probably shit a brick if he knew where I am. He likes to keep me locked away with plenty of decoys around me just to stave off Riekki's would-be assassins." Margo's gaze doesn't meet my eyes. "He doesn't treat me like Kassam treats you."

I manage a small smile at that. "Like a person?"

Margo shakes her head again. "Kassam treats you like you're an angel that he's been tasked to keep safe." Her voice becomes soft and awed. "The way he looks at you is just... incredible. And how he kisses you. It really looks like you're more to him than just a problem." She sighs. "Seth doesn't treat me like that. He acts like I'm a puppy he's being forced to babysit. I think if he could snap my neck to be rid of me, he would."

I stare at her. "Really?"

"Really," she says with a little nod. "We don't have a bond like you guys do. It's strange to see, but it's nice." She leans in conspiratorially. "Are you guys...lovers?"

I want to laugh at her hushed voice. I lean in just like she did. "We're married, remember?"

"You really are? I thought that was just for show." Margo seems surprised.

I don't point out that I thought it was, too. Kassam has never considered it to be for show, though, and that thought kinda makes me warm and gooey inside. It's like he's been all-in since the moment we first met, and I'm appreciating that more by the day. "It's not for show. We're really a team."

"And not a stray dog. Must be nice." Her expression grows wistful again.

I don't know how to answer that. Margo's tied to a murdering jerk, but she's not exactly disavowing him. She just came over to apologize for him, not to turn against him. If she's still on his side, I can't trust her, even as much as I want to. I want to ask her what she wants out of this conversation, but if I'm too pushy, she might not answer at all. So I decide to play it cool, to let her lead the dance, so to speak. "Can you send over one of Seth's scribes when you leave? We really do want to give the innocent a chance to leave the city." I gesture up at the silent, dark trees in the distance. "Just because Riekki is there doesn't mean they all have to go down with her."

She nods absently. "I'll tell him you need a scribe and that we're waiting a day. He...won't be thrilled."

"I don't really care."

Margo smiles. "I know. He's an impatient sort. I'll tell him and he'll just have to get used to it. He's not going to move ahead without Kassam, anyhow. He feels like that's his safety net. As long as he's working with one god in this world, the others won't attack him." She fusses with her skirt again and then looks at me. "Hey, Carly?"

Here we go. "Mmmhmm?"

"What happens to us after all this is done?" She waves a hand in the air. "After the big battle and Seth either wins or loses? What happens to you and me?"

Should I be surprised that Seth hasn't told her much of anything? Because I'm not surprised. "I guess it depends on if we win or lose."

She blanches. "Seth says we can't lose, but he also said he was an accountant, so I don't take everything he says to heart. I wanted to come to you and get the truth. Just tell it to me straight, okay? I can take it."

I feel a little bad for Margo, because she really was dragged into this without her consent. "Well, I don't know if we can lose, but Kassam is confident. If we do lose, though, I imagine you end up like me." I tug the collar of my tunic down, showing her a hint of my stitches. "The walking dead. What that means, I don't really know." I think about how Death showed up in my dream and offered to yank me to his realm, but I don't bring that up. I don't know if it applies to Margo, who's been anchored to an intruding god, and I also don't want to mention it if Kassam is listening nearby. "So your guess is as good as mine. Maybe we undead ladies have to go to the Fates—somehow—and ask to be returned...provided Riekki doesn't trap us in some way."

Margo grows paler by the moment. "Okay, that all sounds terrible. I'm going to assume we're going to win, then. What did Kassam tell you is going to happen after Riekki is vanquished? Seth's version changes all the time."

"Well," I say slowly, considering this. "Since Kassam and I are married, and now I'm dead, he's going to go to the Fates and ask them to fix this for me. He wants me to stay with him at his side, forever. Has Seth not indicated what he's going to do with you?"

"First he said he'd send me home, but when I've asked about that recently, he's been vague." She toys with the hem. "I'm trying not to get too worried. You don't think he's going to kill me the moment he doesn't have to keep me, do you?"

"I can honestly say I don't know what goes through Seth's head." If I did, I probably wouldn't have a big hole in my chest. "You know him better than I do."

She shakes her head. "He's impossible to know. He's spent so long with a million secrets that I don't think he knows how to tell the truth. He's just constantly looking for the next angle. Did you know he's almost five thousand years old?" She hops down from her seat and dusts her clothes off. "If you lie for that long, I'm not sure you'll know truth when it bites you in the ass. Which is why I came to see you."

"Does it match up?" I ask her. "What he told you about what happens afterward?"

Margo grimaces. "Of course not. Like I said, he's a liar. Good thing he's trying for god of knowledge and not truth, or he'd really be fucked." She pats her hands against her sides, as if she doesn't know what to do with herself, and then looks at me. "He told me that the moment he ascended, I'd automatically be sent home. It sounded a little too good to be true."

"He might not be wrong?" I venture.

"Yeah, but now we both know he's guessing." She snorts and then pulls her hood back over her hair. "Well, I'd better run back before he notices I'm gone. I'll get those scribes sent over and let Seth know that we're delaying. Day after, you say?" At my nod, she gives me a big, genuine smile. "I wish he hadn't fucked this, Carly. I'd have loved for us to be friends. I could use one right now. I'm over my head and the water keeps climbing higher every day." Her bright smile wavers. "But if you ever need to talk, well, you know where I am."

I return her smile, but that's it. I wish we could be friends, too. But even though Seth and Kassam are supposed to be on the same page, we clearly can't trust each other. I can't be sure that she won't turn around and race back to Seth's side with everything I tell her. I like Margo, but I don't *trust* her.

In fact, the only person I trust in this world is Kassam.

Margo gives me one last sad-eyed look, then turns and leaves. "I'll send the scribes over shortly." She traipses back through the woods, her footsteps as heavy leaving as they were when she arrived. I watch her as she disappears, feeling a little guilty for not being more welcoming. I'm a bartender. I'm used to being a friendly type. But I touch the stitches between my breasts and wonder if she's going to take what I told her and confront Seth, or if she's playing her own game.

If Margo's wise, she won't trust Seth at all.

The moment Margo disappears, Kassam melts out of the woods, his antlers twined with fresh vines. It's like he was lurking nearby, just waiting for her to leave, and I give him a skeptical look. "Your timing is convenient."

"Isn't it just?" He grins at me. "I was busy scavenging food for your guest." He holds out a withered leaf with a sly smirk. "Mmm, delicious."

"You're ridiculous," I tell him, but I'm grinning. I pluck the wilted leaf out of his hand and toss it to the ground. "You're supposed to be the bigger man here."

"Oh, I am much, much bigger," he purrs, sliding an arm around my shoulders and pulling me close again. "Shall I show you just how big?"

I poke his abdomen. "I've seen it a dozen times already." I glance back where Margo left, and I can't help but wonder. "Do you think he sent her over to suss us out? Or was that genuine?"

"It is impossible to say. We will not trust them. Not in the slightest." He says it easily, as if it's as simple as hitting a switch.

I'm not so convinced. "How do we know he won't turn around and betray you with Riekki?"

Kassam shrugs. "Because he needs her gone. And we cannot trust him. But we can keep him close. You know how to hold a snake, do you not?"

I bite back a laugh. "Of course not. I'm a bartender from Chicago. Why the heck would I need to know how to hold a snake?"

The god of the wild grins back at me. "If you grab them by the tail," he says, nudging one of my boots with his bare foot, "you might think you are safe because you are giving yourself enough distance, but you're also giving them enough room to attack." He moves forward and curls one hand around my throat. "But if you take them by the jaw, as close as possible to the fangs, you give them no room to strike. Understand?"

I think I do. We're keeping Seth as close as possible so we can control him. "If that's the case, then Margo should ride a griffin with me on attack day, don't you think? As extra security? It'll be the safest place for her." I flutter my lashes innocently. "And of course, if anything should happen to you because Seth betrays you, she can be griffin food."

"I like the way you think, my little light."

I don't. I'm actually sad that I have to put Margo's life on the line like that. But this is a desperate gambit, and there's no room for another betrayal. My heart has not only been stabbed, it's been hardened. If it gets Kassam through this, though, I won't care. All that matters is getting him back to where he belongs. He's waited long enough for his return.

46

*D*espite our scribes and their best efforts, no one leaves Hrit Svala.

"She will not let them go," Kassam says to me from atop griffin-back the next evening, as we circle the city over and over again, looking for trails of people abandoning the city, but there are none. "Either she has reassured them they are safe, or they are too afraid of her wrath to flee."

I hate it. I hate that everyone is staying, because I know innocents are bound to get hurt. We have two armies waiting at their doorstep, one full of wild animals, and the other of soldiers looking for a fight. I want to scream with frustration at the tiny plumes of smoke drifting up from the trees—cookfires from a thousand chimneys. We've warned them that they're on the verge of attack, and they've ignored us like we don't matter.

It makes me worry. Does the goddess Riekki know something that we don't? She's the goddess of knowledge, after all. Does she already know that we lose this and thus has told everyone to stay put? Or is this all a ploy to make us think twice?

"You are overthinking it, my Carly," Kassam says to me as

the griffin circles around the city nestled in the trees once more. "You are assuming that these people mean something to her. They mean nothing to her, so she will keep them close and use them as a shield to protect herself. She thinks that as long as there are innocents in her city, there is a chance we will hold back."

"And is there a chance?" I ask, because I have to.

"No." Kassam's voice is flat. "We have warned them. If they stay, they know the consequences. They would rather stay than risk Riekki's wrath, so they will feel mine instead." He steers the griffin away from the deepest part of the forest city with a touch of his hand, flying us back toward the waiting army.

I hold tight onto his waist as the griffin wheels about, and try not to get upset. We did offer them a choice. We've done what we can, haven't we? Even so, I hate this. I hate that everyone is nestled down in their homes with two freaking armies camped at their doorstep, and no one seems to be moving. "So what do we do now?"

Kassam is quiet for a moment, then glances over his shoulder at me. "Normally I would not ask, but you are my wife, and I value your opinion. I can be swift but brutal, or I can take a slower approach that might cost more of my army's lives but might save humans...humans that did not choose to flee when given the choice, I remind you."

I'm almost afraid to ask what he means when he says "swift but brutal." "Go on."

"If I am swift but brutal, I harness my magic and use everything I can against them. I wilt the trees so their homes tumble from the branches. I turn their livestock against them. I speak to the worms that live in their guts and demand that they chew their way out—"

"Okay, okay, I get it," I interrupt, shuddering.

"Or we take the army in and we see how much they fight back as we approach. Perhaps they are forced to stay by Riekki's minions. Perhaps not. My army will be whittled down because we will not have the advantage, but it will be, perhaps, fairer."

I swallow hard, because I try to picture the elk, the snakes, the wolves, and what they'll do to someone holed up at the top of a tree. Fling themselves at the bottom until they surely die? That doesn't seem like a good solution, either. Even so...I would hope Kassam would direct them to find an access point. That it's still the kinder option than having someone's intestinal parasites rise up and attack them. "You know which one I'm voting for."

He pats the hand I have clutched to his waist. "I know, my soft one. I know."

I rest my cheek against his broad back, trying not to think too much about the terrible choices ahead. "How long do you think it'll take? To conquer the city?"

"Mmm." Kassam considers this. "It depends on how fiercely they wish to protect Riekki. I do not think they will—her fiercest devotees have always been her scholars and wizards, not the common people. I do not think a siege is likely, but if they try it, we can use magic to force them out of hiding." He pats my hand again, then rubs his thumb across my knuckles. "We will know more by the end of the day tomorrow. If all goes well, we will ride in and they will hand us the goddess without a fight."

"I hope you're right." Something tells me that the longer this goes on, the worse it'll be for everyone.

∼

I DON'T THINK anything or anyone sleeps that night.

I'm starting to get used to the fact that nothing happens when I close my eyes, no matter how tired I am. I don't even try anymore. Instead, I just lean on Kassam and breathe in his woodsy scent. In the distance, the heavy forest is dotted with fires from Seth's army as they spend the evening preparing. The sounds of the wild army are a familiar clamor, as if they're unaware that tomorrow, we attack.

I'm both grateful and terrified when dawn approaches, when Kassam gets to his feet and makes a soft clicking sound in his throat, and his favorite griffin approaches. He pets it, scratching at the small feathers near the edge of the beak, and then holds a hand out to me so we can mount. We do, and ride over to Seth's army, me behind Kassam, to start the war.

When we get to Seth and his army, though, we're met with an angry tirade from the other god.

"You gave her time to prepare," Seth says in a bitter, furious voice as he struggles to control a prancing horse. "She has put a magical barrier around the city itself. This would not have happened if we attacked yesterday morning. She wouldn't have had time to direct her lackeys to craft such a spell."

Kassam stiffens against me, his head whipping to glance at the distant tree city. I do, too, but I can't see anything. "How do you know?" I ask.

"Go and look for yourselves," Seth retorts, shooting me a withering look. "The time for being weak has passed. Everything depends on this. Everything. We cannot come this far only to have our armies thwarted by—"

"Silence," Kassam snarls.

Seth looks as if he wants to murder both of us. His horse whinnies in terror, on edge, and Seth slams his legs against its sides, trying to calm it. That only makes Kassam angrier, and with a look over at the horse, it goes still.

The god of the wild glares angrily at Seth and then turns his griffin and instead of taking to the air, he sends it pacing through the trees. I hold on tight, afraid to even ask what the magic barrier would be. Kassam is practically bristling with fury, and I don't know if it's at Riekki or Seth—or both.

Sure enough, as we approach the city itself, the path feels

charged with electricity. The small hairs on the back of my neck stand up, and as the road widens and skirts around the bases of the trees, it's surrounded by a series of poles that weren't there before—carved poles with runes dancing up and down their lengths. Something intangible shimmers between them, almost like a force field from an old sci-fi movie. The closer we move to the barrier, the more it prickles against my skin in an almost painful fashion, and the griffin becomes agitated and upset. Kassam strokes a hand down the griffin's feathers, guiding off the path, and we circle the outskirts of the city. Everywhere we go, we see more poles. There are carts parked down upon the roads below the trees, emptied of their contents. A distant stable looks empty. High above us, the platforms and the houses block off the dawning morning sunlight, and I get the impression that everyone is watching from way up high as Kassam circles the city, eyeing their magic barrier.

Kassam grunts at the sight of it, then stares.

Just...stares.

"What do we do now?" I ask after several long minutes pass.

"I am thinking." He gets quiet all over again, just staring thoughtfully at that barrier.

"Well, don't strain yourself," I joke, poking him in the side with a finger. It's my job to get him out of his head, after all.

He grunts again, but this time his hand slides to cover mine where it rests on his stomach. "This is my fault."

"What, you're going to believe Seth?" I scoff. "Just because we didn't attack the moment we got here? It's not a crime to be kind, you know. You gave people a chance to leave. There's nothing wrong with that."

"And now we are blocked by magic." Kassam sighs, gazing at the barrier. "And our army is upon the ground, so this is yet another way she defeats us."

"How so?"

He gestures at the barrier. "Because she is willing to corrupt the rules to get what she wants. Can you smell the death on it? Likely three or four of her wizards have given their lives to erect this, just to please her. And now we are blockaded, and she will gloat upon her victory unless we figure out another way in."

I gaze at the barrier, my thoughts racing. Is this my fault? Because I asked Kassam to think of the innocent? At least it explains why no one left over the last day—they were probably reassured by the goddess that they would be safe. With a barrier in place—and something tells me that if anyone touches the barrier, it'll do more than give them a warning zap—Seth's army of fanatics is useless. So is the vast majority of Kassam's army. The wolves, the massive wildcats, the elk with the dangerous antlers and trampling hooves, all pointless. There are birds, of course, but most are small and can't do the damage that one of the tigers can. The griffins remain dangerous, but there's only a handful of them—a fact which has saddened Kassam, since he said there used to be many of them when he went to "sleep."

We also have zero dragons, which disappointed Kassam as well. I know he's thinking about that lack of dragons as he gazes at the barrier. Just one good dragon and he could probably take out the entire city. Riekki would have known we'd have no dragons. She'd know that a barrier could fuck us over. I stare at the trees, the massive, massive trees...and an idea occurs to me. "How far up do you think this barrier goes?"

Kassam twists, trying to eye me. "Why?"

I gesture at the city high above our heads. "They're trees. You're the god of the wild. Can you make the branches curve? Give your army a pathway up to the city itself and go over the barrier?"

His hand clenches over mine. "I cannot use my magic, Carly."

"You have before—"

"And I hurt you," he growls, voice harsh. "I hurt you badly. I am not supposed to do that. I am supposed to realize that you are more important than using my magic, and I do. I vowed to keep you safe. That is not an option."

I ignore the decisiveness in his tone. "But it would work, right? You *could* build a path and go over the barrier? It doesn't go all the way up to the trees?"

"If I used that much magic, it would hurt you," he says again, firm. His hand clasps mine tightly.

I want to hug him. I want to hug him for how protective and sweet he is...but we didn't come this far to only come this far. "I'm dead, Kassam," I say in a gentle voice. "Seth killed me. The only reason I'm still here is because Lachesis is playing some game. You can't hurt me, all right? Just like I don't need to eat or drink or even feed your hedonism, I don't think it'll matter if you pull on me for magic. If you can make the bridges, you should do it."

His hand tightens on mine again. "Carly—"

"I know," I say. I know what he's going to say before he can say it. "But again, I'm dead. You can't hurt me more than Seth already did. And you need to win this. Fuck this magic barrier. You're the fucking god of the wild, and it's about time you showed her she's not safe in a forest, because that's your domain."

He grabs my hand and presses a fervent kiss to the palm. "I do not deserve you, my wife."

I chuckle. "Just kick her ass for me, baby."

47

Turns out, I'm a liar.

When Kassam pulls on his magic to twist the trees, it hurts. Dear god, it hurts. It hurts like I'm being roasted alive from the inside. It's like my head is a melon being squeezed in a vise. I sit atop my griffin, and when Kassam pauses and looks back at me, I somehow manage to give him an encouraging thumbs up. He turns back to the barrier and the trees, and I watch through a haze of pain as the trees warp and twist, a woodland bridge extending from the biggest of trees down toward our army.

"Your nose is bleeding," Margo points out.

I nod and swipe at it with my sleeve. It's just a trickle, but that might be all the blood left in my body. Who knows at this point. I watch as Kassam moves his hands like a glorious, naked conductor, and the trees sway and move, crawling toward him like the living things that they are, bending to his will.

My griffin shifts underneath me, agitated and impatient, and Margo's does, too. Once the bridge is established, the army will surge forward and Margo and I will take to the air, safe atop two of the griffins, high above the reach of any arrows.

We're to wait while Seth and Kassam invade Hrit Svala and remain securely away from the battle, just in case. According to Kassam, they will send a white dove to us when it's safe for us to land.

I'm not going to think about what happens to us on griffin-back if Kassam and Seth are defeated and Kassam loses control of his animals.

Staying in the air atop a griffin seemed like a logical plan, but that was before my brain was being squeezed out of my ears. Dizzy, I clutch at the griffin's feathers as hot wave after hot wave of pain ripples through me. I burned my hand once as a kid and had to go to the emergency room, and I thought that was the worst pain imaginable. That's nothing compared to this. This eats at me, shredding me from the inside as my vision gets blurry and swims with red.

"Carly?" Margo asks, her voice sounding hollow and distant, as if she's down a tunnel.

Something hard snaps inside my head—at the base of my skull. I let out a shattered gasp, choking as another round of blood gushes from my nose.

"Little light?" It's Kassam's voice, reaching me through the dark haze, and I focus on him. I feel strangely light and heavy at the same time, like I was after Seth stabbed me, and I realize it's happening all over again. If I was alive, Kassam would have killed me just now.

But I don't want him to know that, because I'm still here, and it doesn't matter. I raise a shaky hand and put my thumb up again. "I'm good. Go kick ass."

Kassam hesitates, searching my face. I swipe at the blood streaming down my lip and give him another thumbs up. Either he's reassured by my expression or he decides that it's too late to do anything, but he nods at me. "Wait for our dove, my wife. I will send for you."

"I'll be here," I croak, and all the while, my head pounds and pounds.

He flicks a hand, and then the griffins take to the air. Margo screeches in surprise, clinging to her bird-lion. I'm used to the sudden movements of them at this point and I manage to hold on admirably, even as hot needles shoot through my head. As we fly upward, the trees keep twisting and twisting, creating a thick, leafy bridge. The animal army surges forward, and a cheer rises amongst Seth's army, thousands of voices strong. They too far away to see what's happening, but I suspect that the sight of the griffins rising—and the movement of Kassam's army—tells them that things are happening.

My griffin keeps flying higher, until we pass the leafy canopy and I can see nothing but green below. The plumes of smoke from cookfires are absent this morning, the skies an inappropriately cheery blue. Even through the pulsing agony of my head, the noisy madness of the combined armies is everywhere. The men are shouting, the lions roaring, the birds twittering and calling, the woales honking. It's all maddeningly loud, and I peer down at the branches, desperate to see a pair of vine-covered antlers rising from a tangled brown head of hair.

We're too high up, though. I can only hope for the best as the cheering of Seth's army grows louder and my griffin flies away.

∼

It's impossible to tell time atop the back of a griffin high in the sky. It doesn't obey my commands, of course, but waits for a silent order from Kassam. I'm simply a passenger (or a hostage) waiting for orders. The griffin circles lazily over the forest, over and over again, so high up that the wind constantly rips at my hair, and my dry lips feel like sandpaper. The day grows hot and plumes of smoke appear in the trees below—not small, friendly cookfires but larger, darker, ominous plumes that speak of larger structures burning.

I hope that's a good sign, and then I feel like an asshole for being excited to see a city burn.

It's just that...up high, the only thing I can see is blue skies and smoke. I can see Margo pull the hood of her cloak over her head to protect it from the relentless sunlight, but I'm so broken down at this point that it feels like too much effort. I barely manage to cling to the griffin as it circles over the trees, over and over again. My nose eventually stops bleeding, but I don't know if it's because Kassam has abandoned his magic or if he's hurt, or if I've just run out of blood.

I hate that I can't see anything from up high. It makes sense, of course. An anchor is theoretically a god's only vulnerability, so it makes sense to keep us out of reach where we can't be used as hostages or targets. Even so, I wish I was down there, at Kassam's side. I don't know how to fight or hold a shield or a sword. I doubt I'd have the energy to do either...but I still want to be there.

Waiting just sucks.

The pain eventually ebbs a bit, going from shards of jagged glass in my head to a low, unpleasant throb. My vision clears, and while the hollow feeling remains, I can more or less concentrate again. The day drags on, and as it does, the fires in the forest grow larger and more plentiful, until it seems that everything below us is ablaze. The scent of burning meat drifts up with the smoke, and my heart aches for the animals that traveled with us for so long.

At least, I hope it's the animals. A sick clench in my gut tells me that it could be anything.

As the day wears on, my anxiety increases. There's no word from Kassam, no white dove flying up to meet us overhead. My griffin continues to circle, and so does Margo's. When I look over at her, she's slumped in her seat, drooping in her makeshift saddle. She looks pathetic and weary, and I wonder if she's half as worried over Seth as I am over Kassam. I rub my stitches as we fly another leisurely circle overhead, the smoke thick in the air. By now, it's so smoky that everything seems to be burning—everything except the trees themselves. Kassam said they didn't burn, so I guess everything else must be on fire.

"Be safe," I whisper on the wind, and hope he can somehow hear it. "Please, be safe."

The sight of all those fires below terrifies me. Kassam says he can't die, but that doesn't mean he can't burn, that he can't hurt, that all the wild animals that pledged their allegiance to him can't die horribly. My throat grows tight with worry as the smoke invades my lungs, and still the fucking griffin flies circle after endless circle.

I feel like I'm losing my damn mind when a small white speck flies out of the dark, choking smoke, and circles around the griffin's head. Rubbing my watering eyes to make sure I'm not dreaming, the dove lands on my shoulder and I want to kiss the damn thing in gratitude. "Is it time?"

As if it can understand my words, the griffin underneath me lets out a mighty cry and tilts its wings, alternating the pattern it's been silently keeping for hours and hours on end. Another shape flies out of the shadows, this time Margo's griffin with her clutching its back. Her face is dark with soot and she coughs as her bird circles mine. "Are we going down?"

"I think so," I croak, my throat shredded by the smoke I've inhaled. "I—"

The griffin dives before I can finish my statement, and then we're plunging through the trees, heading on a crash-course toward the center of all that smoke. Coughing, I squeeze my eyes shut and hold on tight as the griffin plummets, crying out in that noisy screech of his. When I feel him shift under me and slow, I peek an eye open just in time to see a massive central platform amongst the trees. It's burning, and the sight makes me want to cry. Houses are up in flames, people are running for their lives, and everywhere, everywhere, there are dead bodies. I see corpses of Seth's soldiers, their white tabards stained and torn. I see dead wolves and the corpse of one of the great wyrms, with a half-dozen pitchforks sticking out of it. I see the spindly legs of a deer hanging over one of the platforms, dripping blood. Somewhere in the chaos, there's a baby crying, and as I watch in horror, a man chases down a screaming woman, who rushes into a burning house.

Everywhere is carnage, and it makes me ache with the horror of it.

It's hard to comprehend just what war means until you see it, but as the griffin flies through the platforms, I see far too much. Everything is burning, the trees showing the strain. Branches are broken, platforms sagging and dumping their contents onto the ground below. As I watch, a rope bridge burns, a fleeing man falling to his death. There's so much screaming, so much despair. Sobs choke me, until I close my eyes, because I don't want to see any more. I can't and remain sane. I can't.

The griffin cries out, the sound different from before, and I open my eyes to see that we're heading directly for a new platform, larger than most, and it seems to be in the heart of the city. Less is burning here, but the smoke remains everywhere. The massive tree at the center of the platform looks as if it's hollowed out into a dwelling of some kind, and I can feel power pulsing deep within, like I did when we first met Seth, back on Earth. It's the pulse of another god.

This must be where Riekki is.

I twist, looking for Margo's griffin, and it's a short distance behind us, heading in the same direction. I can't see her face, but I suspect her expression is the same as mine. Life in a modern city on Earth hasn't prepared us for this devastation.

I'm horrified that it's come to this, and even more horrified that I've had a part in it. How could Kassam possibly want this? How could Riekki?

"Carly!"

A voice calls my name, clear and loud above the chaos. The griffin swoops lower, toward that platform, and I see a lone figure with tall horns and bronzed skin. One of the horns is broken down to a stump, and soot and blood streak his body. He holds a staff in one hand, covered with the biggest thorns I've ever seen, and waits at the edge of the platform for me, one of the *conmac* at his side. I've never been so glad to see him. Sobbing, I clutch at the griffin, wishing I could get it to move faster as it carefully picks its way down into the madness.

When it finally alights on the platform, I tumble to the ground and stagger to my feet. My legs are stiff and my body feels that curious light-heavy that tells me things are Wrong Inside but I ignore it. All I care about is Kassam. I stumble my way toward him, even as Seth's army surges onto the platform, flooding forward from one of the bridges.

Kassam rushes toward me, and when I fling my arms around him, he tosses aside his weapon and grips me tight. His head rests atop mine and he holds me so, so close as I weep and weep in his arms. "You're safe?" I manage. "You're all right?"

He holds me closer, as if he wants to somehow squeeze me into his chest and never let me go. "My body is well, but my spirit hurts at what we have done this day," he tells me. "Most did not fight. The goddess lied to them and told them they would be safe, that she had seen it. And she is Knowledge, so they believed her."

I moan in horror. "So many dead—"

"Seth's army is out of control," Kassam says harshly, stroking my hair. I don't know if he's comforting me or himself. "Once they burst into the city, they went on a killing spree and he will not contain them. They are the ones responsible for this chaos.

I realized what he was doing and scattered mine. The wild are leading those that flee to safety and returning to the woods. I will not have them be part of this." He holds me fiercely. "This is not what I wanted."

"I know," I say, gulping back my tears. I gaze up at him, at the devastation on his face. "I know."

Kassam loves life in all its forms. He wants the natural process, not this...disaster. He will not flinch at wolves taking down a deer, but as we watch Seth's men surge onto the platform with captives and loot stolen from the people here, laughing and shouting with glee, it's hard not to feel responsible. We needed Seth to win, but I'm not sure all of this is worth it. I cling to Kassam, fighting the horror I feel, and look around for his army. There are a few scattered animals, but like he said, most are fleeing. The griffins remain, and a limping striped cat hurries away as Seth's troops swarm forward. Now that I look around, most of the dead aren't the wild army, and as I watch, birds flutter away into the trees. The griffin remains near us, fluffing its feathers and glaring balefully at anyone that approaches, and the *conmac* are near, but that's all.

As I hold tight to Kassam, Margo's griffin lands and she slides off its back, landing amidst Seth's men with a dazed expression. They grab her, cheering, and pull her toward the front of the army. She looks a little confused by their excitement, but it becomes clear what they're doing when a tall figure strides through the crowd.

Seth.

His white robes are spotless despite the smoke and the chaos. He lowers an equally spotless white hood down from his head and assumes a pious expression as he gazes at his army. "Inside this last domicile," he says in a lofty voice, gesturing at the hollowed-out tree, "is our enemy. Let us find her anchor quickly and bring him to me."

The men cheer and head for the treehouse, their weapons

raised. As they do, Seth continues to give them that munificent smile, as if they're his children on a playground and he's the doting father watching over them. Never mind that they're carrying swords and are covered in blood.

Seth looks over at us, and his smile becomes a little more predatory as he approaches. "It is the final hours. Are you not pleased with how today has gone?" He gestures at the tree. "When we take this, we will have completely broken her under our heels."

Screams erupt from inside the house, and I bury my face against Kassam's chest. "Can't you make them stop?"

"Make them stop? Why would I want to do that?" Seth laughs, and the sound is cruel. "We have her exactly where we want her. Our armies have won. Is this not what we fought for? Is this not what we came to do?"

I look up and glare at him. "You could be kinder about it."

"Kinder?" He sneers at me. "There is no 'kinder' in war, you idiot." He gestures at the tree. "How shall we politely wrest power from her? Shall we curtsy and shake hands before slaughtering her people? Shall we—"

"We shouldn't slaughter at all," I snap back at him. "We're better than that."

"Are we? I thought we were here for vengeance." Seth turns to Kassam. "Is this not what you wanted? What you planned for? To seek your revenge on this betraying, selfish goddess? Here it is." He spreads his hands and gestures at the burning, destroyed city around us. "Your vengeance. Is it not sweet? Is it not what you dreamed of?"

I look up at Kassam, and his expression is...odd. He gazes at the burning platforms around us, at the bodies massacred, at Seth's gleeful men swarming over the fortress built into the tree itself. "I do not know what I imagined when I sought to avenge myself on Riekki," he says, his words slow and thoughtful. "Perhaps I dreamed of this once, but no longer. I am different. I see this, and it does not fill me with joy. It fills me with sorrow, instead." He shakes his head. "I wanted to avenge myself on Riekki, not all of these people."

"These people sheltered under her wing," Seth snarls. "They are her creatures. They would kill your woman just to get rid of you."

"As you did?" Kassam's voice hardens. His arms tighten around me, and I can feel the tension brimming in his body.

Seth's mouth flattens as he flicks a glance at me. "That was different. It was to benefit both of us. We could have won this war quickly with you at your full strength."

Kassam gestures at the trees, their twisted branches that he manipulated to create bridges. At the flames and smoke and dead bodies everywhere. "This was not quick enough for you? There was no siege, no long, pitched battle. We came in here and we slaughtered." He shakes his head again, his silver eyes full of sadness. "And I am filled with regret."

Oh. I take his hand in mine and squeeze it.

"Regret?" Seth spits. His face is contorted with fury, no longer handsome. "Over what?"

My husband sighs heavily, gazing at the carnage around us. His focus moves from the trees, warped and scarred, to the dead scattered on the platforms. "I am supposed to be the god of life. This is not what I am. I have let my need for vengeance turn my focus away from what really matters, and that is what I regret." He looks over at me, his expression soft. "Luckily, my anchor has been steadfast. She shows me the true way of things. She supports me even when I am being selfish."

Seth just rolls his eyes. "You are a god. These people, this place, they're nothing to you."

"You are right," Kassam says, never taking his gaze off of me. "And perhaps that is part of the problem. Perhaps this is the lesson I am yet learning. That I must care about all if I am to do my job properly." He straightens his shoulders, his tired expression turning to one of focus as he looks squarely at Seth. "I have scattered the wild army. They will aid us no longer. The city is now yours. Carly and I will be taking our leave as soon as she is rested and ready."

That catches Seth by surprise. Me too, if I'm being honest. "You're not going to wait to meet Riekki? You don't want to rub it in her face that she has lost?"

Kassam's brows furrow. "Why?"

"Because you have won, you fool," Seth snaps. "At the very least, do you not want to show her who it was that defeated her?"

I watch as Kassam's lip curls with distaste. "You think I am proud of this? You think this pleases me?" He gestures at the burning city. "I am ashamed of what we have done here today. I will take it as a lesson and learn from it." He gives Seth a contemptuous look. "You should do the same."

Seth's expression is pure ice. "You are a fool. We were here to seek power, and we have grasped it in our hands. Take your victory lap. Watch as I strip the power from your most hated enemy and revel in her despair. This is what we have worked so hard for. This is what we have strived to attain!"

But Kassam ignores Seth's rantings. It's like he tunes him out completely. Instead, he turns to me and gently cups my chin, studying my tear-stained face. "Are you tired, little light? Shall we go?" His voice is incredibly gentle. "Say the word."

Oh. "I'm ready if you are," I promise him. "I'm not too tired to leave." The thought of getting back onto the griffin again makes my sore butt want to scream, but if the alternative means we stay in this madness, I'll gladly climb onto the back of anything that will fly me out of here. I want nothing more than to leave this horrible, slaughtered city behind.

And if I do, I can only imagine how badly Kassam wants to get away.

He nods, then gently kisses me on the lips. "Then we will go."

"Fool," Seth calls again, furious, even as more screams arise from the treehouse. "Weak fool!"

Kassam ignores him, leading me over to the waiting griffin. He climbs onto its back with ease, then holds a hand down to help me up. As I wrap my arms around him, I see the *conmac* melt into the shadows, slinking away, and it seems to me that for the first time, there is approval in their yellow eyes. Then the griffin takes off and we are into the air once more.

I hold tightly onto my husband, and I'm glad this day is over.

48

We don't fly for long. I'm weary, and I can only imagine Kassam is, too. The griffin lands again a short time later, back into the forest. He settles us into a clearing near water, then begins to preen his feathers. Kassam glances around, turning, and then nods. "We will head north in the morning," he tells me. "Tonight, we will stay here and rest."

I glance around. It seems peaceful enough, but there's an angry stain of smoke in the distance that tells me we're not all that far from the burning corpse of Hrit Svala. I watch the griffin as it smooths its feathers with a sharp beak, as if it's just another day. I'm glad he can recover so quickly, at least. I think I'm going to be dreaming about the bodies dangling off the platforms at Hrit Svala for years to come.

Or not...since I can't dream.

I eye Kassam. He's covered in soot and his tangled hair looks wilder than ever. He's still naked—always is—but there's something hollow in those silver eyes, something tired and weary. It calls to me, and I move toward him, taking his hand. "Are you all right?"

He shrugs, his shoulders slumped. "I do not know, little light. Today, I did not feel like myself."

"Do you want to talk about it?"

"No."

"Do you feel like you should, though?"

"Probably." He gives me a ghost of a smile. "Is this a mortal thing? Talking about when you are troubled?"

I shake my head, taking his hand and pulling him toward the stream. "It's a husband and wife thing. You tell me your concerns and I'll tell you mine. Sometimes sharing them helps ease the burden a little." As I move to sit by the stream, a small songbird flutters toward us, heading straight for Kassam's horns. It pauses at the missing one, as if surprised to find it gone, and then settles in atop the other. For some reason, the bird seems to cheer Kassam up a bit, some of the tension in his shoulders easing. "What happened to your horn?" I ask. "Did someone attack you?"

"Many did," he admits. "I defended myself. After a while...I no longer saw faces. It is one of many things that bother me about this day." His thoughtful gaze turns to me. "And you."

"Me what?"

"I felt your pain. When I was in the city, I felt the agony tearing through you. You smiled so bravely for me and said nothing, even as I wrenched and wrenched from you, taking more than I ever should have." He settles down onto the grass next to me, and I notice his hooves are scarred and one is split. "I hurt you for my vengeance. I did not stop to think about how wrong this was, until much later. And now I cannot stop thinking about it."

"I'm okay," I say automatically.

"Are you?" The look he gives me is knowing.

I shrug. "I mean, I'm already dead, so it's not like things were worse. It hurt, but it hurts less now. And I didn't want you to come this far just to have everything fail. I wanted to help you see it through." I pull off my shirt and swirl it in the water so I can wash him off. "I wanted to finish something, you know?"

"Then we were both wrong."

Maybe we were. I shrug and lift the sodden shirt toward him, taking one arm and wiping it clean of ash and blood. "So what happens now?"

"To you and me, or to Seth and Riekki?" His tone is flat. Tired.

"Let's start with Seth and Riekki," I say, wiping down his bronze skin. He's covered in scratches and bruises, and my heart aches for him and all he must have seen today. "Unless you don't want to talk about it."

"I thought talking helped," he muses.

"Yeah, but they're assholes. I get it if you'd prefer not to dwell on them." I move the wet shirt over his chest, trying not to wince at the deep gouge he has across one shoulder.

Kassam chuckles. "They are indeed assholes." He lifts a finger and the songbird hops onto it, and he brings it to his face, rubbing his nose against its feathers. In the distance, I see a hesitant doe creeping forward, heading toward Kassam, and it makes me happy. He needs nature around him to heal, I realize. This is what he should have been doing for the last few weeks—communing with nature, not going on some crazy vengeance quest. I'm such an idiot for not realizing it sooner.

So when the deer moves over toward us and noses me, I scratch her side and then turn her soft black nose toward Kassam to pet. He immediately brightens, tugging the deer against him and tucking it under his arm as he rubs her flanks. Some of the light comes back into those silver eyes of his, and it makes me want to race through the woods, scooping up every animal and flinging it at him, just so he'll smile again.

I don't know when I came to rely on his smile, but my world doesn't feel quite right without it.

"You asked what Riekki will do now that she is cornered," Kassam says, petting the deer. "She will not bend, if that is what you are wondering. She will refuse to back down, because by now, she will have heard that Seth is coming for her position. She might insist upon having her anchor killed so she can ascend back to her realm, but since she has not done that yet, I suspect she knows the High Father would be displeased if she arranged for his or her death."

"How can he take her job from her?" I ask, curious. "How do you transfer godhood from one to another?"

Kassam rubs the deer's neck thoughtfully. "He is going to use her very nature against her." At my confused look, he continues. "He knows the High Father will not be looking upon her approvingly after she has attacked me. She is vulnerable and weakened. She needs something impressive to happen in this Anticipation to get back into the High Father's good graces. Instead, she will likely be put into chains and dragged about the countryside as Seth shows all of Aos that he is the new god of knowledge. That he has defeated Riekki. The more people that believe in him, the more his power will grow and hers will diminish. Then, when he is strongest, he can petition the High Father and the Twelve will decide if he should be the god of knowledge, or if it should yet remain Riekki. And if it goes to that, Riekki knows she will not triumph."

"And that plan will work?" For some reason, I'd thought all this time that we were going to kill Riekki. But of course she can't be killed. She's a goddess. Her anchor can be killed, but that will only send her home. "Just...holding her hostage and dragging her around the countryside until everyone decides that Seth should take her place?"

"Seth is clever. I suspect he has wormed his way into many seats over time." Kassam shrugs. "He knows that the strongest power for a god is that of belief. If no one believes in her and he spreads his name as the new god of knowledge, it will not matter if Riekki is willing to go along with it or not. The truth is always written by the victors."

So basically, he tells everyone that Riekki is powerless, and in doing so, makes it happen. Clever, and awful at the same time. Riekki will be forced to sit by and watch as Seth steals power from her, and because she's been a naughty girl, she can't even get help from the other gods, because she can't be trusted. "That's just so...subtle."

"Is it? It is effective, though. If someone had thought to take my seat amongst the gods while I was missing..." He trails off.

Poor Kassam. No wonder he was so very delighted each time he saw he had worshippers. Each person that remembered him brought power to him. No wonder he wanted to parade the animals through the countryside as we headed toward Hrit Svala. All of it was to tell people that he's returned. "So Seth has stepped on everyone and gets what he wants. And Riekki loses because she's a bigger asshole than Seth."

"Seth is the new asshole," Kassam corrects me with a wry smile. "Riekki is the one we know. If we must decide upon a known betrayer or a new power, we will choose the new power in the hopes that things will become better."

I digest this. "What happens to her anchor?"

"He—or she—will be kept alive until they are no longer needed."

"And then...because Riekki is not going to be a goddess any longer, the bond will be broken?" I ask hopefully. "And that person can go on their way?"

He's silent. I know what that answer means. "So they're condemned to death," I say, swiping at his dirty chest. "They're fucked, just like me."

"Her anchor chose to serve," Kassam says gently.

"You mean like I chose?" I raise an eyebrow at him. When he's silent again, I shake my head and dip my shirt into the stream once more, wetting it. "It's an unfair system, don't you think? Even if her anchor chose to serve, they probably think they're serving some goddess of sunshine and roses, right? She's knowledge, so she's in charge of her own spin. She's not going to let all of humanity know that she's a huge dick. They're going to think she's a sweetheart, and then whoever serves her is fucked over." I grit my teeth and lean in, wiping away rivulets of ashy water that trail down his chest. I can't even appreciate his washboard abs tonight. I'm too tired, too sick of all the machinations. "Is this what I have to look forward to?"

Kassam grabs my hand, his expression intense. "You and I are different."

"How? How are we different?"

"You are my wife," he growls. "No one will dare take you from me."

I stare at him, not entirely believing this. It was just a quickie ceremony performed by my mother. A handfasting to force a stronger bond between us. Will that matter to anyone other than us? Is it truly as binding as Kassam—and my mother—think it is? "Kassam...what if it doesn't matter that I'm your wife? What if I have to be killed off anyhow?"

"It will matter," he says firmly. "I am the last of my Aspects. In order for me to ascend back to my realm, you must die. But because you cannot die, and because I do not want you to die, we will take my griffins and we will go to the Spidae."

"The Fates," I echo, remembering his plan. "And they'll help us?"

"I will demand their help," he says, expression stubborn.

I fight back a wince. Kassam thinks that because he's important, it somehow makes me important. I know I'm not, though. People die every day. People that have families, people that are wives or husbands. People that are loved just as fiercely as Kassam claims to love me. There's nothing that makes me special enough to thwart death other than Lachesis had a bone to pick with Seth. It's enough to keep me alive for now, but something tells me it's not going to be enough. That my fate-strand is too frayed, like Death said, and then I'll never see Kassam or my mother again. The knot rises in my throat and I press my lips to his palm, feeling the desperate need to touch him. To reassure him.

"Carly," he says in that firm, authoritative voice, as if it's all already been decided. "I will not let you leave me." He nudges the affectionate deer away from him and pulls me forward, until I settle in his lap.

I wrap my arms around him, breathing in his scent. Sure, he smells like smoke and blood and sweat, but he's Kassam underneath, and after the day we've had, I'm grateful that I get to smell him at all. What if something had happened and Riekki had set a trap? What if he hadn't been able to walk away? What if she'd trapped him? I hug him tighter, worried. For a moment, I want to go back to that awful burning city and make sure that Riekki is in chains. That she can't hurt Kassam again. "Promise me you're safe, Kassam?"

"We are both safe." He presses a kiss atop my head. "You worry too much."

"And you don't worry enough!"

"Of course I don't. I am Hedonism. It is in my nature to just enjoy." He kisses my forehead again and then nips at my ear. "And you smell delightful, little light."

I clench my teeth at that nickname, the reminder that I'm a lesser being. That my "light" is smaller than a god's. "I smell like a griffin."

"As if I care? Shall I lick you clean?" When I rear back, squealing, he chuckles and rolls onto his back, dragging me down with him into the grass. "You are so fussy, my Carly. It is just a body. Just dirt. I—"

"Do not dare tell me you've licked worse, because I don't want to hear it," I warn him, fighting a smile. I like it best when he's happy and playful like this. It makes me feel like everything in the world is not so dreadful. Like we're not in this shitstorm up to our necks. Like I can forget for a few more days that I'm now twice-dead and stuck in this realm and I'll never see my mother again... I force the thoughts away and sit up, touching his broken antler. "You broke this today."

"I did." He props up on one arm and watches me with appreciation, and I remember that I'm now topless and my boobs are probably jiggling all over the place. "I tried to get a blacksmith to leave the city using my bridge, and he attacked me with his hammer."

I suck in a breath, picturing the worst. "Were you hurt?"

"Bah. I am a god."

I touch his head, where the horn is broken in an ugly manner, and then trace my fingers along his brow. "I know you're a god. I asked if you were hurt."

He captures my hand in his. "I hurt all day," he admits. "I hurt when I realized how badly I had pulled magic through you. I hurt when I felt your pain. I hurt when I realized how selfish I was to do this, to harm you in my quest for vengeance. I hurt with every elk that fell, every wolf that was stabbed, every wyrm that fell at my feet because the mortals were trying desperately to protect their homes. I do not think they were protecting Riekki. They were protecting the only homes they knew. I realized this, and I realized I was the invader, and I hurt. I hurt and I hurt." He rubs his mouth against my palm and then presses it to his cheek. "But most of all, I hurt knowing that I was disappointing you. That I had done all of this for my vengeance, and I no longer wanted it."

49

He thinks I'm disappointed?

I shake my head. "I'm not disappointed at all, Kassam. I wanted this so you could have closure. So you could feel safe. I don't care if you shake hands with her and call it a day. I just need you to feel good about it. She fucked you over and you wanted revenge. I get that. I understand that completely. It's a very human thing to want revenge, you know." I chuckle, running my thumb down his cheek. "So don't worry about me. I'm fine."

"Are you, my wife?"

I hesitate. Do I tell him the truth of what happened today? Will it worry him? Should I confess everything? That I stayed for him to get his vengeance and frayed my own thread? I don't know what to say. It feels like too much to throw at him, when he's already feeling guilty...and I don't regret my choices. I knew what I was getting into, and I'd choose the same all over again. So I simply say, "I love you, Kassam. No matter how all of this turns out, I love you and I want you to know that."

Those silver eyes narrow and he loses all casualness.

Kassam jerks upright, no longer lounging, and when I pull back, he grabs my hand and tugs me toward him, searching my face. "Why do you make that sound like goodbye?"

Oh. I guess I'm as terrible at hiding things as he is at revenge. "It's not goodbye," I say. "Not yet. But you have to be prepared for the worst."

"I will not let you leave me, Carly." His entire body grows stiff with determination, a scowl on his face. "You will stay at my side forever. That is what we vowed."

"I know we said that," I say to him. "I just...might not have a choice. What if the Spidae don't want to grant us any favors?"

"Then they are worse than Seth, and they will have my undying vengeance." His jaw flexes, and I can tell he's upset. "You...would you stay with me if you could? If it was your choice? This is not your world, and I know I have pushed and pushed for many things, but I am no longer pushing, Carly. I am asking."

And asking is significant for one like him. I understand that completely. He's a god. He demands and his wishes are fulfilled. He's not used to getting thwarted, and I can tell it bothers him. "Of course I'd stay with you." I give him a teasing look. "I need to one-up you again after that last round with the toys. I still can't believe you demanded those from the vizier."

I wait for his eyes to brighten with teasing. For him to pick up the thread that I've dropped at his feet, and to play around. To smile and become my laughing, sunshine-filled Kassam again. He doesn't, though. He simply gazes at me with those intense silver eyes, so bright in his bronze face, and watches me. "I love you, my Carly. Perhaps you do not understand how significant that is—"

"I know it's a big deal," I interrupt, chuckling.

He shakes his head again. "No, you don't. I am a god. A god that has been punished by the High Father many times over for my infractions. With immortality and power, you are used to getting what you want. Anything you ask for is yours. Anything you say is law. It ends up affecting how you think. The High Father has been trying to make us realize that for a very, very long time, but we are stubborn children. Resistant. I have had many anchors, and none of them have affected me like you do. None of them have talked to me as you do. They were either afraid of me, or so fiercely determined to do my bidding and please me that they lost their own way. It did not help me." Kassam gives me an earnest look. "But you, Carly, you help me."

I'm silent. Astonished, but silent.

"You make me realize when I am being selfish, or foolish. You point out when I am not thinking of others, only of myself. And you make me think. You make me realize when I am thinking only of my needs, and you make me consider other ways. For the first time in my long existence, I worry about how another being will perceive me. I have never cared if the High Father thought I was aimless, or useless. I have never cared if the dragons suffered under my rule, or if the *conmac* were angry at being forced to serve. I thought it was my right as a god. As their god. But when I am with you, and I see your disapproval, it makes me think. It makes me try to see it from their eyes. To realize that just because it is something I want, that does not make it right." He clenches a fist over his heart. "I have known many humans, my Carly, but you pierce my soul."

Oh.

Wow.

No one has ever said such sweet, such earnest things to me. I'm a little shell-shocked to hear this coming from laughing, carefree Kassam. Flustered, I manage a smile. "You make it sound like I'm special, but I'm not, Kassam. I'm just an average woman from Earth. It's not like I did anything unusual. Maybe...maybe you were just ready to have your soul pierced.

Maybe after what you went through, you were ready to listen. It doesn't mean that I'm special."

"You are special to me." He devours me with his eyes in that hungry, hungry gaze. "Surely the Fates will look kindly upon that."

"I hope so," I say softly. I want that, more than anything. I want to stay with him and help him restore himself to power. I want to watch him grow in his awareness of how it is to be human. I want to play more one-up games with him. I want everything that being with Kassam has to offer. For the first time, I realize that I don't want to go back to Chicago. That I miss my mother, that missing her is like a dull ache in my breast that throbs daily, but I don't want to return.

Not if it means I lose Kassam. I want to be his wife. I want to be his partner. His everything.

I hope we can figure it out.

Kassam studies me, his expression thoughtful. "Your head still hurts you, does it not? I can feel it."

Does it? Everything feels so "off" and unsettled in my body at this point that it's hard to tell. I can't decide if things are broken inwardly or if they've always just felt a little hollow. Maybe "busted" is my new norm. At any rate, it doesn't matter. This is what I've got to work with. I shake my head at him and pick up my tunic once more, determined to finish washing him off. "You're the one that fought a nasty battle today. I should be taking care of you."

He snatches the tunic out of my hands. "Carly," he warns.

"Kassam," I mimic his scolding tone and reach for the tunic.

"Do you think your path was any easier? I was the one in the city, but you were the one fueling me. It was your power that created those bridges. Your strength that allowed our army to move forward. I felt how much it drained you. I felt your pain." The anguished expression returns to his face. "I felt all of it, and

I still kept going, because I thought I had to. I thought I needed it, until I saw your face and realized how much it had cost you."

I bite the inside of my cheek. Everything in me says I should tell him that he pulled so hard that he broke something inside me. That I felt a snap—oh god, I hope it wasn't my thread—and I've felt unmoored ever since. But I don't want him to think I blame him. I don't. This was wholly my choice. It was my idea for the bridges, my idea for him to pull his magic, and I'm going to own it. "Let's just agree that we both had a shitty day, hmm?"

He grunts and then gives my sodden tunic a squeeze. "Then I will allow you to wash me, but only if I get to wash you, too."

"Deal." I don't mind a bit of pampering, and I'm itching to touch him. Something about just being close with Kassam eases some of the anxiety inside me. I slip my pants off and then step into the stream, not entirely surprised to see that it's only about knee-deep. At home, I'd probably be afraid of snakes or curious fish, but Kassam controls the environment here. There's nothing to fear. With that, I gesture for him to join me, and when he stands in front of me in the water, I take my time wiping the tunic over his skin. I tsk over every cut and scratch, even though they're healing. He tells me of how the day went, of the people he fought despite his efforts. He only wanted to seek Riekki, but defenders kept getting in the way and blocking him.

"I tried to kill no one, Carly. I truly did. They were just doing as the goddess commanded them."

"I know," I soothe. He's not a killer, my Kassam. Maybe the old Kassam was, but he's had his eyes opened, and he sees things differently now. He sees mortals as people, and I know each time he had to defend himself, it hurt him in his spirit. "It's over with," I promise him. "It's done. You've closed that door."

He nods slowly and cups water to spread over my skin. Instead of using the tunic as a washcloth, he merely spreads his wet fingers against my skin. It's both erotic and comforting, just touching one another, and when his hand moves between my breasts to touch the thick, obvious stitches there, he looks so stricken that I ache for him.

Sometimes I wish I could turn off everything he's feeling, because it's clear he's struggling. *I do not like this, Carly,* he told me once. *I do not like feeling all this guilt.*

I don't want him feeling all that guilt, either. He didn't ask to be trapped, after all. He didn't ask to be transported to my world. He's just coping as best he can, one day at a time. So I distract him. "How far is the journey to the Spidae? Are they close?"

He bends down, cupping another handful of water and trickling it over my breasts. I want to point out that they're not dirty, but he seems to be enjoying himself, so I just bite back my smile. "They live at the edge of the world."

"So...not close."

Kassam's gaze flicks to mine, and his playful grin returns. "No, not close. It will take some time to travel there, even on griffin-back."

I bite back a groan at that. Goody. More days on griffin-back. "I guess it's too far to walk."

"I suppose we could," he says, brushing his wet fingers over my nipple and watching it with fascination as it hardens. "But I worry it will put you in danger again. I am tired of you getting hurt by my choices."

I thwack him with the wet tunic, savoring the splat it makes on his chest. "Oh, I'm sorry, is it beat on Kassam time? I must have missed the memo."

He looks surprised, clutching at the tunic. "Did you just strike me, wife?"

"With a tunic. Don't be a baby." I reach over and flick a finger at his nipple, enjoying his outraged expression as he moves to protect it. "Are you done castigating yourself or should I see if we can find a whip in the next town and you can just beat yourself directly?"

Kassam stares at me, then throws back his head and laughs. "Well said, my pretty wife. I hear your words." He tosses the tunic aside and cups my face in his hands, grinning as he bends down to kiss me. "I am sorry if I am moping. I just don't like you getting hurt."

"I don't like getting hurt, either, but I know you wouldn't do it on purpose." I slip my wet hands around his waist, then reach lower and behind him to cup his firm ass. I'm not being eaten alive by hedonism's curse any longer, but I can still appreciate a delicious ass. And man, his is *nice*. "So let's stop with that, all right? Let's just enjoy our time together."

He smiles and leans in to kiss me again, brushing his lips over mine in a gentle promise. I close my eyes, savoring the feel of him, when he chuckles against my mouth. "Look. Little lights."

I blink up at him, slightly confused. When he gestures behind me, I turn to look at what he's pointing toward. It's the dark forest, shadowy with deep dusk, the sky above a rich purple. As I stare at the darkness, a tiny light flashes and disappears. Then another. And another.

Fireflies.

"Little lights," Kassam murmurs, sliding an arm around my shoulders and hugging me back against him. "Are they not a joy to see? They are some of my favorites, I think."

Little...lights. "You call me little light. Because of them?"

"Yes." His voice is rich and pleasant behind me, and in front of me, another light blooms in the darkness and zips away. "You are my light in the shadows, helping me see clearly when I am lost."

Oh. All this time I thought he was insulting me. Being just a cocky god who thought of all humans as lesser lights. Instead, he's been complimenting me. Calling me sweet things.

To him, I'm not less. I'm his light in the darkness.

It might be the best thing I've ever heard. Ever. I turn toward him, ferocious, and push him to the muddy banks of the stream.

"What are you doing?" He asks, amused.

"I love you," I say, even though it's not an answer. Instead, I put my hungry hands on his warm skin and touch him everywhere, stroking his cock as I give him another push toward the banks. He settles onto the mud on his back, propping up on his elbows as I climb over him. "I love you, Kassam."

"I love you, my little light." His gaze searches mine, perhaps looking for answers as to why I'm suddenly so ravenous for him. "I will not let anything happen to you. You have my vow."

I lean in and kiss him, hard, nipping at his lower lip and sucking on it until he groans. "Wanna make love to a dead girl?"

He doesn't laugh at my joke. If anything, he frowns slightly. "You are not dead, Carly. Your spirit is right here with me."

"Yeah, but my flesh—"

"—is just flesh," he finishes before I can say more. He lifts his chin, angling his mouth toward mine as I straddle him. His cock is hard and aching between us, and I rub my pussy over his shaft, teasing, as his lips nip at mine. "The flesh does not matter, my little light. My spirit loves yours."

And that's another reason why I love this man so much. Beneath the tangled hair and the laughter is a gorgeous spirit. I kiss him again as I slide a hand between us, angling his cock against my entrance. When I seat myself upon him, we both groan. I'm a little dry, my body not responding quite like it used to, but Kassam's silver eyes are scorching as I slowly work him into my body. He licks his thumb and presses it against my clit as I ride him, and then we fuck fast and hard on the muddy banks of the stream. When I come, it's the tiniest orgasm, like my body is fighting to show any sort of release, but I'll take it. I rock my hips above him even after I'm done, until he comes deep inside me.

I don't move from my spot, either. I just lean over him and press kisses to his warm, delicious skin. I don't want to think about tomorrow or what comes next. I want to just enjoy my husband amidst the light of the fireflies.

Tonight is enough for me.

50

Two Weeks Later

I thought I'd be glad to see the other side of the mountains, but it looks like I'm wrong.

What's on the other side of the mountains is much, much worse. Ugh. I stare at the gray surroundings, at the enormous, flat gray lake that betrays not a ripple or a hint of movement, and try not to feel alarmed.

At my side, Kassam gives me a brilliant smile. "Almost there. Want to rest a bit longer or shall we get moving?"

I...honestly don't know. I stare out at the desolate gray landscape and blink, trying to decide. I've never seen anything like it. Maybe the last few weeks of travel have spoiled me. We've moved over forests and green landscapes for the last while, all of it lovely and inviting. The weather has been nice, as well, with only the occasional rainstorm to dampen our spirits. It's almost been like a vacation as we've traveled on griffin-back. We're not in a hurry, and sometimes I wondered if Kassam was deliberately taking his sweet time as we moved leisurely north, stopping frequently for no reason at all. We'd stop to see a particularly impressive tree that looms higher than the others, or if Kassam sensed a rare bird. We'd stop at a stream so the griffin could rest for a bit. We'd stop at this particular cliff because the view was spectacular.

Totally felt like a vacation, especially when we stopped just to have sex.

We'd also pass by towns and farms, and while we didn't seek out people, they often came looking for us. Farmers would catch sight of our griffin, or hunters in the forest, and we'd encounter the locals. They were always shocked and delighted to see Kassam, and he enjoyed the brief meetings. I think it made him feel good when they would recognize him on sight. As we've traveled, we've seen a lot of farms where Kassam said there used to be woodlands. He remembers this world from a thousand years ago, with different cities and different roads. It was all new for him, and in this, we're equal, because it's all new to me, too. I know the disappearing forests distress him, but hearing words of praise from woodland hunters helps ease his fear.

As we journey on, the cities and small towns and farms grow sparse and we head into the mountains. Here, it's unblemished and just as remote as the place we first arrived, and I can sense Kassam's happiness. I think he might be crushed if his entire world looked like mine when he'd awoken. He was able to handle the strangeness of modern Earth well, able to cope with finding the wild in downtown Chicago. I'm not sure he'd be able to cope with it on his doorstep.

Even if this world isn't quite as wild as it used to be, there's still plenty of room for a wild god.

This end of the world might be a little too extreme for me, though. I eye Kassam. "Is it supposed to look like this?"

He inhales deeply, that pleased look remaining on his face. "Indeed. Can you not smell it?"

"I don't smell anything."

"Exactly!" Kassam's eyes glitter with delight. "No farms, no mortals, no crops, no cities. It is untouched by humanity."

It's also untouched by a single blade of grass, but I don't point that out. Kassam looks thrilled, and so I try to appreciate our surroundings through his eyes. The mountains are nothing but bare rock on this side, and the slopes are pebbled with loose shale and other equally gray rocks. There's a tiny path winding its way through the mountains toward the water's edge, but the water itself looks hellishly oppressive. It doesn't even look like real water, despite the fact that the lake covers the entire horizon. It's so flat and gray it looks like just one gigantic puddle. Most bodies of water seem to have some sort of life to them—they ripple when the wind touches the surface. They shimmer when the sunlight hits the water. This is just...a void. A big, gray, unpleasant-looking void in the middle of the craggy, equally gray mountains.

Away in the distance, at the far side of the lake, a thin, lone needle points at the sky. Our destination. "That's the Tower of the Spidae?" I ask Kassam, even though we've talked about it a hundred times. It's the only building on this side of the Godspine Mountains. Nothing and no one lives here except the Spidae, who dwell upon the edge of the world. Even our steady griffin who's been with us since the beginning of this journey is unsettled. He prances in place, looking as if he'd like nothing more than to fly away and leave us behind.

Only Kassam looks thrilled to be here. But then again, it never takes much to thrill Kassam—a firefly, a blow job, a full moon, it all works for him. I love that about him. I watch his smile as he breathes in the crisp mountain air, and my heart aches.

I don't have much longer in this world, I think. I haven't seen Death again, but with every day that passes, I feel a little more floaty and disconnected from my body. At some point, I know I won't be able to stay in it any longer. It's just a hunch I have. Whatever life-force tethers me to my flesh has been severed, and I remember what Death said about my thread becoming frayed. I suspect that thread has come completely undone, and it's sheer will alone that keeps me at Kassam's side instead of heading to the afterlife.

I'm trying not to think about it. I certainly haven't told Kassam about how I feel. He'll blame himself, and I don't want him to lose that happy sense of purpose that has been enveloping him since we left Seth's side. He's seeing his world again, he's seeing people rejoice at his return, and I want him to feel nothing but relief and happiness.

Either the Spidae will be able to fix this, or they won't. I absently touch the stitches on my chest, just below the collar of my tunic. Whichever way it heads, I want Kassam to know that I love him and that I did this for him. I don't want him to feel guilt. I just want him to think of our time together with happiness. So I smile affectionately at him and ignore the floaty, drifting feeling in my head. "You think they're expecting you?"

Kassam laughs with delight. "If they are not, we have bigger problems."

"I guess that was a silly question, huh?" Fate should absolutely know what's going on. I think of Lachesis, her world-weary attitude and constant cigarette smoking, and try to picture that in a spider god. Nope. Try as I might, I mentally can't make the pieces fit together.

Kassam looks over at me. "Are you ready to do this, little light?"

Am I? Part of me thinks I won't ever be ready. I move over to take his hand in mine. His fingers are warm compared to my cold ones, and his palm callused and raspy, but pleasant. I lean against his arm and gaze out at the unsettling gray water and that sliver of a tower far on the horizon. Even though this landscape is hideous, I wouldn't mind staying here forever, with Kassam right next to me.

But that's what I want, selfishly. I want to turn around and run, to forget we ever saw this place. Kassam wants to go home to his plane, to his Great Endless Forest. He wants to free the *conmac* from the duty he forced them into a millennium ago. He wants to return to his rightful place in the heavens and take up the mantle of the wild god once more.

And that seems far, far more important than what some crappy bartender wants. So I nod, putting on a determined expression, and memorize his handsome face, just like I have every day for the last two weeks, because I know this won't last. "Let's get this show on the road, shall we?"

51

The tower is even more intimidating up close. It looks to be made of stone...and something very, very much other. It gleams a pearly white against the gray backdrop of water and mountains, with an equally colorless beach lapping at the edges of the shore near the base of it. It's several stories tall, with windows and balconies dotted all up the length of it in no particular fashion, like a drunken architect waved a hand and decided to throw in some ventilation at the last moment. It's unnerving because nothing lines up. It's fluid and without straight lines in the slightest, and like nothing I've ever seen before. The outside wall actually almost looks a porous stone, but when I get closer, I see that every inch is covered in spiderwebs.

That's reassuring.

A long ramp leads up from the beach to the tower itself, and as we approach, I could swear the tower grows taller. The griffin lands on the beach itself and then sits down, as if refusing to go any further, and I can't blame him in the slightest. Kassam turns to him and rubs his feathers one last time, then presses his face to the dangerous, sharp beak of the creature in a caress. "Thank you, my friend. You need serve no longer."

For some reason that surprises me. I watch as the griffin rubs its head against Kassam and then takes a few steps back and launches himself into the air, flying back over the dead waters of the lake. It's on the tip of my tongue to ask why we don't need a ride back, and then it hits me. There is no "back." Kassam expects the Fates to help him ascend back to his home, and me...

I guess it depends on how frayed my thread is.

Kassam turns to me and extends his hand. Wordless, I join him, trying not to cling too hard as we head up the long ramp to the tower's base. Before we can make it to the doors at the top of the ramp, they open up and a woman dressed in a brilliantly red dress steps out. She's got dark skin and even darker hair, pulled back in a thick twist at her nape. Her eyes are bright as she eyes us, her gaze resting on Kassam. She doesn't comment on his nudity, or even blink an eye. "My lord Kassam," she says in a rich voice. "Right this way. Your rooms have been prepared."

Of course they were expecting us. It's that whole "fate" thing again. Even so, she doesn't look at all like how I expected the Spidae to look. She's soft and pretty and her dress is utterly flamboyant, with a deeply scooped collar to show off her impressive cleavage, and her skirt has a jillion tucks and flounces to make it look fluffy and full and ornate. Somehow when he'd told me about the Spidae, he'd made it sound like they were men. Creepy men. They're gods, though. I...guess they can be pretty women in red dresses?

I nudge Kassam, waiting for him to introduce me. When he gives me a puzzled look and says nothing, I decide to speak up. "Thank you for hosting us. We've traveled a long way to meet the Spidae. Are you...one of them?"

Her eyes widen and she chuckles, raising a hand to her

mouth to hide her smile. "No. My name is Yulenna. I serve the Spidae as their anchor. They will greet you once you are settled. It might take a while, however. I will see to your needs until then." She turns toward the tower and gestures that we should follow. "After me, if you please."

Oh. An anchor. I feel stupid. I nudge Kassam again, but he's only gazing at the woman thoughtfully. "They have always lived here in the mortal realm, yet you are the first anchor they have taken. Has something changed?"

"I'm not sure how to answer that," Yulenna says in a brisk tone as she leads us inside. "I am mortal, my lord. I have only served *my* lords for a year now. Anything prior to that I would have no knowledge of."

"But you serve as an anchor? For their magic?" Kassam presses, his brows furrowed.

"I serve as a reminder of the humanity that they serve," Yulenna continues gracefully. "And I tend to all their needs. If you mean that they require my assistance in order to draw upon their magic, the answer is no. They remain as they have always been...in that particular aspect." Her smile grows broader. "You must be Kassam's anchor, then."

"I am." I hold my hand out to her. "I'm Carly."

She gives my hand a puzzled look and then turns to Kassam, as if he has the answers. "Follow after me, if you please."

"Tell the Spidae we wish to see them tonight. Tell them that Kassam is here."

"They know you are here. They will see you when they are ready."

Kassam frowns, displeased at that. "I am tired of waiting. We have traveled far."

I touch his wrist, because I'm willing to wait a few more days if it means I get more time with him. What if the next moment is my last? The Spidae can avoid us for a week and I'd be totally fine with that. "We can wait a bit longer. Truly."

"Time does not flow the same for them as it does for us," Yulenna says, heading up a ramp inside the tower itself. "My task is merely to make you comfortable until they realize you are here. They do not keep you waiting out of a power play. They are simply unaware you are here yet, perhaps."

Kassam doesn't look convinced, but when I touch him again, he focuses on me instead. He takes my hand, and we follow the woman deeper into the tower.

The interior is just as creepy as the rest of the place. It's not particularly well lit, with sunlight streaming in from the windows outside, but other than that, there's no source of interior light. Everything seems shrouded in shadows. Pale stone is everywhere, and instead of stairs leading up into the lofty tower, it's all a series of curling ramps that move up one wall and circle upward. I suppose that wouldn't be too weird except everything —literally everything—is covered with spiderwebs. Huge, alarming amounts of spiderwebs. They cover every inch of surface, dangle overhead and brush against my skin as I walk, and to make matters worse, there are big "clumps" of web of various sizes that look like cocoons. In addition to that, the ramps lead to what look like thick curtains, parted in the middle. It isn't until I peer closer that I realize that the "curtains" are made entirely of webbing. I touch one, and Yulenna is there immediately. "Touch nothing," she says, her tone firm. "There are things behind these doors that are not for you to know."

Oh...these are doors? I shudder as we walk forward again, and then I can't stop noticing just how many doors there are, and Yulenna passes all of them. I frown to myself, wondering why there are so many rooms for only four people, but it seems impolite to ask. For all I know, the Fates here are big entertainers for the other gods or something.

The tower seems to go up endlessly, far past the height I thought it would be from the outside. I'm relieved when Yulenna finally pauses near another heavy set of curtains and opens them, revealing the room inside. "These are your quarters. I hope you'll find them to your liking. I'd also like to ask that you not go wandering without an escort. My lords are very private and don't wish to have their things disturbed." She turns to us. "If you need anything, I will be by several times a day to check in on your needs."

I glance over at Kassam, but he's not looking at me. Rather, he's frowning at the shadowy recesses of the tower's ceiling above the door, almost as if he sees something there. To my horror, the webs crisscrossing every inch of the tower seem to shiver. It's not the shiver of something small, but something heavy moving through them.

"The spiders will not harm you, Lord Kassam," Yulenna says, as casually as if describing a painting. "They answer to my lords only. Think of them as no more than a flea."

Out of the corner of my eye, I see what looks like a long, pale white spider limb disappear into the shadows. It's more the size of a small horse. "That's not a flea," I say faintly.

"They will not harm you," Yulenna says again, and gestures at the room waiting for us. "But again, I encourage you not to wander unescorted."

Message received. When Kassam puts a hand on the small of my back, escorting me in, I'm more than ready to go. I'm also relieved to see that our room is brightly lit despite the shadowy interior of the main tower. We have a window and a balcony, and warm sunlight streams in through the curtains open to the outside. There's also a fire burning in the enormous, oversized fireplace made of the same soft-looking rock (also covered in spiderwebs, which worries me a little). If you get past the whole "spiderwebs" thing, though, the room is lovely. The blanket atop the large, oddly puffy bed is made of a soft-looking weave with all the colors of sunset, and bright throw pillows are tossed atop the head of the bed. Comfortable chairs are perched near the fireplace for warmth, another vivid blanket casually draped atop one, and something tells me that Yulenna is the one responsible for all the colors. There's another pair of curtains off to one side that probably lead to a bathroom of some kind.

Yulenna moves in after us, heading to the bed and adjusting one of the pillows. "There is a bathing tub with piped water in the privy closet," she says, her voice brisk. "I insisted that we give our guests the privacy to bathe after their long journey here. I think you'll find it to your liking. And I will bring you food and drink shortly."

I can't imagine what they have to drink if the water out there is gray, much less food. "I don't need anything, actually. No food, no drink."

That brings Yulenna up short. A flash of understanding crosses her face and then she gives me a look of pity that makes me ache. "Of course."

She knows, I realize. Somehow she's seen how frayed my thread is and that's why she's looking at me with sympathy. I glance over at Kassam, but I don't think he's noticed anything yet. He moves out to the balcony, drawn to the sunlight, and stands out there, drinking in the fresh air as if addicted. "You will tell them I have arrived?" Kassam asks Yulenna.

The anchor inclines her head. "They know already. Or... they don't. Time flows differently for them. They will be here when it is appropriate." Her hands smooth down her dress and she gives me another curious look, then turns back to Kassam. "If you do not require anything else, I shall leave. I have much to do. I shall return in a few hours to see if you need anything." With that, she turns in a flounce of fancy red skirts and heads for the doors, shutting them carefully behind her.

52

I sit on the edge of the bed and then immediately curl my legs up onto the mattress. "You don't think there's a spider in here, do you?"

Kassam moves back inside, heading toward me where I sit on the bed. "They are not normal spiders," he says, a thoughtful look on his face. "I cannot feel them. They are not part of my realm."

"Then what are they?"

He shrugs, seemingly puzzled, and moves to my side. "Do not worry, little light. I won't let them harm you."

"I wasn't worried until you said that," I grumble. I set a hand on his knee and squeeze. "You okay? You've been very quiet."

Kassam studies me, putting his hand over mine. "I just want you to know that I have not forgotten our pact. You are my wife. I made a promise to you, and I intend to keep it. If the Spidae will not help us, we will seek assistance elsewhere."

Uh oh. "You think they won't help us? I thought they were your friends."

His smile is wry. "Can any god truly have friends? I thought Riekki was harmless and she imprisoned me for a thousand years. I do not trust my own instincts at the moment." He shrugs. "And a lot can change in a thousand years. It seems they have an anchor to make themselves more understanding of humanity. That is new. They have never been included in the Anticipations before." Kassam looks thoughtful. "I just worry that too much has changed and that I can rely on nothing and no one...except you."

My poor Kassam. I lace my fingers with his, smiling to reassure him. "It will all be fine," I lie. "Wait and see. And this isn't just about me, remember? This is about you returning to your realm, too."

"Mmm." He sounds unconvinced. His gaze lingers on me. "Carly..."

The doors to our room open and I jerk in surprise, even as Kassam moves to his feet, protectively stepping in front of me.

"Brother," says a cool, echoing voice. "You are overdue."

I touch Kassam's hip and peer around him to take my first look at the Spidae. I'm actually a little surprised, because I thought the god before me would look a little more...spidery. The tall, lean man standing in the doorway looks a lot like the rest of this tower—strange and slightly colorless. His face is elegant and austere, haughty like the elves in storybooks. He's got high cheekbones and a straight nose and soft mouth, and it seems like the only color to his face at all is in his eyes, which glimmer a faint blue. His hair is loose and resembles the spiderwebs that cover this entire place, silky and long and colorless as everything else. He wears a robe that seems to be the same pale shade as everything else, but it seems oversized —it's so long that it tangles and pools around his feet.

A horrible thought occurs to me—what if he doesn't have feet? What if all he has are a bunch of spider legs under there? I imagine that, and then I imagine Yulenna hanging out with this guy, serving him the way anchors "serve"...and...I just can't. But maybe she's lucky and he doesn't suffer from hedonism or anything along those lines. Maybe he's just perfectly normal and I'm reading too much into his appearance.

Then, the Spidae's gaze slides to me where I peer out from behind Kassam. His head tilts, the motion quick and jerky and unnatural, and I'm reminded of spiders all over again. Fighting a shudder, I slip behind Kassam again.

His big warm hand brushes my shoulder, as if to reassure me. "Greetings, brother. It has been a very long time."

"Has it?" I can hear confusion in the Spidae's voice. "Time does not mean much to our kind, unless one is trapped inside a glacier, I suppose."

I bite back a hiss, because that's a low blow. I feel Kassam stiffen in front of me, and I put a hand on his back, giving him the same reassurance he just gave me.

Kassam relaxes, as if my touch soothes him. "I seek to bargain for a favor. You know me. You know my word is good, and that I am a fair god. I would bargain with the Fates for—"

"No," the Spidae says, swift and brutal.

"You have not even heard me ask yet," Kassam growls, his body vibrating with anger. Gone is the easygoing, hedonism-loving god of the wild. He's furious, the air around me practically crackling with his rage. "I have traveled far. Crossed worlds. And you—"

"No." Just like that, the curtains whisper, and when I look out again, the Spidae is gone.

Kassam gives a snarl of pure rage. "Arrogant, selfish pricks," he seethes, turning toward me. His silver eyes are blazing with anger, and I've never seen him so upset. "They think to make me beg?"

I swallow hard. "Maybe it's a bad time to ask? Maybe... maybe they're having a bad day? We can hang out here for a while, relax for a few days, and then try approaching the subject again?"

"Do they not realize all that is at stake?" Kassam storms

toward the door, pauses, and then moves back to me. He grabs me by the shoulders, kisses me hard, and then gives me a firm, determined look. "Wait here, my Carly. I will talk sense into them. They will not dismiss me as if I am nothing. Even though I am in Aspect form, I am yet a god. They had best remember that."

"Oh, but Yulenna said—"

"Wait here," he repeats again, and then heads out the curtains after the other god. I'm left blinking after him. I understand Kassam being upset—considering we've traveled for so far, only to have a thirty-second interaction with one of the Spidae and get shut down—but I'm a little worried for him. Somehow I don't think the Fates are ones you want to make enemies out of. I like that he's defending me to them, but perhaps he could have gone about it better. When he comes back, we'll sit down in bed and plan out our next move, I decide. We haven't thought beyond getting here, and I shouldn't be surprised that our original plan didn't work out. Heck, I don't think any of our original plans have worked out. Doesn't matter. As long as we're together, we'll figure something out.

So I sit back down on the edge of the bed again and pull one boot off, deciding to get comfortable. My traveling clothes are filthy and smell like griffin, and my hair is so tangled from the endless winds as we rode that I might have to shave my head and start over. I wonder if Yulenna left a comb somewhere around here. Tossing my boots aside, I head for what I assume is the bathroom. The moment I step inside, I see an enormous mirror and I'm drawn toward it, ignoring all other plumbing.

Oh god, I look like absolute hell. I touch my face, astonished that Kassam hasn't pointed any of this out. My eyes are hollow, my skin drawn tight over my normally rounded face. My mouth looks chapped and colorless, and my hair like straw. I don't look travel-ravaged. I look...unhealthy. Like there's something wrong inside me...and isn't there? I touch my mouth, horrified at the changes.

"It will get worse," a quiet voice says behind me.

Gasping, I turn around and see one of the Spidae behind me. This one doesn't have the blue eyes as the one did before. Instead, this one has eyes as black as night, and they look like holes in his pale face. He looks unnerving as he cocks his head at me, watching.

"Hi," I manage to croak out. "I'm, uh, Carly? I'm with Kassam."

He takes this in with an impassive look, and for a moment I wonder if he heard me at all. He gestures for me to follow him, then turns and leaves.

"Wait," I call out, trailing after the tall, mysterious figure. "I have to stay! Kassam told me to remain here for him."

The Spidae turns his head slightly, but I don't feel as if he's looking at me. "Time is limited. When he comes back, there will be much sadness. Best to get this done first. Follow me."

What the hell does that mean? Much sadness? Anxiety seizes me and I'm suddenly afraid for Kassam, and also for myself. "Wait. Explain, please." I trot after him, abandoning my promise to stay put. Kassam would understand, I tell myself. We're here for help and answers, and surely that's what this man is going to provide. "Where's Kassam?"

"Home. He returns home. There is much sadness." He pauses, drawing himself up. "Or much joy. I cannot tell which way it will go." His black-eyed gaze grows vacant and he sways in place. "The trees. The trees. I did not want to see the trees doing that." He scrubs at his face with a sleeve. "Hedonism..."

I hesitate, confused. "There's something wrong with the trees? Or is it something to do with Kassam's return? Please, you have to tell me." When he ignores me, I reach out for his sleeve, to touch his arm and get his attention.

The god lets out a shrill cry, as if pained. "No!"

I immediately clutch my hands to my chest. "Sorry! I didn't mean to. But you're not making sense!"

Another figure comes racing down the hall, and to my surprise, it's not Kassam or another Spidae, but Yulenna. "Zaroun," she calls at the sight of him, moving directly toward the god who even now claws at his hair as if he's in pain. "Zaroun, it's all right. I'm here." She approaches him like one would a skittish colt and holds her hands out, palms up. "Do you see me? I'm right here with you."

"Yulenna." The god pants, pressing his palms to his eyes. "Has to see. Has to know," he mutters. "Trying to help."

"I know, my lord," Yulenna says in the most gentle of voices. "Come. Let me guide you back to the web. Is your brother there, waiting for you?"

"My brother. Yes. My brother is there." The god lowers his hands and focuses on her face. He grabs the sleeve of her dress and twists his long, spindly fingers into it. "You will lead us. This is the help we need to get it started. Her questions are too much for me."

Yulenna nods. "I am here, my lord. I will handle all your needs." She heads back up the ramp and gestures that I should follow. "Come. They're looking for you. But stay back and don't —don't touch Zaroun. He sees too much when that happens. It hurts him."

"I'm sorry. I didn't know. The things he's saying, though... they frighten me." I need to know what happens to Kassam. I race after Yulenna's swishing skirts, taking care to stay a good distance back as she leads the god up the ramp. "Please, you have to tell me what he's talking about. He said there would be much sadness? Is something wrong with Kassam? I have to know. *Now.*"

She shoots me an impatient look. "Zaroun sees visions of the future, but most of the time, his visions are nonsensical because he sees all possible versions at once. He's trying to warn you, to be helpful." The gaze she casts him is oddly affectionate. "He's doing his best."

"So no one's in danger?"

"Not yet." Her voice is tart as she leads the Spidae—Zaroun—forward. "Ossev is with him, hearing his requests. You will speak to Neska."

Neska? I don't know who that is, but I suppose it's one of the Spidae. "Should I get Kassam? He'll want to hear this, I imagine—"

"They separated you deliberately," Yulenna says, all impatience. "Whatever Neska will say to you, it is for you to hear alone, without influence. Now come, or they might not want to see you again for quite some time." She gives Zaroun a gentle smile, full of affection and completely at odds with how she treats me. "One more landing, my lord, and then we will be there."

"The trees," he says, his voice distant. He trails off, lost in thought.

"I will make sure Neska warns them of the trees," Yulenna replies.

"Warn?" He chuckles, then shakes his head, and for a moment, he doesn't look so lost. Those black eyes are unfocused, but not confused. "No warning. Just...startling."

Yulenna glances back to me, and at my confused expression, she shrugs. "No warning, then. Come, my love. We will send her to Neska and I will see to your needs."

The look he gives her is heated and alert, and I suddenly feel like I'm intruding. Would it be inappropriate for me to clear my throat? Because I feel like I should remind them that I'm right here.

But then we reach the landing, and Yulenna points at the thick cobweb curtains. "You are needed in there, Carly. I will go on with Zaroun."

"Oh. Okay. Thank...you?" Should I even be thanking her? I

got no answers. Zaroun spouted a bunch of confusing things and scared the shit out of me and now I'm more lost than ever, and twice as worried. I touch the curtain, trying not to recoil as the sticky webs cling to my fingers, and step inside into a narrow hallway. As I do, I hear a low thrumming sound, like machinery that's working in the background somewhere. I move toward that sound, and as I do, it sounds less like machinery and more like...a harp. Or a fleet of harps. A gentle golden light spills into the hall, and when I finally step into a room, the breath escapes me.

This must be the heart of the Spidae's powers.

53

I stare in wonder up at the massive, multicolored web that fills the room. It's the source of all the lighting, a million threads all tangled together in no particular order, hanging in midair like a starburst or a nebula of sheer color captured inside the tower. I take a few steps forward, my feet cold on the stone floor, and I clutch my hands to my chest as the strands seem to move, fluttering and weaving themselves amidst each other as I watch. They look close enough to touch when I move to the middle of the room, but I don't dare. I know what this is, and I stare at the strands with awe, trying to pick out Kassam's and my own.

The melody is thicker here, amidst the strands, a thousand songs all floating together at once. It's not discordant or jarring, just...a lot to take in. No wonder Zaroun is lost in his own mind so much. If he's seeing the stories of all these threads...I can't imagine. I take another step forward, and the threads part around me, giving way. They're all slightly different, this one coarse and yellow like yarn, this one silvery and so thin I can barely see it. I'd bet they all have different sounds, too, each life playing its own melody.

It's the most beautiful thing I've ever seen, and I just stare and stare.

"Most people reach out to try and touch," comes a voice to the side of me. I'm not entirely surprised that when I look over, I see one of the Spidae. He looks exactly like the one that just left, clothing and hair and all. Only the eyes are different. These are so pale that they might be colorless, and piercingly focused on me.

I shake my head. "I've messed up enough stuff lately. I just want to keep my nose clean at this point."

He makes a sound that might be laughter, might be derision. "But you are looking for your thread, are you not?"

"Or Kassam's," I say. "I'd like to see his. Mine would be close by, wouldn't it?"

The god inclines his head, still watching me with those intense eyes. "Do you think you can find them on your own?"

Is...this a test? Because I don't know that I can, or even if he truly wants me to. But if I say no, will I be condemning us to some sort of awful fate because I didn't even try? I hesitate and take a few steps, watching the threads drift through the air, caressing each other and separating, drifting close and knotting, then sliding apart once more. There's no focus, no rhythm, and yet it all seems perfectly orderly in its own way. I stare at the threads, looking for one that seems strong and sure and full of joy like Kassam is...and I look for a janky, torn thread to be attached to it. The sheer number of threads feels like an avalanche, though, and I quickly get confused and overwhelmed. "Do I lose some sort of bet if I say I can't find it?"

"No. This is no test. I am simply humoring my curiosity about how mortals behave." He continues to watch me from afar. "Would you like to see?"

"Are you Neska?" I counter, even as I move toward him.

"Who else do you think I could be?"

That's a shitty answer, considering that there's two other

people that look just like him here in this tower. I suspect he's just being a dick, so I ignore it. "Yulenna said you wanted to talk to me?"

That icy gaze—funny how Kassam's silver eyes can be so warm and these so cold—focuses on my face. "I don't recall saying such a thing. You wished to speak to us, yes? Here we are." He spreads a hand. "You have a request, and I am benevolent enough to explain why it will not work."

I flinch, my heart feeling as if it's shattering at his casual words. "What do you mean, it won't work?"

He indicates I should follow him. "Let me show you your thread. All will be made clear."

Anxiety flares through me again. Something tells me I'm not going to like what I see. I remember Death approaching me, and his warning about fraying my thread. I rub my arms, feeling chilled despite myself, and follow after the Spidae. I can't *not* look now. I have to see for myself.

He moves through the tangle of threads as if they're water, and they part before him. He lifts a hand and a few threads surge forward, others curling back as if repelled. He holds his hand out, palm up, and as he does, I can see two threads. They pass over his palm, stretching out from the web itself and pulled taut. One is a vivid green, thick and strong and beautiful. The other is...obviously mine.

It's colorless and faint, stretched thin even as it is attached to Kassam's thread. There's something about it that looks incredibly fragile, as if it'll break if I so much as breathe on it. "Oh," I say, because what else can I say? "It...doesn't look good."

His mouth twists, as if he's just dying to mock my lame-ass answer. "Would you like to see a healthy pairing?" At my nod, he lifts another hand, reaching through the mass of strands and pulls downward. Two other strands emerge, one a healthy, pale blue and the duller, smaller thread tugging tightly on it. They run parallel to one another, whereas mine looks more like I T-boned Kassam's thread at an intersection and am now clinging to him. Which...really might not be far from the truth. "This is Lord Gental and his anchor, a young mother from Glistentide. Note how healthy and strong her strand is as she anchors him."

My lips feel like sandpaper, but I lick them anyhow. "So why are you showing me this? I think we both knew it was bad."

The Spidae—Neska—regards me. "Because you know what Kassam is asking for. I am showing you why it is not possible. He is going to insist that you stay at his side. He is going to demand it. And I am showing you why it will not happen. I am not trying to be cruel. I am trying to help you understand."

There's a knot in my throat the size of a boulder. "But you're Fate. If anyone can do it, it's you."

A bitter smile curves his mouth as he gazes down at me. "I am Fate. I am not all-powerful. I can only work with the confines of my duty. What you ask for is impossible." Neska gestures at my thread again, so frail against Kassam's strong one. "Right now, you are tied to the mortal realm of Aos, pulled taut from your world. For me to do as Kassam would like, I must pull you free and remove you from your world entirely. Then I would be able to transfer you to this web and attach you at his side." His hand moves alongside the threads without touching them. "But if I touch your thread, it will snap. You will return to your world, only to die there because your thread has been severed. It does not matter how badly Kassam might wish for you to join him in this world. There is simply no way around it. Your thread is not strong enough."

"Oh," I say softly. I feel like I'm being shattered inside, but I should have known, shouldn't I? The moment Death reached out to me and I turned him down, I knew this was going to go badly, and I did it anyhow. "So if I want to be with Kassam, I have to stay...like this." I gesture at my not-quite-alive body, which even now feels floaty and strange.

"As an unnatural thing, yes. You wait for your thread to snap on its own."

I flinch at his words. An unnatural thing. But that's how I feel. Like my soul is trapped inside a body that no longer responds the way it used to, like it doesn't quite fit anymore. Like a puzzle piece that's been jammed into the wrong spot. And yet...it's not so bad, is it? Being a puzzle piece beats dying, and I don't want to do that for sure. I'm not ready to give up on living...or on Kassam. "I can stay like this, then. How long before my thread snaps?"

Those painfully hard eyes narrow at me. "It could be ten years."

Ten years with Kassam? Ten more years of loving under the trees, of touching each other, enjoying each other's bodies, laughing together...suddenly I want that very, very badly. Ten years is a little selfish, of course. It's ten years that Kassam can't return to his realm, ten more years of the *conmac* trapped in wolf form. Ten years of floating and dry lips and not eating, but I want those ten years. I can squeeze a lot of living into them, I know I can.

"Or ten thousand," the Spidae continues.

"Ten...thousand?" I choke out, horrified. "And my body?"

"It will wither. The life force that keeps it vibrant will fade, and the elements will tear away at a body that cannot repair itself." He shrugs. "But you will live on, as you are, until your thread snaps on its own, and Kassam will be trapped in the mortal realm with you until then."

The thought tastes sour in my mouth. I've seen how Kassam hungrily eyes the forests. The guilt in his gaze when he looks at the *conmac*, who we left on the far side of the mountains. I know he wants to go home desperately. He's been away from his realm for a thousand years, and every day more must eat away at him.

And here I'm selfishly hoping for another ten years of this

because it suits me. I slump with the realization that it can't happen. "I see."

"They sing his praises in Chandrilhar," Neska says in a soft voice. "Even now, those that flee Hrit Svala spread the word of the wild god, who did not take lives, who sought only to find his enemy. The peoples of the eastern mountains speak of the arrival of Kassam, and how he marched through their lands with a parade of animals to announce his return. For a thousand years, there has been no word of him, and now he is on the lips of every trader in every city, every farmer who yokes his cattle, every hunter who hopes to bring down food to feed his family. Do not take this from him."

I'd cry, but I don't think there's any tears left in my body. I just feel raw. Raw and aching for my lovely, wonderful Kassam, who deserves to have people praying to him again. I ache for the people of this world, too, who deserve to have a laughing, gentle god answer their prayers instead of dicks like Seth or Riekki. "He needs to return."

The Spidae gives me a look of approval. "You have worked well with him, you know. He is a different sort than he was when he last walked this realm." He pauses and then adds, "The High Father is learning that mortals from your realm do an excellent job of teaching our gods humanity, because you both must learn this world together. It changes the bond, makes it stronger. He is very pleased with the results."

He makes it sound like we're lab rats. "Great. Glad he's thrilled."

"You should be. It will be a very, very long time before Kassam must go through another Anticipation, and it is all because of you." He tilts his head in that insect-like way, studying me. "It is one reason why I give you this choice. Do you choose to stay on in the mortal realm, or shall I snap your thread now and set him free?"

I blanch. I'm not ready, but maybe I'll never be ready. "I... don't I get to say goodbye?"

The Spidae arches one thick, colorless eyebrow. "You think he will let you go? He will do his best to get you to stay, because he made a vow to you. He feels duty-bound to keep you at his side, even if it's not what he wants."

For some reason, that hurts. I understand duty, but I thought Kassam wanted me with him because he loved me, not because of our stupid wedding vow. "I guess I should..."

I trail off, because I can't make my throat form the words. It doesn't seem right to just vanish on Kassam, after all we've been through. Haven't I said that I wanted to see this through to the bitter end? For once in my life, to finish something? It feels wrong to skate away in the eleventh hour just because it's *easier*. Nothing about this has been *easy*.

"Decide quickly," the Spidae hisses at me.

"You're rushing me," I hiss back, suddenly angry. "This is a big fucking deal and—"

"No," snarls a new voice. "Whatever you think you are about to do, the answer is *no*."

Kassam.

54

I turn as my husband, the god of the wild, strides into the chamber. I devour the sight of him with my eyes, because this might be the last time I look at him. His thick, loose hair is as tangled as ever, a few strands caught on his branching horns. One is broken a few inches from his scalp, a remnant of the battle at Hrit Svala, but it only makes me love the sight of him more. He's naked, a few vines curling around his hips and one arm, and his expression is fiercely determined as he storms through the room toward me, his silver eyes flashing with anger.

The colorful, singing threads part as he heads toward me, his hooves smacking on the stones with so much intensity that I flinch. The moment he reaches my side, he touches my cheek, searching my face as if to reassure himself that I'm well, and then he positions himself in front of me, like he always does when he's feeling protective. "Leave her alone."

"I merely seek to do my job," the Spidae answers in a cool voice.

"You seek to manipulate us to serve your own ends," Kassam

retorts, even as his hand reaches for mine behind his back. "You think I don't know the games you play?"

Neska makes a sound that is pure exasperation, his expression annoyed. He crosses his arms over his chest, staring down his nose at us. "This is no game. I seek to help you return to your realm, just as you do—"

"At the expense of my wife." His fingers clasp mine tightly. "I made a vow to Carly to keep her safe. She's my wife, and her life is not on the bargaining table. If you will not help us, we will leave this place and seek assistance elsewhere."

"Keep her safe?" Neska's tone is mocking. "Did you keep her safe when you broke her back at Hrit Svala? You have fractured and pulled upon her thread so much that even Death cannot take her."

Kassam stiffens and whirls about to look at me. His gaze searches mine. "Is this true?"

I give him a guilty smile. "I wanted to see it through to the end, Kassam. You needed my help, so I gave it."

"Oh, Carly," he murmurs, cupping my head in his big hands. His handsome face is stricken as he looks down at me. "You have given too much. I would never ask that of you."

"You didn't. It was freely given."

"You should have said something."

I cover his hands with mine. They feel so warm and comforting that I close my eyes, leaning into his touch. "Like I said, it was freely given, and you had enough to worry about. I don't regret my choices. They helped you."

"Helped me burn a city and put Seth on Riekki's throne?" His voice is bitter, even as his touch is so, so gentle. "It is not worth it, Carly. It is not worth your life. I promised—"

"It's okay," I say softly, and press a kiss to his palm. "Really."

But the look in his eyes is inconsolable. Kassam stares at my face, no doubt at the circles under my eyes, my cracked lips, my wan skin. He breathes deep and then presses his brow to mine.

"I am not ready to lose you." His voice is ragged. "You are more than my anchor, my Carly. You are my wife—my friend. My partner. I can't do this."

I choke back a sob, my eyes burning but still dry. "I don't want to leave you either, okay? I love you. I want forever with you...but I can't ruin your plans—"

"*Fuck my plans*," he says raggedly. "Fuck them all."

"No." I shake my head. "You're going to return to your realm, and you're going to be a kick-ass wild god, and you're going to free the *conmac*, and everything will be back to normal."

Kassam looks incredulous. "There is no 'normal' without you, my little light. My normal is in your arms. My normal is hearing your sweet voice. My normal is laughing with you, spending time with you, learning from you. I do not want to go on to a different normal. If they take you from me, I will no longer have a normal. There will only be sadness. There will only be loss, and I will be nothing once more."

"That's not true—"

"You are my wife," he says in the most gentle, most heartbreaking voice imaginable. "My love. My little light. And I promised to protect and keep you, just as you promised the same to me. So I am not going to let you leave me, my Carly. You made a vow."

I sob, holding his hands tightly. "I don't want to leave you. But there's no choice—"

"There is always a choice," he tells me, an intense look in his silver eyes. "Just because it is not an obvious path does not mean it is not there." He leans in and kisses the tip of my nose. "Trust me to fix this?"

"My thread—"

"Trust me?" he asks in a hushed voice. "Please?"

I nod. Surely he knows at this point I'd give him anything he asked?

Kassam smiles, a look of relief on his face. He kisses my

nose again and then turns toward the Spidae. "You will not bind her thread at my side?"

The Spidae looks icy with disdain. "As my brother has already told you, it is impossible. Her thread is too frayed, too destroyed by the fact that she has died *twice* now in your care. Let her go, or you risk damaging her thread further."

"It can be repaired," Kassam says, a stubborn expression on his face.

Neska looks ready to spit nails. "Only the High Father—"

"Then we will wait for the High Father," Kassam says immediately. "Send word to him. I know you can. You are his favorites." He scoops me into his arms, bridal-carry style, and calls over his shoulder, "My wife will be waiting in my chambers with me. You are not to approach her alone ever again, or you will face my wrath."

My eyes go wide as I stare up at Kassam. I've never heard his voice so hard and so flat. He breezes past the singing, shimmering threads and out of the chamber, passing another Spidae who looks on with an equally displeased expression as my husband carries me away. As we head down the ramp and away from the Spidae, I touch Kassam's chest, worried. "Should you be pissing them off?"

"They will not test me," he says, all cheer once more. "If they do, they will find their lands full of biting flies and the smelliest of skunks. I will fill their lands full of nettles and bees." He gives me a sly look. "Or even better—I will drain their forbidding lake and make this such a verdant, enticing place that mankind will show up on their doorstep."

"They do look like they'd hate that," I admit. "But...Kassam, love, what if he's right? What if my thread is too broken?" I bite my lip, hating that I have to confess it all. "Death approached me in a dream and told me if I stayed to help you get your vengeance, I'd be screwing myself over."

"And yet you stayed," he says softly, "Because you wanted to finish something. My sweet Carly."

"I stayed because I love you," I correct. "I didn't want to give Riekki the opportunity to hurt you again, so I stayed."

"You gave much for me, and I will do the same for you," he promises. "Trust me." He sweeps aside a curtain and we're in our room again. Kassam marches over to the bed, and before I can wonder what he's thinking, he settles me onto my back and flips my skirts up. He claims my mouth in a hungry kiss and settles between my parted thighs. "My Carly. My love. I will not let this be our ending."

And yet when we make love, it's with a fierce desperation, as if he's not entirely sure he believes his own words.

55

I lie in bed with Kassam atop me, my legs wrapped around him. He's still seated in my body and hasn't moved from our fierce fucking some time ago, and we just... cuddle and touch. I run my hands over his back, tracing his muscles and relishing the feel of his weight atop me. He presses lazy kisses to my neck and my jaw, and I love this position because I can feel his every breath. His heart doesn't beat, but that's all right, because mine doesn't, either. His long hair tickles against my fingers, and I draw tiny circles on his butt as he shifts his weight over me, murmuring my name.

"Am I too heavy?" he asks at one point.

"Never." I make another tiny circle with a fingertip, right over the spot I imagine his butt is dimpled. I can't see them, but I know there are dimples there. "If you move, I'm going to be very upset with you."

"Can't have that," he teases, nipping at my ear. "My sweet, lovely Carly. My little light. What if we stay like this forever?"

I'd been thinking the same thing, and hearing it makes me smile. "I mean, there might be some chafing at some point, but I'm game if you are."

"I'd lick your chafed parts for you," Kassam murmurs between kisses. "Rest assured that I'd keep you good and lubricated."

My smile widens. I know we're stealing moments before everything falls down around our ears, but that's one of the things I love most about Kassam—that even in the darkest moments, he makes me smile and forget about all the terrible things in the world. It sounds like there is an afterlife (I did meet Death, after all) so I want to take these memories with me when I'm parted from Kassam. Until that moment comes, I'm going to spend every blink just drinking it all in. I dig my heel into the back of one thigh, squeezing my inner walls around him, and I'm rewarded with a gasp from Kassam and a full body twitch that I feel deep inside.

I give a little wriggle, just about to ask for another round... when I pause. It feels like someone's watching us.

I go still, because surely the Spidae would grasp the meaning of privacy, right? They have curtains over every door, after all. I peer over Kassam's shoulder—

And make eye contact with a stranger.

I yelp, squeezing Kassam again and making him groan when I stiffen. He surges into me with a rakish grin, grabbing my hips. "You're insatiable, my little light."

My hand goes over his mouth and I squirm underneath him, trying to get free. "Someone's here!"

Did I think that was going to deter Kassam? This is the same man that flipped my skirt up and fucked me in front of Seth. I should know better. He only pumps into me again, rearing back before dragging his cock slowly in once more, seating himself to the hilt. "This is all part of my plan, you see," Kassam murmurs. "He will not take you from me while I am balls deep inside you."

I screech in horror, pounding a hand on Kassam's back. "Get off me, you oaf!"

"I thought you were game for staying like this forever?" He nips at my jaw, one hand sliding up to cup my breast.

"That was before someone came in to watch!"

Kassam chuckles, his breath warm against my skin. "You think the High Father has not seen fucking before?"

That's the High Father? I peer over Kassam's broad shoulder again, trying to concentrate as he drives into me again. The person watching us is…young. Horrifyingly young. I hammer a fist on Kassam's shoulder, because he should absolutely not be making love to me in front of someone with that young a face. "Please," I wheeze, and I have to specify when he flicks my nipple, teasing it erect. "Stop now. Stop. Cover—"

"You are foiling my plans," Kassam murmurs between kisses.

"She is shy," the newcomer says. "If this makes her uncomfortable, I can go."

Go?! He can't go. We need to talk to him. "Kassam—"

With a sigh, Kassam turns his head. "Promise you won't take her if I get off her, Father?"

The young person—god—behind us chuckles, the sound hollow and ancient and young all at the same time, like voices layered over each other. "I promise. Let her relax so we can all talk, my son. And stand up so your father can look upon you. It has been some time."

Kassam presses one last fierce kiss to my mouth, winks, and then climbs off. I quickly fix my skirts, my face burning with embarrassment as I sit up on the bed and try to smooth my sex-snarled hair. God, my nipples are like beacons against the front of my dress, and I'm pretty sure my skirt is wrinkled and stained and my face is scratched from Kassam's beard stubble and this is *not* how I should greet a god that is my husband's father.

But if I'm all awkward shyness, Kassam is not. He gets up from the bed, naked and sweaty and sticky, and crosses the floor to drop to one knee in front of the stranger. "My father," he says, and his voice is full of emotion.

The High Father gazes down at Kassam, his expression fond, and he touches his cheek. I can't help but stare. I pictured the High Father as something a bit more like the Christian version of God—an old dude with a long white beard, and possibly some angel wings. Maybe a harp. This boy—and I only say boy because they refer to him as the High Father—is sweetly androgynous, with a cap of thick curls that are a shade between blonde and brown. His skin is the same warm bronze that Kassam's is, and his eyes are a thick, rich brown with long lashes, his mouth soft. He wears a simple tunic belted at his waist and is barefoot, his frame slight and feminine. He also looks as if he's ten years old, max.

It's jarring.

Those deep brown eyes turn to me, though, and my throat closes. I want to suddenly sink to my knees in front of him as well, because those eyes are...ageless. They are deep and full of both sorrow and joy, and looking at him like this, I realize his form is just a trapping for the powerful god underneath. He's making himself sweet and harmless, but something tells me that the actual being is neither. He's old and powerful and so, so strong that my skin prickles in his presence.

I sink to the floor and bow my head, because it feels important to acknowledge him.

"I'm not here for you to bow and scrape," the High Father says in that soft, mellifluous voice of his. He touches Kassam's broken horn, an amused expression curving that youthful, full mouth. "I came to see my son, and to hear his request. What is it you require, my son of sunshine and joy?"

Kassam closes his eyes, basking in the presence of the High Father. He looks blissful, like he does when...well, it seems a little blasphemous to think of that right now. I give myself a mental shake. "I have a favor to ask of you, my father. I have taken a wife."

"This woman," the High Father agrees, gazing over at me again with vague interest.

"Yes," Kassam continues. "She has been a good, loyal partner and an excellent anchor. She's made me see new things, and brought her wisdom to me, even when I didn't want it. And when her life was being ruined, she still supported me and was a good wife. So I wish to be a good husband to her." He swallows hard and glances back at me, then turns to the High Father once more. "I promised Carly that we would be together after the Anticipation. The Spidae say that her thread is too frayed for her to move into this world and remain at my side... so I wish to join her in her world. I need you to make me mortal and to send us both back there, my father."

"Wait, *what*?" I yelp, horrified at what I'm hearing. "Kassam, what the fuck?"

"Can you do it, my father?" Kassam gazes calmly at the High Father. "For me?"

"It is an enormous change," the High Father says, and he touches Kassam's cheek. The look on his face is both knowing and sad, as if he expected this. "You are certain this is what you want?"

I scramble forward, determined to slap a hand over Kassam's mouth before he can answer. "He's not certain," I blurt out. "He's not certain at all, and we need to talk about this."

Kassam looks over at me as I wedge myself in between him and the High Father. Is it a good idea to push in front of a god? Probably not but I'm doing it anyhow, because Kassam can't do this. "Carly," he says, clasping my hands in his, a gentle smile on his face. "It will be all right. You said you trusted me, yes? Give me that trust now and let me do this."

"No, Kassam," I say again, shaking my head. "I'm not going to let you do this. You've dreamed of going back to your forest.

This is what you fought for. This is what you've struggled for. And you're needed. Look at how excited everyone was to see you when we approached Chandrilhar. When we traveled to Hrit Svala. They weren't like that for Seth. They wouldn't be like that for Riekki. People love you. They *need* you."

"But I need you," he says simply, and presses kisses to my knuckles. "I made a vow to you, and I want to keep it."

I grip his hands tightly, wanting to smack him with them and kiss him at the same time. "You made a vow to the *conmac*, too." That makes him hesitate, and I press on. "Think of all the good you can do when you're restored, Kassam. You don't need me—"

The stubbornness returns to his face. "That is where you are wrong, my wife. I do need you. You have taught me things. Things like grief and regret." He places my hands over his heart. "Things I am feeling right now, and I do not like them. I want to go with you, Carly. Because I cannot lose you. I do not want to spend an eternity of regret without you. I would rather spend a few decades at your side in happiness."

"You big idiot," I say, even as I sob and throw my arms around his neck. "Don't do this."

"I love you, my little light," he says, hugging me tightly. "You have been at my side through all of this. Let me be there for you, as well." He strokes my hair. "It will be all right. No matter what happens, as long as we are together, I am content."

"You're lying," I say, sniffing hard and leaning back to search his face. "You need to return to godhood. You're good at it. And now you'll be even better. You don't need me." At his stubborn expression, I turn to the High Father, who is watching us with those sad, dark eyes. "He's lying. Don't let him do this. He's amazing at his job and you need him."

The High Father turns his gaze toward Kassam. "Do I need to find a new god of the wild?"

Kassam's hands tighten on me. "The Spidae say they cannot

keep Carly with me if I ascend once more. That we will be separated for all time if they interfere. I do not want that. I want to be with her." He holds me against his chest, practically squeezing me. "She has taught me about so many things, but mostly how to be a better, more thoughtful god. How to really pay attention to those that ask for assistance, instead of simply chasing after my own pleasures. I have been learning with her at my side, and Carly is my conscience. If she cannot stay with me...I worry I will turn into Riekki...or Seth."

To my surprise, the High Father smiles.

"The very fact that you worry about such things tells me you will not," he says to Kassam. "You have truly grown and I am pleased. This Anticipation has taught me much. It always pains me to punish my children, but I like to hope that the rewards will be as sweet." His smile broadens. "This Anticipation is showing the true colors of all. Riekki welcomes war on her doorstep to cling to power, and Magra abuses her anchors by draining them of life to prolong her own and then switching them. Vor thrives on creating chaos, and Gental has set himself up with a harem of women and men eager to do his bidding. I fear they are lost."

His expression grows sad, and the questions I have—like who Magra is, what sort of chaos Vor is causing—die in my throat.

"Others have shown me that even though things are changing, it is not necessarily bad. So I have decided that we, too, shall change...if you are willing to try?" The High Father gives Kassam a fond look. "Or is your heart set on abandoning this world?"

I can feel Kassam hesitate, but his answer is firm. "My heart is set upon being with Carly."

My eyes burn with tears, because I'm not sure what I did to deserve such a sweet, perfect partner, but I'll take him. I hug the arm he has wrapped around me, never wanting to let go.

The High Father watches us, and I could swear that fondness in his eyes flickers over me as well as Kassam. "Aron of the Cleaver was given an anchor from the other realm, as well. It was an experiment that the Spidae and I came up with. Perhaps lessons will be learned if they are learned together. An anchor that is mortal, with all its failings, but who is also yet unfamiliar with this world can help point out some of the problems, and bring new ideas with them. It worked very well, and Aron was restored quickly. What I did not anticipate was that he would fall in love with his anchor. He was furious when she was taken from him and stormed Death's realm to retrieve her." He chuckles. "Rhagos was not pleased."

"What happened to her?" I ask, unable to remain silent.

The High Father blinks at me. "I have decided that the Aspect that ascends shall keep his anchor at his side, to allow that anchor to continue influencing their partner—their god—just as they did in the mortal realm."

"Forever?" I'm breathless at the thought. Kassam squeezes me so tightly I swear my ribs are going to pop, but I get it. I feel the same way he does.

"Forever." The High Father casts an amused look at Kassam. "But you must promise to listen to her advice and not spend all your time in orgies with dryads."

Kassam chuckles like a naughty boy and presses a kiss to my hair. "I am only interested in touching Carly. All others have lost their appeal."

I rub my ear. "I'm sorry, did you say orgies with dryads?" Am I going to have to kick a bunch of dryad asses if they try to touch my man?

"Will you stay, then?" the High Father asks, not looking at me. His focus is entirely upon Kassam, and for a moment I could swear his emotions show through, and I get the impression that he doesn't want Kassam to leave at all. That if Kassam turns him down, it will hurt him unbearably. I wonder if even the High Father has favorites. It's easy to love Kassam, so I get it.

Kassam turns me in his arms, his gaze seeking mine. "Will you stay with me, Carly? Be my wife and my anchor? It will mean that you will remain here in my world forever. You will be forced to endure me, day in and day out." His expression grows flirty. "Though I promise we shall continue our one-up games."

I grab him by the ears and kiss him. "I love you, you idiot. Of course I'll stay. You didn't even have to ask." I kiss him again and then pull back. "But you have to promise to keep off the dryads."

"Did I not just say that I only have eyes for you?" He arches a brow at me and sticks a finger in my ear. "Is your hearing going, my little light?"

I push his hand away and grab a fistful of his permanently tangled hair. "I'm just warning you. If there's an orgy on your plane, it had better be an orgy of two. Me and you. That's all."

The smile he gives me is one of delight. "All holes filled by me shall be yours. I understand."

I squint. I'm not sure if I should agree with that. "Can we focus, please? You need to give your father an answer..." I turn around, trailing off, and then frown as I realize we're in the room alone. "Did he leave?"

"He did. He knows my answer." Kassam settles me in his lap, tucking me against his chest. "You swear you will not mind staying with me? I do not want you to be sad, my little light."

Sad? How can I possibly be sad? I reach up and caress his jaw, at the short beard that's been coming in slowly. "You and me forever? You getting your powers and your realm back? How could I possibly be sad?"

He gives me another fierce kiss, and then another, and another, as if he can't stop kissing me. "Because you're forced to stay with me now. You will be at my side for all eternity. You will not be able to go back to your world." He kisses me again, each one more fervent than the last. "I will make it up to you, I promise."

Am I sad about that? I won't miss tending bar, or drunk customers. I won't miss being behind on rent payments, or the smells of the city, or when my car breaks down on a snowy day. I won't miss a lot, actually...but I'll miss my mom. My mom, who I've been too busy to fret over, and who is probably losing her mind with worry over her only child. "Oh, Kassam, my mother—"

Kassam nuzzles my face, all affection. "I will speak to the Spidae and make a bargain with them. It won't be the same as your thread. Hers will be whole." He draws up, suddenly remembering. "If I ever hurt you again, you have to tell me. I had no idea I'd pulled so hard that I broke you. It wasn't worth it. Nothing is worth your pain, my sweet Carly."

"There's nothing to be done over it," I say. "It's in the past. All of that is." I touch my chest, where my stitches are, and to my surprise, they feel loose. My skin suddenly itches, and when I scratch at the stitches, they fall away, revealing smooth, bare skin. "What—"

"He has healed you."

My skin prickles and I sharply look up at Kassam, because that's his voice, but...it's different. Richer. Full of strange, deep, echoing tones like the High Father's was, tones that remind me of the forest. As I stare up at my husband, his silver eyes seem ablaze, his bronze skin luminous, as if he's glowing from within. The broken horn atop his head repairs itself as I stare, surging out and then branching tall and proud. He suddenly looks like more. He radiates power, his scent that of open air and flowers and pine trees. Vines crawl up his skin, twining in his thick hair, and he's the most gorgeous, most untamed thing I've ever seen. Kassam takes my hand in his.

I can tell the moment the bond between us kicks in again. After weeks of feeling not much at all, the moment our fingers touch, my stomach growls, my mouth feels like a desert, and my libido rears its head. I orgasm immediately.

Just like old times.

The look he gives me is positively devilish as he kisses my fingertips. "Come, my little light. Let us go home."

56

We stay at the Spidae tower for a few more hours, as Kassam works out a bargain with the Spidae in order to bring my mother over into this realm. Yulenna keeps me company, and now that all the tension is gone between her masters and mine, she's a chatty thing. She gossips with me about the other anchors of gods that came over to this world as we eat a feast of food that I try not to think about the origins of, and I tell her about Seth.

It seems the High Father is making a lot of changes. Seth is poised to take Riekki's spot and the High Father is going to allow it. Both Death and War have permanent anchors (in addition to Fate). The goddess of magic's city has been destroyed. And of course, Kassam is returning.

"It's been quite an eventful Anticipation," Yulenna says between bites of the world's worst bread.

"Are most not like this?" I sop the hard crust of bread with a bit of oil, avoiding the sausage set out for both of us. Yulenna admits she's not much of a cook and they have a trader that brings them goods every now and then, but most of their diet is...meat-based thanks to the spiders. I stick to bread, as hard and stale as it is.

Yulenna pops a bit of meat into her mouth and shakes her head. "My masters let me peer at the threads sometimes and I've seen many of the past Anticipations. They had some big events, like when Lady Tadekha took over the Citadel and launched it into the skies, or the War of Thirteen Lords, but nothing like these events."

"What about the future?" I ask, gnawing on a bit more bread. "Do you ever ask to look at that?"

Her eyes go wide and she shakes her head. "No. Not after I've seen what it does to poor Zaroun. He can't tell what timethread we're in, or what is truth and what was a possible event that never happened." Her mouth pulls down into a frown. "I stick to the past and present threads. Everything there has happened in the past or is happening now, so I feel comfortable watching them while I knit or sew."

I guess when you don't have television, you have a lot of spare time. I'm about to comment on that when there's a tickle in the back of my nose. I sit up, blinking...and then I sneeze.

"That'd be Kassam working on my garden," Yulenna crows happily. "I guess they reached an agreement."

I rub a finger under my tickling nose. A tickle in my brain is better than a nosebleed, at least. "I guess they did." Here I'd thought that the Spidae would make all kinds of crazy demands in exchange for bringing my mother over to this world, and instead, all they want is a couple of gardens for Yulenna. One for her to grow fruits and vegetables in, and one for her to have pretty flowers. Both gardens are to be selftending and grow without too much care, because the Spidae want to keep Yulenna busy with other things.

I can guess what those other things are.

They bickered over the exact "price" for a bit, and the Spidae wanted a dryad attached to the gardens themselves to tend to them, and Kassam argued with exactly how big the gardens should be. To me, it seems a silly thing to argue over—it's a freaking garden and he's the lord of nature, it should be a cakewalk—but Yulenna assured me it's all for show. "No one wants to cave too quickly," she'd told me. "It sets a bad precedent. So even if they're completely agreed, they'll argue and moan about what's being asked to make it seem like a bigger deal."

So we continue to eat and gossip, and I sneeze a few more times, and as I chew on the last bit of oil-soaked crust, the pleasant scent of wind and leaves touches me. I straighten, molten desire pulsing through my body even before Kassam can put an arm around my shoulders and pull me against him. I close my eyes, reveling in the feeling of him touching me, of feeling whole again, and feeling that thick, heady pulse of desire instead of a pinprick.

I'm never going to take this for granted. Never. "Is it agreed?" I ask, snuggling back against him. God, he's warm and smells amazing. It's making me crazy.

"Agreed," he says, and nips at my ear, sending a shiver up my spine. "She will be here soon. Do you need anything else, my little light? If not, we shall take our leave."

"Dresses?" Yulenna asks. "Clothes? Bread? I'll share what I have."

Before I can answer, Kassam makes a soft, dismissive noise. "She needs none of that. The forest will provide."

Oh. Okay. He's the expert. I shrug, smiling at Yulenna. "I'm good, but thank you." I rub a hand over Kassam's arm and then get to my feet, stepping away from the table in the tower kitchens. The sight of Kassam takes my breath away. I'm not sure I'll ever get used to looking at him like this. He's gorgeous, his skin glowing with inner magic and his eyes so intensely silver that they're otherworldly. More vines are twined in his hair and up one arm, and it's like he looks a bit more unearthly every time I see him...and I love it. I wanted this for him so much that it made me ache, and I'm aching all over again at how good he looks. "I'm ready when you are."

He grins, roguish once more, and tilts his horned head at me. "Shall I take you home?"

I nod. "I'm ready."

"Hold on tightly to me."

I move forward into his arms, pressing my cheek to his warm chest even as I'm grumbling a little. "If I get any closer, I'm going to be on your jock."

"And this is a problem?"

I reach down and pinch his naked butt, because he's such a twerp and I love it.

"I hope you enjoy your garden, Yulenna," Kassam says, and then my hair lifts off my head as a rush of wind encircles us. It's like a tornado has formed around us, and I squeeze my eyes shut as debris and leaves pick up in the buffeting wind. I hope we didn't just make a mess of Yulenna's kitchen. My shift dress flaps and blows against my body, and then, everything goes still once more.

The scents around us change, and the air pressure, too.

I hear the sound of birds calling out to one another. Of a monkey chittering somewhere in the distance. The thick fragrance of greenery and fresh air hits me, cool and ever so slightly sweet. When I open my eyes, Kassam's expression is one of pure joy, his eyes streaming with tears.

He doesn't have to tell me where we are. I know he's home.

It's my home now, too. Still clutching at him, because part of me never wants to let him go again, I look around. It's a forest, which doesn't surprise me, but like everything to do with Kassam's magic, it's like a forest on steroids. The leaves are so green that they could be carved from glossy jade. Thick flowering vines hang down from massive trees, and birds flutter past. As I stare at my surroundings, a deer pokes his head out from behind a tree, quickly followed by a figure that looks like it is made entirely of plants, right down to the cascading vines and flowers where hair should be. A dryad, I assume. They gaze at us in wonder.

"It has been so long," Kassam whispers, his voice raw. "I thought I'd never be able to return."

I step out of his arms, and when he extends his hand, I immediately take it. We move forward a few steps, and there's a rocky path covered in mossy stones, and in the distance I can see a lovely waterfall with a rainbow over it. The sky is an endless, clear blue peeking through the leaves, and up ahead, I see a berry bush so laden with fruit that the branches droop. As we move forward, a rocky outcropping shifts, and a sinewy neck raises a triangular, reptilian head to gaze at us.

A dragon.

Welp. I guess I should have expected that. "This is amazing, Kassam."

"This is your home now, too," he tells me, his eyes bright with excitement. "Anything you want, anything you need, I will provide it for you. Simply speak it, and it shall be yours."

"The *conmac*?" I ask, because I feel we have to think of them.

He nods. "They will arrive shortly, and I will remove the rings that bind them."

I squeeze his hand. I imagine he's going to have a lot to answer to the moment they get their voices back, but something tells me it'll be fine. "I have you," I say. "I'm good for now."

"Are you tired? Hungry?" His gaze searches mine.

I'm probably all of those things, but it doesn't seem important right now. I don't want it to be about me. I want him to revel in the fact that he's home again after so long. "Let's just explore for now? I want to see everything. Does your whole realm look like this?"

Delight curves his mouth. He likes that I'm asking about his home. "Not at all. This is one small corner, but I thought you might like it."

Oh, I do. I squeeze his hand again, smiling as another shy dryad peeks out from behind a bush to gaze at us. Kassam grins down at me, too, as if he's got some sort of secret he's dying to share.

"Carly?"

I gasp, my eyes going wide. That voice—I know that voice. I drop Kassam's hand, surging in the direction of it. "Ma?"

"Carly!" Up ahead, there's a thrashing of bushes and then my mother—my beautiful, silly, wonderful mother—steps out of the forest thicket in her favorite pink pajamas. She looks just as I remembered, healthy and strong.

The moment I see her, I burst into tears and run toward her. "Mama. You're here."

"Oh, my baby," my mother cries, and then we're hugging and she strokes my hair, and I sob and snot all over her pajamas, and it's wonderful.

We're home. All of us.

EPILOGUE

"Today is an adventurous day for you, Carly!" my mother sings out as I approach her favorite lily-pad-strewn pool. "I saw it in the scrying waters." She beams at me. "Got anything planned?"

Sharing eternity with my mother as well as my lover is awesome, but it also makes for awkward moments...kinda like right now. At least the whole hedonism thing was broken and my mom no longer feels attracted to Kassam, or things would be *incredibly* weird. I debate how much to say to her about my naughty plans for the day and decide to fudge it. Trying not to look too guilty, I sit down by the pool with her and put on a chipper smile. "Oh, Kassam and I are going to have a date. Nothing much. How's the scrying thing going?"

My mother lights up, her eyes full of excitement. It's the right thing to say to distract her. For the next half-hour, my mother tells me all about the water-scrying network she's been working with Kassam to set up, as if it wasn't my idea in the first place. The Great Endless Forest is a paradise, and all of our needs are met by either the plants or by the magical dryads that dwell in the forest. We have food, water, and shelter, all by simply asking the forest to provide. Kassam keeps me busy—I help him with his duties and offer advice, and we spend a lot of time thinking up ways to spread the word that he's returned and is answering prayers.

We also spend a lot of time in bed. Which is awesome, but I quickly became worried that my mother would feel like a third wheel. She ran a shop back home, after all. She's a businesswoman and is used to staying busy, even if that business was fortune-telling and tarot cards. Kassam and I brainstormed a way for her to apply her abilities, and thus water-scrying was born. Through any of the pools here in Kassam's plane, my mother can view people, and places. I thought she'd use the scrying windows to chat with Yulenna or Max or Faith—the other anchors—but my mom is clever. She decided she was going to pass hints to Kassam's priestesses (of whom there are few but are growing in number). It's started a bit of a frenzy, with new supplicants sending up prayers and requesting water-scrying constantly, but my mom loves it.

"...so like I sent to that woman Rudith," my mom continues, dragging a finger through the ripples of the pool. "She was asking about her boyfriend again and I can't exactly say through the water, 'Girl, he's no good for you.' So I sent her an image of a shoe."

I frown, my attention snared. "I'm sorry, you what?"

"Sent her an image of a shoe. You know, so she'll boot him to the curb."

That's...random. I chuckle. "You think she'll figure it out, Ma?"

Mom shrugs. "I don't care if she does. I'm not spoon-feeding them here. I have to keep an element of mystery in things. Make them work for it, you know?" She pats my hand. "I'll do that man of yours proud, wait and see."

I hug my mom. "I know you will." I'm always hugging her lately. I think it's because I came so close to not seeing her again that having her with me gives me a fresh appreciation for our relationship. "I love you."

"I love you too, pipsqueak." Mom hugs me back. "Have you eaten lunch? I have some nuts here."

Just like a mom, always trying to feed me. It works, though, because I'm always hungry. Part of my bond with Kassam, I suppose. I don't mind it, though. Thanks to his magic and this plane, there's an endless supply of fruits, vegetables, and nuts to eat. Mom has turned vegan, just like me. Sometimes I miss a good steak, but it's hard to think about eating those kinds of things when you're surrounded by deer and foxes and squirrels, all with big, beautiful eyes and all of them acting like pets.

So nuts it is. I crack a few and eat, and we talk a bit more. Once I've finished eating, I brush off my mossy skirts and get to my feet. "Oh, Ma, I almost forgot. Kassam asked if you could watch over the *conmac* for him? Just keep an eye on what they're doing and report back if any of them even look as if they're trying to shift?"

Her expression grows sad. "No progress there, I take it?"

"Nope." The *conmac* have been brought to the Great Endless Forest, the magic rings removed from their noses and...they disappeared again. They haven't changed back to their human forms (or fae forms, I guess), and it's another thing that eats at Kassam. He worries over them, but they've been wolves for a thousand years. They probably need time before they're ready to change back, or they need to remember how. Either way, we'll keep an eye on them. "So if you could peek in on them, he'd appreciate it."

"I'm on it," Mom says with determination.

I press a kiss to the top of her head. "All right, I'm off. Love you." I pause, and then snap my fingers, hoping my acting doesn't look too obvious. "Oh! One more thing, Ma." As if this isn't the thing I came over here for in the first place. "Can you uh, stay out of the deep thicket this afternoon?"

"Absolutely."

Whew. "Thanks—"

"I'm still scarred from the screeching you were doing in your last sex game," my mother says, cracking another nut with a squeeze of her palm. "Trust me, I don't want to hear anything."

I wince. So much for subtlety. To be fair, I was screeching *quietly,* hoping my mother wouldn't hear her son-in-law railing her daughter. Guess I wasn't as quiet as I'd thought. Today is probably going to be just as noisy, too. "We're just having a date. But like…yeah. Don't come near the deep thicket."

"Earplugs?" my mom asks.

"Probably a good idea?"

"Will do." My mom leans in. "But I have another good idea for him if you're willing to pass it along."

"What's that?"

Mom grins. "Tell him to wear a fig leaf. He's a lovely-looking man, but I still feel weird every time I see his balls."

My face feels bright red as my mother discusses my husband's balls. "Fig leaf. Got it."

∼

THERE'S a particular deep thicket that Kassam and I like for our "dates." There's a thick, blooming hedge around the perimeter, and inside, the trees are close together and draped in flowering vines. It's very pretty and feels private, which is why I've chosen it for today's activities.

We're having a date tonight.

Not that we don't see each other every day and I sleep curled around him. Not that we don't fuck like bunnies every chance we get. Not that we don't spend hours and hours together just talking and enjoying each other. That's all the normal stuff.

Date nights are for our one-up competition, for when we try to raise the stakes for the other person.

Kassam is no longer cursed with hedonism, but I think it's a big part of who he is at his core. He loves pleasure. He loves watching me eat and nibbling on things, or tasting my lips. He loves bright, colorful things and scents. He loves sex—god, does he love sex—and his addiction to pleasure and fun makes me a bit more adventurous, too. While most of the time, there's nothing crazy, Kassam upped the stakes on me a few days ago by turning himself into a tree and then fucking me on his branch-cock.

That...was odd. And hot. And I might get a little squirmy every time I see a particularly thick knot on a tree.

But that experience reminded me that he's winning our little game, so I've got to up the ante. And I've come up with the perfect solution. So today, while Kassam is running with the herds at the far edge of the forest and answering prayers from below, I'm preparing. The thick hedge parts when I touch it, closing behind me once more and then I step into the thicket.

The dryad that's been helping me finishes setting a few items down on a makeshift table made out of a fallen tree. She gives me a shy smile and melts into the trees before I have a chance to say anything. "Thank you," I call after her. They're not normally that shy—maybe we scarred them a bit with our tree-sex last time, too.

I check over the items on the table, touching each one. There's a pitcher of sweet berry wine, a bowl of fruits and nuts, and several small bowls of various oils. Just looking at them makes me blush, even as my body tingles with excitement. At the far end of the table, in a pile of vine belts, is the shiny, shaped wood phallus attached to a belt that I requested. It's smooth under my hand, not quite as long as my forearm, and more slender than Kassam's thick cock. It'll be perfect for our date and I know Kassam is going to love it.

The man is absolutely up for anything and everything between us.

I pick up a woven mossy blanket and spread it out at the perfect spot, then wander over to a glossy pool and check my reflection. My thick, straight hair is entwined with a few vines and flowers like it always is, and my short dress is a mixture of more vines, big, blooming flowers, and moss. Like Kassam said, the realm provides for everything, and because I'm his wife, the plants obey me to a certain extent. I finger one of the flowers on my dress, making the petals unfurl, and then I go back to the table and rub one of the berries on my lips, reddening them. And because I know my wicked Kassam will appreciate the touch, I redden my nipples, too.

When I'm ready, I lie down on the blanket and wait. The forest is cool and lovely, the scents as magical as my surroundings. I gaze up at the swaying branches overhead, and this seems like the perfect spot to take a nap. Instead, I decide to call my lover to my side. Hiking up my dress, I slide a hand between my thighs and touch myself. I'm not surprised to find that I'm already slick with arousal. I've been thinking about our date all day. So I brush my fingertip in circles around my clit, moving my hips in time with my finger.

I'm pretty sure Kassam has a sixth sense that tells him when I'm touching myself. He always seems to show up the moment I do, and today is no different. I hear the galloping thump of hooves on the forest floor before a magnificent stag charges in through the hedge, then immediately shifts forms into my husband. His hair is wild and tangled in his horns, and he gives me a look of pure molten silver as he storms to my side. "Did you start without me?"

"Just warming up," I purr, teasing my clit again. "Wanna watch?"

He growls with pleasure, dropping to his knees in front of me, and pushes my thighs apart, gazing between them. "If you are giving me a show, I absolutely want to watch...unless I can do it for you?" He gives me a hopeful look.

I know how that goes—he'll do it for me, and then we'll get so distracted from him eating me out that we'll just charge right into things and then I won't get to play. It's happened several times. Neither one of us has any ability to resist the other. So when he leans in, I put my foot against his bare chest and eye his gorgeous body. His cock is growing harder by the moment, and as I watch, he reaches down and strokes himself, working his shaft. "Hey now," I protest. "That's mine."

Kassam gives me a sly smile. "If you can touch yourself, I can do the same."

I immediately draw my hand back and sit up, mock-frowning at him. "We're here because it's my turn. Now are you going to play with me or not?"

He arches a brow at me, amused. "You are bossy today, little light. I like it."

He has no idea. "I'm just getting started," I say, getting to my knees. I slide my arms around his neck and press my breasts against his chest, my dress of flowers and moss prickling between us. "Did you want to play or shall I save it for some other time?"

Kassam grins. "You know I want to play."

I did know that. I knew the answer before I even asked. "Then I'm going to need a few things from you today," I say in a light voice, tangling my fingers in his wild hair. "Say, 'That sounds like a good idea, Carly.'"

Laughing, my husband gives me a sly look. "That sounds like a *delicious* idea, Carly."

My pussy thrums with excitement. I love the way he says *delicious*, like he's referring to *me*. Oh, today is going to be so much fun. I beam up at him. "Did you have a good day today, love?"

"All of my days are good."

Such a Kassam answer. He's the happiest sunshine personality, and I know what he'd say if I pressed him for a better answer—he has his realm, he has his powers, and he has his wife. He needs nothing more. "You know it's my turn, right?" I scratch at his scalp. "And you'll do what I like? Whatever I like?"

"Mmmm. Did you have something specific in mind?" When I nod, his look becomes mischievous. "Don't I get a word?"

"Of course you do. What word do you want?" I slide my hand out of his hair and brush a finger over his lips, not surprised at all when he nips at my digit. "Pineapple?"

"How about...tree branch?"

That naughty son of a bitch. He's still pleased with himself over how much he startled me with that move. He smirks at me, and I try not to think too much about how it had felt, how woodsy and hard and foreign even as he'd wrapped himself around me and whispered naughty things in my ear. Sly devil. "Tree branch it is," I say, not taking the bait. "Now, I need you to wear a blindfold."

Kassam chuckles. "Your games are adorable, my little light. A blindfold? Very well." He obediently closes his eyes, and as he does, the vines he wears in his horns slither over his brow and temples, forming a mask. "Does this suit your needs?"

He's still all smiles, this smug beast, as if all I'm going to do is blindfold him and tickle him or something. Being his wife is forcing me to step my game up, though, and I'm loving it...and I love that I know he's game for everything. But I'll let him go on thinking that it's just going to be a bit of blindfold play. I make a big show of tugging on the vines to make sure they're in place, and then flip one of the leaves up to check his eyes. "No peeking."

"None. I am your humble servant today."

I snort at that. "There's a lot of things you are, husband, but humble is not one of them." I'm rewarded with his grin, and then I get to my feet. I move around him, circling, and then take my dress off, tossing it to the forest floor. He's already undressed, his cock hard, so it's not as if I have to spend a lot of time preparing him. "How are you feeling?"

"Hungry," he says, reaching for my hips and pulling me toward his mouth. "I smell your fragrant cunt and my mouth waters to lick it."

"Mmm, just one lick," I tell him. I'm feeling benevolent.

He pulls me against him and nuzzles at my pussy, his tongue skating over my folds. The breath rushes out from my lungs and I whimper, which makes him chuckle. Oh no, he is not taking the upper hand again. I reluctantly pull him away from the cradle of my thighs.

"Mine," he growls, pushing back against my hand when I tug him away.

"Later," I promise. "I get to have my wicked way with you first."

Kassam chuckles again as I rub my hands all over his broad shoulders. "I am eagerly awaiting it, my little light. Do your worst. It will all be pleasing to me."

"Anything I want?" I trail a fingertip over his clavicle.

"Anything."

"Can I oil you up?"

His mouth twitches with amusement. "You do not even have to ask, my Carly. Oil away."

I tilt his head back and lean down to kiss him, just because he's such a sweetheart. I love this man so much. "Don't worry. I'm going to make you feel so good."

"Because you're going to throw me down on this blanket and ride my face?" he asks hopefully.

That makes me pause, because my pussy is throbbing with want, and indeed, that sounds like an awesome idea. "Later," I say, breathless. "I want to do this first." I trot over to the table that he didn't even look at when he came in, thanks to my distraction, and reach for one of the bowls of oil. It smells like flowers, and another smells like berries. I got several different kinds in case we wanted to try them out in multiple rounds, but that might have been ambitious of me. I glance over at Kassam. He reaches down and furtively strokes his cock, smiling into his blindfold.

Nah, not too ambitious, I decide.

I bring the bowl over to his side. "Oil incoming," I warn him. "Remember your word if you want me to stop."

"You think this is the first time I've been oiled up, my Carly?"

I arch an eyebrow at him. "You think now is the time to tell me that?" I reach over and pinch his nipple.

Kassam groans and his cock twitches. He reaches for it, stroking himself, and a bead of wetness gleams on the tip. "I tell you everything. You are my wife and the most desirable person I have ever met. You are all I could possibly want."

Okay, for that, he gets a pass. I eye him and decide the easiest—and funnest—way to grease him up is for both of us to stand. "Can you get to your feet for me? I want to make sure I get all of you really well."

He laughs again, a curious look on his face, but does as I ask. I tip the bowl and spill some of the oil down his bronzed chest, rubbing it in with my fingers, and then move to his back, doing the same until he's slick, rivulets cascading down his glorious body.

"Can I touch myself?" he asks.

"No. From here on out, you can't touch anything unless I say so," I tell him, deciding to be bossy again. "You have to ask permission for everything."

He grunts, as if slightly irked. "Then may I touch my cock?"

"Nope. That's mine." I set the bowl down a fair distance away and then run my hands up and down his slicked chest. Once they're good and greasy, I slide them lower and cup his sac, then run a hand along his shaft. Kassam's groan is powerful, and heat surges through my own body in response. "God, you have a pretty cock," I breathe as I work his length. "I could touch it all day."

Kassam's breath hitches, lifting one hand out to touch me, and then lowering it again as he remembers our bargain. "It is yours, little light. Touch it all you want."

"It's a shame I had to grease it up," I tease, leaning in as I work his cock, running one slick hand down his shaft and then the other. "I'd love to put my mouth on this beauty and drink you up." When he groans again, I lean in, deliberately brushing my nipples against his chest. "But I guess I should move on to my other plans."

And I grab his ass with my oily hands.

He huffs, the sound both laughter and slightly startled. His hands move to my shoulders as he struggles to keep his balance, and then Kassam gently removes them from me, trying to stay true to our game.

I slither up against him, rubbing against his chest and hard cock as I stroke his buns. God, here I thought I'd be getting him off and I'm crazy horny just from prepping him for what I'm going to do to him. I rub his ass, and then delve my fingers into the cleft of his ass cheeks and press a finger there.

Kassam grabs my shoulder again, groaning. I know he likes this. Every time I blow him, I push a finger into his ass and tickle his prostate and he fucking loves it. He's completely not shy about ass play, and that's another reason why I think today's play is going to go over so well. "Can I go back here?" I ask, stroking the spot in question. "Or do you need to use your word?"

"I need to touch you," he manages, his voice ragged. His cock slips against my belly, leaving a wet trail, and my pussy clenches reflexively. His hands grip my shoulders as I press against his backside, greasing up that spot in particular. "Let me lick your cunt, Carly. I'll make it so good for you."

I wriggle out of his grasp, giving his ass one last squeeze. "I need more oil," I whisper as I get to my feet. He groans a protest, but it only encourages me. "Actually can you do me a favor? I'd love it if you got on your hands and knees."

Most guys would probably refuse, but Kassam isn't like most guys. He's a god, for one, and from what he's told me, he's led quite an adventurous life. He's secure in who he is, and he's tried a lot of stuff, so he simply cocks his head and thinks. "Are you going to fuck me?"

"In the ass," I agree. "With a dildo. That okay or do you need to use your word?"

A wide smile spreads across Kassam's laughing face. "Ah, my Carly. I love the way your mind works." He pauses. "And then after I come, I get to lick your cunt and make you come too, yes?"

I adore that he's thinking of me. "As if I'm not gonna like doing this to you?" I tease. "But yes, we'll do both, I promise."

"Excellent." He moves forward and braces himself on his elbows, presenting the best backside in *two* worlds for me to oil up. His skin gleams with the oil, and when he spreads his thighs, he shows *everything* to me. The man does not have a shy bone in his body.

I get the oil bowl again and dribble more down his backside, then slide one finger into his ass, caressing his slick balls with my other hand. Kassam groans as I dip my finger in and out of his hole, working it. I'm pretty sure I have to stretch things for him to take the strap-on, which I worry might be too large. As I work his bottom, he clenches around my finger, squeezing, and it sends hot prickles of awareness through my body. Is this what it's like when I clench around him? God, that must feel amazing.

I add a second finger and work his sac as I prep him, and I love the noises he makes. His breath hitches with every movement of my hand, and his hooves dig into the blanket. "Too much?" I ask, checking in. "Should I stop?"

"Keep going," he growls.

"Think you can take my strap-on? It's pretty big...though not as big as you. I didn't want to give you a complex."

He huffs with laughter, which turns into a groan when I push a third finger into his ass. His butt clenches, his cheeks tight, and I'm fascinated by the sight. He's just so damned gorgeous. "I can take it."

All righty, then. I slip my fingers out of his bottom and give him a light smack. I wipe my slick hands on the blanket, then put on my harness. The moment it settles around my hips, the vines tighten and move, settling everything in place. Kassam's magic is handy, even for such decadent things. I fix the belt in place and then give it an experimental wiggle. Everything seems secure, and I grab a bit more oil and grease up the wooden shaft of my "cock." "Remember your word if this is too much, Kassam."

"You forget who I am already?" he calls back, slightly breathless as I move behind him. He's smarter than I am at this, or more experienced, because he's lowered his upper body to the mossy blanket, raising his hips in the air at the perfect height. I run the peg along the crease of his ass, getting him used to the feel of it.

When his body clenches and he shudders, it fills me with a giddy excitement. Fuck, this is going to be so damn sexy. I smack it against his ass cheek, trying to mimic his movements when he fucks me and all the ways that he drives me crazy. "You ready?"

Kassam groans again.

All right then. "Coming in hot," I murmur, and then press the head of the shaft against the opening to his body. My first thought is that nothing's going to fit, but then I remember there's a tight ring of muscle there that has to be pushed past. "Remember your word," I tell him, as I press in. "I can stop at any time."

He lets out a ragged growl. "Don't."

Fair enough. I anchor one hand on his hip and lean in, and when his body relaxes and lets me in, I surge forward, until I'm seated at the hilt. Kassam's breath stutters, and I'm panting, frozen in place. I've never pegged a man before. I hope I'm doing it right. "How's it feel?" I ask, rubbing his hips with tiny circles.

"Amazing," he manages in a thick voice. "My clever, sexy Carly. You are amazing."

I mentally preen at that. I thought he'd be a little more reluctant to do this, but he's into it, and honestly, so am I. My pussy is so slick I can feel my juices running down the insides of my thighs as I slowly rock against him. I gasp as the fronts of my thighs smack against his and it occurs to me I don't know how to move my body to fuck him properly. "Give me a sec to figure this out," I tell him. "I've never fucked a man before. Been fucked by one, sure. But doing the fucking is new to me."

Kassam's only response is to groan. The trees above us shiver with a stiff wind, the leaves rustling.

Right. Okay. I pull my hips back, and then gently push them forward again. He doesn't make a sound of distress, so I try it again, and after a few fumbles, I figure out a rhythm that works for him. Shorter, quick bursts that involve me snapping my hips elicit groan after groan from him, whereas the deeper, slower strokes don't seem to do much at all. I rock into him, using one hand to grip his hip. I try smacking his ass, but it knocks me out of my rhythm, and feels a little too porny anyhow. As I work him, I lean over his bigger body, pressing my skin to his, because I love the sight of him like this, and I love the way he feels. I love the sounds he makes, and I love that I'm giving him this pleasure.

God, is this how it feels to be a man? No wonder they strut so much, even with all that shit dangling between their legs.

On a whim, I reach underneath him and grip his cock as I

push deep. Kassam growls again, and his body clenches up underneath mine. Oh, he likes that. I keep my hand on his cock, my fingers loose as I continue to snap my hips, fucking him with the strap-on, and the movements cause his cock to shuttle in and out of my grasp.

"Carly," he snarls, thrusting back against me. "*Carly!*"

"Are you going to come for me?" I coo, moving my slick hand harder over his cock, squeezing as I do.

Kassam lets out a ragged groan, and then his big body shudders. An unearthly sound rips out of him, and hot cum spurts on my hand as I work him with my fist. He comes so hard that his body quakes, and overhead, the trees tremble just as violently as my lover does.

Something hard the size of an apple hits me atop the head, and I yelp, pulling back and shielding my head. It's...an acorn. An acorn the size of an orange. I stare up at the trees, and they're all ridiculously overgrown, the nuts hanging from above massive. Kassam must have let out an intense surge of magic as he came, and I giggle wildly at the realization. "Your powers..."

He just lets out a happy groan.

Chuckling, I ease off of him and pride myself on the fact that I only gave his ass one more loving slap. Then I remove my toy, rub Kassam down with a fresh, mossy hand towel, and remove the blindfold. He's got a sated look on his sweaty face that pleases me greatly, and I offer him a drink of water. "Wanna snuggle?"

He ignores the water and pulls me down next to him, blissful. "You know I need no water. Just you. All I need is you."

I wrap my arms around him, tucking his face against my tits. Holding him close, I let my fingers drift over his back as the minutes pass and we drowse under the now-thicker-than-ever trees. He's still got a bit of oil clinging to his skin, but I like the scent of it. I'm proud of myself as I wait all of a good five minutes before I ask, "So how'd I do?"

"You will never be able to fuck for hours," he tells me, languidly thumbing one of my nipples and watching it harden. "But your enthusiasm was delicious. That was quite enjoyable."

"You didn't think it was weird that I fucked you?" I ask, because I want to be sure.

Kassam runs his hand down my stomach, caressing. One of the good things about him being a god is that his recovery time is practically nil. The man has supernatural stamina. "Why would I think it is weird? I am proud that you are so creative and take our games so seriously." The look he gives me is downright mischievous. "And I will have to think of a suitable way to one-up you for our next date."

"Just no animal stuff," I tell him. "The tree was weirdly hot, but I draw the line at animals."

He shrugs, then slides a hand between my thighs. "Did you enjoy it?" The moment his fingers touch my sopping folds, he gives a rumble of pleasure. "Ah, yes, yes you did. My sweet little deviant light." He lifts his head and gives me another teasing look before slipping down my body and settling his shoulders between my thighs. "Such a fucking deserves a reward."

"You just want an excuse to lick my pussy," I say as I obediently spread my legs apart.

"I need no excuse." His tongue drags over the seam of my folds, sending an arching tremor through my body. "This cunt is mine. I will lick it and tease it as I please. And since you were such a clever wife today, I feel it deserves a lot of pleasing." He lowers his head, and then his wicked, wicked tongue seeks out my clit.

My legs jerk, and I settle them in their favorite place—over his shoulders. I moan, settling my hands in his hair. "We'll... have to practice..." I tell him between gasps. "So I can get good at fucking you. And then you can reward me like this." His tongue moves fiercely against my clit, and then he sucks on it, his mouth fierce and full of purpose. "Oh, okay, wow, that feels really...amazing." I arch, quivering as he does this tickling thing with his tongue that makes me wild. "I must have been a really fucking good girl."

"You were incredible, little light."

"I need practice," I pant.

"Lucky for you, we have all the time in the world." And with a wicked smile, he dives back between my thighs again.

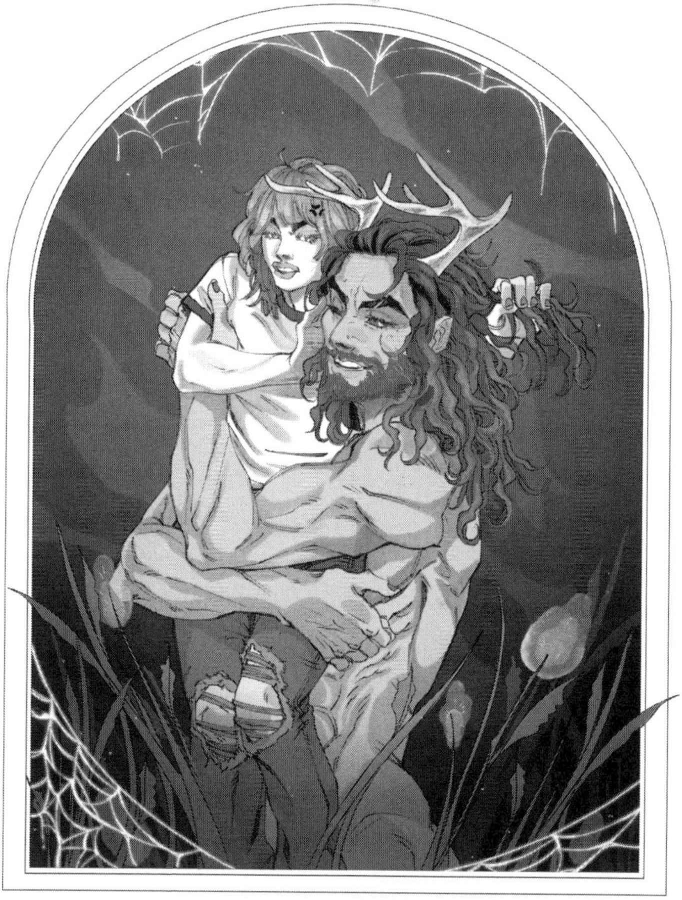

AUTHOR'S NOTE

Hello there!

Thank you for being so patient in waiting for this book! The Aspect and Anchor series always feels like a big undertaking for each book, so they need a bit more time to bake. This one is slightly shorter than the others in the series, but I hope Carly & Kassam's story feels just as epic as the others.

In each of the books, I try to bring a little something new to the world that I've built. Aron of the Cleaver was Arrogance, Rhagos was Lies, and I wanted to explore making one of my heroes Hedonism. Kassam was a very FUN hedonism, but it made me think about what we would consider up for grabs in the pursuit of pleasure, and what that would mean for each person. Kassam, being an old soul and a sunny sort, has very few boundaries. I imagine if you live for thousands of years and have tons of power, there's very little you haven't licked, sucked, or fucked by the time you reach his age. Carly is the one in the relationship with boundaries, and I realized early on that I was writing a reverse grumpy-sunshine trope, where the hero is the one that's sunshine and the heroine is the one putting her foot down constantly.

(I still hope it was fun to read!)

This story also had a bit of a different angle in that Kassam starts out in our world. Since I was snatching heroines from our world, it seemed only fair that I shove a hero into my heroine's world for a while and see how he liked it. Turnabout is fair play and all that.

Speaking of heroes, this book is a tiny bit more adventurous than standard Ruby reads in certain aspects (no pun intended). If that's not your jam, I totally get it! But I also didn't want to make Kassam the most straight-laced, vanilla man out there, because I didn't feel it would suit him and his history. Hedonism was a fun aspect to write, but exhausting in other ways, because everything he did, I had to stop and think, "Would this be enjoyable? Would this feed hedonism's need for pleasure?" Much like writing Rhagos as a liar was a challenge, this was challenging in different ways. But I like a challenge!

The only Aspect I haven't written yet is Apathy, and I don't know if I have a story for that particular sort of Aspect. Stories tend to involve movers and shakers, and while psychologically it might be fun to dive into pulling an Apathy aspect out of that hole, reading it might be hella dull.

But! Things in Aos are far from dull, and I have more stories in my head if it looks like readers are interested in more. I'd love to do a Yulenna and Spidae book. I'd love to explore how Seth and his anchor Margo handle the world they now find themselves in and how Seth shoves himself into Aos's pantheon (and how the pantheon shoves back). I would really love to write a story or two about Kassam's wolf-sons, the *conmac*. Then there's Kalos, Rhagos's dark brother, who isn't the nicest sort but might turn a bit of a new leaf for the right woman...

The stories there are already writing themselves in my head, but it depends on so many things - my schedule, sales, etc. We'll see what springs to the forefront!

AUTHOR'S NOTE

As always, if you're into the books, please review or spread the word. Authors like me are constantly juggling the projects we want to do with what we think readers want to see from us. Your 'vote' is important, so even something as small as a review on Goodreads or sending a message on Facebook about how much you enjoy a story can bump a 'Not right now' story higher on the to-do list. We're led by what does well, but we're also easily influenced creatures, we authors.

(And if you know me, my to-do list is HUGE.)

You guys are wonderful, and I hope you enjoyed the story! <3

Ruby

WANT MORE RUBY DIXON?

Interested in more of my books? Here's a smattering of my works that might interest you! Everything is Kindle Unlimited, so borrow to your heart's content.

BORROWS = LOVE
:)

Want the first two books in the series?
Bound to the Battle God
Sworn to the Shadow God

Want a slow-burn with a wounded hero and heroine?
When She Belongs

More Fantasy Romance in Aos?
The King's Spinster Bride

Dragons? Did someone say dragons?
Fire In His Blood